ALSO BY CAROL EDGARIAN

Rise the Euphrates

The Writer's Life: Intimate Thoughts on Work, Love, Inspiration, and Fame from the Diaries of the World's Great Writers (coeditor)

THREE STAGES OF AMAZEMENT

A Novel

Carol Edgarian

Scribner

New York London Toronto Sydney

SCRIBNER

A Division of Simon & Schuster, Inc.

1230 Avenue of the Americas

New York, NY 10020

First Scribner hardcover edition March 2011

SCRIBNER and design are registered trademarks of The Gale Group, Inc.,
used under license by Simon & Schuster, Inc., the publisher of this work.

For information about special discounts for bulk purchases,
please contact Simon & Schuster Special Sales at 1-866-506-1949
or business@simonandschuster.com.

The Simon & Schuster Speakers Bureau can bring authors to your live event.
For more information or to book an event contact the Simon & Schuster Speakers Bureau
at 1-866-248-3049 or visit our website at www.simonspeakers.com.

Manufactured in the United States of America

1   3   5   7   9   10   8   6   4   2

Library of Congress Control Number: 2010044448

ISBN 978-1-4391-9830-8
ISBN 978-1-4391-9920-6 (ebook)

For you, TJ

Silence

One

The modern marriage has two states, plateau and precipice, and in the winter of our recent crisis—with markets plummeting and even rich folks crying poor; with the dark reign of one tinsel president finally ending, and the promised hope of a new man about to start; yes, with hope rising like a cockamamie kite and fear more common than love—Charlie Pepper forgot his wife.

He didn't mean to. That much Lena knew. She paused at the kitchen sink on New Year's Eve morning, the last day of the lousiest year of their lives, and considered what she needed and what she knew. The crab needed to come out of the fridge. What about butter? She'd forgotten candles. She needed another bag of ice. It had been a year since they'd even thought about hosting a dinner. Since then the world fell down one black hole and she and Charlie fell down another; as yet no one had come back. But Obama was taking over in twenty days and Lena had hope. She also had a sick baby and no lettuce. And if years ago Lena and Charlie promised that their hearts would always be in sync, well, it was a fool's promise, wasn't it? For now their hearts were a cacophony of chuffing and banging, with Charlie's motor driving like a great battleship and hers a bubbling alchemist's pot. Then there were the children's hearts: Theo's drum sounded like quick boots pounding up the stairs, while Willa's was more skittish, the flap-flap of gossamer wings. And there was a third heart so silent it took away sound.

"Usted está mutada en el burro, tiene que seguir," Glo called, on her way out the door after tending Willa half the night so Lena could sleep. "You're on the burro, you might as well go."

In quick-fire Spanish, Lena answered, hoisting the baby onto her shoulder. "The burro is strong. Now why can't he have an extra pair of hands?"

Glo chuckled, her girlish, brown fingers covering her mouth. Seven years ago, Glo crossed the border at night led by a coyote, leaving her two kids and her mother behind in Guatemala. Every Sunday Glo called home, and sometimes her youngest, Rosella, refused to speak to her. Yet here she was talking of Lena's burros. It was life, this crazy life, and if you didn't laugh it broke you. It broke you anyway, but it was better if you laughed.

All day Lena made lists and as she carried Willa up the stairs she started a new one. Butter, candles, ice. If, while working feverishly, Charlie forgot her and the kids, it was never for long. He forgot them repeatedly, at moments, across days, in time. Lena, five years younger but dog-aged in matters of love, likewise misplaced Charlie, with all the worry and push she had to nudge up the road. *I ought to write it down: butter, candles, ice,* she thought, when Willa started coughing again. Lena ran. Charlie was forty-seven, she was forty-two. They had five years between them and eight years of marriage to their backs and to say they were committed was to say they were in deep.

Yet they missed each other.

And Lena wanted—oh, she wanted—to be touched inside her bones. But Charlie was elsewhere—it might be Uganda, or Boston, or an hour south at the office, or asleep in the bed beside her. Dear Charlie, grinding his jaw.

"Theo," Lena called, grabbing the newspaper as she pushed down the hall on her heels. "I'll have the door closed. Come find me, honey. Don't shout."

She kicked the bathroom door shut and flipped on the shower. As it roared to life, Lena whispered into Willa's tiny ear, "That's it, breathe."

Willa, ten months old, weighed just eleven pounds. In her short life she had been to the hospital a dozen times. With pneumonia, seizures, surgeries, not to mention those four months at the start. The doctors talked gravely of cognitive delays, and worse. *Cerebral palsy* was a term sometimes used. Lena stopped her ears. It wasn't that she didn't believe, it was that believing took her only so far. What Willa needed, Lena felt sure, was time. Lena's job was to seize time.

As the steam built, Lena first stripped Willa to her diaper, then peeled off her own sweats down to her panties. Making a bed of towels on the tiled floor, she sat—for the first time all morning—with her knees bent, her back against the wall, showing the cabinets her real face, the face she let no one see. Lena Rusch was irreverent, good-looking, plucky. She had a fine if exhausted brain. This meant she couldn't always recall the lists she made, or the ends and even the middles of her sentences, but she always started out with a bang. She was a romantic and, worse, an optimist. Fate had forced her to be practical and stolid, too. The two sides rubbed. She was crazy for her children, her friends, chocolate, and news of any kind. She might be crazy for Charlie, too, if she came across him in the daylight once in a while. In other words, Lena Rusch was extraordinarily ordinary: she worked and reared and hardly slept; she began each day prepared for a surprise.

Preemies did best skin to skin. Lena laid Willa's bare chest like a cloth over her own, and making sure her baby was upright with the world, she gently drummed on the tiny back. Willa moaned, burrowing her face in the cave of Lena's neck. "Sweetheart," Lena murmured. "Come on, come on."

"There you are!" Jesse cried, throwing open the door. They were sisters, and though Jesse was much, much younger, they entered rooms as their mother had taught them, like a storm. "I've been *shouting* a lung out downstairs. Theo finally—"

"Shut the door, you noodle! You're letting out the steam!"

Jesse did as she was told. But between the blasting shower and the stifling heat, she wouldn't stay long. "What? Is she sick again?" Jesse folded her arms. "Poor pup. Poor *you*."

"Nah. We're fine."

Technically they were only half sisters. Jesse, sixteen years Lena's junior, was the product of a love affair their mother had, one of many, after Lena's father died. She was as long-limbed and blonde as Lena was curvy and dark. Their mother told everyone that Jesse was helping out with the children until she found a job, but Jesse was a child herself.

"So. What are you wearing tonight?" she asked.

Lena tipped her head against the wall and laughed. "You've got to be kidding."

"Wear your green dress," Jesse advised seriously. "It's about time. And how 'bout I wear your black?"

"Cheeky girl!"

"Am not!"

"Oh, yes." Lena smiled wistfully. It wasn't so long ago (in truth, it felt like a minute) that Lena was the one flying out the door to get wasted at high school parties while little Jesse flapped her hands from her bouncy seat. And while that was long ago, Jesse still manipulated like a child—openly, as if she were the only one playing for keeps. Sighing, Lena rubbed circles in Willa's back. "I gave the black dress to Glo."

"You what? You gave it to the *nanny*?"

"Not nanny. Glo."

"Christ, Lean."

Truthfully, Lena would have given Gloria Angelica Cardenas anything—anything—for Glo saved Lena's sanity every single day. And besides, the rapture on Glo's face when Lena handed her the box was worth a hundred, maybe a thousand, black dresses. Lena looked up at Jesse, trying to decide if she should take the trouble to explain. But Jesse was looking at herself in the mirror, continuing that frank, daily conversation women have with their faces. "Ugh. New Year's Eve and no guy. I hate my life!"

"Fa."

Jesse turned. "OK, Miss Veteran. When. When is *he* going to show up?"

Lena's grinned slyly. "They always do."

At last Willa coughed, good and wet. It was enough. Jesse escaped, slamming the door behind her, as Lena put Willa to her breast. They would be there another hour. With one arm hooked under the baby, Lena spread the newspaper across her knees, where the steamy ink would stain her black. She didn't care. This was the moment she'd been waiting for— her reward being four full pages in the *New York Times* on Bernie Madoff and his colossal Ponzi scheme. Lena was in awe of Madoff, who, by promising steady returns of eighteen percent, had perpetrated the largest stock fraud in history. He'd swindled at every level, from the Wall Street fat cats, to relatives, to Palm Beach society, to grieving Jewish widows, to the mistress who claimed he had a small penis, to Mort Zuckerman, the media titan, to Elie Wiesel, the Auschwitz survivor, to Zsa Zsa Gabor. Yet in the photo on the front page Madoff showed no remorse. He walked the streets, a Jew with a George Washington haircut; he smiled like a shark for the paparazzi.

Her guests arrived all at once. They tossed their coats over the banister and pressed wine and chocolate into Lena's hands. There was much hugging. Lena made a robust effort to herd them into the living room, but they ignored her, following her into the small kitchen, where they grouped like stupid, happy cows.

"Get the fuck out of here!" she cried, laughing helplessly, but they only smiled and kept on talking. These were the beloveds: Lee Swanson, showing off his new baby blue suede jacket, and Josh Klein, Charlie's roommates from college, and Sandy, Josh's wife. When Jesse appeared, having spent the afternoon talking on the phone, tweeting, Facebooking, and smoking a little grass, she made a beeline for Swanson, to tell him that his jacket was his best awful. Laughing, they all agreed.

Meanwhile Lena had four things she couldn't remember and perhaps one of them was burning in the oven. She was about to check when Vi arrived. Violet Vesuvio, dear Vi, was Lena's flag of joy, her best friend since they were sixteen, the year they each lost their virginity, one to a girl and one to a boy.

"Oh, god. The fucking traffic." Vi gripped Lena's shoulders and looked deeply into her eyes. "What. What is it?"

Lena wrinkled her nose. It had been a day.

"All right. We can fix this," Vi said. "Start at the beginning. What have you been eating?"

Lena had a deep, womanly, shit-kicking laugh. "Oh, hi, Maude." Turning, she greeted Vi's new girlfriend, who appeared to be in costume, a men's gray suit and fedora. "You look—"

"Rakish?" Maude tipped her head. Maude was a painter, a decent one; her oversize portraits sold best in Santa Fe and Miami. She was large-boned, mannish, with a small, pretty nose. Vi thought she was tremendous.

"Yes, rakish," agreed Lena, and though undecided about Maude, she hugged her warmly. Everyone was here; they only lacked Charlie. For the next half hour, as she threw dinner together, Lena kept an anxious eye on the door. And when at last Charlie walked through it, she was so startled she nearly dropped a bowl. She plowed into him, backing them into the hall.

"Well, Doctor, I do like to see your face at the end of the year. Remind me, what's your name?"

"Lena's husband," Charlie said, kissing her quickly. He'd been pushing toward this moment for more than two hours in traffic. But now that it was here, and Lena was beside him, Charlie couldn't slow his molecules enough to enjoy her. Instead, he dropped the bags of butter, lettuce, and ice she'd asked for on the floor. "Hey. Can I talk to you a sec?"

"Sure." Lena fiddled with his collar. She was pretending to ignore the gray hollows under his eyes and the smudge on his coat. What she wanted was a good kiss. A good kiss could restore them. Didn't he know? A good kiss could sail them into the New Year just fine. But even as she longed for this, they headed in another direction—she watched with wonder, seeing them go—and instead of saying something romantic she asked, "Did you get the champagne?"

"Damn."

"It's OK. I screwed up on the groceries, but I remembered the booze!"

"Charged it?"

"Course." She frowned. Now, why ask a thing like that? She shook her head and all but moaned. "Charlie, I want it to be . . . lovely. One night. Can it be lovely?"

"It is."

She tried her best to smile. "All right. What do you want to tell me?"

For two hours fighting the traffic on 280, Charlie had practiced his lines. *I got a call today, out of the blue.* He had his speech ready and there would be no deep kisses until he got the words out. Until he came clean. But the way she was looking at him, with those yearning green eyes, well, you'd have to be heartless.

"You look great," he said, and meant it. The truth was she looked wan and her hair seemed sort of wild. But even a wan, wild-haired Lena was sweet relief.

Lena patted her hair where Charlie's gaze landed. Did she really look like hell? She wanted so much from the night. If only desire were enough to take them there. "OK," she declared, brushing his lips with hers. "The bar first, then I need five chairs."

Klein wiped his plate clean with a hunk of bread. "God, this is good. Lena, what'd you put in the crab?"

"Butter and butter. A touch of garlic."

"No, something else."

"Jalapeño. The thinnest of slivers."

"Jalapeño! You are a witch, Lena-love. Pass that bowl."

Lena, because she was nursing, had just the one glass, but it burned nicely in her cheeks and in the tops of her ears. She passed the crab to Klein on her right and the salad to Swanson on her left. Now where was Charlie? She looked down the long table, past the winking candles and rosy faces, to the opposite end. He wasn't there. The thought of Charlie absent caught in Lena's throat. And just like that she knew something had happened—something more.

She moved a candlestick aside, the panic rising—as if her heart had been zapped and the ceiling dropped lower. Where was he? From the far end of the table Sandy caught Lena's eye. Sandy was a gynecologist, not a shrink, but since the twins' birth she'd made it her business to keep tabs on Lena. Worse, Lena knew from Vi that Sandy believed that had she been the doc on call she could have prevented the twins' early delivery. It was more than Lena could stand. The hubris. The exposed nerve. It wasn't only her fatigue or pride that Lena didn't want poked. It was a question of luck and unluck—and the tenderest, most unspeakable sorrow. It was, finally, a question of the heart. Lena's heart was tired. And a tired heart is a susceptible one.

"Lena, help me here with Swanny," called Sandy. "The *eshag* thinks he can cure a chronic sinus infection with amoxicillin!" *Eshag* was Sandy's favorite word—Armenian for ass—but she applied it to all her favorites. "See that, Swanny—Lena agrees. Listen to me, *esh*: you have to go in there with napalm."

Lena tried to stand but Josh Klein took her hand and pulled her into her seat. "Don't even think about it," he said kindly. In the wife department, Josh Klein considered Charlie one lucky dog. Then, too, with the market down fifty percent and no bottom in sight, Klein had been wondering all evening if this wasn't the end of the world. He decided that was OK. It was OK if the world ended. He would chat with Lena, drink a little more and see if the forecast changed. Last year he'd brought Lena pots of caviar left over from the Goldman Sachs holiday party. This year couldn't have been more different. A week before Christmas, he'd been forced to fire half of his department—guys and women he'd brought along. His dreams were haunted by their faces. And so Klein filled his and Lena's glasses to the top. "Talk to me. Where were we?"

Lena smiled dimly.

"Come on, Helena. Pretend there's no kids, no worries, sex forever. Money? Well, let's leave money out of it." Klein squeezed her hand. "What are you excited about? Is it Obama? Of course you love him. You and everyone are in love. The man is going to kill what's left of the markets, but let's not go there either. No, not Obama. Too shiny, too glorified. Let's talk about a real skunk. Bernie—Bernie Madoff."

Lena blushed. "Kleiny, are you obsessed with him, too?"

"No. I met him once and that cured me. A few years ago a friend of mine was thinking of investing with Bernie. When my pal asked to see a prospectus, Madoff's people said, 'Bernie doesn't do that. It's a trust thing.' Please. You know, Lena, there's a saying, If it sounds too good to be true, it is."

In fact, Josh Klein had been thinking about Bernie Madoff almost as much as Lena had, but for different reasons. For Lena, Madoff's business was beside the point; it was his motive, his character that intrigued her. For Klein it was just the opposite.

Meanwhile Lena was having what could only be called an inside-outside experience. She was talking with Klein and passing Vi the salt, while her heart searched the house for Charlie.

Lena looked deep into Klein's soul. "What about Madoff's sons?"

"Those two? No question. They did exactly what Daddy told them. Bernie wasn't a guy who rewarded people for using their brains. Did you know that on the day he turned himself in one of the sons' wives filed divorce papers?" It had been the talk on the street all week.

Klein refilled his glass. He'd drink until there was no more. And as he drank he was thinking, Boy oh boy, Charlie, get your ass back in here. She's lonely, lonelier than she knows.

"OK. Tell me this," Klein said. "The wife, Ruth Madoff. Did she know?"

"Kleiny, please." Lena gave his arm a push. "The wife knows—even if she doesn't want to know."

This much Charlie heard. He'd gone upstairs to check on the kids, and come down to get more wine from the garage. He'd been standing in the doorway, behind Lena, long enough to catch the gist. What he heard made him sick at heart. For something indeed had changed: that morning Charlie received a call from someone who could save his faltering company—this man happened to be the one person in the world Lena loathed. Charlie hoped he could explain it to her. But somehow she knew. My god, she knew.

Lena, unaware that Charlie was behind her, kept talking, and in that way dealt with her nerves. She was telling Klein about a woman who got arrested for shoplifting that morning at Whole Foods. "It was terrible.

Theo heard the whole thing. The woman, she wasn't young. Kleiny, here's the strange part: she was wearing a sable coat."

"Really? What'd she take?"

"It's not what."

"Oh no?"

"Yo, *eshes*!" Sandy called, rising from her chair. "Charlie, what are those two conspiring about now?"

"Thieves," replied Klein. "We're talking about thieves."

A sable coat wasn't something you'd expect to see, not even in January, and certainly not on a bright morning at the grocery store.

Motown blasted over the speakers; the aisles teemed with the holiday harried. Some economic downturn, thought Lena, hitching Willa higher in the sling so she was snug to her chest. Lena took Theo's hand firmly and, hoping to keep him jolly, pretended they were doing a Viennese waltz as she led him into the crush. But as they took a shortcut down the shampoo aisle, the woman in the coat blocked their way.

"Mama," Theo said, backing up.

"It's all right, Theo."

"Yes, little fellow, I won't bite," the woman said.

Something about her looked familiar. Lena guessed that her picture had been in the society pages. She had dyed yellow hair and white powdered skin and black kohl drawn under and above her pale eyes. She wore a large sapphire on her middle finger; her nails were frosted pink.

Unlucky, Lena decided, and she squeezed Theo's hand to keep him from asking one of the questions she knew wanted to bust out of him. Theo wasn't wrong to wonder. For despite all that glory, something about the woman signaled that she was past the good times. It wasn't her saggy coat or shoes exactly, and it wasn't the forced fact of wearing sable on a clear California morning; nor was it the bad dye job or the contrast she made to the young clerks stationed nearby—short, round girls with their nose piercings and tattoos. It was something else. On New Year's Eve all she had in her basket was a box of pasta, a jar of marinara sauce and a screw-top bottle of red wine. She was studying a jar of cream, no bigger than a large thimble; she held it between her thumb and index finger.

"It's called Pot O' Gold, and they want ninety dollars for it," she said, looking Lena square in the eye. "Can you imagine?"

Lena could. Even as she rolled her eyes, tsking, "It's a crime, such a crime"—she could easily believe that a pot of nothing cost ninety dollars, and that this woman was going to steal that jar. There are all kinds of thieves in the world, and one sort always knows the other.

From inside the sling Willa coughed, barky as a seal.

"Oh, that bark!" the woman cried. "It's a sound you never, ever forget. I remember with my middle boy." Lena could see now that she was older, in her seventies at least. "Dear, have you dealt with croup before?"

Nodding, Lena slid a protective palm under Willa's tiny rump and gave Theo's hand another reassuring squeeze.

"Ah, of course," the woman said. "Scares the heck out of you, doesn't it? With my boy, when it got really bad at night, we used to drive him around in the car with all the windows open. The wet air did the trick—calmed him down. Well, it's always something. Me, I've just got to quit being *stunned* by these prices. And you— Good luck, dears. Happy New Year, all that lala." The woman waved a jeweled hand as they pressed on.

It was a madhouse at the registers. The lines snaked into the produce aisles and doubled back. Lena and the kids took their place behind two Asian women, sisters no doubt, dressed in leggings and high boots and glossy ponytails that fell down their backs and swished their behinds. To kill time, they were perusing the magazine rack, snapping pages and commenting on the stars, as if they were their old friends. "Look, Madonna. Doesn't she look better since she left Guy?"

"Hmm. She has excellent skin."

"Botox up the yinny."

"And how."

Their chatter distracted Lena, and it wasn't until Theo gave a sharp pull on her hand and cried out, "Mama!" that she turned to see the commotion in the Express line.

A security guard had stopped the woman in the fur as she was leaving

13

the store. He demanded that she empty her pockets. Moving ever so slowly, she complied. From the depths of one pocket, she produced a wallet, a bunched silk scarf. Keys.

"Now the other one," the guard said, opening his palm and wiggling his fingers.

Of course, by now everyone on line was watching—including Theo. Lena looked at her son. Theodore Pepper's mud-brown eyes were already a bit wild with dark imaginings. Now this. We should all be embarrassed, Lena thought, dread weighting her heart.

It wasn't the cream after all but a bottle of probiotics.

"Fifty-five bucks," declared one of the Chinese girls.

"It's a silly misunderstanding," the woman explained, her voice unnaturally high. "I put the bottle in my pocket, you see, so it wouldn't fall out of my basket. I had every intention of paying, of course." She lifted her chin and sniffed. But despite that little bit of anarchy, the face couldn't hold. It collapsed. With a world-weary sigh, she searched the crowd for help. "My husband. He needs them for his digestion. The doctor *insists,* and, well—"

She sighed—the husband, the doctor, all the trouble. "I don't know what else to say. Honestly, I don't. You are standing there looking *very* severe, my fellow. You have to know that I have been an excellent customer since you people first opened these doors." She seemed to be operating under the assumption that for everyone's sake this regrettable incident must be put behind them. She looked over her shoulder longingly, toward the parking lot.

The guard held out his palm and once again wiggled his fingers. The gesture was gross and she ignored it, her eyes fixed on the floor.

He dove that large hand into the silk-lined depths of her coat and took out a brick of Parmesan cheese. "Did you think this was gonna jump out of your basket, too?"

"Oh, god," Lena said.

"Well, I couldn't be more embarrassed, or feel more stupid," the woman replied, her shoulders rounding. "No, it's not possible. You have done your job, young man, no one can blame you for that. Oh, how stupid!"

But the guard didn't think she was stupid, and he whispered as much in her ear. Her face broke with a fresh horror. "No!" she cried, sagging visibly, as he gripped her elbow, lifting it unnaturally high, and led her, unsteady in her skinny cocktail heels, toward the back of the store.

"Come on," Lena said, feeling sick inside. She covered her mouth with her hand. Abandoning the cart, she marched them toward the door.

"But Mama—the groceries?"

"Leave them," she choked. There was nothing certain in Lena's life, not the bags of ice or the butter, not the credit card on which it would all be charged—not one thing certain, except the lump that was Willa, hung round her neck, and the hot, ardent squeeze of Theo's paw.

Lena managed to steer them across the parking lot, even as her heart boomed and her legs felt spongy. "You don't reduce people like that," she said. "You just don't."

When they reached the car, she turned to Theo. He was awfully short and she had no choice but to bend down. This involved a fair act of balancing, what with Willa in the sling and Lena sort of swoony, and Theo himself only a few feet high. Squatting like a sumo wrestler, cursing under her breath, Lena tried to take the worry from her face. There would be no salad at dinner, and without butter the crab would be bone-dry. "Theo, honey. What is it?"

He narrowed his eyes. And weighing his words just like Charlie, his lips moving as he set his thoughts neatly and precisely in a row, he said, "That lady. Are they going to put her in the dungeon?"

"Don't steal, Theo." Lena tugged on the bunchy hem of Theo's jacket.

"I won't," he said, pushing her shoulder lightly with his hand. There was something wiggly in Theo's stomach and his mother was ignoring it. "That lady. Are they gonna . . . I mean do you think she's bad? She's bad, right?"

Squinting hard, Lena tried to think. From the beginning she understood that she didn't own her children; at best, she hoped to be their worthy shepherd. Besides, Theo had come with his own urgency, an oddball directness, an urgency that had nothing to do with her. Here he was, eyeing her intently, proving that already he possessed all the faces he would ever use in this world—the lover, the worker, the goony bird and, my god, the judge.

"What do you think, Theo?"

"I think most grown-ups would say she's bad, but you might not."

Lena smiled. So true, so disarmingly true. She turned away to look across the parking lot. She would have to make it simple for him, to put his mind at ease. For one day soon Theo would know that his mother was also a thief.

Lena Rusch was a thief stealing time.

"Here, Theo. Give me your eyes."

While Lena and the kids drove home, an hour south of the city, in Mountain View, Lee Swanson padded down the corridor of Nimbus Surgical Devices to look in on the only other soul working that afternoon of New Year's Eve. Charlie was seated behind his desk, an unpainted door held up on one end by a sawhorse and the other by a chipped file cabinet. The cabinet was several inches shorter than the sawhorse, and so a book entitled *Colonoscopic Procedures* had been wedged underneath. With the next round of funding they'd get new furniture and Swanson, whose own setup was an L-shaped slab of Formica framed with two-by-fours, had a certain dream of maple burl.

"Hey, Chah-lee, you doin' any good?"

"I doubt it," Charlie admitted, the shock apparent on his face, for he thought he'd been alone. Lee Swanson was a house of a man: timber-boned, colossally footed, but he moved through the world in whiffles and whispers.

"Yeah, slow day," Swanson agreed. "Anyway, I ran the tests with the new cables. Friday, I'll have the boys jimmy the robot for the umpteenth time."

Charlie nodded. The robot: the instrument of their dreams, the beast that consumed their lives. Charlie wasn't thinking about the robot. He had a thornier problem to solve. It had to do with the two irreconcilables in his life: his desire to succeed and his desire to be good to his wife. But not wanting to hurt Swanson's feelings, he said, "All right."

Swanson took that as invitation and sat down.

They'd been best friends since college, when both landed scholarships at Harvard. Sinks, toilets and miles of copper pipe had raised Charlie Pepper, a plumber's son, to the land of guileless trees and isles of pachysandra; of summers cutting lawns and laps in the pool, slow days of mounting ambition, to Harvard. For Lee Swanson it had been South Boston meat. Both would have struggled that first year had the gods of Harvard not seen fit to put them together in a quad inside Wigglesworth with a view of the fabled Square and a brotherhood of unlikelies: Lee Swanson, Lou Papadopoulos, Josh Klein, Charlie. A Swede, a Greek, a Jew and a Pepper.

Behind them were raucous dinners at Grendel's Den followed by dancing to Little Feat and Earth, Wind & Fire with bright young ladies. There were Red Sox games, scores of them, and the pride that came from years of devotion to a hopeless cause. The Swede, the Greek, the Jew and the Pepper shared an unwavering loyalty, hilarity and an assumption of success. They were, after all, part of a generation of winners, and as such possessed a certainty, hardly imaginable now, that given their education, connections and ambition, they had every reason to expect that with a little luck and a whole lot of push, they would have everything.

Charlie had gone on to become a surgeon while Lee trained as a bio-mechanical engineer. By any measure, they'd done exceedingly well. Yet here they were, starting over again. They had a patent and a prototype for a surgical device whereby, using a robot on one end, fiber optic cables in the middle and a console of instruments at the other extreme, a boy with a harelip in Mbarara could be operated on by a surgeon in his office in New York. The potential, if they could get there, was tremendous. That had to be good, since neither man had slept in a year.

Now Charlie, deep in thought, was grinding his teeth. Swanson stretched his legs out in front of him and waited for his friend.

Their employees called Charlie "Papa": the old-fashioned great man— ye ole buffalo hunter. In an era when everyone came on too loud too much, saying in effect, Don't you know who I think I am? Charlie said nothing until he was right. People liked him, even his inferiors, and there

17

were plenty of those, according to Swanson. But he was hard on himself, Charlie was. Already smart, accomplished—a surgeon, for chrissakes— now Charlie had to be brilliant and rich. That, and he had to save all the little children in the world, too.

"So, Chah-lee, there's like a couple of minutes left to kill in this for-shit year. You want to tell me what's up?" Swanson, whose Irish mother raised him a Catholic, made a church of his hands.

"Go away, Swan."

"I'm outta here," Swanson replied, digging his head deeper into the sofa. He removed a candy bar from his pocket, split it, and lobbed the larger half across the room. "Here, Cap. Lunch."

Charlie caught the bar and popped it into his mouth, hitting his back molars with a *thock*. Like spent dray horses, the two men chewed.

"Did you hear the latest with the banks?" Swanson said at last. "Citi, B of A, the whole can of worms. After the inauguration they're going to nationalize the bunch."

"Says who?"

"The pundits."

"Yeah. I don't buy it. Obama's got another plan. You'll see."

Swanson chuckled. "You think so, Charlie? You think while he's at it, Obama can part the seas, too?"

Charlie didn't answer. He seemed scarcely to hear Swanson. But, yes, Charlie believed. He believed with his whole soul that there must be someone, let it be Obama, smart enough, straight enough, wise enough to fix the current quagmire upending the nation. The thought of anything less made Charlie irritable. Moving swiftly, he marched to the window, opened it wide and let the cold air blast him. Swanson was the gizmo-maker, but perseverance, drive, clarity—these were Charlie's levers. As a surgeon, he lacked the magical hands of the plastic or neuro realms, but was hugely capable with the difficult and bloody jobs. Beginning each morning with the thought *I can do better,* from that happy challenge Charlie plunged. Women liked him because he listened. He hadn't thought about his soul in years. He was the kind of man you'd want married to your sister or bucking up your soldiers or guiding the mission to tramp uncharted land, should tramping be required. It was, true enough, but also required were timing, luck, verve.

"This morning I got a call from Cal Rusch," Charlie said at last. "Seems he's interested in being the lead investor on our next round. And I've been sitting here most of the morning trying to figure out a way to tell the twenty mil we sorely need to go to hell."

Whenever Swanson was confronted by phenomenon, whether a handsome woman or a gorgeous string of code, he blushed, from his strawberry blond curls down to his wrists. He blushed now. Cal Rusch was one of Silicon Valley's oldest and most savvy venture capitalists, common knowledge. He was also a famous curmudgeon.

"Jesus, Charlie, what the hell's your problem?"

"One word: Lena."

"Lena? Come on!"

Charlie nodded, the severe look on his face fading to sorrow as he went on to explain that Cal Rusch was Lena's uncle. Her estranged uncle. When Lena was a kid Cal Rusch invited her father to put some money in a deal. The deal tanked; Lena's family lost nearly everything. A year later Lena's father had a heart attack and died. Uncle Cal sent a wreath, not much more.

Charlie sighed. "Lena's mom and her sisters, they had a rough time. When it got real bad they had to show themselves at the uncle's castle and then maybe a few bucks trickled down—all of which Lena took as insult. When we moved back here Lena made me promise up and sideways he'd be the one source we wouldn't tap. I gave her my word."

"Sweet Marie," Swanson said to his hands, meaty as they were, folded primly in his lap.

"Right. And just to put the cherry on it, an old boyfriend of Lena's works with Rusch. Lena doesn't know he's there, but I do. I do. Christ, Lee, what kind of guy would I be, I mean, to put her through—Lena, you know she's—" Charlie waved his hand.

"She's every bit that," Swanson agreed, his crush on his best friend's wife hardly a secret. "Especially given, I mean, what you guys have been through this year."

The color drained from Charlie's face. Not for the world would he put another heartache in Lena's pocket. Not for the world.

He turned to the window. At the far end of the parking lot, a couple of runt apricot trees stood like tuning forks in the wind. They were all that remained of the abundant orchards that had filled the valley when Cupertino and Mountain View were farm towns. Today, the valley's cash crops grew indoors, in rows of nondescript office buildings such as this one, where folks like Charlie and Swanson worked feverishly, digging themselves in deep, which was why, in the end, Charlie would accept Cal Rusch's money, though he absolutely must not.

"You know, there are worse things than taking a bastard's money," Swanson mused. "Redemption. Vindication."

"Yeah. I thought of that."

"And what do you say is Uncle Cal's motive now? I mean, calling out of the blue and all."

"His motive? He said a friend at Stanford told him about our trial with that gallbladder in Des Moines. He said that his interest was pure business. But I suspect . . . I don't know, this type of guy—maybe he's after some peace in the later years."

"Ah, screw him."

"Yeah, but Swan—" The men exchanged a look that didn't require words. Two years ago they'd been stars; during lunch at Buck's they would eat their chicken California sandwiches as one by one the venture capitalists came over to the table to shake hands. But then, last summer, as they were preparing to raise their second round, the bottom fell out. The newspapers were calling it the Great Recession, but in real life it meant that the glad-handing VCs stopped returning Charlie's calls. By late autumn, funding in the Valley had all but ceased. Nimbus had a few months of capital left, and then the lights went out.

"You should have heard the old man," Charlie said. "Two minutes in and he's talking about the patent issues, bang; the software piece, bang—hell, what the other firms took months to see, he got at the first go." Charlie recalled the gravel in the old man's voice. It had been easy; Cal Rusch made it so.

"If he mentioned the other guys—"

"Oh, he mentioned Midas right off. He said he had a plan."

Swanson spread his hands like meat pies across the shelf of his wide-boned knees. "So. We going there, or is he coming to us?"

Charlie managed a smile. "Those trees out front," he said. "We might feed them. Give 'em a boost."

"Meantime you'll tell her."

"I imagine there will be a discussion."

"My advice, tell her quick, before she reads the thin film of your man-brain. Women can do that, don't I know." Swanson climbed wearily to his feet. "Buck up, Charlie. It'll turn out all right. That, or we're screwed." Swanson paused at the door. "OK, see you in a couple of hours. And, hey, in the spirit of things looking up, I bought a new jacket sure to impress the ladies."

"Oh, god."

"Yeah, well. Just wait. You heading out?"

An hour later Charlie locked the doors to Nimbus and walked to his car. It had been a year since he left the surgical faculty at Mass General—a year of push. And all that time he'd been gone—in Africa, Boston, or late nights at the office—while Lena managed everything solo. But tonight, they were throwing a dinner like normal folks. A new year, a new president: the papers were full of wild predictions and doom.

Charlie turned on the motor and reached for his phone. He would have to tell her—Sunday at the latest.

On the voice mail, Lena sounded younger and bright.

"Sweetheart," he said.

Two

Charlie Pepper wasn't Lena's first love, but he counted on being her last. He counted on it from the beginning—when they met, in the nineties, in a different world.

The party was in SoHo. Klein, having been named a partner at Goldman Sachs, was throwing himself a bash. Lena, a producer for an ABC news show, had come to research a piece on post-yuppies, whose avarice she intended to skewer in four parts.

Charlie noticed her by the windows. She was wearing a black dress that announced her intention to go to the next level, while her face said, But here I am—why's that? It was the disquiet in Lena's face that captured Charlie. Dark hair, pale skin, Audrey Hepburn neck. As she scanned the room, her eyebrows peaked as if asking a fundamental question. Charlie wondered what it was. He hoped he had the answer. There was a bit of the fairy about her, a bit of the witch.

"Obviously, it's an excellent time," Bill Hungerford told Charlie, by way of explaining his recent move into private equity. Bill played squash with Klein and he seemed to be under the mistaken impression that

Charlie was also a mover in financial circles. "My pop's putting up the initial nut, if you're wondering about that."

Charlie wasn't even remotely listening. "What color?" he mused. "Green?" He was talking about Lena's eyes.

"Green? Oh, sure, man: green as Ben Franklin!" Bill Hungerford laughed. By then Charlie was halfway to the windows.

Oh no, Lena thought, as the buffalo hunter approached. They weren't alike at all. She was impatient to his patience; intuitive to his one foot in front of the other empire-building logic; she was mercurial, proud, thin-boned, quick to slight, long to suffer, ardent. In other words, Lena Rusch wouldn't likely fall for Charlie Pepper unless she were recovering from his opposite.

As he came closer, Lena's gaze dropped to the whirls in the pickled oak floor. She'd been thinking lately that if she didn't do something amazing and soon, she'd become the thing most dreaded: ordinary.

"Hungry?" Charlie asked, wanting everything, advertising nothing.

He offered her a strawberry dipped in chocolate perched on a dainty white napkin.

"That's your name. Hungry?" She took a large bite, showing him two versions of a smile, one with the lips closed, the other with an endearing line of gum. As a matter of fact Lena *was* hungry—that, and date-wise it'd been a dismal couple of months. Love has built its house with less.

Want burned in Charlie's lower brain, while upstairs he wondered if maybe she wasn't Greek or French. In fact, Helena Rusch had been named for an actress of some merit in the Irish National Theatre. Great Great Aunt Helena first crossed the family blood by screwing the fair Norwegian actor who was playing Bassanio to her Portia. Following Great Great Aunt Helena, subsequent generations, now in America, included a slave-owning Virginian, an Ohio Episcopalian and a handful of Jews, who forgot they were Jews once they reached California. This all took place on Lena's mother's side. On her father's side, there were the money-fixated, unyielding Germanic Rusches, who every few generations produced a dreamer unable to earn a buck. Lena's father.

Nice but too nice? she wondered, glad that Charlie wasn't pretty, not with that hawkish nose and small English teeth. Age and some sleep would be kind to the face of Charlie Pepper, adding gravitas here, softening there—bettering. Lena could see that map as far as it went.

Her gaze shifted to Charlie's capable hands. A sigh of girlish hope escaped her. She'd been holding herself safe, tied up in knots. Every so often she would undo a part; let it down, have a fling. In the beginning, they all wanted to marry her. That would go on for a time. Until one or the other would put the fork in. Her friends were all career women, pretending not to be looking for husbands, while looking for them every night. But Lena never pretended, she'd done away with love.

"Where to?" she asked, taking Charlie's arm.

A low current ran through her as they moved across the wide-planked floors. Look at this, she thought, I'm completely calm. She'd gone off with a stranger once before. But that had been different. That had been entirely different. She was nowhere near that trouble now.

Stop grinning like an ass, Charlie warned himself, smiling anyway, as he led Lena down several flights of stairs. At one point he let her get a few steps ahead. Her hair was thick and her ears very small and he had to keep his other hand in his pocket so as not to touch; not to cover her bones, her cheeks, her nose with his mouth. He had a tremendous urge to crush her.

"Here," he said, once they were outside, nearing the corner. He tucked her close like a package that must be kept out of the rain. "We're going here."

Even after the wedding they still believed that marriage was a flexible, romantic sort of agreement, which they would shape and polish over time. It was not. Marriage was a stone on which far tougher than the likes of Charlie and Lena had been shaped and polished unto vapor and salt.

Theo arrived a few years later and soon he was a sweet-faced kid who asked too many questions, but that just made him more like his mother, and more loved. They took up housekeeping in a three-bedroom condo in the Back Bay of Boston. Charlie joined the surgical faculty at Mass General, leading a push in robotics. Lena was a senior producer for special projects at Boston's famed PBS station, WGBH. She'd produced a winning series on the evolution of the presidency and had won the plum assignment of making a documentary on the global AIDS crisis. Lena took Charlie and Theo on that first trip to Mbarara, Uganda, to a teaching hospital with a small HIV clinic. The surgical unit had just one full-time doctor and an overflowing population of sick and wounded. It lacked an X-ray machine, and the one wheezy generator only intermittently supported the lights and a ventilator. Charlie believed he could help. Soon they were spending their vacations in Mbarara. Charlie brought over some residents from Boston to help the staff; he built systems. Lena, toting Theo, worked with a local woman to start a school. At night they ate dinner at the Lord's Bar. Grilled goat, chapati, salsa. Beer. That first year they traveled to Mbarara twice. They were happy, as singularly happy as they would ever be.

Meanwhile, back home, Lee Swanson kept bugging Charlie. "Hey, what the hell are we doing?"

"A robot," Charlie answered—musing, but sounding sure.

"Say more," Swanson replied.

"A device so simple you could set it up in a field hospital or in a mobile unit."

Then one night, as Lena and Charlie made love, at the climactic moment she heard the ripple in the river. Straddling Charlie, locking him with her thighs, she put a cool finger to his heart and asked, "What is it?"

"What is what." Charlie truly believed he'd only been shooting the breeze with Swanson, that's all.

Lena nodded encouragingly. She gave him plenty of time. She had looked inside him, to the lamplight there. Seeing the lamp, Lena also spied the secret box he kept beside it—as everyone did, as she had one herself. His heart beat up through her finger.

"You know," she said.

He didn't quite. Not in so many words. Having marched straight through med school into his internship and residency, and then on to the daily grind of a high-speed surgical career, Charlie Pepper hit his forties wanting something more. Something more woke him in the night like a lover calling his name. But he hadn't really put it into words.

Smiling knowingly, Lena climbed down from the bed and walked her high ass out of the room. She was never casual with her intuitions and she never liked to waste time and, besides, the lamp and the box were hallowed things not to be messed with.

What the hell just happened? Charlie sat up, pulling the covers discreetly to his waist. He felt stunned, enlivened and, yes, some afraid. Lena was in the kitchen now, banging cabinets, opening the fridge door—his small-boned girl with a bit of a heavy hand.

Loving always made her starving, that he knew as well.

She returned with a plate of chicken, grapes, bread, pickles, cheese and a six-pack of Guinness. Climbing into bed, she daintily arranged the picnic around her. She tore off a hunk of bread, laid it across her palm and stacked it with a slice of chicken and a log of cheese. Biting down, Lena groaned with pleasure. Then she fixed him with those grass green eyes.

Once Charlie started talking, it was hard to stop. His thoughts tumbled out, fully formed, like neat bricks set in rows. Of course, he drank a bit, too. "We'll talk of this time," he said, "as the revolution."

Charlie had already convinced Mass General to invest in a million-dollar robot called the Midas. He had made himself the go-to guy, training doctors up and down the East Coast. This much Lena knew. But the Midas proved to be an Edsel, overly technical, fussy. And through his work in Mbarara, Charlie had imagined a more simplified robot that could be used in remote locations, a battlefield, say—a smaller robot that could be wheeled in on a cart and cost a tenth of the price of the Midas. Any surgeon anywhere would want to use it.

In a long life together, who says what the key moments are? When love knocks you on the head and shouts, Hey. Listen up. This is our chance.

Lena understood desire; she understood it in her bones. She ate all the food and drank a beer then put her plate aside. She'd been listening carefully. And when her mind wandered, she counted the crow's-feet around Charlie's eyes, making certain they were the same number as yesterday and then she listened a little more. They would have to move out West to join Swanson, who had deep roots in the medical device world. San Francisco would be a leap backward, to a place she'd run from years ago. She saw the sharp, unhappy faces of her mother and her sisters, and putting them aside, she hugged her ribs and focused on the pleasant cadences of Charlie's voice. Lena considered the sweet fragrance of San Francisco in March, when the hills of Marin and Oakland were greenest and the sea air mixed with the pungent flowering privet; she recalled those tawny afternoons of her childhood, when the sun cast its golden veil over the city. But was she ready to go back? From here Lena's thoughts returned to the shadows. She fretted over housing prices. She hated the thought of leaving the job she loved. She knew it would be hell to get Theo into one of those snotty private schools, but the public schools, which she preferred, were broken. So instead Lena imagined calling Vi, whom she missed terribly, to say she was coming home. The picture brightened again. By the time Charlie finished, she had decided they'd keep the piano but sell the car.

"You OK?" he asked, for there were tears in her eyes.

Then again, she had a piece of arugula stuck in her tooth. With the tip of his finger, Charlie removed it. He kissed her deeply, holding her face in his capable doctor hands, and pledging in so many endearing, silly phrases his undying love. Then he sat back to listen. He knew she would have lots of questions.

At first she said nothing. She got out of the bed and, throwing on his old sweater, sat in the one good chair across from him.

Her eyes tick-tocked. Finally she said, "We could lose each other." It wasn't a question. She had hefted the largest boulder from the river and flung it on the floor between them. She expected him to examine it with her. "We're different," she said. "That's fine when it's just us together, but the distance, Charlie." She shook her head.

Charlie didn't want to think about them being different. "With you, Lean, that's what I'm saying. It's always going to be us."

"We're talking years, Charlie. You won't do this halfway. I wouldn't want you to."

"What—do you mean schedules? We can figure that out."

"Now. Let's figure it out *now*." And once again she pointed to the rock he could not see.

"Weekends," he ventured. "I'll be home on the weekends, and three out of five nights during the week."

"And Mbarara?"

He thought for a long moment. Finally, he hung his head. "I'll have to cut out Mbarara."

"Cut it out?" she cried. Didn't he understand Mbarara was hers, too?

Charlie opened his mouth and shut it like a fish. "OK. I'll cut *back*. Whatever it takes. Honestly, babe." His heart was racing. "Three years. Let's agree we'll give it three years. I'll build it, then sell it. We can do this, Lean. We can be big."

"How do you know we can be big?"

"My god, I just know."

Feeling it, too, she nodded. Her hand went to her heart. She'd been thinking lately it was time they had another child. "Charlie Pepper."

"Come over here and say that."

She smiled but stayed put.

"I said come over here."

"Mmm. I heard you."

Maybe now, Charlie thought, I should offer her something equally bounteous. "Hey," he said. "Let's make a girl this time."

When scared or surprised, her ears moved back, like a horse's. "What, Pep? Then I'd have two to raise on my own?" But she was beaming, and Charlie knew he had hit on the very thing.

They had no limits. Together they had no limits at all.

They laughed as she crawled back on top. "Come *here*. Come here."

They were as ordinary as any two people wanting more. When Lena's boss heard that her radical, save-the-world and nail-the-bastards producer was pregnant with twins and moving to San Francisco, Kay Higgins let go a world-weary sigh. "Why is it," she asked, "in a boom economy, it's always the women heading back to the kitchen?" Higgins was fifty-five and a spinster. What besides a lifetime of work did she know? She fixed Lena with a self-justifying smile that was the purview of politicians and maiden aunts. "My door's always open, sweetheart. I'm just so disappointed that I won't see your star walk through it." Again Kay sighed, a sigh that had everything to do with her old loneliness, but that part Lena missed. Instead she heard a warning.

"I'll get there," Lena protested. "It might take a little more time."

"It'll be harder. Kids feed off the primary vein."

"Fine by me."

"Oh, it'll be fine. It'll be wonderful. Just different."

But Lena wasn't sure she wanted different, if different meant being less. What had she been doing all these years, if not striving to become someone? She wanted to have her children and still be the mighty star. "What's this, Kay? Didn't we agree that there should be a special place in hell for women who didn't help other women rise?" Lena was already on her feet, heading for the door. "You know, for women who don't let other women choose."

"Oh, honey, by all means choose. By all means *rise,*" Kay agreed, but there was something new in her voice that sounded to Lena a lot like a door closing.

Lena was halfway down the hall when she remembered where she was going and, feeling better, she shouted behind her. "Life, Kay. Life!"

So, Lena and Charlie made their deal. Charlie would give everything to Nimbus and Lena would handle the rest. Their children would be well, their love would advance, and nothing would impede them. They arrived in San Francisco ready for luck. At first they were tentative in their arrangements. They looked at houses, appalled at the prices, and then the prices seemed not quite so appalling anymore. They looked at smaller houses, well beyond their budget, and then these went for more than they had and they adopted a new stance. They were flexible, Lena and Charlie. They were hopeful. They bought a small bungalow they didn't love that was painted an awful shade of pink. What did it matter, pink or otherwise? They'd paint, first thing. It had three small bedrooms upstairs and an unfinished room with a bath in the basement. It had a small deck outside with a magnolia tree and room enough to put in a set of swings. The previous owner, a stage actress turned lesbian singer, left her crystals lining the edge of the upstairs tub. There they stayed.

Charlie went to work. Lena pushed through the first trimester feeling awful, to the sweet spot of the middle months. She settled the house and launched Theo into preschool. Each morning she dropped him at school and set off on a walk toward the Bay. The early-morning breeze was bracing, but Lena had the twins inside, her own private furnace. Filled with wonder, she felt as close to life as she had ever been.

The city was different from the one she'd left long ago. The dot-com money of the nineties had turned San Francisco around. The funky girl city of Lena's youth had grown up, becoming a fine lady in linen and heels. All across town houses had been renovated, sparing no expense. There was new paint and gold detailing and brilliant landscaping. Large SUVs filled the narrow driveways of Noe Valley and Cow Hollow. In the Mission, block after block along Valencia had a restaurant with a big-name cook and parking was impossible. Even the shoreline had been gentrified. At Crissy Field, there was a crushed-granite walk leading to the Golden Gate Bridge. There were cultivated wild grasses and native birds dip-diving in a man-made marsh, and signs marking what's what. Lena's walk ended at the Warming Hut, where Alice Waters, the famed chef from Chez Panisse, had designed a menu featuring organic, sustainable coffees, and croissants. Lena looked back at the city aglow in its morning whites.

Of course, Lena didn't see Charlie much and they were tight on money, with Charlie's salary half what it had been in Boston while their mortgage had doubled. Lena joined Violet's PR firm as a freelancer working part-time, writing commercial documentaries. It was soulless work, but temporary. On weekends, she showed Theo the town; together they painted the new nursery green.

One night early in March, twenty-four weeks into the pregnancy, Lena found she couldn't sleep. She curled around Charlie and planned their lives. She went shopping in the store inside her mind to buy the next few years. When Charlie climbed out of bed for an early surgery at Stanford, Lena had an excuse to get up as well. Feeling wifely, she made coffee and buttered his toast, and after breakfast she stood on the front steps in Charlie's running shoes to say good-bye.

"You OK?" He was looking at her seriously, the way he did. He ran his hands along her back, knowing the bones and nerves.

"I am not missing you," she said, covering his face with kisses. "I'm not. I'm not."

Later that morning, while getting Theo dressed, Lena felt the first contraction. Theo was doing somersaults on the bed and the thump and bounce sank her to her knees.

"Theo, please. Hold still."

She waited, her fingers linked under her belly. "Theo, honey, I've got to . . . lie down." Aware of Theo's eyes on her, she made for the door, holding her belly with her hands.

"Theo, sweetheart. Get the phone."

Sober, clear-eyed and, like his father, believing that if he were vigilant, no wrong could happen, Theo ran to the master bedroom and back.

An hour down the road, at Stanford, Charlie was using a robot to excise cancer from a fifty-six-year-old schoolteacher's bladder. As he cauterized vessels deep in the pelvis, he explained to the residents and surgeons watching in the theater above, that while man's hands were limited tools, his mind could fashion a device that turned his fingers into a needle, scissors, fire and a wand.

Lena had him paged. When he called back she sounded more mystified than frightened. A day earlier at the doctor's everything had been fine. "It's only twenty-four weeks," she cried, pausing for another contraction. "Shit! Charlie, my water just broke."

He told her to stay on the line, while on his cell he called their OB and an ambulance.

"Charlie, Theo's here. He's standing next to me. What do I do? Oh, god, what do I do?" Panic rose in Lena's voice.

"Send him over to the Brandts' until I get there."

"Who?" Her knees were buckling. She closed her eyes.

"Next door. The guy with the leaf blower. His wife's name, what was her name?"

"Charlie, we don't know them."

"Of course we know them. They're our neighbors. We're talking a couple of hours, Lean."

"Don't you remember, Charlie? That time with Theo's ball? They kept calling him, to his face, 'the child.'"

But Charlie wasn't listening. He was issuing orders. And when he was done issuing orders, he grabbed his keys and tore up the highway.

The firstborn twin, Sylvie, was just too small—all the wonders of technology and medicine couldn't save her. Willa, only slightly larger at one pound six ounces, had trouble breathing. She needed immediate surgery on her lungs. Lena, drugged and exhausted, had a tear in the wall of her uterus and had to be hurried to the OR and stitched. Like a seal she slipped under the surface, to where it was cool and safe, and there she stayed for the next several hours.

Charlie named Sylvie. He stood at the foot of Lena's hospital bed holding his baby. At last he opened the blanket. With skilled, tender hands he smoothed the bottom of Sylvie's feet and counted her fingers and turned her over and saw that she was covered in down. Twice the nurses came for her; the first time he sent them away and the second time he had them bring a basin. He bathed her, wrapped her in another clean blanket, then he walked her around the room, the heartbreak coming in waves. It affected his knees. Charlie, the able doctor, folded to the floor and begged the gods. The gods were silent. At last, when he couldn't put it off any longer, he woke Lena so she could hold her dead baby.

Lena opened her eyes. The morphine made her thoughts loopy and the lights too bright. The thick hedge of Charlie's hair appeared winked with silver. She smiled—there at the holy gates, high as a kite. With trembling hands, she reached for her prize.

"Charlie?"

Three

Grief was a stalker. It lurked in the china cabinet and in the waiting room at the dentist's and behind the switch on the hall light. It twined itself inside the tongue of sneakers and the click of pens and the heels of socks. Tea bags were infused with it, as were cereal boxes, board games and the mail as it passed through the slot. Contrary to reputation, it never looked drab; it didn't care a whit about time. The hummingbird had it, flapping furiously, as did the weary-faced gorilla eating its banana at the zoo. Ferries crossed the Bay with it trapped inside their cabins; container ships carried it in their hulls. It wasn't elegant. It wasn't easy or smooth. It rose with the sun and hid in the corners of fog. Surprisingly, it preferred hello to good-bye. It showed up on the beach and acted churlish in the park. It frayed the nerves in the manner of a gunshot or a siren whizzing by. It was big, hairy, inarticulate, possessing just one word, *why*. It was brain freeze and sour lemons and a knife to the belly and a thrum-thrumming of the heart—combined. Grief made Lena clumsy. She was always falling, and attempting to rise.

On the nights they spent together, she and Charlie lay side by side like swimmers capsized by a rogue wave, hurled onshore. They lay on their backs, breathless, speaking in clipped half sentences of other things. Other things consumed them. There were Willa's ongoing health crises, and the accompanying medical bills, and the applications and interviews required to get Theo into a decent kindergarten. There was work, unyielding. The presidential election and the economic crisis were distractions. And all the while Lena and Charlie were living another secret life, a life of amazement. And that life was changing all the time.

Swanson spent the night on the sofa and the next morning, New Year's Day, he helped Charlie put out the trash. "Are we good then? What did she say?"

Charlie was tossing empty wine bottles into the recycling bin, where they made a satisfying crash. He went on that way for a while. "Swanny, how many meetings have we had that haven't amounted to a hill of turds?"

"Too many."

"This is my point."

"What the hell's your point?"

"My point," Charlie said, tossing another bottle, "is why upset her for nothing? We'll do the meeting and then—I'll tell her when there's something to tell."

Several minutes later, the door to the kitchen swung open and Lena appeared with another bag of bottles. She eyed the men carefully. "So."

"Oh, hey." Swanson waved as if she were across the street instead of five steps away. He took the bag from her.

Lena nodded. "Am I interrupting you guys?"

"Jesus," Swan whispered. "They can't all be mind readers, can they?"

"Yep," Charlie said.

"Yep what?" Lena asked.

"Lena," Swanson dodged, "last night I forgot to ask: What's your New Year's resolution?"

"I don't know." She tipped her head in a way he found both charming and unnerving. "I'm lousy at giving things up. What's yours?"

"Better wardrobe might be a start."

She laughed. "I can help, Lee."

"Nah. It's part of my charm."

She nodded. Dear Swanny, blushing so sweetly while Charlie stomped those boxes, ignoring them both. Lena narrowed her eyes. "Grace. I want grace."

"Oh, god, you have it," Swanson said.

"No. Not where it counts." She sighed, folding her arms. "Just ask Charlie."

"Chah-lie?"

Charlie slammed his heavy boot on a carton, splitting it at its seams. "You have it but you don't know."

"Doesn't count," she said quietly. "Doesn't count." And she disappeared into the kitchen, shutting the door.

Later that morning Jesse was drinking coffee at the kitchen table when they heard a bang on the back door.

"Oh, god," cried Jesse. "That would be Mom."

The door, swelled by the wet weather, hesitated then gave way with a crash, and a small woman wearing a plastic hat appeared out of the rain—Beverly herself. The castanets of her many bracelets *tinck-tincked* as her bright eyes surveyed the room taking in the surface of things. She had only a few minutes; friends were expecting her. She dropped a bag of lemons on the counter. "And how is the little bird?"

"Fine," said Lena from the floor. She had Willa seated in a Boppy and was trying to get her to track a large red ball.

"Oh. I tell you, that child breaks your heart." Beverly's hand indeed went to her heart. "But she doesn't fool me. Uh-uh. She is her mother all over—another drama queen."

As if to prove it, Willa looked up at her grandmother and grinned, showing four new rabbit teeth.

"See that!" cried Beverly, satisfied. And eyeing both her grandchild and her daughter from a distance, Beverly ran quick hands down her tight knit dress and up through her hair. She had weathered an uneasy life, Beverly.

She had done the best she could. But this middle one, this Lena—what to do about her? She was superior and downtrodden both, too high and too low, and nothing Beverly possessed, not a single thing in her bag, could help Helena Rusch. "And how are *you*?"

"Oh, I don't know. A little tired, Ma," Lena admitted.

"Please. Raising you three on my own? I was tired for thirty years."

Lena turned to Jesse and the two sisters exchanged a deeply historic eye-rolling glance. But Beverly, whose daughters gave her nothing but trouble, shooed them like flies. Did they know what she suffered? To have raised three girls on the whiff of a rat?

Beverly moved a pile of Lena's mail to a new spot on the counter. She looked around, a small bird on the hunt for something shiny. "Well, I know you made a nice dinner. You always do. Was it great, Jesse?"

"It was, Ma."

"Me, I expected to be sitting home all by my lonesome, but as it turns out a couple I met just yesterday invited me to tag along. Wonderful people. He's into imports; she's made a killing in real estate. Anyway, if they ask me to visit them in Del Mar, I just might go." At the thought of a new adventure, Beverly's face assumed a far-off happy look and this she trained on her youngest daughter.

"Now, Jesse, tell me. What do you have going?" By *what,* Beverly always meant *who.*

"Nothing, Ma. Not a damn thing."

"Don't talk that way," Beverly scolded. "You could write your own ticket. Lena, help your sister."

Lena was building Willa a tower of blocks. Slowly, she picked up her head. "I'm sorry. What'd you say?"

"Fa! You girls," pressed Beverly. "Come on! Shame one and shame two! Twenty-six, my friends, becomes thirty-eight just like that, and a very nice girl is disappointed." Beverly snapped her fingers.

"Wow," Jesse said, "just like that."

Then, as if to save them, Charlie came in from the garage.

"Let me say hello to the traveling man!" Beverly cried, clapping her hands and pushing her way round the island to take Charlie's shoulders in her tiny, fierce grip. She rose on tippytoe to be kissed. Men still loved her, of course they did. "Charlie, what's doing? Lena, Charlie looks worried."

Lena squinted at her husband. "Where's Swan?"

"Gone."

"Charlie," Beverly went on. "Charlie, last night I had dinner with some folks who might know someone. Tell me, how is it going with the funding? Have you gotten any traction?"

"Ma," Lena warned.

"Well, has he? He said by Christmas, for sure, and it's New Year's." She studied her son-in-law, who looked as exhausted as his wife. "Charlie, people ask me, 'What's Charlie up to?' I don't have a clue how to answer. I mean I used to say, 'Why, he's a fabulous surgeon.' Which, of course, you are. But now this Nimbus business—with the sky falling and these hard times—here you people are! Charlie, I know you must have a plan. Of course you do. Tell me what to tell them."

"Ma, stop torturing the man," said Lena, picking Willa up from the floor and bringing her to the table.

"You, stop. Charlie's happy for me to ask. We can talk about anything, can't we, Charlie? Go on." Beverly lifted her chin to get him going faster.

"Tell them Nimbus is solid," Lena said.

"Is that right—or is that Miss Moonbeam, hoping?" Beverly fixed on Charlie.

But Charlie had eyes only for Lena. "Tell them Nimbus is solid," he said.

Lena smiled triumphantly.

Beverly was having none of it. "Charlie, you should call Uncle Cal. Don't give me those eyes, Helena; yes, yes—there, I'm saying it. Charlie should call Cal. It's high time he does a good turn for this family."

"Does he know that, Ma?" cried Lena. "Does Uncle Cal know it's high time he does us a good turn?" Lena's anger was fierce and quick, which was lucky, for she missed the shock on Charlie's face at the mention of Cal Rusch. "Charlie Pepper wouldn't take a *dime* from that man—"

"Then Charlie would be foolish," snapped Beverly, and she leveled a very brown look at her daughter. "And I'm sure he's not. Are you, Charlie?" Beverly adjusted her bracelets. "As for you, Helena Rusch. Pride is the thing the bird drops on your nose."

"If I'm proud, Ma, it's because of Dad. Remember?" Lena's voice shook.

"Hey, Lean," said Jesse, "I think Ma's just trying—"

"Of course I remember," Beverly cried, jabbing her finger. "I don't need *you* reminding me! Lena, I hope for your sake you never disappoint your children. God knows, they won't let you forget it. That was a long, long time ago."

Lena's face was blotched with feeling. "You brought it up, Ma. Please, and I say this with all kindness, don't mention that man's name again in this house." And with that, Lena took Willa upstairs. Charlie followed.

Beverly looked over at Jesse and nodded.

"Ma, don't do it. Don't stir the pot."

"You, be quiet. Someone has to stir that pot." Beverly pointed at the ceiling. "I'm sure."

Upstairs, Charlie found Lena lying facedown on the bed, weeping. Willa sat in the hoop of Lena's arm, sucking on a stuffed elephant.

"Tell me that didn't just happen," Lena mumbled.

"All right, that didn't just happen." Charlie sat down on the bed and put his warm hand on her back.

"But it did." Lena rolled over and studied Charlie. "You're a good man."

"Well, don't go bananas here. I'm OK."

"Nope, you're more than OK. Charlie, is it going to be all right? I mean, no BS."

"I think so."

"And if there's something I need to know, you'll tell me, right?" She looked at him with yearning eyes.

"Right."

"OK then."

"OK." He stood. "You want me to sit in the shower with her?"

"Oh, god, would you? Here." Lena kissed him.

That was Saturday. Soon it was Sunday night, and Charlie had to hurry to catch the red-eye to Boston. He put Theo in bed and came downstairs with his suitcase. He was putting on his coat when Lena hurried from the kitchen with Willa in her arms. "Charlie, I think her cold's turned. Look, she's a little blue around the mouth. Can you listen to her?" Charlie unpacked his kit and fitted the stethoscope to his ears. Lena held her breath as he moved the scope across Willa's chest and onto her back, nodding, as he heard the unmistakable crackles of pneumonia in her lungs.

Lena ran up the stairs to get Theo.

So, the whole family raced from the house to stand on the front lawn in the fog-spooked dark. The damp wool of San Francisco winter closed around them. The patch of lawn, tricked by early rains, was a shock of green. Foghorns, or digitized renditions of horns, mourned and mooed from the towers of the bridge. Theo, his frog pajamas showing frankly above his boots, leaned against Charlie.

The family car was parked in the driveway; Charlie's cab waited at the curb.

I love her, he thought, while noting that the lawn was soaking his shoes. And I will do whatever it takes—that phrase, exact and neat, played in his brain like a mantra, a happy loop, bucking him to do more and soon. That Charlie was deeply devoted to his family was not in question. There was nothing he wouldn't do for them, nothing he couldn't manage. And if it didn't occur to him to cancel Boston, where he had a shot at getting Mass General to prototype the Nimbus, and thereby impress Cal Rusch, it was because another song played on a second track, its lyric being, "Twenty million by April, Bud, or the lights go out."

Theo spotted the bird.

Overhead, in the limbs of the magnolia bordering the neighbor's yard, a wild parrot perched, with his tuck lime jacket, cherry epaulettes and cap, his white-rimmed eye cocked. They all looked up, and the beady caviar eye looked down.

"Theo," Lena called over her shoulder, "he's flown all the way from Telegraph Hill."

"He's only after the fame and gold," Theo replied, repeating a line he once heard his mother say to Vi.

Theo's habit of plucking the bald spot from the truth had already convinced the boys at school that he was a bit odd.

Lena turned slowly, her eyes bright. "Theo!"

Of course she'd been talking about Charlie. He was the one, after all, who'd brought them back here, the one who taught Theo about the gold rushes one and two, the third being the gold rush they'd just missed.

"Lean."

"Oh, come on, Pepper," she said. "We're fine. This is just, well, what it is." Lena turned into the wind where they could not see and wiped her cheek.

At that moment the cabbie, watching them stand there, flagrant in their inaction, blasted the horn.

"Christ!" Lena shouted. Hiking Willa higher in her arms, she walked to the car.

Theo, at that fleeting age when his mother seemed almost perfect, dropped Charlie's hand and followed. If there were sides to be taken, he took hers. Nothing could alter his good opinion of that person upon whom his every comfort depended. If she no longer looked exactly like the mother he remembered, if her hair was oily and unbrushed, if her skin was dry and her lips so pale they almost disappeared, if she forgot to put on earrings or any adornment, and if under her breath she vividly cursed, these details did not so much detract as amplify Theo's impression that once not long ago they had lived a grand life.

And what a life it had been when her arms were the cathedral of one Theodore Finnegan Pepper. Instead of Willa, floppy and feverish, who had to be taken to the hospital—again.

Theo climbed by himself into his booster, clipped the seat belt and sighed like an old man.

Meanwhile, the cabbie, a white-turbaned Sikh with a Burberry scarf, watched Charlie as he went back for his bags. And everything I do, I do for them, Charlie went on, addressing the surgical review panel that traveled at all times inside his head. The panel, Harvard class of 1984, were hardly immune to the pleasures of life—windsurfing, drinking, screwing around—nevertheless they were on the clock. Recently the panel suggested to Charlie that perhaps he had missed the revolution. Those days in Silicon Valley when mere kids in T-shirts and baseball caps took a great idea and went all the way. Why wasn't Charlie Pepper one of them? Why wasn't he? The house leveraged, credit cards maxed, first-round financing shot; the former surgeon living on half what he used to make, plus his wife's freelance earnings; he'd missed school functions, Willa procedures; he'd been home in time for dinner only twice in six months.

Lately he'd been thinking about age. Forty-seven wasn't the forty-seven of his father, whose children had finished college by then. No, forty-seven today was a wife, work and young kids. Forty-seven was debt. Forty-seven was having the stamina of your father at thirty, with the stress of a peasant carrying bricks on his back.

Charlie strode across the fog-drenched lawn. Eight hours from now, in a locker room at Mass General, he'd unpeel damp socks from his puckered feet and hang them on a hook to dry. All right, guy, he cautioned himself. Buck up.

"I'll call you," he shouted.

Doors opening and banging closed, Lena, of the fairies and the witches, waved. Charlie's heart was quite certain she waved.

Four

Lena took a deep breath, pushed open the heavy doors, and made a quick path to the bulletproof window at the reception desk. "Betsy," she said in a loud voice. Betsy had been working the nightshift in the ER the last time, and the time before that, but there was no recognition in her dull eyes. She had turquoise beads woven into her cornrows and two-inch, multicolored nails. She was typing in slow mo.

"Hello, Betsy." Lena took pains to modulate her voice. Holding Theo's hand, she hefted Willa higher on her hip as a bead of sweat ran down her face into her scarf. She ignored it. Oh, they had been such innocents, she and Charlie, a year ago.

"Name?" Betsy droned.

"Not me, my daughter. Willa. Willa Pepper. We've been here many times. Look, please, look up her chart. She's eleven months, with a history of pneumonia. She was sixteen weeks preemie. Her breathing is strident. Her oxygen level low, dangerously low. I would bet eighty-five, maybe eighty-four. We'd better check it now. I'd like to see Dr. Carr immediately. He's on, Monday nights, no?"

Betsy turned from her computer screen just long enough to see who was talking at her with that uppity tone. "Name? Insurance?"

That was all it took. Instantly, Lena was back inside her nightmare, that fortress of hell where some babies die and others never quite heal, and mothers never forget. She returned to that first afternoon when the nurses took Sylvie from her, and then, abruptly, Charlie said they had to go tend to the other one. Lena refused. Charlie told her she had no choice. He lifted her from the bed like a bride, but a bride with a catheter and a stitched womb, and he settled her into the wheelchair he'd parked alongside the bed. She begged him not to. She said please, she couldn't. But he had to be the doctor, he had to be Charlie, always assuming he knew better. He pushed her in that wheelchair down the hall past the rooms of the deeply satisfied new mothers, with their bouquets and balloons, round the nursery with the large plate-glass window and all the good babies there, on past the nurses' station and down another corridor through several sets of doors to the locked world of the NICU. They were buzzed inside. Charlie rolled her to a sink and the nurse scrubbed her hands and dried them. Then Charlie did the same, washing like the surgeon, hand over hand. Oh, his proficiency. She tried not to hate him.

He rolled her past the first isolettes with the tiny, tiny babies, to the still smaller ones, beaked like chicks, to the tiniest of all.

Lena supposed she'd feel relief to see her baby girl alive. She supposed she would be captured by a fierce maternal love, as she had been with Theo. She was ready. She had it coming. Despite the pain, she raised herself up and looked inside the clear plastic box that was part atrium, part vacuum and part coffin. As she began to shake, Charlie held her.

There was such a confusion of wires, tubes and alarms leading in and out. Lena looked past them, to the tiniest of tiny birds, all curled limbs and pointed bottom, the blue pulses visible, the waxy pink lips, the dry skin of a wizened elder, the heaving chest, the huge lashless eyes.

"Oh god." Lena covered her mouth.

The nurse, a large-bottomed gal from Wales, understood. She had seen scores of first-time mothers hit bottom in the NICU. She had witnessed their astonishment, fear and reasonable disgust. The trick was to push

43

them past the shock, to get them invested; it was her job to turn them into fighters.

"It's all right, love," she said, gently.

"How? How can it be all right?" Lena cried.

Sometime during those four months Willa spent in the NICU, Lena decided to change her character. She may not have delivered her twins, not the way she planned, but she understood the years in front of her, of labor and push. Whereas in the past she was impetuous, now she was constant; once impulsive, now well reasoned. Whereas she had been melancholic, she kept her grief private.

She had no patience for self-pity or whining; she refused envy.

But her dreams proved more difficult to control. Each night, as Lena closed her eyes, a symphony of bare-chested men greeted her, their deep-river voices calling for her to come over.

It took several hours, but eventually Lena, Willa and Theo moved upstairs to a private room on the pediatric ward. The room had two empty beds. Lena rolled them together and directed Theo to the one by the window. She handed him his Game Boy. As she arranged the blankets, the nurse came in with the IV. Seeing the needle, Willa, shrewd veteran, threw back her head and squalled.

"That's all right," Lena said. She lifted Willa in her arms and climbed onto the other bed. And tucking Willa into the side of her hip, she motioned the nurse to come forward.

The nurse approached, the needle hidden behind her back. "That's fine," Lena said soothingly, wincing as the nurse shoved the needle into Willa's small bony hand then taped the baby's arm up to the elbow onto a board. "No matter," Lena cooed, tears rolling down her cheeks. She kept her voice jolly even as Willa whimpered beneath her oxygen mask.

The nurse left them to it.

"Here, Big," Lena said, and Theo scooted from his bed to theirs, where Lena tucked him close under her other arm, one and two.

She wouldn't sleep, not that night or the next. Every four hours the pulmonologist banged through the door with the next dose of albuterol—adrenaline to dilate Willa's lungs—and the lights had to go on and they were all awake again, Willa high and fussing, climbing Lena's skin. Then Theo had to use the bathroom but was too afraid to walk the short, scary distance across the room by himself. Lena tried to unpeel her arm from around the baby, but Willa woke and the whole thing started again. So it was another hour to settle.

Outside, the staff marched to and fro, a regular late-night talking parade. They chatted in raised voices, sometimes laughing. Across the way a boy cried out for his mother. Elsewhere in the world people slept, they made love, technology was on the move, but in the corridors of the pediatric ward, mothers in greasy ponytails and comfortable shoes hunted for chipped ice.

They were on a trip; they were in the belly of time. Lena talked her children to sleep by telling happy stories, and then, of course, Theo wanted to hear about the dogs.

"Gus!" Theo cried. Gus being a Great Dane—the biggest, dumbest and most lovable dog—who had gotten Lena through her stormy childhood. "Tell about the time Aunt Didi was getting ready for her first boy-girl dance and Gus peed all over her new paisley dress."

"He soaked it, didn't he," Lena said, turning her gaze to check on Willa. The baby was watching Lena, her eyes atop the oxygen mask flicking open and shut.

"Aunt Didi was *pissed*!" whooped Theo, burrowing his large coconut head deeper into the crook of Lena's arm.

Lena arched her brow. *Pissed* was a word Theo knew he wasn't supposed to say, though, to be honest, he'd heard it more than a few times. She didn't want to raise a son with a garbage mouth, but on the other hand the ability to use a word cleverly, knowingly, daringly seemed all right.

"You know, Theo," said Lena, "I've always wondered . . . well, maybe old Gus, in his way, was simply expressing his opinion about that dress." Her smile was full of mischief. "What do you think?"

Theo covered his mouth with his hand. There was a square of light in the door leading to the hall; he focused on that. "What is paisley?"

"Ah," Lena said, and kissed the top of Theo's head. She had to thank the gods he had an uncommon mind. Loving them was one thing, but liking them was a bonus.

"OK, Theo. Willa's asleep. Do you want to try?"

She felt him touch bottom in her arms.

By the next night, Lena knew she had to get them home. Theo was increasingly restive, and with the nurses waking Willa up every few hours to check her vitals, the baby wasn't getting any rest either. Yet there was no one home to help. Glo was away on a trip with her church; Jesse wasn't answering her cell; Violet was meeting a client in Chicago. Charlie had another two days to go in Boston. Beverly was not a possibility, not at all.

Lena had her canvas bag packed when the morning nurse came into the room. Lena informed her they would be going home. A discussion followed, with one side saying you can't and the other saying, Oh, yes. The nurse retreated, and outside Lena could hear her on the telephone, informing the pulmonologist that Lena was difficult. A half hour later Dr. Chang appeared, as Lena knew he would. She hadn't seen him before. He was young, maybe just out of residency, and as he bent down to examine Willa, who was seated on Lena's lap, Lena noticed he had a hunk of wax in his ear. She made a face, she couldn't help it, but that wax gave her strength, too. Believing he was superior, Dr. Chang jiggled the keys in his lab coat pocket as he told Lena she was dangerously unaware: Willa needed at least one more day on the oxygen and IV.

Lena stared at him intensely, allowing him to think she was listening. In fact, she was visualizing getting them from the parking lot to the car to the front door to their own beds. Her body ached deep inside her cells, and she had a frightening itch underneath her ponytail—then, too, there was a whole set of nerves inside threatening to snap if Theo didn't stop bouncing that damn ball.

That this young doctor, himself stupid from exhaustion, didn't share her urgency, wasn't a problem for Lena. So long as he didn't get in her way. She smiled contritely, her voice sounding oh so reasonable. Hearing her,

Theo stopped playing with his ball and watched his mother, as if she were an actress on stage. "My husband is an MD. I know the protocols; I know how to administer the treatments—all night if necessary—at home. This baby—my baby—needs rest."

Much more was said, of course, and at a point Lena unwisely did curse, embarrassing them both. But it was all a show and even Dr. Chang played his part gamely, knowing that Lena was prepared to make herself a real pain in the ass until she got her babies home.

It took all day. The house was dark and cold and, coming after the relentless squawk of the hospital, eerily quiet. Lena put Theo to bed first, tucking the covers tight across his chest the way he liked it, even though she was so tired her teeth were pulsing. She changed Willa, nursed her and put her down. It was eight o'clock. Lena would be getting up every few hours to give Willa the albuterol treatments and that was how it was going to be.

Lena crawled on all fours into her bed. Crashing to sleep, she thought, Isn't the heart, isn't the heart a curious thing?

The next morning Charlie's call woke her from a sound sleep.

"You, sir," Lena said in a voice that would have been reasonable had she not been fast asleep, "have no guarantee."

"Boy." Charlie laughed. "Don't I know." He sighed deeply, from a world away. "How are you? Lean?"

Lena had fallen back to sleep.

"Sweetheart—" he said. "Lena!"

"Charlie?" Her voice sounded high-pitched and happy, for she was dreaming. Her voice nearly broke him with longing. It was a magical thing, her voice. For Charlie it had become the sound of home. He closed his eyes and pictured her in their large, white bed. He could smell her, if he tried; he could knock himself out with the thought of her morning musk, her leg making contact first and then the lips and then the rest. Lena's voice was the mirthometer of their lives, and when she was happy he believed he must also be happy.

"Charlie, I was dreaming of . . . men. They were crossing the street."
She yawned loudly. "Why? . . . can't tell. Guys, these guys, in thick over-
coats, were crossing the street at odd angles." Lena paused, the map of
her dream sketchy. More than anything, she felt curious. No matter how
terrible the night had been, Lena Rusch always began the day with hope.
"What do you think?"

He thought he'd like to keep her talking just a little longer. But they
were paging him over the loudspeaker; he was due in preop and so Charlie
let go of pleasure, and spoke to her out of duty. "I'm between cases," he
said. "I'll finish here, give my pitch, and catch the last flight tonight."

"Pepper, talk yourself home *now*," she begged.

"Baby, I wish I could. Hey, before we go, how is she? How is Willa?"

Lena opened her eyes. Back in the days of the NICU, he made her a
promise: as long as she had to handle the front lines of Willa's care, the
surgeries, the therapies, the cardiologists, immunologists, pulmonologists;
the eye folks, the trinity of the gross motor, speech and hearing folks; the
sleepless nights, the medicated days, not to mention Theo, he couldn't
demand that she also be like one of his interns, spouting updates whenever
he demanded. He'd have to wait for her to tell him.

With a start she sat up. "Oh my god. Oh my god. What time is it?"

Hearing Lena's panic, Charlie tried to help. He flicked back his cuff
and read his watch. Forgetting to translate east to west, he announced that
it was nine—nine o'clock in the morning.

"Fuck!"

He heard the drum of her feet as she ran down the hall. Lena was
gone.

Please god, please god, please god, she whispered, knowing she'd be accorded
no favors, and could at best hope for only a bit of clearance from the gods.
Please.

Willa was curled on her side in the corner of the crib and Lena knew
she was dead. *Oh, no, oh god no.* Her hands shook as she picked up the
baby and pressed her lips to Willa's hot, sweaty skull. *Oh thank—OK.* Lay-

ing Willa belly down across the length of her arm, Lena thumped firmly between the baby's shoulder blades. At last Willa coughed. Weak, but still a cough. *OK. OK.* And turning Willa over, working quickly now, Lena hosed the nostrils first with saline, followed by the suction bulb, extracting ropes of green snot. Willa, limp with the effort of breathing, had her eyes closed; Lena might as well have been trussing a chicken.

Lena dropped into the one good chair and flicked on the nebulizer at her feet. She hoisted two large pillows from the floor onto her lap, added the baby, and hovered the plastic mask with the medicinal plume in front of Willa's face. "Breathe," she commanded.

The third pillow, the one necessary to support her arm for the next forty-five minutes, had demonically found its way across the room. *Get over here. Get. Over.* The nebulizer thrummed at her feet. Lena sighed and adjusted her mouth, removing as much of the grimness as she could. The tears rolled down as she looked into her lap.

"Will-a," Lena whispered. "Quick. Brave."

Willa, glassy-eyed, locked onto her mother's face.

"Curious. Wise. Funny. Will-a."

As the albuterol took hold and Willa's lungs opened, she began to nurse. Lena's milk dropped to her breasts as through a trap door. She tucked in her lips and moaned. The other side of the room was coming up from the night shadows, the window and its curtain.

"All right," Lena said.

She was moving Willa to the other breast when downstairs the brass hinge on the mail slot wheezed open then shut. Lena lifted the window shade to see who could be at the front door. A man in a black overcoat was walking briskly down the stairs and crossing the street in front of the house.

From the next room, Theo cried out, "Who's that?" his bare feet hitting the floor. As he reached the hallway Theo caught sight of Fummer, his stuffed rabbit, who'd been missing for days and days. And all that time Fummer had been wedged behind the wicker hamper. Theo hugged him fiercely, and stuffing the bunny under his arm, he hurried downstairs, his heels heavy on the boards. At the bottom, he turned the dead bolt and threw open the front door.

"Hey!" he boomed to the great world. "Hey-hey!"

The street was silent, fogbound. The man in the coat had reached the corner. He turned round. "What did you say?" he shouted.

Theo didn't know what he said. "I found the bunny!" he called and waved Fummer high overhead. Then, for good measure, Theo repeated himself, this time louder. "Commander, I found the bunny!"

He slammed the door, threw the lock and bolted into the kitchen where he took one of the big chairs and dragged it across the floor.

Crackers, thought Lena, tracking Theo's movements by the thuds and shudders he produced. Now he was opening the box, no doubt leaving crumbs everywhere; now he was pouring himself a glass of milk.

A few minutes later, Theo came upstairs.

"Look! Look! Fummer." He held the stuffed rabbit in front of him, his hand with the crackers hidden behind his back. Recently, Theo felt compelled to enter a room with a feint and a charge.

She laughed. "Hey, Big."

He winked. Where did he get that? Reading her mind, Theo shot across the room to fetch the pillow, wedging it under her arm.

"You," she said, "are my glory."

Theo beamed, the difficulty of the last few days rising like steam from his thin shoulders. He stood close beside Lena, his heart beating into her arm. And then, forgetting himself, he ate his crackers. When the crackers were gone, he remembered the envelope that had come through the mail slot. He'd stuffed it into the waistband of his pajamas.

"It's just an advertisement," he said.

"What is, Theo?"

"I'll throw it away in my room."

Lena wasn't really listening. She was studying the clock, trying to figure out how to get all three of them dressed and fed, and get herself caught up on emails from work. Glo wouldn't be arriving for another hour and a half. Lena needed to tell her about the new meds, and then, somehow, she had to leave with Theo on time.

Theo went to his room, took out the envelope with its thick, cream paper and fancy script and drew on it. He made a dragon with a boy beside it, and signed his name. Then he tiptoed into the hallway and slid the envelope into Lena's briefcase.

"Theo, let's get you dressed."

He was downstairs, playing on the floor with his model airplanes when Lena swung into the kitchen with Willa nestled in the sling. Lena, in a hurry now, moved as though possessed.

"Theo, honey, where are your shoes?"

Theo looked up. In fact, his feet did feel icy.

Lena turned on the stove. She was cooking eggs when Jesse appeared, yawning loudly as she stretched up and upward, waving her arms high above her head, her mini T-shirt rising to show off her flat belly.

"Theo, come," Lena barked, her mouth tight with all the things she wouldn't say. She took Theo by the hand and led him to the table. "I thought you were in Tahoe."

"What's the matter with you?" Jesse helped herself to a large glass of juice.

"We called you," Lena went on, her impartial tone damning. "Willa was in the hospital. We called."

"Oh, god." Jesse's thin shoulders sagged, making her appear all clavicle and baby skin. She gave her sister a pleading look. She had been at a friend's house in Mill Valley. She'd forgotten to take her cell.

Jesse paused, her face shifting. "And Charlie was where?"

"Oh, shut up," Lena said. She was not about to discuss that. Tasting her lip, she moved slowly, setting a plate with a fried egg cooked inside a hole in a piece of toast at Theo's place.

"Len-a, come on, it's the crack of dawn." Sighing dramatically, Jesse reached up and released her heavy hair from its clip. She did not have the singular gifts of her elder sisters: not beauty or wit or, for that matter, vocation. But she had hair. "It's too early in the day to make me rotten."

Jesse avoided her sister's gaze. Lena liked to give the pious hausfrau eyes, but, really, not so long ago she had been the family lark; it was a shame, Jesse felt, to witness the change. "Look, I have an interview this morning, yes indeedy, but hey, let me help you this afternoon. No, wait. I can't." Jesse puffed out her cheeks then let the air go. "Ah, what am I going to do with you? What am I going to do? I can't stand you being such a . . . pillar. You make me look like . . . fluff."

Lena sighed. Much as she tried, she just didn't have the heart to stay mad at Jesse. Jesse would always be the baby. Being mad at her was like holding a grudge against a puppy.

Instead Lena announced, "I made one-eyed gypsies."

Jesse clapped her hands. "Yes! Yes! Oh, aren't you starving? You know, I once heard them called Egyptian breasts, which has got to be stupid, but a guy I met last year in Aspen, his family calls them toads in a hole."

"Really. What guy? What was his name?"

Thinking hard, Jesse screwed her mouth to one side.

"It doesn't matter," Lena sighed.

"No." Jesse banged the table. "Give me a sec."

The phone rang then, and Theo, who'd been trying hard not to listen to the women, caught it on the last ring and handed it to his mother.

At this hour, it had to be Charlie. "Chaos," Lena sang by way of greeting.

The man said her name.

Lena's mind refused to know the voice, but the body, the body remembered.

"El-ena," he said, her name in his mouth always sounding like a ride up and down a hill. "El-ena," he went on, but she couldn't make sense of the words.

By the stove, Theo hovered jealously, shoes in hand. "Mama, I need help."

On the other end of the line, Alessandro Corsini sighed like a surfeited king.

"Oh," Lena said, dropping to the floor.

She'd been twenty-four. They'd lasted just a few months, of which she could remember only the perfection, the endless skin. When they ate, it was also in bed, stretched on their sides like Romans. It ended terribly—a firecracker gone off too close to the eye. One morning he said he had to go to Florence to see his family. He didn't know when he'd be back. He left

Lena the key to his apartment. Weeks later, when he failed to return, she went through his desk and found the wedding invitation with his name embossed as the groom.

She couldn't be so innocent twice.

Now Alessandro Corsini was telling her how delighted he was to be working on a deal with Charlie and her uncle Cal.

"I remember!" Jesse cried. "His name was Jack." She pounded the table. "It was Jack!"

"No," Lena said evenly. "No."

Alessandro laughed. "Bella Lena, you haven't heard my question."

Lena knew better, the heart being a curious thing.

Five

Perhaps, thought Alessandro Corsini as he stared at the phone, it had been a mistake to call so early. Alessandro had never lived a conventional life, and he was always flummoxing the rules. On the other hand, by any measure of the heart, he was years late.

It was half past seven and Alessandro had been awake for hours. Well before dawn, he climbed out of bed, saw his girlfriend (who got up early with the market) to her car, and took a long run in the woods behind his house. He came home, showered, dressed and cooked himself a breakfast of espresso, fruit, Parma and eggs. He did all these usual morning things while keeping an eye on the clock. But the clock, not caring a thing for love, hardly moved. At last, when he couldn't stand it any longer, Alessandro went to his study and was shocked to find the garden outside the windows still covered by shadows. To dial Lena's number, he had to turn on a lamp.

They'd talked no more than a few minutes but, look, his hand was trembling. How could it be, after so many years? He shook his head with wonder. In that house where no one could hear him, Alessandro cried out, *"Ma che scemo!"* What a dope!

Helena. Helena Rusch.

Losing her, he now realized, had been a colossal mistake. He'd been young and stupid; he'd been a boy. No, he'd just been stupid.

Sliding his phone into his pocket, Alessandro paced from the study to the living room and back again. Of course, he'd thought about Lena from time to time. She was the touchstone of his youth. But life had moved on, and Alessandro had moved with it. Returning to the living room, he put his hand on the stone mantel and judged the room through her eyes. The house, though new, looked to be a hundred years old. Just four large rooms up and another four down, he'd designed it himself not long after his divorce. It was a monk's retreat, should the monk have the means to carve a small Tuscan villa into a choice hillside in Portola Valley. The house was the highest chic in that it was simple, with Venetian plastered walls, high ceilings, dark burnished floors and only a few sofas and a couple of antiques that talked to his eye. He had a table in the dining room large enough to seat twelve, and a still larger table under a walnut tree for summer dinners in the garden. Otherwise, he left the place empty—this house of reclamation, this gift for someone who never arrived. In the stable down the hill past the garden Alessandro kept half a dozen horses. He and the horses were the property's only permanent residents.

Now Helena Rusch. Alessandro grinned, thinking of his old lover. Something stirred inside him that he'd assumed was dead. It wasn't her voice so much as the possibility she awoke in him. It made him want to act, however recklessly or boldly.

It had been that way from the first moment, some twenty years ago.

That morning, Alessandro boarded the commuter train heading from the city south to Palo Alto. He was late, as usual, and there was just one empty seat left in the car. Alessandro had his trombone in a large black case, which he balanced between his knees.

"Ah, excuse us," he said apologetically, rapping the side of the case. The instrument within echoed.

"I've always wondered," Lena mused aloud. "You know, where *is* the Tin Woodsman's heart?"

"*Cosa?*"

She bit her lip and turned her smile to the window. At a young age, Lena had been told that she was smart, the judge's decision final, and that little piece of knowledge was always getting her into trouble. Didi, four years older, had been awarded the crown for beauty—that got Didi into trouble, too.

Alessandro didn't know about rivals. As the only child of elderly parents, all prizes were automatically his. He acted as if he were always in the right, and the world agreed; it was that way with golden boys. But early in Alessandro's graduate stint in mechanical engineering at Stanford, his parents were killed in a plane crash off Corsica. The prince was left with no immediate family, a small inheritance and a trunk of clothes that smelled of his father even after they were washed. Alessandro dropped out of school, mooched off friends, slept on floors. He got stoned; he dropped acid. He was moony, drifting, fucked up. That went on. Eventually, he grew bored. He climbed out of his sleeping bag to tinker with stuff, take stuff apart—everything from software to go-carts to coffeemakers. In an abandoned warehouse in Palo Alto, he discovered a like-minded group of friends. They were straight, pretty much, and Alessandro pretty much got straight, too. They had just designed their first product—a self-standing toothpaste dispenser. Alessandro, being the only one with a suit, was voted the front man. He had come to the city to make his first presentation—to a representative of Procter & Gamble.

"I'm sorry, what did you say about *tin man?*"

Lena looked out the window, her face alive with emotion, both shy and bold, this girl dressed in a new silk blouse, high-waisted skirt and black pumps—interview clothes—all bought on sale. She had thirty-two dollars left in her checking account and the rent due in five days and no job. Her wrists were very thin and she hooked them on top of the leather satchel she held in her lap.

She'd already gotten the Italian part, but what about the baggy cashmere sweater and the uncombed hair; and the crust in one eye and the cheeks smooth as a child's? What about that fancy watch? Lena wondered with a pang of desperation if she'd ever own such a nice watch. But she turned away from the familiar gulch of worry. Clearly he was a different breed from the California boys she'd known; from Billy, cute as a bug's ear, who kept dollar bills balled up in his pockets and who'd awakened her that very morning by announcing himself as a large stick pressed against her thigh. Billy had driven her to the station, all the while searching tracks on the stereo, nearly forgetting to stop at lights, and she never did get to hear his new great song. She wasn't going to think about Billy either.

Before they reached Redwood City, the train hit a patch of old track and down the length of the car, the heads bobbed. Lena was knocked back, her hair brushing Alessandro's face.

"Xanadu," Alessandro whispered, close to her ear. Out the window, where they were both looking, an office building was being built in a vast, empty field, as if civilization had colonized a part of the moon. "Do you know Xanadu?" He had a way of de-emphasizing a word, so that he was often misunderstood.

Lena beamed. Oh, yes, she understood.

"I'm Alessandro," he said, having decided. He had no idea what he was getting into, but he knew absolutely, as if standing at the edge of the water and already knowing the water, that the jolt to the system would be profound.

He offered his hand. By evening they would be together in his bed, handing themselves over, open-palmed, as if they were slices of ripe fruit.

It didn't matter that as Alessandro rode that train, a wedding was being planned in Florence. Sweet Ava, the daughter of his parents' best friends. Alessandro had known her since childhood; they were like brother and sister. Alessandro was expected in Italy the first of July. At which point, having no other road map or adviser, he would choose the path with the deepest groove. But that was three months from now—three months being a lifetime.

"Who *are* you?" he asked.

Lena shook her head. He was not going to believe who she was.

"Helena," she said at last.

"Oh my god," he cried. "It's Helena di Troy."

Alessandro walked through his kitchen, grabbed the last piece of toast and munched on it as he went out the back door into the garden. With his wife, Ava, he understood his blunder immediately. In fact, he panicked. He called Lena to explain. She cursed him and hung up. She wouldn't reply to his letters. So he tracked her from the West Coast to New York, where she'd fled. He went to see her, but she refused to talk to him. Meanwhile, Alessandro and Ava made an accommodation. They were great friends and even at a low temperature, a happy-enough couple. They shared history and the same acquaintances. Then one day, a few years into the marriage, Ava announced that she had fallen for a Norwegian architect. Alessandro couldn't blame her. He packed up his things and returned to Palo Alto. Eight years ago, in a touch of payback, Lena sent him her wedding announcement. In this house with its thick walls he roared, yet out of respect he left her alone.

But as for the American notion of "getting over it," an Italian, he assured himself, never does. On the other hand, a Florentine makes sure that the rest of his life doesn't go to hell. Using his small inheritance, Alessandro and his buddies bought the old warehouse, where they launched a design firm that was part incubator, part idea factory, part Silicon Valley tech shop. On the side, he dabbled in the mystic and Tantric arts. There were women, always women. Alessandro's girlfriends, each one more complex and stunning than the last, observed the house, with its pots and plates and the large empty closet in the master bedroom next to Alessandro's, and heard the notes of a most promising song. Each was certain that she would become the next Mrs. Corsini. Alessandro did nothing to dissuade them, for he was a generous, passionate lover, if not a steadfast one. But in reality Alessandro was cruising; he was an unmoored star falling through the sky.

Early on, through the small, incestuous network of the Valley, he met the legendary Cal Rusch, whom Lena had mentioned in passing. Cal recognized in Alessandro that rare confluence of arrogance, intellect, curiosity and detachment, which the elder savant understood in his marrow. Cal was an early investor in Alessandro's firm, and many successful collaborations later he made Alessandro a partner in Rusch & Co. Cal thought of Alessandro as an adopted son.

Because Alessandro was particularly adept at picking new technologies,

Cal often turned to him when vetting new projects. So it was only natural that on New Year's Eve, Cal sent Alessandro the background on Nimbus, with his notes nearly indecipherable in the margins. Alessandro saw the problems immediately, beginning with the robot, which was overdesigned and would require years of development before there'd be a dime of profit. Still, the concept was inspired, and if Swanson's software could be adapted to an existing robot, like Midas, it was a huge advancement, even genius. As he read over the documents, Alessandro, deeply engaged, nodded in agreement. Then he turned to the page with the principals' bios. One name caught his eye: Dr. Charles Pepper.

Alessandro took the phone from his pocket and dialed.

"So?" Cal barked, puffing and snorting. "Rough strokes: What's your hit?"

Alessandro smiled. He'd caught the old dog bashing his daily few miles on the treadmill—it would be a short call.

"Elegant," Alessandro said, noticing that the jonquils along the drive-way were showing their happy, crowned heads. He held the phone away from his ear. "Of course you're right, the telesurgical aspect is at least ten years out. But the robot and the software, that's the piece we'll run with."

"We" was all Cal needed to hear. "You know," he said, "the partners are going to give me hell on this one. Even in this suck-hole of an economy they want to hold out for the ten-baggers of yesteryear. We have to show them the way, eh, Sandro?"

Alessandro paused. His history with Lena had never come up, and he supposed Cal didn't know, just as Cal supposed Alessandro didn't know his niece was the chief medical officer's wife. Both men considered such personal issues beside the point. Alessandro would help Charlie because his idea was sound and because the company would make money and because he, Alessandro, was curious about the other thing, too. "So, this Charlie Pepper," Alessandro said. "What's he like?"

"Smart, obviously. A surgeon. So you know he's a control freak," Cal replied, thinking aloud. "Course we'll have to minimize him, and also put in a CEO with manufacturing chops, but first let's—"

"But is he flexible?" Alessandro insisted. "What's his mind?"

"His mind?" Cal cried. "His *mind*? Sandro, the doctor's got thirty people on payroll and he's out of dough. What the hell, his mind." Cal paused, his voice dropping low. "I'm bringing him into the office on Friday. Why don't you join us, and then you can tell me about his mind."

The morning light peeking over the hills of Skyline was *incantevole,* bewitching. Alessandro punched the gas as he zipped past the horse farms along Portola Valley Road.

Still, he thought, I'd have to prove I'm a better man than I was. Am I better? If Lena didn't want to hear from him, she didn't say. It was the not saying he had to read.

Alessandro drove into downtown Palo Alto and parked on a side street off University, in front of the converted warehouse he'd purchased as a playhouse for his geek friends. Over the years they hired product engineers, designers, psychologists and even more coffee-addicted, badly dressed eccentrics who, on a fee basis, retooled companies and products, and otherwise kicked the ass of corporate America. In Alessandro's church of ideas, nothing was fixed, not even the stainless-steel walls, which rolled in and out of the way. Overhead, a World War I prop plane and a panoply of surfboards and the skeleton of a whale hung from wires rigged from the rafters. In the music room, there were some fifty guitars.

Alessandro met Jimmy Sachs at the front door. Jimmy ran the firm, though he hardly looked like a president-somebody, not with his Beowulf T-shirt, goatee and Kangol hat. But Jimmy had a certain groove and in this, the worst business climate anyone could recall, he had managed to keep the news upbeat for Alessandro.

"Ah, Jimmy," Alessandro said, wrapping him in a bear hug. It wasn't that Alessandro failed to notice the strain on Jimmy's face, but he thought it would be rude to mention it.

"Uh-oh," Jimmy said, smiling with obvious amusement. "The man's got his *loca vita* face on. Look out."

Alessandro laughed. He had just enough self-awareness to appreciate his own paradoxes: he was conceited and self-deprecating; arrogant and vulnerable; adored and lonely; ambitious and Zen. When he veered too much in one direction, the other side took over and redeemed him. The sight of Jimmy, standing at the door with his bicycle and his ancient Labrador, Peaches, restored Alessandro's faith—at least for the moment. Beaming, he bent low to whisper a few endearments into fat Peaches's ear. The dog sniffed joyously at Alessandro's neck and face, a moan-growl of pleasure vibrating her black lips.

All this merriment they took with them inside, where Alessandro greeted everyone with his infectious banter and robust hugging. At the same time he carried on a conversation with Jimmy. "*Allora*. Are we still in contract with Midas?"

Jimmy shrugged. "I pitched them the next phase—basically a rough design of the next-generation robot, but they didn't bite."

"How are they doing?"

"Still hung up on the software. They'll need to buy it, or get someone else to design it. Why? Did you talk to them?"

Alessandro shrugged, which meant he may have talked to them or not, and when the time was right he would tell Jimmy.

They made their way to a large room in back with white boards and maps covering two walls. In the center of the room a dozen beanbag chairs encircled a table that was loaded with bowls of markers, stacks of paper, Post-its, glue guns, X-ACTO knives and duct tape. Here, over the past few years, Jimmy and fifteen employees had designed or improved, among other things, a computer mouse, various laptops and video games, a tape dispenser, an adult diaper and the Midas.

"But do you believe a person can change?" Alessandro asked Jimmy, as the staff drifted into the room. "I mean *vitale*."

"Man or woman?"

"Well, either."

"Na, you can't talk about 'em together. It's like wolves and apples."

Alessandro nodded pensively. "OK. Apples."

"Forget it, man. The apple never changes. She just becomes more apple." And removing his hat, Jimmy patted what was left of his hair. "On the other hand your wolf—"

"Wolf?" said Paula da Sardo, the Brazilian psychologist, who'd been eavesdropping as she hung up her coat. Looking through her black spectacles she appraised Alessandro, his Jesus hair, his baggy sweater and his fine, black shoes. "Exactly what," she said, the mischief and naughtiness Alessandro always inspired lighting her face, "did the wolf do now?"

They all laughed. Alessandro beamed back at them out of a face that belonged on a coin.

Jimmy called the meeting by initiating a discussion, pros and cons, of a phone they'd been hired to design, with no visible buttons or dials. Alessandro followed along halfheartedly. His gaze wandered from Jimmy's boots, which were practical but inelegant, to the painting on the far wall, which Alessandro had brought back from his parents' house in Florence. He would not want to take advantage of anyone's unhappiness—certainly not Lena's. On the other hand, if this Charlie Pepper were stupid enough not to care for her properly . . .

Lena was wrong about one aspect: Alessandro was not yet surfeited, not yet king.

Six

The king wants what the king wants, and the queen wants hers, too. That being the way of it, all down the line, the Rusches' butler, Paco, made a quick business of delivering the invitation to Lena's house. The morning air was bracing and damp as he marched down the ski-slope of Pacific Heights with the cashmere coat the missus gave him for Christmas buttoned up to his throat. At the bottom of the hill, he turned right and approached the little house. It wasn't much of a thing, now was it? Paco removed the thick, cream envelope with the invitation to Paige Rusch's engagement party inside and shoved it through the brass-plated slot in Lena's front door. Turning quickly, he started back, his face the mask of patience and decorum for which the butler was known.

It was this face that would one day greet Lena, should she, in fact, arrive at the great house. Paco would lead her across the Botticino and Negro Marquina marble foyer into the salon, and there, as she settled into a seat by the window, he'd serve her a cocktail in a handblown glass on the smallest of hammered Jensen trays. She'd gaze at the fancy-work ceiling, or down at the magnificent Aubusson rug, or out the French doors, the city laid before her as if spread out on a picnic blanket; she'd sip from her glass and certainly never suspect that she was hated there.

A few strides down the brick bordered by shaggy grass and over the curb, Paco crossed the street midblock. Behind him, that little house was painted a truly hideous shade of pink. From this lapse in judgment the Rusches' niece would have to rise. Paco had his doubts anyone could.

He walked quickly, stressed by habit. The gardeners were due at eight and Mrs. Rusch wanted no misunderstanding: the roses and delicate anemone beds must be kept from their trampling hooves.

As Paco reached the corner, he looked skyward. A small moan escaped his lips. What had been a swift twenty-minute lark into the lowlands of the marina, with the wind a firm, helpful push on the back, now called for a brutal ascent into a singing wall of fog. Seven blocks straight up. There at the top, above the clouds, Paco made out the implacable mansions of Broadway. He knew those faces as if they were his sweethearts. Reading right to left: Jewett, Rosekranz, Getty, Ellison, Rusch. Inside each, a world complete, a world few understood as well as Paco. It took an army to maintain their beauty inside and out: their salons and Aga stoves, their Tut tombs of silver and glass and gold, their miles of hand-waxed floors; their cellars of Pinot and blancs and bruts; their media dens and squash courts and gift-wrapping nooks; their double pantries and HEPA vacuums and eight-car garages; their swarms of children. It took a rare headman to drive such an army—a fine-tuned individual, for sure. A person of delicate sensibility yet Herculean constitution, who saw everything but said nothing; who fetched and finessed; who, after twenty years of service, delivered on foot invitations to estranged nieces before the blasted sun was up. Oh, this life! Oh, these behemoths, these big-busted old ladies, these jack-o'-lanterns set in a row up there in the clouds. How Paco loved them.

But his love came back as a fragile caution, for the world Paco adored was on the verge.

First the stores along Fillmore began going belly-up, and then the shops downtown. Barneys, even post-Christmas with everything slashed seventy-five percent, had less foot traffic than the Columbarium. On Tuesday, Paco learned that his friend Victor, majordomo for thirty years with the Tabors, had been let go. No warning, just three months' severance. The Tabors were dead broke—or so a weeping Mrs. Tabor explained as she hugged poor Victor. They'd put it all into the Fairfield Greenwich Group, and Fairfield Greenwich had put it all into Madoff. Everything had to go: the house in Umbria, the lodge in Aspen, the five-bedroom town house at Esperanza in Cabo, the winery in Napa—all the properties were put on the selling block. And Victor, he was on the block, too. He called Paco for help. Of course, Paco would do what he could.

But what would become of Paco should the Rusches fall, too? Last night at dinner, as Paco served the steaks, Mr. Rusch told Mrs. Rusch she would have to cut back. They were not immune, he said. The subject was their daughter Paige's engagement party. Ivy had been planning the event since Paige was a child, but she and Paco had been full-tilt conspiring for more than a year. Seven hundred guests were expected.

"It's obscene," Cal growled. "Spending that kind of money now. Ivy, hear me. We're down fifty percent at Rusch & Co. The Valley is panic city. My partners, they're all suffering lemming-paralysis, the likes I've never seen. And you want to throw a ball."

"A party to celebrate the marriage of our *one*, not-so-young daughter."

"Jesus H, hear me, Ivy—it's over!"

"What is, duck?"

"This!" And he pounded his fist on the good table. Cal Rusch was a man of unique distortions. He lived in a castle and captained three yachts, but he wore his button-down shirts until they frayed, and then he had them patched. Same for his shoes and suits. He wore a wristwatch that had been his father's and the garnet ring Ivy gave him when they'd started out broke. He liked simple food—the steak and potatoes in front of him— anything more upset his stomach. In another year he'd be eighty. He had hardly begun. "Ivy, how to get through to you? You will look as if you've lost your goddamn mind."

"Well, if it's lost, I'm sure Paco will find it." She nodded at Paco and sipped her wine. Ivy did not require a lecture on money from her husband. She had grown up poor as well, a ranch manager's daughter with one coat and a pair of Sunday shoes and two skirts she wore all through high school. Of course, that was a long time ago. For every one of Cal's patched shirts, she had a dozen couture. "Darling, I can't make this out. Paige, for one, she has her heart set—of course she does. But putting Paige aside, if we were to cancel, every vendor, from the cooks to the napkin makers to the tent people to our own people, will suffer. They have all made it clear to me that they're relying on this night and this night alone to see their staffs through this dreadful winter."

"Then pay for their time, but cancel." Cal's voice, pinched normally, sounded more strained than usual. "We'll give 'em a low-key thing here, at home—couple of people, Paige and Le Chapeau."

"*James.* You know his name is James."

"Yah, yah." Cal waved his fork in the air like an emphatic maestro.

For a few minutes, Ivy remained silent, concentrating on migrating her haricots verts, bean by bean, from one side of the plate to the other. Her plans included a ballroom and a tent that enveloped the street. The party was in four weeks. Ivy raked the beans back to where they'd started. "Fine. I'll call the Pelosis tomorrow. They rejiggered their calendar—you can imagine Nancy, as Speaker, had a million reasons to stay East; well, they can rejigger some more. Same thing, the Gores. Everyone planned to do the inauguration in D.C., then end up here. I simply thought—"

"Oh, hell, don't I know what you thought?" Cal dropped his knife on his plate. "Ivy, listen—"

She held up her hand. "No, no. I get you."

"Listen, I'm all for being bold."

She looked up brightly—she was every bit his match, Ivy was. Every bit as gay and cunning a force as her husband was a mercurial and loud one.

"Look here—" Cal studied Ivy over the rim of his scotch.

She met his gaze while chewing a tiny bit of bean.

"Ivy," he said chuckling. "You—you are a conniver. You know that: a conniver of the first rank."

Ivy shrugged. "Darling, what can I say, it's done. Blow as you like, it's done." She sighed, visibly relieved.

"All right then." He drained his glass, shook the ice and held it out for Paco to refill. "But on the subject of bold, there's something we need to discuss."

"I'm on the edge of my chair."

"Surgical robots, Iv."

"Of course," she said. But she was a little winded from before, and as Cal went on, giving her a primer on telesurgery and mitral valve repair, Ivy's gaze lifted to the crown molding, whereby, Paco knew, she was deciding if a truckload of French tulips would be redux after last year.

"I'm looking into an outfit called Nimbus—remember the name, it's a good one—I'm telling you it was as much a surprise to me as it will be to you, Ivy, who is behind the thing."

"Bud Cope?"

"No. No!"

"I can't imagine."

"The world is a circle, Iv, isn't that what you say?" Cal cleared his throat and as he did, in that moment of verging, Paco and by the looks of it, Missus, too, smelled the ripe fish. The turn happened very quickly, but the road had been set from the start. Now, Boss, thought Paco, don't.

Cal fixed his deep, crystalline blue eyes on Ivy. "Are you ready for a shocker? Are you? The guy behind Nimbus, this doctor, why, he's married to our niece—that's right, to Lena Rusch." And with that, Cal forked a large bite of steak and chomped on it fiercely.

Paco nearly dropped the chafing dish of scalloped potatoes. In the kitchen, Paulette set down her spoon and hurried to the dining room door.

"Say that last part again," Ivy insisted. "The part you *shoved* under the tail."

"I said I'm putting together a deal—"

"*Why?*" she cried. "Why would you want to bring *that* element—that god-awful *element*—back into this house?"

"I explained," he snapped, pushing aside his plate with such force it nearly flipped off the table. "I walked you through so there would be no mistake—"

"No mistake," she said direly. "Then no mistake."

Ivy rose from her chair like a well-glossed narrow board. And going upstairs, she disappeared into her rooms, where she spent the night alone.

In the morning, she summoned Paco and dispatched him with the invitation. But the house car, the Mercedes wagon, was in the shop; Paco would have to walk.

He checked his watch. Any minute Raoul, Mr. Rusch's body worker, would ring the front bell. If no one answered, would the Latino lover-boy have the good sense to go around back and try the kitchen door? And what then? As Paco went out through the kitchen, Paulette, the cook, had been at the sink, crying into a towel.

Paco turned the corner, setting his nose into the blasting wind. Just then, he felt eyes on his back. He turned, his choirboy heart tapping quick beats. A light was shining in the upstairs window. It made Lena's house appear, well, rosy. What? Paco asked himself, in danger of changing his mind. *Paquito, what?*

The front door opened and a small boy in pajamas appeared on the stoop. He called to Paco.

"What did you say?" boomed Paco.

Theo repeated himself.

This time Paco heard him clearly. He said, "Commander, I found the *money*." And waving a brown rag in salute, he disappeared.

Every morning, after his workout and before his massage, Cal Rusch stood in the wide arch of his bedroom window and observed the hills his butler now climbed. The northern tip of the city, veiled by fog, lay at his feet—that, and the unmitigated drop to the sea.

Cal tuned his binoculars. He was a short man with a barrel chest and chicken legs, a tyrant in a shabby robe and athletic socks. His white hair, spiny with sweat, stuck up in places. His jaw was tight and his lips dry, but the hands tuning the binoculars were disconcertingly soft, like a girl's. If Paco were to look up again toward that enormous window, as tall and wide as a single-story house, he would surely miss the small man standing at its center. Even so, what Cal Rusch lacked by way of physical packaging, he more than made up for in brain. His mind, you see, was gorgeous. It was also rabid, highly disciplined, lightning quick and ruthless. It was a machine of a mind, its food every figure, code or image it encountered; every factoid, including the Byzantine pathways of cities and semiconductors, genomes and species—down to the little fishes, too. This thrill-seeking noggin had pushed Cal unceasingly for nearly eighty years, blowing him across oceans and thrusting him out of planes. It had made its fortune on the riffs and dreamscapes of humans. Had such a brain been twined with as large a soul, Cal Rusch would have been a Mozart or a Tolstoy. But his soul was less like his brain, more like his knees and jaw. Tight. And so Cal spent a lifetime binding his dreams to the dreams of others—to the real conjurers, gadget-masters and geniuses he encountered. But first, he had to find them.

This morning being no exception, Cal stood before the glass and dared to ask the world what it had to say for itself.

Pinnacles and crashes, the world said.

Cal picked up the phone and dialed. Of late he had been feeling old. He needed nothing so simple as one more ride.

"Charlie. Cal Rusch. Good morning. Where am I finding you?" Cal's mouth dropped open as he listened. "Boston? Are you doctoring, or selling? Talk louder, I can't hear a damn thing."

Three thousand miles distant, in the corridor of Mass General, Charlie Pepper felt the heat-burst come toward him. It was Cal Rusch's singular form of courtship.

Charlie shouted vigorously into the phone.

"Whoa, horse, not so loud, man!" Cal boomed, his voice a thin tube pinched on all sides, with a heap of sand thrown inside. "There. That's better. Now tell me: How's the Nimbus?"

Cal was proof that civilization could profit from one person's fixation on the things that irked him. In the sixties, working at Fairchild, it irked him that mainframe computers had to be bulky and loud; why couldn't he have something tidy and quiet in the office, say, on his desk? And why couldn't he carry that machine around? And why couldn't one machine talk to another?

Xerox, National Semiconductor, the microprocessor, Apple, Intel, Jerry Sanders, Steve Jobs, AOL, Google—such was the long list of irritants Cal Rusch had backed with money. He owned office buildings, banks, oil and gas positions, barges, a winery, an airline, a large stake in several media companies, his yachts. He was broadly invested with firms in China and the Middle East. He owned a solar company in Denmark and a cheese operation in the south of France. Back when Netscape went public, he'd earned a hundred million on paper in a single hour. It hardly mattered. Of late, his irkometer had quieted. The Internet, in which he had been an early and keen investor, had its Tweets and Facebookers, but overall it left the taste of sticks in his mouth. His bones bothered him; his guts acted up; his prostate was a rotted fig that had to be plucked. At night, in his dreams, Cal's younger partners came at him with knives. Even so, his finicky gut had convinced him that the medical realm was the next thing.

Cal nodded while Charlie explained himself. He was in between surgeries at Mass General, having made the trek so he could teach a team of docs several new procedures using the Midas. Then, later in the afternoon, Charlie would pitch the administration on piloting the Nimbus.

"Smart," said Cal, snorting appreciatively. "You cut 'em in the morning and sing to 'em in the afternoon. Good for you, Charlie. You're on the hoof; I admire that. Just more reason for us to be brief."

Cal attached a headset to his ear, freeing his hands so he could make another sweep with the binocs. The view out of the bedroom never failed to stir him: the gorgeous sugar-cake of the city, the hillside houses of creosote and stucco, the blue, irrational sea. His gaze turned to the landmark of the St. Francis Yacht Club flag and the mast of his boat, *Thirst*. Jogging east to Alcatraz and to the tip of Angel Island, he noted what boats were out and the state of the wind; then west to Marin, he paused to take in the touchstone bridge.

"Jesus, Charlie, I wish you could see this. The view, I mean. A year ago—it was the second week of January—I was standing in this very spot, tuning the binocs, when I saw a guy jump from the Golden Gate Bridge. How many mornings have I stood here? I have never seen a thing such as that. It was terrible. Terrible. The guy's name was Don Lester; Ivy read the obit in the paper. Turned out he worked in mortgage-backed securities and it is my guess his conscience got to him. Who knows? Up and over he went, and you know my first thought when I saw him jump? I thought: the correction, here it comes. Charlie, I've been in this business a long time. I've seen nine cycles—that's nine highs; more to the point, nine downs. And if I learned one thing, it's that there are no coincidences, none. I told my partners as much, but they didn't believe me. Still don't, in their way. Don Lester, poor sap, was my sole guide. That same morning I converted as much as I could to cash. Of course, the Rusch & Co. funds, well, we were fully invested and so, like everyone, we took our trouncing. But I'm telling you, Charlie, it is the same lesson: who hears the call, and who doesn't. Isn't that so? The game isn't now, it's five, ten years out, and it doesn't have a damn thing to do with luck. Not for you, not for me. You got to grab it, 'cause when it goes, man, it's Don Lester falling like a scallion into a bucket."

A world away, in Mass General's urological surgical unit, Dr. Charlie Pepper stood with a badly needed cup of coffee cooling in his hand. He was listening intently, his shoulders rounded, one hand cupping his ear. Around him patients rolled by strapped to gurneys. The intercom blasted a series of pages—Dr. Rosenberg was wanted in the second-floor outpatient clinic. But what were these words he was hearing? And who was this man, this Cal Rusch, all of a sudden at the center of Charlie's life? Was he a wacko or a prophet? Charlie, sleepless from the red-eye, had been on his feet for hours. He had vivisected a cancerous liver, and was due to perform a prostatectomy on the half hour. But first he had Cal Rusch, barking like old Jeremiah in his ear.

Charlie ducked into a nearby linen closet to get out of the larger noise.

"All to say, Charlie . . . I'm impressed. I've read your numbers. Got a few things to clarify, and such, but overall, your plan makes sense. My gut says within ten years there'll be a robot in every operating room, and it might as well be yours. Eh? My end, Charlie, I'm going over the deal with my partners this morning. They'll want to give you and Swanson a good grilling when you come in on Friday, just their way of saying how-de-do. You know the drill. From there, we'll bang out a term sheet we can all live with. At least we'll come close. Then the lawyers will do their thing, papering the deal and so on; we'll do what we can to push it through. I'm assuming you'll be after some kind of bridge financing—we'll cover that. It's harder now, every which way, financing is frozen. But if everything looks kosher, we're good. Frankly, I don't see what would stop us. I wanted you to hear it from me. What do you say, Doc?"

It was the moment Charlie had been building toward all these sleepless months, that's what he thought. And wasn't it fitting that it should be at Mass General, where Charlie started as an intern, and where he ran his first department at the singularly young age of forty—wasn't it fitting that in these halls Cal Rusch, a savant of an investor if ever there was one, should tell him that Nimbus was twenty million more possible. And yet . . .

"Cal," Charlie said, trying to maintain an even tone. "Your interest, your conviction, it's fantastic. It is—well, stunning. But I have to be straight with you. I cannot—I cannot consider next steps until you and I discuss, well, until we clear up the family dynamic."

"The family dynamic."

"That's right," Charlie said with emphasis. "I mean, given how things stand between you and—"

"—Lena," Cal shouted, relieved to have said the name aloud, believing immediately and wondrously that he and he alone had put the topic forward. And with such relief his voice dropped almost to a whisper. "How's she doing, by the way?"

"She's fine. She's . . . great. But, sir—"

"Sir! Good Christ, Charlie, none of that." Cal tossed the binoculars on the nearby sofa. "Look. I'm glad I put it to you. We could have waited, but I'm glad it's come up."

Charlie nodded. "Right."

"What, by the way, does she think of me?" asked Cal.

Charlie paused. "She hates you, sir."

"Hates me?"

"Yes."

"Well, that can't be forever, can it?"

"I'm hoping not."

"Charlie, what can I say? I like the directness—I appreciate it. Families, listen, what a fucking mess." Cal grunted, agreeing with himself. "But we are politely tiptoeing around the question, aren't we, Charlie? That is: What the hell are my intentions, given the history you have against me. On the other hand, you've got your gizmo, and you're a novice. And given the state of the world, not a soul is going to look at you until, best case, second quarter two thousand ten. How am I doing so far, Charlie?"

"Well—"

"No shame!" Cal shouted. "No shame! Both of us, we're saying, is this guy for real? And you're also saying to yourself, what's my move here, given that she's not likely to move at all. That pretty much cover it?"

Nodding, Charlie held the top of his head. "Look, Cal, I have to believe—"

"Me, too, Charlie! Me, too," Cal cried excitedly. "Going in, I have to believe. So let me make this easy: you've got my attention. All you've got to think about right now is what are you going to do with it. Your job is this: come Friday amaze me. Then it's my turn to show you what we can do. Nobody's getting married tomorrow. All right, Doc?"

The conversation soon ended and for a brief moment Charlie lingered, grinning, among the blue starched gowns, dressings and drapes. Son of a bitch. Son of a bitch! They were waiting on him in preop, but they could wait a minute more.

He called Swanson. "Hey. Nothing's signed yet, Swan. And we won't jinx it by saying another word. But fair to say, go ahead and pick out those new desks."

After Swanson, Charlie thought of Lena. He had to tell her. He had to hear her splendid, volatile song the moment she realized they were going to be all right. He shifted his weight, taking a deep breath, the smallness of the closet making it hard to breathe. In equal measure to the elation, he felt a deep longing for his wife. He found a narrow perch on a stack of hospital gowns, sat down and dialed.

But before the call went through, he closed the phone abruptly. To tell her, he'd have to go back days, to the beginning, and explain why he hadn't been up front the first time Cal called. And that would require a long conversation he couldn't do justice to right now (they were paging him over the intercom). But why not call anyway, and just say hey? He redialed. The phone beeped, but the call wouldn't go through. Charlie examined the phone—he was out of juice. Traveling all night, he'd forgotten to recharge it.

He pocketed the phone and returned to the corridor.

"Charlie goddamn Pepper," called Jack Bost, who'd replaced Charlie as head of urology; he'd been hunting for his friend in the halls. "Is it true what they say about start-up CEOs being like babies. You know, up all night, crying?"

Cal tossed the phone on the sofa and picked up the binocs. The irritation was full on him. It was the sweetest thing.

"Hoping for another jumper?" asked Ivy, who'd been listening from the doorway of her bathroom.

No reply came from the window.

So, putting the mad on, are you? she thought. He was far across the room from her, wearing that tattered robe she swore she'd thrown in the rag pile. From the side, he looked like a plucked eagle. But he's *my* plucked eagle.

"I said, are you hoping?" Ivy, seventy, almost ten years Cal's junior, had stepped out of her bath a few minutes earlier and was wearing a black lace thong and bra. Where her left breast used to be she wore a pad, which she nervously adjusted.

"Nah," he said, though he was focused on the very spot where Don Lester jumped. But to admit that to Ivy was to indulge her favorite question, What are you thinking? She'd been asking and he'd been denying for nearly fifty years. "No jumpers today, Iv. Those guys want clear skies. See or be seen, that's their thing. Why else do they jump *toward* the city, instead of the ocean?"

"Funny. You'd think the opposite. You'd think they'd want the eternal view."

"People, Iv. P for peculiar. Now, where the hell's Raoul?"

"He's late?"

"Thirteen minutes."

"Well, shoot him."

Cal turned then, just as she knew he would.

She smiled bravely. Forty-five years earlier, Beverly, Cal's brother's wife, put her hand on the back of Cal's chair and Ivy knew. She *knew*.

"Hi," she said. "How'd you sleep?"

"Great."

She smiled, knowing otherwise, and for the simple fact that he never bored her. "Cal."

"I don't want to talk about it."

"Me either."

"Good."

Ivy nodded. "Just so you know—I've invited Lena and her husband to Paige's party. Paco is walking the invitation down now." She paused, feeling the heat of those blue eyes on her. "Darling, if you're so determined to wreak havoc, I'll thank you, *this time* let's bring it through the front door."

There was a knock then coming from the hall. Startled, they turned from their separate stations in that enormous room. Raoul, the bald masseur, beamed at them. "Mr. Rusch, I am so sorry. I rang, but no one—"

Cal held up his palm like an emperor, and out of deference to the fact that Ivy was dressed in only her underwear, he motioned for Raoul to look away. "Twenty minutes you owe me, Raoul, and in my world that's a fortune. Think on that."

Raoul gave a slight bow and retreated into Cal's dressing room, where the built-in massage table was made from hand-carved cherry.

"Good Christ, Ivy," Cal said. "Are we done with this, then?"

"Darling, may we never be done."

Cal grunted. He took several steps toward the dressing room. "Iv, I think I'm tired."

"Are you?"

He tucked his thumbs into the belt of his robe and rocked on his socked heels, feeling himself, to be sure. He was turning eighty and what did such a number mean? He'd raised himself from the flats of Santa Rosa by way of the Valley to the highest window of Pacific Heights. Yet his hungers did not cease. They were wide and deep and could not be stopped. Not by a little irritation in the tummy, or a little weakness in the manly knob. He wanted, as ever he'd wanted.

"Nah," he said, and disappeared into his dressing room.

Within minutes, Cal was naked, his legs tucked under the softest of chamois covers. Raoul rubbed his palms vigorously, gathering the heat he applied along with good intention and a generous amount of lavender oil to the parched hide of one Calvin Rusch. The body, always vulnerable, spoke eloquently to Raoul of its estrangement: the liver enlarged, the diaphragm constricted, the shoulders, neck and head stacked like so many bricks. The body's story was written and in time, like character, it would show itself.

"*Bueno,*" Raoul said. "The shoulder from yesterday, still snug?" He pressed his thumbs knowingly into the socket.

"Holy Mother of Christ!" Cal gasped.

"We should work less, Mr. Rusch."

"We should live on this earth while we can, Raoul."

Pretty was the first thing Ivy Rusch knew about herself. Everything had been built on pretty, as if her life were a house built upon the foundation of a single rose. The briny wit and irreverence came much later, as a way to shore up the roof and the walls.

And so, this morning, alone in her dressing room, Ivy approached one of many mirrored doors. She'd made her point, but what did she win? A skinny, old gal stared back at her. Ivy hardly recognized herself. She'd had a little work done, starting in her forties, and then a little more. This last round the doctor got carried away. They'd lifted and pulled too much, turning Ivy into an almond-eyed sphinx. Oh, god, she cried the first time she saw this new Ivy, her face frozen in a look of perpetual expectation. Oh, heck. Recently, in *Vogue,* she'd been named an icon, but Ivy told her friends that just meant she was ancient.

She moved to the next closet—there were twelve in all—opening doors and greeting her many selves. "And who is my bride tonight?" Cal used to ask when she would come downstairs dressed for a party. "Are you Cleopatra or Madame X or Annie Oakley?" The size 2 Oscars hung with the Lagerfelds, the Dolces with the Herreras; the polka dots with the sheaths—her clothes were the story of her life.

As she rooted to find a shirt, Ivy longed for her two great vices: cigarettes and love. The cigs she gave up a decade ago. And love? Cal was impossible; half the time she couldn't stand him. Yet she knew she adored him anyway.

Downstairs, Paige Rusch, thirty-two and happy for the first time, slammed the front door, sending a tremor through the upholstered walls.

Moving quickly, Ivy slipped a cashmere sweater overhead—this was shaping up to be no day to dress like a peacock. Hearing Paige's voice coming closer, Ivy grabbed an ancient St. Laurent safari vest and zipped it, feeling the sure embrace of an old friend.

"There you are! Why didn't you answer your phone?" Paige was born eight years after her brother, a last hurrah as Ivy neared forty. Mother and daughter talked at least several times a day, and for that reason every conversation was a continuation of the last one, and very little got decided. Agitated and worried, Paige raced to her mother's side and, meaning to kiss Ivy's cheek, missed and knocked her instead on the nose.

Ivy winced, tears springing to her eyes as she held her nose. "Fine. Everything's fine."

Paige collapsed into Ivy's favorite Louis XVI chair. She was a tiny thing, with the sharp, odd bones and smarts of her father. "So, what, it's all better now?"

"Of sorts."

Paige groaned. Then she spotted Ivy's new crocodile Hermès bag. She lifted it with a finger, as if it were sticky. "Mommy," she scolded.

"I know. I know—" Ivy protested. "Lee Radziwill and I ordered them over a year ago. You know—*before*—" Ivy waved her hand. "Now what am I going to do with it?" Ivy sighed. "Isn't it gorgeous."

Paige sighed. "If only it made you happy."

"Oh, is that what it's supposed to do?" Ivy shook her head. "Don't be a brat. Hand me that belt, there." Ivy cinched the belt high and tight over her slacks and vest, turning herself into a chic urban huntress.

"Well," Paige announced, "I'm fed up with him."

"Who? Your father? No, you're not. I guess I'm not either. When we are, then you and I will be having a different conversation." Sighing, Ivy dipped into another closet for boots. Paige had Cal's bones, quick temper, and bluster, but underneath she was pudding. It was the pudding Ivy had to protect. And so she'd told Paige that Cal wanted her to cut back, but she didn't dare mention Paige's party. Ivy looked behind her in the mirror.

Paige's eyes tick-tocked. Her father was a trick, wrapped in a riddle, thrown down a well. She wasn't his darling, no one was. Yet while her older brother, Christopher, had packed off to India to become a yogi, Paige stayed. She did what was expected of a smart girl—BA in art history, then two years at Oxford. Her father collected the Impressionists and Postim-pressionists, and she went one better and started her own gallery with him as backer. First she worked to find him things, and then she began develop-ing artists of her own. Being Cal's daughter she was good at it. Very good. But it wasn't enough. He didn't seem to like her. Even when she thought to sell art on the Web. She'd worked on a proposal for months, with Cal's tepid encouragement. But last night, without any apparent reason, he sent her an email saying in effect that come the partners meeting, he was going to vote against her deal.

"Did Dad tell you he's going to tank ArtShop?"

Ivy winced. "He said it wasn't far-reaching."

"It'll reach to the bank, for chrissakes. Everyone thinks so. James cer-tainly does."

"James is very true."

In the mirror, Ivy watched as Paige picked among her stacks of secrets and items not-to-be-discussed to locate her heart. James, Paige's fiancé, was perfect for her, the problem being that perhaps he liked her too much. And then Cal had to belittle the man by zeroing in on his massive head of hair. He couldn't help calling his future son-in-law Le Chapeau. Morn-ings, when Paige woke in James's arms, she wondered what was so wrong with being . . . she could hardly shape the word . . . happy?

The two women sighed, feeling each other. Knowingly, they silently agreed to move on.

"But I'm not going to forgive Cal for ArtShop, Mommy. I'm not."

"Forgiveness is overrated," Ivy replied. "Find another way." And, confessing her own bit of revenge, Ivy told Paige the part about sending Paco down the hill that morning with the invitation.

Paige took it all in, her eyes huge. "Are you mad?"

"Probably. Yes!" Ivy laughed.

Paige nodded, clearly impressed. She wondered if she would have thought to be so daring. She folded her legs beneath her, wrapped her thin arms around her ribs, and making herself a knotty ball of twine, looked at the business before them. "Lena. What's she like?"

Ivy shrugged.

"Well, I know. The snide thief."

"Oh, Paige."

"Come on! Mommy, she was absolutely going to steal that statue! I mean, she had her *hand* in the cabinet. I was what, five? I saw the whole thing. And I wasn't going to tell—not a soul. Let her take it, I figured, if she needs it so badly. But calling me a cow? Now, that was *mean*."

"I believe she called us all cows," corrected Ivy. "And a few other choice words for your father." Ivy recalled that feisty package that was Lena, all of seventeen, jabbing her finger in the air and telling them all deliciously where they could get off. Lena had discovered the affair between Cal and Beverly and in high dudgeon broadcast the news. Then she conveniently disappeared. It suited Ivy to have her gone—and with her went Beverly.

"I can't believe Cal's going to fund *Lena* instead of me." Paige's voice shook.

"Well, duck, actually it's her husband."

"Same thing." Paige hugged herself more tightly, her thoughts shifting in odd directions as she chewed her lip.

"What," Ivy said at last. "Come on, out with it."

"Alessandro."

"Alessandro Corsini? What does he have to do . . . When did you start seeing him?"

"Mommy, stop. We're friends. He's helping me with ArtShop."

"Really? Alessandro?" Ivy raised her brows.

"Yes, Mommy, and you can quit giving me those eyes. I swear, I'm maybe the only girl in the world who doesn't live to see the David in Alessandro Corsini's pants. We're more like, I don't know, brother and sister. He helps me; I help him." But Paige was blushing and her mouth didn't quite match her words. "Oh, cut it out. You don't understand."

"Duck, I do." In fact, all of Ivy's life, she'd been in the business of understanding. She was very good. "So what about Alessandro?"

"That's the thing: I don't know. One night we were watching a movie at his house, and out of the blue he asked about Lena. He wanted to know if we'd seen her since she moved back. It wasn't what he said exactly—"

"You mean . . . they were lovers?"

Paige shrugged.

"Well, he's handsome, that's for sure." Ivy grunted as she shut a drawer. "Me, I've always found him to be too much work. Give me a man with a little grit under his nails. Like James."

"Do you really think James has grit?"

Ivy smiled into Paige's questioning eyes. "Don't you?"

Paige thought a bit. She had been certain that morning when she woke up in his arms, but now she wasn't sure. She wasn't sure of anything when she was in this house.

She searched the top of her mother's face, the gorgeous bones, the black hair skunked with silver, pulled tight in a chignon. Cal's affair with Beverly had never been discussed, but it had lived in the house just the same. And swearing never to be like her mother, though how else to be she wasn't entirely sure, Paige nodded.

"Mommy, you are certainly no cow," she added.

Ivy smiled, relieved. "Neither are you, babes."

"On the other hand—La Beverly," Paige growled.

"Oh. God."

What more could I have done for her? thought Ivy, as she watched Paige thread her way down the limestone stairs to her car. Would it have mattered? Of course it mattered, not the moments, but the general line. All those days when Ivy had been at lunch, at dinner or dressing, or on the phone. She'd been running the corporation that was their lives. She'd been hosting dinners, picking out fabrics, arranging fund-raisers; she'd been planning Christmas, ski week, Easter break. Meanwhile, under her guidance, in the hands of others, the children were fed, educated, indulged. Had she snorkeled with them in Mexico? Of course. Had she gotten on the floor and played rummy and hearts? Sure. Had she been to every recital and volleyball match, every potluck, and every play? Absolutely. But the first love, the one that consumed her, wasn't Paige or Christopher. It was always Himself.

Ivy called the dogs.

The pair of them, Angie and Finn, mother and son harlequin Danes, were the fourth pair raised in the house, starting with the first Dane, sired by Gus, who'd been a present from Lena's parents. Ivy leaned against the wall to absorb the welcome of the massive beasts. Finn, the rascal, went straight for her crotch, his black nose homing in, making Ivy laugh. But Angie, the introvert, hung back, dipping her head while her tail thrashed the wall.

"Come on, come on," crowed Ivy, as Angie tiptoed nervously toward her, whimpering as she dipped her huge head under Ivy's arm. Ivy kissed Angie above the eyes, where the dogs always smelled of woods and rice. She smacked Finn's thick haunch as he touched her wrist with the large black licorice knob of his nose.

The dogs herded Ivy into the breakfast room. "Settle," she commanded, snapping her fingers. With a satisfied groan, they folded themselves like living ladders to the floor.

On cue Paulette, the cook, pushed through the swinging door with Ivy's breakfast arranged on her favorite Spode.

The women greeted each other somewhat stiffly this morning, and Angie, sensitive to any shift in routine, nudged Ivy under the table with her nose. Ivy patted the dog as she turned to address the cook's swollen eyes.

During the night, Paulette's son, Jean-Claude, had wrecked the family car. He was unhurt, but that was the least of it. He'd been drunk, and the girlfriend, it turned out, was wanted by the police. Paulette, who tended to confront life with a French bourgeoise's flair for drama, was devastated.

That the car, a gift from the Rusches, had been totaled; that the police, called to the scene, had taken the lanky boy into custody and booked him for DUI—all this news Ivy received first thing, before her yoga. It was taken for granted by all parties that following breakfast Ivy would make some calls and fix everything.

But that meant another hour's endurance for Paulette, who'd been awake all night. She turned Ivy's coffee cup a quarter round, so the curved handle was closer to her fingers.

"He's a good boy, Paulette," Ivy said.

"He kiss off his advantage," Paulette cried in a high voice. "For what?"

A maid, hired to help with preparations for the party, passed through the foyer with an armload of linens. Paulette hissed at her and wagging an impatient finger sent her in a new direction. Paulette had an army to run besides.

Ivy tried not to smile. Truth was, while Ivy had a multitude of friends, there were few people she liked as well as Paulette, all bun and buttons, a schoolmarm who cooked like a wanton.

"A good boy," Ivy said authoritatively, "who followed his heart."

"*Shhha,* the heart," hissed Paulette, rolling her eyes. The heart and its hungers had been at the crux of Paulette and Ivy's understanding all these years. The heart was impossible, you could at best only feed it. And so, with a final shake of the head, Paulette disappeared into the kitchen, leaving Ivy alone with her breakfast.

She was starving. She attacked her plate with a kind of gusto that had to be kept private. In truth, she shoveled. The velvety poached eggs dusted with Parmesan were just the way she liked them. But no sooner had she dug in, than the dogs lifted their massive snouts and barked. It was Cal and, having heard him, it was impossible not to respond, if only to assert that one wasn't a total loafer.

Ivy quickly scanned the *Times* fashion section, noting that lips that summer would be bloodred and accessories would emphasize gladiator sandals and pelts. The wide shoulder was trying to make a comeback, as it always did when women and the markets were downcast. Ivy picked up another section. Each morning Cal liked to take some new fact with him on the road. Ivy never stopped trying to amaze him. But when you are the wife of nearly fifty years, how many different ways can you spin on your ear? She turned from the *Times* to the *Chronicle*.

Hillary Clinton was going to be Obama's secretary of state. Ivy lifted her head to see what she thought of that. Ivy liked Hillary and, over Cal's strong objections, had sent her money during the campaign. (Cal was from the first an Obama man.) A photograph of Bill and Hillary, Cal and Ivy hung on the powder room wall in Napa. It had been taken just prior to the Monica Lewinsky business. Stupid boy, thought Ivy, recalling that silly drama. Who wanted to begin the day thinking of Bill Clinton's penis? For a time, over lunch, it was all the women talked about. Sally Dubens claimed, "I have it on good authority he's hung like a pipe. Balls down to there."

"I don't know about you, Sal," Ivy replied, adjusting her Verdura cuffs, "but I've always been partial to a man with a pipe."

Well, the girls loved it. If society were divided into women who talked of cocks and those who didn't, Ivy's friends talked. They smoked and told dirty jokes and hardly ate and had their faces lifted and their tummies tucked and otherwise it was on their skinny, no-nonsense backs that the soft belly of society rested: not just the running of the opera or the arts, but the public library, the humane society, the free clinics, and the abused women shelters. The women discussed Bill Clinton's penis until they were bored, then with a wave of their jeweled hands, they turned their attention to the plans for Sally's new guesthouse in St. Helena.

"What have you got?" asked Cal, coming up behind her and chucking strawberries into his mouth from the large bowl on the sideboard.

"Geithner wants to nationalize Citibank and Bill Clinton isn't sure he can forgive Obama for winning."

"Geithner won't and you bet, for expediency, Clinton will act as if he did. What else?"

"They've given this whole nightmare a name: the Great Recession."

"Lousy name," Cal said. "Not big enough."

"What would you call it? The Great Comeuppance?"

At that moment Paulette banged through the swinging door to hand Cal his espresso, which he bolted. There was no misunderstanding between Cal and Paulette; they spoke only when necessary. Paulette traded the empty cup for an egg sandwich, which Cal also ate standing, followed by a glass of juice. His whole breakfast took only minutes.

"All right," he said, eager to get on with the day—to the office where fates were decided, a million here, a million there. To another eight hours, Ivy supposed, of working alongside Maggie. Before Maggie, there'd been other assistants—Constance, the Brit; and before her, Penny. Of course, Ivy had her friendships, too. But Maggie, Cal's executive workhorse, had lasted the longest. Except for Ivy.

"Cal."

"What."

"Paige," Ivy said. "Take care there."

"Oh, hell."

Ivy held her coffee cup close to her lips. "She's not as squared as we'd like to think. This thing with ArtShop is a big deal. She's been working on it with Alessandro. Now, lo and behold, I think she has a crush on him."

"What? I thought she was gaga for the other guy."

"Right. And everyone is just one thing," said Ivy.

"Well, if it's Alessandro she wants then she's a fool. That man will never marry. Why should he? He's got his horses, his dames, his house. He'll never settle."

With a tick of her head, Ivy let the remark pass. "Darling, stay with me here. Did you know that Lena, yes, Lena, was once involved with Alessandro?"

His face proved he did not. "Please, no more scenes like last night. This is the kind of piddling shit I cannot deal with. And neither should you."

Which part, she might ask, should she not deal with? His diverticulitis, his food allergies, his stiff knees, the nerve in his back? His nightmares, his hopes, his fears? She had her dryness, her obsessions with clothes, the wasting of a whole life just wishing to be liked. From behind the paper, Ivy said quietly, "You belittle the things that make the larger engine go. You always have."

"Oh, fuck."

Cal didn't care much for humans, though he'd married this one, and from her and him, two other beings had grown up in this house. Cal had no interest in *understanding* their pressing feelings, their needy-needs. He'd planned to move this thing with Charlie along at a certain pace: deal first, chums later. And to deal with Lena after that. Now, thanks to Ivy, the whole game was bollixed.

"You mean Lena. Don't worry, she'll take the deal," Cal blundered on. "If she isn't thick, and I don't believe she is. My brother was a fool, but among those girls Lena always had the wits. Her husband will get the funding he needs and, god willing, go on to glory. That should be sufficient balm for the righteous."

"I don't give a fig about *Lena!*" Ivy threw the paper aside to prove it. "You. In *my house.* Your brother's wife, goddamn you." Ivy gulped, she could hardly breath. "Ted went to his grave—"

"Happy and ignorant as ever, as there was nothing to know," Cal said.

"That's your story. I suppose you want credit for sticking to it."

"No, I want credit for sticking to you."

This stopped them both, for in fact it was true. They had both stuck, more than stuck.

"Then please tell me, Calvin Rusch, what exactly are you doing."

"My thing, which has done us just fine."

Ivy blinked. A few steps back, she'd wanted to say, but what about our Paige? What about us? The moment had passed. She looked at Cal for the first time since he came down.

"What is that shirt?" she cried. "You calling on Swish Jones?"

Cal regarded his buttons. For starters, both of them knew Ivy would never buy an orange shirt. Orange turned Cal's skin sallow. At a certain age one had, at least, the consistency of one's taste. And if Ivy didn't buy it, it had no business being in the house. He struggled to explain. No, it would have been Maggie at the office—Miss Autumnal—who'd trundled up her pennies and bought Cal a tangerine check.

"Ivy."

"Don't bother."

"Ivy," he said, as two of the gardeners passed through the foyer carrying an enormous bamboo tree. With the party only a month away, a wonderland was being built in and around the house, yet until today he hadn't noticed. "Who do we have on tonight?"

"Just us," she said glumly.

"Thank god." What he meant was thank god with you and he turned back to show her. To Cal's way of thinking, that should have been enough. Years of experience with Ivy had taught him otherwise, but he would go down believing it should have been enough.

She let him get as far as the front door.

" 'My thing' isn't an answer."

His eyes lifted to the ceiling. "Nope. And yet I go." Cal opened the front door.

On the other side, Paco was just arriving at the stoop. The two men nearly collided. Stepping back, Cal waved Paco inside then went out, shutting the door with a bang.

Ivy dropped her spoon, sending it crashing to the floor. Under the table, the dogs barked wildly as they climbed to their feet.

"Missus?" Paco hurried toward her, while inside the kitchen, Paulette stopped counting the bills in her wallet and burst through the swinging door. *"Qu'est-ce que c'est?"*

It was there on Ivy's face—for them all to see. The most basic question no one could answer.

Paulette cupped her hand to her chin, and sighed. *"Bien sûr. Bien sûr."* Of course: love.

Driving south, to the exit just after the airport, Cal turned off the highway and parked in front of a small café. Beverly was waiting inside. As he approached the table he was confounded by the same spark that had touched him and his brother, too, when they were just kids at Santa Rosa High.

"Thank you," Beverly said, looking up. She wondered if he was going to stand there, or sit. He didn't know himself.

"You are full of surprises," Cal said, pulling out a chair. "Sixty-some years ago, forty-five, and now."

"A girl uses what she has," Beverly said lightly, "when need demands."

They both knew that over the years need had demanded many times, yet she'd held off. Telling him now, when it could only benefit someone other than herself, went opposite her character, and that was why he didn't doubt her.

"You kept a secret a long time," he said.

"It got your attention."

"Well, it would."

She was silent then, nodding in the face of it. Women are far braver than men, he thought. And for a moment he took up Ivy. In all his years of dealing with hotshots, Cal had known but three great generals: Ivy, Maggie and this one. And each of them wasted on the war that was him.

"Ted had only his girls," Beverly went on, continuing a conversation that had played out in her mind many times. "I wouldn't want Lena to lose him. I'm not sure she could handle it. She's got a thing for lost causes. And besides—"

"Why complicate things."

She breathed in and out in short sips at the top of her ample chest. "And what do you think of Nimbus?"

He stiffened at the question. "Good. Your son-in-law's concept seems top shelf."

She smiled privately. There was nothing to be said that wouldn't require a whole lot more of saying. Collecting herself, Beverly nodded at his shirt.

"I knew that color would suit you."

"You shouldn't send me stuff."

"Oh, for the holidays, I like to give a little something to remember me by." Beverly laughed loudly, ignoring his embarrassment, his cellular reticence, which even when he was a poor kid made him seem fussy. And because there was no good reason to hold back, she reached across the table and gave his arm a squeeze. As her hand darted away, he caught it and held on. Her palm was padded, like a child's, and was surprisingly cool and dry; his were not. The bangles made their own music.

Seven

"But why wouldn't Charlie tell me . . . ?" Lena's thinking advanced only that far. Theo's shoe was untied. There on the crowded sidewalk Lena bent to fix it, but she moved too quickly and her purse swung from behind, hitting her in the face. She growled and swung it back.

They were late for Theo's kindergarten interview. All the pressure was expressed in Theo's shoes.

"How's that?" she asked, giving the lace a final tug.

Theo tapped the sidewalk. "Now the other one's wiggly."

Citywide, there was one spot for every twenty applicants, and the odds were less if you asked for financial aid. So far the "playdates," as they were called, had gone badly for Theo. During the first two interviews, as all the children played brightly, Theo decided it would be better not to talk. He could shake his head, he could hop on one foot, but Theo couldn't talk. In one playdate, he was asked to draw a star; Theo drew a portrait of Bruce Springsteen. The admissions director at that school grudgingly admitted that this was a creative choice. The next interview went even worse.

Lena sighed. She had to deal with Charlie. And she had to consider Alessandro—the effect of hearing his voice she couldn't say. She couldn't say because she couldn't think because she didn't have time to feel. It was in this state of unaccommodation that Lena's thoughts turned global. Think of the mothers of Iraq, Sudan and Appalachia, she reminded herself. Was it only luck or unluck; only fate? From fate Lena moved quickly to the gods, her image being not one god but a collective of ancients, old Greeks, perhaps—these men and women, all somber, flawed, but mighty, the lot of them in robes and beards (not the women, who had seventies-style cuts) with hairy legs in crude sandals—nodding at her from a higher plane. Lena's gods were lusty, capricious and highly improvisational. They were not above one-upmanship and crude management practices. They were parsimonious and unjust.

While Lena squatted at Theo's feet, she took her phone from her purse and, before she could think, texted Charlie. Damn you, Charlie—WHY??!!!

"Mama."

"Hang on."

"Mama?"

"What, Theo?"

"I think we should cancel."

Lena glanced up at her son then down again. She had her listening face on, her head bowed, eyes focused on the ground. "Theo, we're not canceling. Just be yourself."

"But you want me to get in some place and you're scared I won't."

She couldn't acknowledge this bit of solid reasoning, at least not while squatting near the ground. Lena stood up. "Give me your hand," she said. His fingers tucked into hers felt very strong. She looked him squarely in the eye. "We're trying these schools out, not the other way. We're just seeing what we see, that's all. In the end, we'll decide."

"You really think so?"

"I do."

While the playdate dragged on, inside the school lobby, the other mothers worked to make friends. They seemed to believe that their ability to get along with strangers would have a positive effect on their child's application. Lena went off to a corner and stewed. She checked her phone: no call, no text. She phoned Charlie and was put straight through to voice mail, meaning his cell was turned off. Why wouldn't he just tell her? She lifted her nose skyward and fought back tears.

The moment she caught sight of Theo, Lena knew they were in trouble.

The instructors had asked the boys to make a coffee cup to take home. There were five steps involved: cut a piece of paper, following the lines; draw your best picture on the paper; then fit the drawing into the plastic sleeve on the outer rim of the mug, like so; then fit the top on. When finished, raise your hand. Start now.

The other boys rushed forward to show their cups to their waiting parents. Lena could make out detailed renderings of underwater worlds and houses and families.

But when Theo found Lena he said, his voice shaking, "I'm never coming back here. Ever."

"What happened, Theo?"

"Those people."

"What did they do?"

Theo handed over his mug. He had kept his paper blank, except for a row of five green dots. "It's just like ones we have at home," he explained.

He would never get in now, unless they understood his mind, and why should they do that? Lena smiled at the woman who was the kindergarten teacher. She did not meet Lena's gaze.

On the way to the car, Theo looked soberly at Lena and decided exactly how much truth his mother could handle. "That lady, she smiles with her mouth but not her eyes."

"Oh, Christ." Lena pulled him to her, feeling his small solid back, the man already there in his bones. Theo was a character, and the world would make him pay for that, but she'd hoped to keep him safe just a little longer.

"You are great, Theo. Do you know that?"

"Yeah," he said, his face mashed against her. "But I'm a little weird, too."

"Honey, your dad and I are a little weird."

With his face pressed against her belly, he nodded. He already knew.

The dissection of a person always starts with an unequivocal truth.

"Here comes Lena Rusch," said Lindsay Greer. For emphasis she rolled her eyes and pointed her chin toward the window.

The three other mothers at the table tipped forward in their seats, craning their necks toward the glass, as Lena whooshed by, a clutter-cloud of urgency in her old, black coat, pulling Theo alongside her.

"Late again."

"Late? The other boys got back from the screening half an hour ago. Mrs. Winters will have her head. They've already missed Circle."

"Timmy says Theo's a little . . . odd."

The others nodded; they'd heard it, too. They were not bad women. When the crisis with the twins first happened, each had done her part by dropping off a chicken or a quiche, or offering to take Theo home for an afternoon. In doing so, they felt a rightful claim to the Peppers' tragedy, which necessitated much discussion. They'd told the story to their friends on both coasts and, in telling, found themselves referring to Lena as "my dear friend."

"I called her last week and left a message. She signed up to make treats for the Martin Luther King party but I bet she forgot. She never called me back."

"She will. I give her every excuse. I cut her major slack."

There was nodding all around. They all cut Lena slack.

"But she's aloof."

"You would be, too."

"No," Lindsay Greer corrected, pressing her finger into the table. "If *I* were *Lena,* they would have had to haul me to the funny farm and lock me in a padded room."

Lena felt the sword as she climbed the school steps with Theo. "Whoa!" she cried, her fingers flying to her mouth.

"What?" said Theo.

"I don't know!" she confessed, pausing, checking. She pulled on his hand. "Honey, come on."

Theo refused. He'd been tugged at enough. He was tired. He had been "the best boy" in the hospital and, later, at that school. He thought, at the very least, he had a different kind of morning coming to him. He wanted to run tucked inside the flap of his mother's raincoat with them both pretending he was a baby bat. He wanted to tell her a story and have her listen carefully—a story that had no beginning or end.

"Don't make me beg," Lena pleaded, as the phone in her purse started to ring. Charlie, she thought. You son of a bitch. She dug in her bag for her cell. But it was only Violet, calling to remind Lena not to be late.

Lena hung up and, turning to Theo, said, "All right, I'm begging."

Theo ran up the school stairs. He wouldn't be seen clinging, not like those first weeks of school, when Mrs. Winters dubbed him "the last boy to say a clean good-bye." Theo ran past the room where his schoolmates were singing, to the large playroom. He climbed on a rocking horse and wildly jerked its reins.

Lena motioned for Theo to come back. He ignored her. "Sweetheart, I've got to go," she said, walking toward him. "Glo will pick you up."

"I feel sick," Theo said.

"Oh, Theo. Sick how?"

He presented his face for Lena's inspection. In the hospital, he'd hardly slept. But that aside, Theo was hale as a post.

"Sorry, honey. You have to hang in. Willa has to get better; I've got to go to work; and you've got to stay in school."

Theo looked at her frankly. "And Dad, he's got to sell the chief in Boston. And Glo, she has to work for us, and Miguel and Rosella are mad because Glo lives here while they're stuck in Guatemala."

"You've got it."

"It's lousy."

She couldn't disagree. "Tell you what. Stick it out for today; tomorrow, if you're still tired, you can stay home . . . Sweetheart, that's all I've got."

Mrs. Winters was on her way to her office when she spotted the pair—*negotiating,* of all things. It was the mother's fault, always mooning and clinging, making things hard for the child. Much better to give them a quick peck and out the door you go.

"All right," Mrs. Winters called, her voice preceding her, followed by a cloud of Estée Lauder Beautiful perfume. Mrs. Winters took Theo by the hand, led him down the hall and that was the end of it. Theo understood he must not look back. Lena knew her role, too. She went quickly down the stairs and into the street, where, despite waves of panic, she did not stop.

Lena had no time—not for coffee chats, yoga, spin classes. Not for chaperoning a field trip to the Pumpkin Patch, or baking treats for afternoon Circle, or volunteering for library duty. She didn't get her nails done. She hardly cut her hair. Feminine indulgences were confined to two quick brushes of the mascara wand and the occasional swoop-shave of the legs and pubes. Otherwise, she had to finish the script she'd promised Vi and attend four client meetings—pushed back from earlier in the week when Willa was in the hospital. She needed to bill at least forty hours this week to cover some of their basic bills. She had client calls to return and a half dozen doctor and therapist appointments for Willa to schedule across the next few days. That, and the toilet upstairs in the house needed a jiggle. And what of Willa's seizures? Had they caused irreparable damage? Had they? Lena had a roll on her hips and bags under her eyes. Her black pumps were rubbing a blister on her right baby toe. Meanwhile the heart with its wants—its ridiculous wants—demanded a kiss and a poem.

Lena turned her attention toward an immediate and desperate need for coffee. Was Theo really sick? She closed her eyes. No. From Theo, the obvious jump was to Willa: Would Glo know to give her the antibiotics with food? Lena halted on the sidewalk, waiting, until a bird of relief rose in her chest: Glo would.

And because Glo would, Lena opened her eyes and received the morning. It was a lovely day, the city replete with a spring dampness that kissed the cheeks and brightened the air.

Vi was waiting at the corner. Lena's conscience panged. The sight of her dear pal, now boss, reminded her all over again of the work undone, beginning with the script she hadn't finished. "Oh, Vi," she said breathlessly hugging and explaining at the same time. "I laid down the key changes, I swear. The goddesses and harmonies I'll have to put in later. Tonight. Promise." Lena sighed, for that, too, was wishful thinking. "I'm sorry. I swear, Vi, one day soon you'll stop having to carry me, and I'll carry you."

Violet tipped her head. As yet she'd shared her complaints regarding Lena only with Maude, which delighted Maude and made whole evenings pass amiably. "I have an agency to run, you know."

"Oh, Christ, I'm sorry," Lena said. "There can't be any worse feeling than knowing I'm letting you down. By the way, that's a stellar dress. Makes you look tiny."

Vi looked down at herself. "Do you think? Not too much?"

"Nope."

Vi narrowed her gaze. "Are you trying to suck up?"

"Yep. But I *am* sorry. And I will finish. And the looking thin part is true." Lena smiled.

Nodding, Violet squinted into the future, and the future squinted back. She had any number of urgent work matters she needed to discuss, but one glance at Lena told her otherwise. "I want to hear—Willa, is she OK?"

"Coffee," Lena said.

Inside the coffee shop, the mothers were putting a fine point on things. They had cut a wide swath through the swine flu scare, the impossible parking at Laurel Village, real estate prices, house renovations, kindergarten admissions and Michelle Obama's erratic fashion choices (the wide belts looked god-awful). Diana had the rug man due in half an hour. Lindsay Greer had a Pilates class.

"Do you think she's good-looking?"

"Who?"

"Lena, silly."

Surprise went through the ranks. There were days when it seemed quite obvious that Lena Rusch hadn't combed her hair.

"Well, Bill does," Lindsay continued. "On the way home from the new parents' dinner, he said she was a quiet fox."

The women shifted in their chairs. There was a whimsical quality to Lena, for sure, of something funny or witty on the tip of her tongue, something that ought to be on the tip of yours. But they hardly thought of her as a siren.

"He said that to you?"

"Oh, he says all kinds of things. Don't worry. He's more talk than do."

Around the table, there was silent agreement that Bill Greer was a bit of a putz.

"Attractive," Kate said definitively, honing the question. "But not beautiful. Between the eyes and nose something's off."

"Well, Bill loves 'something off,'" Lindsay admitted. "He loves the Ellen Barkins, with their squinty eyes and crooked noses."

"Oh, I like Ellen Barkin," Diana added rather dreamily.

"There you go."

Outside on the sidewalk the Muni bus released its cargo of some dozen Korean teenagers, all students bound for nearby Newcomer High. They packed into the tight coffeehouse, refusing to form a line. The girls giggled in back while the boys went first—twiggy boys in huge down jackets and oversize jeans, the crotches hanging below their knees. The women at the table pulled their circle tighter, and therefore failed to notice Lena and Violet standing at the back of the line, not two feet from them. Lena didn't see them either.

"Vi," Lena said.

"What?"

"Answer me honestly. Have I pushed Charlie?"

"Pushed him how?"

"I don't know. Say Charlie's piece is a certain do-gooding glory, could the money piece be me? Is he doing all this because he thinks I want more?"

Violet narrowed her gaze. "Wait a minute. What are you saying?"

"He's gone, Vi. I don't just mean he's never home, which he never is. I mean he's . . . *gone*. And I'm thinking, is it just work, or does he think he has to prove something to me?"

"Yikes, let me think." Violet stared hard at the teenagers in front of them, whom she wanted badly to slap or shake, as they were lollygagging instead of moving up. "No, babe. He's working for lots of reasons, you among them, but in the end, Charlie is compelled."

Lena nodded, holding her hands, which were shaking. She couldn't seem to keep them still. "Vi—"

"Lena, honey, what *is* the matter with your face?"

"Vi, Alessandro Corsini called this morning while I was making one-eyed gypsies." There, she said it. Lena nearly swooned with relief.

Violet turned—really, she spun—her face wide with shock, yes, but wonder, too. And for that, as much as anything, for the ability never to stop being impressed and even delighted by the world, Lena loved her.

The women's voices came from behind. "Charlie certainly looks grim. You know, statistically, most marriages don't survive the death of a child."

"And then there's Willa."

"But I thought she was gaining? Lena said—"

"Oh, be honest. Have you seen that baby lately?" Lindsay Greer observed emphatically. "Lies in the stroller like a squash."

They ran from the coffee shop, Violet in her heels and Lena with her bags. Down one block and then another, at which point Lena pulled up, clutching her belly. "Oh god, oh god. Vi!"

"Stupid fucking cats," hissed Violet, pressing her hands to her knees like a quarterback. "Who was that?"

"Lindsay Greer," Lena huffed. "They're scared. They're so damn safe yet scared. She didn't mean it, Vi."

Violet disagreed. She thought most people did believe what they said. That was the trouble. The stupidity that came out of mouths was the stupidity within. "Scared? Well you cured her of *that*. You cursed her, you did. Sort of brilliantly." Violet squinted appreciatively at Lena.

"I did not."

"Come on, I mean, *May you always have luck*? If someone said that to me, I'd be certain a beam was about to fall on my head." Violet smiled. She was not a great believer in modern life, Violet. She did not believe in temperance or moderation, though she did believe most people should shut up. And, most significantly, she did not believe in a casual workplace, but that was another subject. She'd loved women for as long as she could remember, and with her love for women, Vi cleaved to the designer wardrobe, immoderate driving, a pack-a-day habit, and Lena. She cleaved to Lena. "Oh god, honey. I'm so sorry."

Lena hugged her ribs. "How could they talk about Willa that way? How could they—" But Lena's eyes got huge as all of a sudden she realized what they saw. She shook her head at the ground. "How could they not."

"Oh, honey."

"You wonder, too. Don't you?" Lena met Violet's eyes.

Violet studied her friend. There was no point in denying what was true. "I believe what you tell me, and I know what I see; and what I see is that Willa is one lucky baby to have you fighting for her."

Lena nodded, miserable, as the truth was worse than she'd feared. Most of all, she was stung and very proud. The last time she'd seen Lindsay Greer, they were at the Holiday Sing and Lindsay was wearing a ridiculous red velvet blazer. She had saved a seat for the husband, who didn't show, and at the end of the performance Lindsay looked miserable and embarrassed. Lena hugged her. That's all: she hugged her because—because it was easier. Lena didn't care if she was talked about, but she felt at the edge of violence to hear her daughter's name in that silly, lonely woman's mouth. Lena considered herself no more a survivor, no more a victim, and certainly no better than any of them. But lately it seemed to her that there must be something heroic about getting through the day with a bit of grace.

Lena dropped her bag on the ground and rummaged inside for her notes. "Vi—"

"You aren't coming to the meeting, are you?"

"I can't," Lena said. "I'm sorry. I'm always saying sorry, aren't I? Well, I am. I have to—" She stopped herself from saying more. She had to get to Charlie. She fished in her bag for the script to hand to Violet. An envelope fell out of the side pocket. "What the hell?" Lena picked it up. On one side Theo had drawn his favorite dragon. On the other side, Lena and Charlie's names were written in fancy script. She ripped the envelope open. *Join us to celebrate the engagement of . . . Regrets only. Ivy and Cal Rusch.*

"Oh, Charlie," she cried, covering her mouth.

"What now?" Violet demanded.

Lena looked up slowly. Her face was blanched as wood. It seemed to practical Violet, who did not wonder why things happened, only when they would start or stop, that all faces were masks, except this one. Lena's.

"Honey, now you're scaring *me,*" Violet said. "What happened?"

Lena could not say. There were not words enough, certainly not the right ones, to answer such a question. "Help me up," she said.

Eight

Forgetting means remembering at an inconvenient time. This little bit of wisdom could not have been further from Charlie's mind, as he hustled down the familiar corridors of Mass General, where just two years earlier he'd been head of urology, and was now a visiting adjunct with a gizmo to sell and a patient waiting in preop.

Herbert Wilson wasn't thrilled to meet his surgeon. A sixty-seven-year-old African American, Wilson had been ignoring his prostate for more than a year. He had an elevated PSA and a localized cancer, but no evidence of spread—in other words, he was a perfect candidate for a prostatectomy using the Midas robot.

Jack Bost introduced Charlie to Wilson, who was understandably anxious at the prospect of having his privates sliced. Despite two injections of Valium, Wilson's blood pressure kept soaring. The nurses had been trying to calm him for the better part of an hour.

"Dr. Pepper?" Wilson said. "You're kidding me. I'm being operated on by a Dr. Pepper?"

"That's right, Mr. Wilson. Name is destiny—don't you know it?" Charlie fought to keep a straight face, but the nurses were already chuckling. No one had more bedside manner than Dr. Pepper. Charlie took Wilson's hand and checked his pulse. "As Ellen and others here know, I've made a study of proving that point. Let's see, there's a fellow named Al Fresco, he runs a cooling business, and then there's Hy Marx, the scholar, and Les Plack, the dentist, and Bea Minor, second chair violin of the Chicago symphony."

"You don't say, Doc. Isn't that something." Wilson smiled dreamily, the narcotics now flowing through him unimpeded. "I once met a gal, her name was Mary . . . Mary Christmas."

"See that. And what was she about?" Charlie met Ellen's gaze and nodded, the monitor showing Wilson's pressure falling nicely.

"Mmmm, she was . . . very . . . nice," Wilson murmured, his eyes fluttering closed.

Satisfied, Charlie released Wilson's hand. "Of course she was. Mr. Wilson, we're going to take great care of you."

Charlie and Jack scrubbed while an unconscious Mr. Wilson was cathetered, draped and strapped onto the table, his feet bound in stirrups. Above the table, flat-screen monitors had been set up on both sides the way Charlie liked, and the Midas unit, with its four steel arms, hung like an enormous spider at the center. Across the room, at the computer console, Charlie would control the robot as if playing a video game.

Charlie greeted Clyde Dubinski, the anesthesiologist, with whom he'd worked on scores of cases and, as such, had developed a shorthand born of practicality and Charlie's superstitions.

"No nitrous, no twitches," Charlie warned, as he always did at the start, meaning take him down deep and keep him there. Once the robot was docked, he couldn't have Wilson moving, not even a fraction.

"Right-o," said Clyde, and he released a bit more gas.

Charlie started in. The euphoric adventure never lessened with time, and this was a special day besides. It came on Charlie like a drug. Turning to Ellen, he nodded, and she flicked on the stereo, having already loaded the CDs in the special order he liked. To Charlie Pepper's way of thinking, a prostatectomy called for a bit of roar. Midway, they'd switch to Springsteen, and then on to Bobby Dylan for the close. But the start, the start was sacred. At the first three twangs of Keith Richards's "Brown Sugar," Charlie lifted his head and summoned the powers.

Above, in the glass-paneled theater, the chief and a group of residents looked on, as Jack inserted the Veress needle through a small nick just above the umbilicus and the abdomen inflated like a balloon.

"Twenty mills of pressure," Charlie advised. "That's right."

The first trocar, a long, metal, tubelike arm with a camera attached, went in through another tiny incision in the abdomen. Instantly, Mr. Wilson's insides appeared in full color on the flat-screen monitors. Charlie moved the scope, checking for adhesions, and finding none, moved on. He nodded for the next three trocars to be inserted: a pincer, a wand and a cauterizer.

"All right, let's get him in deep," Charlie said. The attending nurse shifted the table and Mr. Wilson was positioned in a steep Trendelenburg position, pelvis raised, head lowered.

Charlie and Jack moved to the console, a large box with 3-D HD binoculars and finger controls like highly tuned joysticks. Charlie sat in the cockpit with Jack behind him. In quick succession, he snipped the adhesions from the colon, manually aspirated the bladder, while providing a running commentary into the microphone for the group watching above in the theater. He transected the vas deferens and moved it to the one and eleven o'clock positions, as the prostate became visible past the neck of the bladder. At that point, Charlie noted, the challenge was to avoid nerve damage.

"We're on sacred ground, folks," he told the gallery. "We are in the nexus of Mr. Wilson's chi, the heat, the sex, the soul. Then again, it is also the piping, and I am a plumber's son."

Two and a half hours in, the plumlike prostate showed itself on the monitor. Charlie netted it like a guppy into a bag.

Dylan's "Like a Rolling Stone" played on the stereo.

"Beautiful," Jack said.

As if released from a meditative state, Charlie nodded. His work nearly done, he was feeling good as he emerged from the zone, moving quickly, mechanically, as the room once again came into focus and the music roared in his ears—as Bob Dylan sang, asking Charlie directly, how it felt to be alone, with no direction home.

With a shudder of heartache and doom Charlie remembered Lena. He picked up his head. "Goddamn it," he exclaimed, forgetting the microphone. "I've got to get out of here."

"What's that?" Jack glanced at the folks upstairs and smiled reassuringly. He put his hand on Charlie's shoulder.

Charlie turned away. Moving swiftly, they undocked the Midas and Sam, the resident, took over, placing Mr. Wilson's drains and closing him.

Jack and Charlie pushed through the double doors. "Hey, Charlie, what the hell?"

"I know," Charlie said. "Let's not talk about it."

"You see the chief watching your show?"

"I did," Charlie replied, but the shine was off him.

Jack tore off his gloves and gown and stuffed them into the bin. "We've got our semiyearly departmental coming up and I just heard that the fellow presenting had to cancel. You want the slot? Do that and come with me on a morning loop through grand rounds. You'd get a twofer. The executive committee is meeting in a couple of weeks, you know. This way, you have the surgical faculty primed first, and then we'll set you up with the board. The memory of you amazing them would be fresh, you bastard. I think the chief has gotten over being pissed you left and may be open to piloting your robot. He's been talking about it enough. You game to come back Friday a week?"

Charlie was having trouble listening, his thoughts ranging. He had to change, talk to the chief there, make a quick stop in Somerville to see his parents. Come Friday, back home, he had the meeting with Cal, and once they had the bridge loan, there'd be piles more work and new hires to make. The contract with Mass Gen would seal things. It was all falling into place. He just had to hold up. He had to sprint. And most of all, he had to make Lena see that it was all good.

"So. You game?" Jack asked.

Charlie nodded. "I'll have to do some dancing back home, but sure."

As they made their way through the double doors from the recovery room to the proc ward, Charlie looked at his friend Jack, who had taken the safe and stable route. But, honestly, was anyone's life sure? Charlie's gaze lifted to the clock above the door. "Hey. That's new." The clock had a distinct blue band around its face with a slogan that read, *Isn't it time to think about Viagra?*

Charlie laughed.

"You kidding me?" Jack said. "These guys have nothing but hope."

Charlie's childhood house in Somerville looked exactly like its neighbors: a split-level painted white with black shutters and a dark green door. Each year, the shrubs beneath the windows grew larger, and the basketball hoop sagged, and the lawn, which used to take him a day and a half to cut with the Toro, grew back with a vengeance. He'd studied for hours in that room with the small, garret windows; he'd smoked his first reefer on the roof of the garage.

The side door was unlocked. A string of bells from Thailand, a gift to his parents from Swanson, hung on the knob.

Each time Charlie came home his parents looked up with utter shock at the sight of this grown son. Charlie carried with him the scent of the world, of occupation far and wide and beyond them. He was their boat that had sailed into the glorious deep, while they remained, with the Coppertone and sandwich wrappers and beach chairs, on shore. There was Charlie; there he was. And there he went—as he was always in a hurry, today being no exception. He'd promised to spend the night, but that didn't mean he had any intention of relaxing.

They had taught him never to brag and so he couldn't start in with the news of the second round. He'd have to wait. Checking his watch, Charlie improvised a posture of ease.

"Who'd you work on today?" his father asked, painfully lowering himself into a chair at the table and turning his bum knee to one side.

"A liver and a prostatectomy," said Charlie.

"Jesus. There but for the grace of god."

Fran, Charlie's mother, carved the roast. Though it was midweek, she had made his favorite Sunday meal: a pork loin with peppers and potatoes, a three-bean salad, cake. She brought the roast to the table. "How's Willa?"

"Better."

"Who took care of Theo while—"

"Mom."

"What? I'm just asking." Fran was fierce, and always had been, with her cropped hair, no makeup—a get in here and don't BS me sort of mother whom Charlie and his friends adored. "What about her hearing?"

"There's nothing new there. We need to put the tubes in, then once the fluid drains and the swelling goes down, we'll see how much hearing she's got." The worry unnerved Charlie; he sensed implied criticism, which was not of him but of Lena. And thinking of Lena, Charlie got up to plug in his phone. "Dad, how come you've got the blower out? I thought you were going to hire that guy—"

"Charlie, you know your father," his mother said. "Before he listens, he's going to first have to bust the other knee."

"And when I do, Fran, you can tell me how right you are. Now how about you stop chapping Charlie's rear." Charlie's father pointed his fork at his wife, but that was as far as it would go. Every Sunday, before church, he made pancakes, bacon and coffee and served her in bed. And every Sunday afternoon, as far back as Charlie could remember, they retired to their room for a couple of hours and laughter could be heard behind their locked door.

His mother cut her meat, then set down her knife and fork. "I'm just saying. If you were closer, I could help. As it is, it's never too much for me to get on a plane and come out. What else are we doing around here?"

"Hey," Charlie said as he wrestled with the twisted charger cord. "You want to hear the latest from Theo?" He was determined not to head down any sad roads.

"Sure," his mother said.

"The other day Theo was riding with Lena in the car and from the backseat he pipes up and says, 'Mama, I feel sorry for god.' Lena says,

'How come?' Theo shoots back, 'He lost his brother.' Lena, she tries to wrap her mind around this. She says, 'Theo, do you mean Jesus?' 'Yeah,' he says in a condescending sort of tone. 'You know, god's brother.'

" 'Theo,' Lena says, 'Jesus was god's *son*. Most people believe Jesus was god's son.' Now in the backseat the wheels are turning. Our man Theo is working this over; steam's coming out of his ears. They drive along. 'Well,' Theo says after a while, 'that's terrible. Poor god. We should send him a card.' "

Charlie's mother chuckled and wiped her eyes. "A pagan, we got there, eh?" She stood to face the dishes.

"Mom. It looks like we got the second round. We just heard this morning. Twenty million in funding with a bridge loan of a mil starting now. We're going all the way."

She shut off the water and faced him. Slowly, thoroughly, she dried her hands. "Oh my god," she said, not wanting to call too much attention to it, the same as when he came home with his report cards, year after year all A's. She tucked in her mouth and nodded twice. The first nod taking it in, the second nod the swell of pride.

"I suppose they wire that kind of money, yeah?" his father asked.

"It depends, Dad." Charlie was checking his text messages and therefore only half heard his father. There was one from Maggie in Cal Rusch's office, confirming their meeting at Rusch & Co. Charlie nodded to himself; it was all working, all moving along. "What's that, Pop?" he asked, scrolling to the next. This one was from Lena—there were several more. *I mean, Uncle Cal?* She'd written. *Damn you, Charlie! DO NOT CALL.*

"Shit."

"Shit, what?" his father echoed.

Charlie dialed Lena's cell, but, of course, she had turned off her phone. He called again and left a message. "Lena, honey, call me. Please. Let's talk. Give me a chance to explain before you jump to anything."

His mother was wiping down the table. She looked up.

"Mom," he said, "let's just say I didn't get a chance to tell Lena about this new deal before it happened."

"She won't be happy about it?"

"It's complicated."

Charlie was her only child, and there couldn't be anything simpler than that. "Charlie."

"I know, Mom."

"What do you know?" She was a foot shorter, so that as she took his face in her still-damp hands she had to reach up. "So smart. I couldn't be any more proud. But, Charlie, you have been in this house less than an hour and I have watched you chew and I have listened to your stories, but your *you* has yet to come through that door. What do you know?"

Nine

The following morning the Great Lakes suffered fierce winds and as Charlie's plane pushed westward, the wind pushed back. Meanwhile, on land, new desks were arriving at Nimbus. A beaten-up truck pulled into the loading zone out front and two men wearing lifting belts climbed out, speaking Spanish. They asked to see the boss. The receptionist, who was also Charlie's assistant, told them the boss wasn't available but that she could handle it and taking their clipboard she scanned the list of credenzas, bookcases and pedestals and a total amount due that was nothing short of astonishing—given that Charlie Pepper checked her biweekly Costco runs to make certain she didn't overspend on Cokes and Kleenex. She summoned Swanson. He hurried from the lab—such a rare occurrence to see him out in the sunshine—and whooping and laughing, he signed the paper with a flourish. The two men proceeded with their task, unloading boxes and crates.

The Herman Miller desks and credenzas were top-of-the-line maple. They came in parts, but even the parts were beautiful. The setup took hours, but the truck and the men were gone before Charlie pulled up in his car.

He went first to Swanson's office, which was closest to the front door.

"Hey, what's this?" Charlie dropped his bags. Swanson was sitting in a new black-mesh swivel chair, his socked feet up on his new desk. "I said pick 'em out, buddy, not buy 'em. We've got to nail the funding first."

"Uh, we did, Cap."

"We have a verbal handshake, no check."

"Charles, sit yourself down lest you abuse my moment here. This, in case you don't know, is a great day. Talk about good tidings. After you called I phoned that guy I knew from the gym and what do you know, someone just canceled this order. They had the truck loaded and everything! I mean, perfect timing. I got us these beauties wholesale. Come on, relax."

Charlie tried. His body was as yet soaring over the Rockies; he met it coming and going. Even so, he dropped onto Swanson's futon and, closing his eyes, attempted to land the lunar vessel of himself on earth.

"I only wish we had the dough in hand, Swan."

"You worried, Pep? I mean seriously."

Charlie thought for a moment. "Nope."

"All right. All right!" Swanson clapped his hands. "On that note, next up we've got Earth, Wind and Fire. Here we go." Swanson nudged up the volume on the remote. Maurice White sang, "Do you remember . . . ?"

Charlie kept his eyes shut and grinned, allowing the song to move through him. After it was over, he said, "So, Lee. What's this thing you have with maple?"

"Grew in my yard. A good tree, the maple." Swanson reclined in his new chair. Home was a small apartment with a bed, a TV, a leather sofa and a set of metal Costco chairs. He rarely visited it. Most nights, he slept right here, on the futon, where he was just a few steps from the lab. He and Charlie hadn't taken a paycheck in months. If the desks made Swanson happy, Charlie would be the last one to deny him.

Swanson turned down the music. "Hey, you want to run over our plan for the meeting with Rusch?"

"Nah. We know the deal. Shuffle ball change."

Swanson nodded. "So. What did Lena want?"

"Lena? You saw her?" Charlie jumped to his feet.

"Just a few minutes ago! Come on. She was in here, then she went back to your office—I figured you guys must have seen each other out front."

Charlie ran down the hall. Lena had left the invitation to Cal and Ivy's party on Charlie's new, blond desk. He hurried through the lab and out the back door into the parking lot, where he spotted her, talking on her cell in the car.

He'd already decided to take what was coming—and to agree to all charges. There was almost nothing he wouldn't do to make peace. He sprinted toward her, across the lot. Seeing him, she climbed out and slammed the car door shut.

"All right," Charlie shouted, holding up his palms. "I screwed up. I should have told you."

"That's it?" Her face was terrible. "That's what I get? The I-fucked-up defense? Come on, Pepper."

He struggled to find better words. The skills he used every day now, the pitching and honing and dance, were of no use to him. The surgeon had nothing in his hands.

"What," Lena demanded, "are we *doing*?"

"The best we can."

"Not good enough."

"Look, Lena. You want the ugly? Here it is: no one is going to fund Nimbus. No one. Oh, maybe in a year or two, when the economy turns around—maybe. Swanny and I, we don't have a year. We've got weeks. If we don't find money—and I mean now—all the work, the patents, everything, it's a hill of piss. I've talked to everyone in the Valley. I've talked to them twice. Out of the blue your uncle calls. Out of the blue, Lena. Should I have put him on hold and asked your permission? No. I thought, let's see what he's about. If he's serious and if we can come to terms—I think we'll know that pretty quick—at that point I thought we'd talk it out—trusting you'd understand and even be *glad*—"

"Glad." Her eyes flashed. "My god! Who *are* you?"

"The guy who's got to pull this off. That's who. Maybe that's all I am." He pointed his chin at her. "Are you with me?"

She presented him with a face of such pure misery he had to look away. "God, we're really lost."

Charlie gestured behind him, toward the office. "What would you have had me do?"

"Talk to me!" she cried. "There was ample time—"

"Ample?" he cried, cutting her off. "Babe, we haven't had ample in a *long* time." He ran a hand through his shaggy hair.

"It's not—"

"What," Charlie said. "Fair? Lena, tell me you aren't still expecting fair."

Lena dipped her head and with the toe of her shoe made an X on the pavement. "From you," she said quietly.

They paused. It was the missing on both sides that made them want to retch. They were in too deep. And if either of them knew a way to hold their ground and also make peace, they would have gladly done it.

"Look," he said, "either I'm a wimp or I'm just enough your husband to think this is my gig."

"Your gig."

"Yes. If we hit the big time, all the credit is yours. But if it fails, it's mine. I've got to do this."

Lena wiped her nose with the back of her hand. "I don't know," she said. Hugging her ribs, she turned in a circle. "You—you don't even ask how she is. You go days."

His face was full of tenderness. "Only to spare you. Don't you know that?"

"I don't think she's getting better, Charlie."

"Yes, she is. I see her. I see you. I don't know how you do it, but you've brought her back, one more time. She'll be fine."

"*Fine.* How I hate that word."

"You pick at the words and miss the comfort. Lean, you're so close to Willa, you can't see her."

"I see you, Charlie. I'm not so close to you."

But saying it, she knew this wasn't entirely true. She did see Charlie, in a way. She saw his belief, his love and his kindness. She saw the ambition, too. He could cut loose when she least expected it; he could mess around.

But then in the morning he was himself again, juicing oranges, biting his jaw and reading the business page. Their life was an operation; Charlie took up the knife and went in. Today it was the gallbladder, tomorrow the appendix. If he was to operate on the foot, he didn't think about the stomach, he didn't think about the heart. He thought about the foot. He gazed at his children with simple affection, and missed completely the turns in their day, the shifts, the crises, the triumphs. If Lena forgot to brush her hair, he didn't care; he decided years ago that she was beautiful and he had no need to reexamine that decision. How could they ever get along, when she questioned everything? When Charlie had forgotten how to be present, in life, and she had forgotten how to believe?

On the other hand, he knew her; he walked into the dungeon of her soul where the witches roared, and came back loving her. There'd been a time when that by itself was a miracle. She'd married him and for the first time in her life, she'd come home.

She puffed her cheeks, and with a soulful cry said, "I thought we were past the hard part."

"Three years," he said, taking her hand. She was close enough that he could smell the soap on her neck—her smell being the scent of their lives. He longed to be with her. "We agreed to give it three years. Babe, we're eighteen months shy."

Thinking it over, Lena looked across the lot. "What's that tree there? Is it dead?"

"No. It's an apricot."

"I thought so. You should water it—"

"Funny, we just did. We got food for it, too."

Nodding, Lena wiped her nose with the back of her hand. "Look," she said. "I'm not saying it's absolutely wrong to take money from the likes of them, money that could turn to good. I can see that line as well as you. But when it comes down to it, what more are you willing to give up? There's always a trade, Charlie. Don't kid yourself. They were the worst people in my life. Remember: Cal came to my father, too."

"That's not our story."

"How . . . how can you say that? Pepper, we're two smart, well-educated people counting our dimes." She raised her palm up to the sky. "What makes you so sure?"

He smiled. "You."

"Well, stop that," she said.

The next morning Charlie and Swanson drove together to Rusch & Co. They took the exit for Sand Hill Road off 280 and headed east past the Stanford Linear Accelerator, down a quarter mile to a two-story wood building reminiscent of an Alpine ski lodge. Pitched roofs, dark beams, large plate-glass windows; there were perhaps a dozen such buildings hidden along the street, and together they made up the largest density of private capital in the country.

Charlie parked his old Saab next to a fleet of BMWs, Porsches and Ferraris. He and Swanson came up the steps and paused to read the sign above the door: *Finis in principio pendet.*

"The end depends on the beginning," Swanson said.

"Christ, let's hope not," snapped Charlie, and he threw open the door.

From the stark sunshine they entered a muted world of dark paneled walls, caramel-colored sofas and floors tiled in brown leather. On the walls hung one of the west's finest collections of twentieth-century photography. The juxtapositions were uncanny and deliberate. Harry Callahan, from his Vietnam series, juxtaposed with "Moonrise over Hernandez" by Ansel Adams—the brutal against the pristine, man against nature. The tension, of course, catered to Cal's tastes. He insisted that each time an entrepreneur walked into Rusch & Co., he must be newly confronted and inspired.

"Good morning, Charlie. Lee." Margaret Gaffney, Cal's longtime executive assistant, offered her hand. A redhead with freckles, Margaret looked to be in her early sixties with a round, moonish face and thin nose. Sparse lashes, straight as spokes, framed her pale eyes. She was Cal's secret weapon, much feared and sweet-talked.

She led them into the conference room, sat them at the far end of the oval table and saw that they had coffee and a plate of cookies. A few minutes later Cal appeared and shook their hands and said let's get on with it. The partners drifted in one by one, Greg Bettor, Bill Shouts, Tony Hatch, Gaspar Neri, legends in their own right, and the newest partner, an Indian woman named Cynthia Dahl. Alessandro arrived last and there were handshakes all around, but the meeting itself was a grilling.

Early on, Cal propped a finger in front of his mouth and, sitting back, let the drama unfold.

Charlie stood to present. At every turn, Cal's partners interrupted his flow, their pointed questions aimed at mining the depths of Charlie and Swanson's thinking and, beyond their thinking, to what they didn't know.

Alessandro in particular seemed focused on the competition.

"Charlie, how far along are you with getting a 510k, so you can skirt FDA testing?"

Cal brightened. "Ah, good question. I've advised Charlie to piggyback onto Midas, the existing technology, that way—"

"Midas won't like that," Alessandro warned. "They'll aggressively guard their turf."

Charlie had already marked Alessandro as a pretty boy; now he looked him in the eye and addressed the point. "Alessandro, have you worked with Midas?"

"A bit," Alessandro replied, rolling his palm open on the table. "The design firm I hold an interest in, we helped Midas a bit with their second model."

"When was that?" Charlie demanded.

"Oh, Sandro here has worked with everyone," Cal said brightly and waved them on to the next point.

The meeting did not go long.

As they walked to their car, Swanson exhaled loudly. "Jesus, I've got to count my nuts to see if I've still got the two."

"Damn straight." Charlie was prepared for the arrogance and the rigor—anything less would have been counter to Rusch & Co.'s reputation. But what he hadn't seen was an opening. Nowhere in the meeting did they cross over to the promised land. He shook his head. "What the hell was Cal doing in there?"

"Letting 'em each take a piece," Swanson reasoned.

"But for what? They never came aboard." Charlie tossed his briefcase into the Saab's backseat.

"The old man seemed jolly enough. In his way," Swanson observed. "You know, I hate to say it, but I kind of like him. He certainly has a knack for cutting to the chase. And that weather-beaten mug he's got. In another life, the guy could have run a lobster boat. Eh, Charlie."

"On the other hand, La Alessandra," Charlie said in a low mocking voice. He rolled his hand open in a fey gesture that made Swanson laugh.

"No worries, Pepper-man. We got the goods and they know it. I mean, who better than us to do this thankless task?"

Later that afternoon, Cal phoned Charlie to say that it had gone better than he'd hoped. All he needed was for Charlie and Swanson to run their numbers again, with a few tweaks, and they'd be good.

The next weeks passed in a blur, with Charlie mostly on the road. Soon it was the night of Paige's party. Charlie never expected Lena to come with him, but when he arrived home to change, the shower was running upstairs and he wasn't about to ask questions.

The kids were having dinner with Glo. Charlie kissed his children and kept on going. Upstairs in the master bedroom, he kicked off his shoes and lay back on the bed, his hands folded neatly on his chest. The sounds of Lena in the shower sang like a lullaby to him. He was so tired. His body begged for him to close his eyes but he had to resist.

"Hey," he said, waking with a start, as Lena walked through the bedroom naked.

"You'll want to wear a tie," she said, sighing. She refused to look at him and instead opened and shut the drawers to her bureau. "Despite all the casual come-on, the Gold Coast likes its monkeys to jump through hoops and it likes its monkeys to wear ties."

Charlie took a quick shower and changed into his best shirt and tie while Lena put on her New Year's dress and heels, and made up her face. They drove to the top of the hill and then Lena told Charlie to park. There was no reason for this. They were late, and they were still a few blocks from the house. The early-evening fog was rolling in on a hellish breeze. Certainly there would be valets. But Charlie didn't argue. He climbed out of the car and followed that familiar long gait and high rump.

The view on top of Broadway was stunning. San Francisco topography reminded Charlie that if you let up, you fell. He took hold of her arm, and for the first time in many days she allowed it.

So they walked a block, then two, along the highest point of Pacific Heights. Charlie pulled Lena close. "Here, at the edge of the world, I want to say, thank you, Helena Rose."

Her green, questioning eyes met his gaze. "See that?" She pointed her chin behind him. Charlie turned. The Rusches' house wasn't so much a house as a castle, its concrete and stone façade built on a base of rock. A house that said from every angle, Do not tread here, don't even think of it.

"Dangerous, Charlie."

He shrugged. "We've been in worse."

She wasn't sure they'd been in worse, and she wondered how he could be so certain when all she did was question—but she nodded just the same.

An enormous tent had been erected in the front garden blocking the street. It was tricked up on all sides by potted trees and garlands. Music boomed from within. The valets, dressed in bow ties and white jackets, lined the sidewalk on both sides, talking amongst themselves. They watched Lena and Charlie approach.

Charlie whispered in Lena's ear. "Hey," he said, addressing a question that had been in the back of his mind. "You never said who told you about the deal with your uncle. Was it Swanson?"

"No, not Swanny."

"Who then?"

She lowered her eyes. It took Charlie a moment to catch on.

"The Italian," he said wretchedly. "Sniffing around."

"Watch yourself, Doctor."

"What, you talk to him?"

"No! Not in a long—no." They parted, taking a step back, with Lena keenly aware of the valets. She turned her back on the castle and all the people there and, using Charlie as a wind block, removed the pins from her hair and shook it loose.

"You look great," he said, stating the obvious.

She wrinkled her nose. "Really? I don't know, the hair?"

A thousand shared looks in a life together, they both knew this one: Lena primped and primed. Suddenly everything was clearer and none of it safe.

"Whoa," said Charlie.

"Don't."

"Lena, your uncle I can deal with. Whatever cards he's got to play, let him play 'em. His motives are not all that counter to ours. But this other guy—"

"I said, don't."

"Well, you don't!"

"I haven't!"

"Make sure!"

"Make sure what?" cried Lena.

It was getting ridiculous. Charlie cut to the bottom. "God, I must be a fucking idiot."

"You don't believe that. If you did, I might not be so . . . confused. Or angry." She shook her head.

"Lena, listen to me. This Alessandro. He thinks he knows you."

She measured her words carefully. "No, Pepper," she replied, her voice filled with a certain regret. "Once, a hundred years ago, he knew a *girl*."

They had come as far as the profusion of roses and tulips that framed both sides of the entry. Hurricane lamps lit the stone stairs. Lena's hair was soft on her shoulders. Her skin was pale and her lips a deep red. By sheer will, she had turned herself into the brightest flower. Charlie would remember that. He would remember, too, that Lena picked up the pace and went in first.

Disbelief

Ten

The Rusches rarely opened their doors to a crowd, but when they did, they opened them wide. The cost of the night would exceed a million dollars. Seven hundred and two guests; ten thousand passed hors d'oeuvre.

The former vice president arrived early. Up the back alley he came, bypassing the tent which, by special variances from the mayor, was positioned in the street, blocking traffic in both directions. The tent held three fully staffed kitchens and seating for five hundred. The vice president missed the hand-waxed walnut bar, the chocolate velvet banquettes and the twenty thousand French tulips.

Paulette wouldn't hear of him passing on her food.

"But," protested tiny Dahlia, who had to stand on tiptoe to be heard over the kitchen roar, "the secret service man said the vice president is on the Oprah diet."

"Tsa, Oprah!" snapped Paulette. "He'll eat, I promise you that." Turning slightly, she barked another command into one of two walkie-talkies she wore in a holster over her apron. "Now, *vite*," Paulette blasted.

Everyone had come. They'd stepped out of the gloom to embrace a new era. The old guard, the new guard, the hot, the rich, the techies, the money, the talented, the stars: Rita Moreno, Jackie Chan, the Pelosis, the Olsen twins, Francis Ford Coppola and his wife, Ellie, and Sean Penn without his wife. Penélope Cruz, in town shooting a film with Nicolas Cage, proved to be even more gorgeous in person; she was tucked into one of the banquettes, kissing Javier Bardem, her Spanish *amor*. Everyone. The bars in the tent and here in the house were packed ten deep, and a corps of waiters carrying large silver trays delivered drinks to the rest of the crowd.

Inside the kitchen Paulette worked her handpicked army: chefs from Chez Panisse, Roses Café and Jardinière to add to her regulars. They'd brought with them their support teams and a hundred waitstaff. The party had taken a year of her life, with Paulette designing the menu during her nightly soaks in the tub. Moroccan lamb meatballs, halibut and shrimp cakes with romesco, brioche panini with fontina and truffle oil, roasted pepper and Serrano ham, fried risotto balls, tuna tartare with chermoula on toast, fried polenta with mushroom duxelle. There was a kitchen with six Japanese chefs for sushi. There were pumpkin gnocchi, truffled pota-toes—mashed and roasted—and an asparagus risotto; there was *bagna cauda* and Paulette's famous Parisian salad, and cheeses in wheels and triple creams and artisan breads. For dessert there were miniature tea cakes and éclairs, peach trifle, Scharffen Berger soufflés, chocolate truffles, cupcakes stacked like the Transamerica pyramid, sorbet and house-made pepper-mint bark ice cream sandwiches. To wash it all down there was every kind of liquor and seven flavors of vodka, a very nice Barolo and a lovely white burgundy from Rothschild, and a river of Cristal.

"He'll eat," Paulette said, "and as for Tipper, she'll fill her plate not once but twice."

Dahlia, being permanent staff, had seniority over the hired hands, and with a look here and there she made certain they knew it. Holding aloft a silver tray with yet more plates and napkins, she pushed through the swinging door into the party.

There, at the center of the civilized world, Ivy saw her approach. Dahl-ia's uniform was too tight across the bum; Ivy made a mental note to tell Paco. Then she turned back to her guests and with a whim of steel, smiled.

Of course Cal had ruined the evening before it began. He did it every time. "Cancel the damn thing! I don't care if I ever see another soul," he yelled from his dressing room to hers, as hundreds of souls were already on their way from the Valley or across Pacific Heights. Then Paige called in tears to say she and James had had a fight. Ivy's heart plunged, and from those depths she'd come back again. Why did Cal have to act like a child? Why was he always pushing back from life and she always pushing him toward? As for Paige, where was she? She was the girl of the hour and she kept disappearing. Ivy smiled. The hour was early and the party still fragile; she had work to do.

"I am so glad you're here, darling." She said it to everyone. Seventy and still mighty enough to do a yogic handstand, Ivy passed through the room in her celestial gold Valentino (from his final collection); her diamonds and pearls perched atop her small chest like a prow cutting the sea. Along the way, she noted crises small and large: a wet napkin ruining the finish on a lacquered Ming table; Dahlia chatting far too long with a handsome guest; Suzy Cummings—well, Suzy Cummings—holding her glass of Pinot at a precarious angle, talking at a frightening volume. And Gunther Pease—the forty-year-old wunderkind who'd just last month landed himself on the cover of *BusinessWeek,* his hedge fund having taken a devastating hit, but not as bad as many—said to Cal, "I'm thinking gold looks good."

At this both men frowned at their shoes.

Ivy left the men to it.

The salon was brilliant. Over the last year, she'd had the walls paneled in ivory goatskin and the sofas redone in caramel linen velvet; she'd gone to Europe and brought back a pair of rare Murano lamps. The suite of Louis XVI chairs she'd done with a vanilla and gold Fortuny, very refined, but on the backs, just for kicks, she'd used a chocolate polka-dot silk. She enjoyed the rooms tonight, as if seeing them for the first time. The candles in the tall amber hurricanes gave the whole room a glowy bang.

The place thrummed. Laughter rose from every corner, and, oh god, they drank. But it was only the first hour. As captain of the evening's cruise, Ivy's job was to look after her passengers. The techies, sucking tiger shrimp with their fingers, had taken over the Fortuny-upholstered chairs. Ivy cringed, but let it go. The Dan Abels and the Chadrick Colbys had arrived. The Kramers, who hated the Farbers, but came anyway, were keeping their distance by the piano. Tony and Ru James and the Macks were laughing uproariously and Ru had to hold her glasses so they wouldn't slip off her head. The Druckers had come up from Woodside on their custom Harleys; they looked like jazzy astronauts in their matching leather outfits, he in black, she in red. Ivy went over, passing the Halls, the Zaldinis, the Bancos, who were on the hunt for the flavored vodkas and sushi. Ivy sent them to find Paige, who, with James, had taken command of the thirtysomethings inside the tent, where they were loading up on Grey Goose crantinis and dancing to Spike May's Jiveband.

"I'm so glad you're here, darling," Ivy said, squeezing arms as she went.

Greg Bettor, Cal's partner, was conspiring in a very odd, intense manner with Cal's former partner Bud Cope. As Ivy passed by for a kiss, they seized up. "What is it, darlings?" she asked brightly, and turning her head just so, caught Cal's eye. He'd also seen the goings-on and scowled. Suki and Gaspar, normally such fun, stood with the rest of the partners and their wives, all of them looking stern. Ivy had heard whispers that there was talk among the partners of Cal's retirement, which he wanted no part of, but after this she was certain they were plotting. She passed through them, mixing and chatting—worried.

Francesca Phipps said she'd come from Florence a day early for the party. The cadre of engineers and wunderkinds, Cal's favorites, having discovered the Chez Panisse buffet, was eating as if they'd never eat again. And Norah Jones, who'd been paid a bomb to perform, had proven to be a lamb.

In the corner, by the salmon sofa, Betsy Jones, the battle-axe defender of the old guard, took measure of the room. "Whatever you think of him, Ivy is a pro. It's a level of class few have anymore. Not too little, not too new, not too shiny." Betsy caught Ivy's glance and blew her a kiss. Ivy smiled: the party was a hit.

The security crew, thank god, wore decent suits; you could hardly pick them out. Why did engineers dress so poorly? The partners had shifted, clotting by the piano, as if they didn't get enough of one another. What were they up to? She'd have to mix them by hand. Francesca Phipps had had her face done. So that was her trip to Florence! Oh my god, she had.

"Those machetes," Doug Layton said gravely, speaking to the French consul of his recent humanitarian trip to the Sudan. "The kids with the arms cut to stumps." He paused. "By the by, on the way back, did you fly through Frankfurt or Paris?"

Pryde Hall, Ivy's great friend, was a mess. Giardia, she'd had it for a month; yet here she was, good girl, white as a sheet.

Ivy kissed her. "Darling, how's the tummy?"

"Awful. What a way to get thin." Pryde looked Ivy over from her toes to her hair and, liking what she saw, smiled. "Ivy, I was just telling everyone about our trip to Cuba. I have the whole thing set up. Your driver is the key." Pryde leaned in. "The Cubans. Ivy, they are a simple, happy people."

"What? I've never met a simple, happy people in my whole long life," said Chas, Pryde's husband, who started as if just awakened. "Certainly not in Cuba."

Pryde wrinkled her nose. "The tummy thing is separate. And a nightmare."

In the corner by the Picasso, Greg Bettor, still locked in deep conversation with Bud Cope, was looking neither simple nor happy. He had taken out his pen and was writing things down. What the heck were they up to?

Artie Green, the judge, Ivy's old beau, wanted to kiss her. "Ivy, you look like a secret." He smiled at her with the patience of the long refused. A million years ago, they'd gone out. Then she met Cal.

Ivy smiled shyly at Artie Green, hoping he'd always adore her. It made her as happy as it made his second wife, Jules, nervous.

"What a party! The best," declared Jules, who was younger by twenty years and wanted Ivy to love her. But Ivy had already committed her love to Artie's first wife, Ruth.

"Do you think so?" Ivy asked. Jules's dress didn't suit her; Jules had too round a face to wear a round neck. She went on smiling at Ivy, who had to say something confiding or Jules Green would turn the night into a sharing of her views on creativity.

"I spent New Year's at an ashram," she said, unaware that her voice rang like a harsh bell.

Ivy smiled and, wrapping a jeweled arm around Artie and Jules, pulled them in. "I'm only telling you—"

"What?" cried Artie.

"This afternoon, in this house, a homeless man came to the door. He nearly killed me."

Artie and Jules were shocked.

"Yes, yes," Ivy continued, her eyes alive with wonder and fright. "It was around three o'clock. I had just finished having my hair done. I'd gone downstairs in my robe to check on the flowers . . ."

She had come down for a glass of wine. Himself called then, as expected, to announce his mood. Nerves. He was in the car, coming up the road. Ivy let him rant, and speaking a few words of encouragement, hung up. She was just passing through the foyer when the doorbell rang. Over the hum and hammers no one on staff heard the bell. Ivy wouldn't have heard it herself had she not been right there. She opened the door.

He was dressed in rags, smelling frankly of Mad Dog, sweat and urine. He looked at her expectantly and it occurred to Ivy that she ought to be frightened. She ought to cry out. But she couldn't utter a peep.

Neither, for a minute, could he. He looked as surprised to find her as she was to find him. He'd gotten this far—how, through the labyrinth of tent builders and cooks and carpenters and florists and the tent itself—how could he have gotten past Paco?

"That's when it always happens," said Jules. "There's a ton of security and a false sense that one is safe."

Ivy nodded. It was true. It was absolutely true.

He was wearing a bit of fur round his neck, like a half scarf or a cravat. He had an old, beaten, black fedora set back on his head—Ivy used her hand to show how. Her first thought was that it must be Davey, the Lessors' boy, who at long last had gotten sprung from rehab. Her second thought was that she'd forgotten to TiVo the remake of Masterpiece Theatre's *Les Misérables.*

"Oh, but I did," said Jules, eager to help. "I'll burn a DVD and bring it around."

Ivy and Artie studied Jules for a long moment.

"That's nice, deary," Artie said at last, nodding at Ivy to go on.

"His face was filthy," Ivy said. "Yet in his eyes there was an intelligence. I can't explain it. But it was as if he saw through me, in the most . . . I don't know . . . peculiar way."

His nose, flat and hooked to the right, was freshly cut, and the teeth, the few that remained, were veined with moss. She didn't know what to do. She was incapable of crying out. "Can I help you?" she finally squeaked.

Ivy learned long ago that a thing said was like a post driven into the ground, the next remark setting the direction of the fence; the question being, did a person want to cross to Rome or Des Moines or just as far as the corner? She had pleased all her life, in her sphere this was still a vocation; her life had been all about remarks, about deciding whether the fence of talk led to the fiery furnaces of hell or to Shangri-la.

"Can I help?" she repeated, just in case he missed it the first time.

She would give him a minute, for humanity's sake, another minute, before she started to shout. Her eye fixed on that flat, scabbed nose. In grade school, Paige studied the herring gull. The female gull, as Ivy now recalled, had a red dot on her beak and when the babies wanted to eat they pecked at it. Ivy, wanting to be closer to Paige, studied the herring gull, too, and this red dot business left a strong impression. (Against Cal's wishes, Ivy sent Paige to a progressive coed school, where every child was a winner and an artist; where Christmas was on par with Hanukkah and Ramadan; where heroes were also sheroes; where the children spent a full six months in study of the herring gull. Ivy herself had served on the board.)

All this passed through Ivy in a moment. That, and a phrase of her mother's—We don't want any—waiting all these years in the wings.

Ram went the first post.

"If a person," the bum said.

"Yes?" Ivy said evasively.

"A towel . . . please." He made a gesture of wiping himself dry. "And perhaps . . ."

"Yes?"

"A-a-a-a pen."

"No!" cried Artie Green. "He didn't want a pen!"

Ivy nodded, "Yes, Artie, he wanted a pen."

The last time Ivy refused to answer a direct question she was eight: Uncle Drew, whom she'd never liked, whose breath had the faint whiff of soiled hay, leaned across the dinner table and asked Ivy if she knew what the capital of Nebraska was, her mother's home state. Any idiot knew that, thought Ivy. Uncle Drew, a wildcatter from Oklahoma, swirled his very wet tongue in his very wet mouth. He must be making a trick, thought Ivy, and she said nothing. When asked a second time, Ivy, glued with pride, again refused to open her mouth, and so Uncle Drew cast her in stone. "Ivy," he drawled, "either creeping, clinging or *poison*."

From that moment, Ivy worked tirelessly for the prosecution of Uncle Drew. She would not be creeping, clinging or poison; she would not be proud. She would do what it took to protect what was hers. She would climb ruthlessly but make certain she was known for her bounty (yet she had a perverse weakness for men who were none too kind). And when Uncle Drew died in an accident on the highway near Auburn, Ivy meant to feel sorry. But Ivy was pleased.

She told the bum to wait and closed the door. It occurred to her that she was safe now. She could summon Paco or the police, or she simply could stay behind the door. Instead, with her heart booming, she went to her desk, found the pen and then, from the powder room, grabbed not one but two towels.

"Gratitude," the bum said as he took the gifts and, stuffing them in his bag, bowed. "Forgiveness," he went on, his hands in prayer, his freckled eyelids gazing downward.

Now, the herring gull chick, when hungry, pecked on a red spot on his mother's nose. Peck. Peck. Then up from the mother's belly came fish, up came worms.

"Simplicity." His voice was magnificent. He might as well have been flaying Ivy, or shooting her belly with nails. "Abundance."

"Abundance, oh, yes," Ivy croaked.

"Heart," the bum concluded, crossing his wrists on his chest.

"Heart?" Ivy said, genuinely moved.

Ivy found some bills in the foyer console and handed them over. She had tears on her cheeks. "Please. Say it again so that I have it. Gratitude, Forgiveness . . ."

"Mary Magdalene and Jesus H Christ," he bellowed, and took off down the hill.

Artie Green had been listening to Ivy's story grim-faced, his head pitched toward the ground. "You know," he said, "he could easily have had a gun."

"No-no-no," Ivy protested. "It wasn't like that. He was all right. Strange. But all right." Ivy frowned. He had come to her like a person in a dream, and just like with a dream she found herself moving through life gripped by its power. She was in its power now. A shiver ran through her and she knew her fear was of a different order, though of what she was unclear. She looked over Artie's shoulder, toward her party, knowing that the night could still veer this way or that. With an effort, Ivy hauled herself back.

Across the room, by the bamboo screen, Barbara Quinn, the empress realtor, known to the world as Bobbie, was talking to Cal. Quinn had the old version of an improved face, pulled tight so the skin was very, very thin, while the new face was on display in the tent, with the young people, who, before the downturn laid down cash for fillers, botox and dermabrasion. The old face wanted to lock in forty forever. The new face aimed to look like a baby.

"I've seen nothing like this, Calvin, in fifty years of selling, there's never been a market this bad this fast. Boy, do I miss the glory days of the nineties. Cash, no contingency. Why, I once had a boy, an absolute youngster-ramous, pull a crumpled check for twelve million dollars from his pocket—and with it came his son's teething ring! Can you imagine? I said, 'Sweetie, I'll take the paper and you keep the silver!' Ha!" She sipped her martini. "Now it's all to shit."

Cal grunted.

"You," said Quinn, shaking her emaciated finger. "Mr. Doomy-gloom. You're going to say you saw the collapse in your crystal ball."

"Well, I did."

"All right. Then tell me, how does it end?"

Nearby, Suzy Cummings was making up her mind. "Oh, you know I miss the fun," she said, her voice projecting across the room. "The late nineties were great. I mean great. They were the eighties without all the drugs. But what are we going to do with this decade?"

"All eyes on the White House, I imagine," replied her dear friend Amy Mudd, who was trying unsuccessfully to catch a waiter's eye. "By the way, where did you come out on the inauguration? We froze standing all morning out there. Absolutely froze, but I wouldn't have missed it for the world."

"He is something. I had tears pouring down my cheeks. Everyone nearby, black, white, purple, the same." Suzy sighed. "Now we have to pray some cracker doesn't shoot him."

"Oh, god."

"It is a real concern, honey. I think about it all the time."

"Me, too," said Amy. "I'm just afraid to say it. Did you like Michelle's dress?"

Suzy Cummings made a sour face.

Amy Mudd agreed. "My downfall," she said, seizing an hors d'oeuvre from a waiter's tray, "is *cheese*."

Ivy sailed across the room, in search of Himself. Ivy squeezed Cal's hand. "Darling, it's time."

"Too early," he said.

"No, darling. Now. Here we go."

Cal eyed the packed room contemptuously. The room looked back, hopeful, wanting desperately to know how the story would end. Cal cleared his throat. He raised his glass of whiskey and slowly, slowly, the voices of several hundred revelers fell silent.

"Well. I won't bore you with talk of good times or bad—yah, yah," he said, his raspy voice trailing off. "You, lucky bastards, have drunk your fill at the trough." Cal cut the laughter short. "On that score, I'll say what many have said before me: Here's to the new man in Washington. Let him be wise. Let him be bold. Let him put no stock in the timidmeisters. As Churchill said, belief is strength." Cal raised his glass high and for a moment it looked as if he would end there, as if he'd forgotten the real reason these people were gathered in his house. Cal's mouth opened, but no sound came out. And then, finally, he said, "I've had one wife and one daughter and they've each cost me a pretty penny. And if I told you I made my pretty pennies for them, well, it would be true. Paige, you are—" he looked at his drink, his lips jutting. Paige with her James stood nearby, in her off-white Comme des Garçons creation, all veils and skin. Cal nodded at her. "You are a father's pride . . . James, be strong, take no guff, have hope, go fishing when you need to and, with your best, love her."

Relieved of his burden, Cal turned his back on the applause and drained his glass of scotch.

Lena and Charlie arrived in time to hear Cal's toast.

"You OK?" Charlie asked, squeezing her hand.

"No." Lena smiled dimly. Even so, she felt the heat rising in Charlie as he scanned the crowd, and she wanted the best for him. "It's a who's who, isn't it?"

He shrugged appreciatively. "If a bomb were to go off right now, most of the city and all of Silicon Valley would cease to exist."

"Well, that's impressive," Lena admitted. "Go," she said, pushing him onward. "Go, dog, go!"

Charlie, having also spotted Swanson, smiled at her gratefully. "Hey. What do you want me to bring you?"

"Your soul," she replied.

Lena watched Charlie disappear into the crowd. She assumed she would be OK. But the last time she'd been in this house she was alone, and alone was how she felt now. She required a drink. Paco noticed her moored by a column in the foyer and he approached at once. "Hello, Ms. Rusch," he said. "May I get you a drink?"

Shocked, Lena looked beyond the Filipino mask, into the butler's eyes, and finding a willing spirit there, laughed. "Well, somehow, you know my name," she said. "Now what is yours?"

"They call me Paco." Paco couldn't help himself, he smiled and his eyes all but disappeared.

"Hello, Paco. Tell me, please, what do you have in terms of real booze?"

"Anything the lady wishes."

Lena pointed to the bright yellow drink on Paco's tray. "What's that?"

"A lemon drop."

"Lemon drop?" Lena wrinkled her nose.

"Quite lethal."

Her relief was certain. "A lemon drop sounds perfect."

The room looked even more beautiful and opulent than she remembered. Lena took hold of her lemon drop and drained it. Ignoring the faces surrounding her, she retreated to a quiet space between the foyer and the grand salon, where she made a real effort to buck up and to quell her envy. Her eye fell on a small photograph hanging on the wall. It was of white deer in flight.

"They fear," said Lena aloud. "How smart they are."

"Sorry, dear, what was that?"

Lena turned to find Artie Green's spectacled frog face looking down at her. She hadn't seen him since she was a little girl, and she couldn't be absolutely certain it was he, except that no one else in the world looked like Artie Green.

"The animals. In the photograph. The artist caught them just as they were about to run. Look at them. Fear, from their noses to their tails. How appropriate." Lena laughed.

Artie peered through his thick black spectacles at the young woman before him. He had seen that face before. It was a long time ago, perhaps in a movie, or maybe back East. "And what's that yellow thing you're almost done drinking?"

"A lemon drop. They're lethal." Lena shuddered, for the drink was moving like acid down her pipes. "This is only my first and I can honestly report that it packs a wallop," she went on. "But getting back to . . . fear . . .

what I was saying, oh yes, it's like that woman in Mozambique. You know, the one in the newspaper?"

Being a judge, Artie learned long ago that if one held still, the world assumed you knew things. Holding still was hard for the world, but it was not hard for Artie. He held still right now, happy that this pleasant-looking young woman, whose green eyes were going one way while the mouth went another, was talking about the newspaper, which might, somehow, bring them to firm ground.

"You saw it. I know you did. On the front page, just recently?" Lena's gaze narrowed. She was concentrating very intensely on the judge's eyebrows. Incredibly, they may have been dyed. "This woman, she climbed a tree to escape a flood. In Mozambique. The river overran its banks and her whole village was swept away, including her parents, her husband, everyone. It poured rain for four days, but she managed to stay up there. She gave *birth* up there—remember? In the photo the tree was just a spindly thing. And she was just a spindly thing, too."

"Terrible," Artie said.

"No! No! No!" Lena protested. "Fantastic! Incredible, really. I mean, what a thing to do."

As she spoke, Paco stealthily removed the empty glass from her hand and replaced it with a fresh drink. Lena was now in possession of a second lemon drop, the first already working its magic, heating her profoundly from inside. She was on her way to becoming her own nuclear reactor, her own band.

Lena swatted Artie playfully on the arm, and some of her drink sloshed over the rim of her glass. She sucked her fingers. "Of course, it quickly turned dicey. Our girl didn't think twice about cutting the umbilical cord with her teeth. She gave birth, by herself, up in a little swaying tree, surrounded by a sea, and then she has the wits enough to cut the goddamn cord with her teeth?" Lena was in danger of weeping.

"My dear," Artie Green said, looking longingly toward the rest of the party. "Are you new to the city?"

Lena squinted at him. It was Artie Green all right, and he had no idea who she was, which was proving to be sort of fun. On the other hand,

131

Artie's face color didn't match his neck. Lena couldn't make sense of it. Was it a spray-on tan? Did men this age actually do that? Artie Green was speaking sentences, his mouth moving, but the sentences didn't make sense either.

"No, I'm not," she said.

"I see."

"In fact, you could say I grew up in this very house," she admitted.

"Really. Now explain that."

"I can't."

"You can't."

"I can't explain it any more than you can explain to me, Judge, the randomness of luck. Can you? I mean really. Why do some have it and others—equally positioned—not. What is luck when you get right down to it? How exactly does it differ from fate? Are we really the stories we tell? This, Judge, is just the tip of my iceberg. Grace—I need it—I need it badly. But the thing is, I can't find it. Is it enough to be just a decent mother, a wife, or do I have to do something big?" She tucked in, her lemony hot breath puffing in his face. "Answer me this: Do you believe today everyone has the goods to be a champion?"

"Ah," chuckled Artie Green, "a liberal."

"Of course I'm liberal. Aren't you?"

"Yes and no."

"That's unlikely," Lena snapped.

"Common sense, my dear."

"Well, it's common, I'll grant you, but I don't see the sense."

Artie smiled.

Lena smiled back.

"To your question, Is everyone a champion?" Artie Green continued, "Not by half."

"Artie. Artie. Artie," Lena slurred. If tipsy were a quick car trip from Eureka to L.A., she was whizzing through Modesto, on her way to Vacaville.

Lena searched the room for Charlie. She looked longingly for him. Would she choose him again if he were a stranger? If the world were new again, and they were new again, and they found themselves at this party on this night, would they be capable of something grand, something hopeful? Lena wasn't sure. At last she caught sight of Charlie. He and Swanson were surrounded by several men and one woman, all of whom looked self-satisfied and bored. Lena squinted. No, worse than bored, they looked harsh.

Lena turned to Artie. "So, what have we decided?"

"My dear, do you have someone you can talk to?"

"You mean a shrink. I did. Now I don't."

"Someone else then."

Lena shrugged. "I used to talk to Charlie."

"You mean your husband? Oh, no. Husbands are no good for this. A woman could die from lack of real talk. I've seen it. I've seen it a hundred times. And it's not the kind of thing a man can or should provide. In fact, any fellow who doesn't worship his wife's girlfriends is a fool. What you need is a girlfriend." Artie patted Lena's shoulder and smiled, showing his gold crowns.

Lena suppressed a lemon drop burp. "I have great girlfriends. And sisters. What I'm missing . . ." She wagged her head, her voice trailing off. "I don't agree with you, Artie, I mean what you're saying underneath all that . . ." She waved her hand. "Bull."

"Oh yeah?"

"Men talk." She pointed her finger. "They talk all the time. The truth is, in normal daily intercourse, men never shut up. Let me give you a for instance: three men building a stone wall. Talk, talk, talk. Artie, they go on and on. Every rock and angle has to be anointed with talk. Ad nauseam. People: it's a lousy wall. Throw the damn thing up and be done. But no. When they finish and it's time to relax, that's when they shut up. Have you ever seen workmen eating lunch? Staring into the distance, chewing like zombies, not one word. With women it's exactly the opposite. We get down to work, and we don't want anything pleasurable to get in our way. Think of the grandmothers in the kitchen rolling dough. All business, only shorthand talk allowed: put that here; no, not those; roll it thinner, that's the way. But when the pies are in the oven, they sit down with their cups of tea and the fun begins. To a man, talk is work; to a woman, it's reward."

Artie Green removed his glasses. "Dear, I think you've just summed up the essential problem in the bedroom. I don't know what the hell you said, but I think it may be profound."

Lena grinned as he went on talking. "Now, tell me how is it you grew up in this house."

"Artie. Artie. Artie," Lena sang. "It's Lena, Ted's girl. Lena Rusch."

His eyes opened wide with shock. "I don't believe it." He turned to find someone to tell. Cal was making his escape, heading for the library. "Cal! Cal! Do you see who this is? Lena, Ted's girl."

Fortified by lemon drops, Lena pivoted at a dangerous speed. She wobbled and only at the last second righted herself.

Cal took hold of her elbow and steadied her. He looked her over, heel to hair. The more he liked something the grimmer and more unimpressed he appeared, but how was she to know that? Only his eyes gave him away. "The last time we spoke," he said, "Lena here was telling us to fuck off. There wasn't much conversation after that."

Artie sighed. "Leave it to you, friend, to salt the sore."

"Glad you came." Cal nodded, tucking the hand that had touched her into his pocket.

"Don't be," Lena said. "I'm here for base reasons, as you know."

"Didn't you come with your husband?"

"Yes."

"Bah. Look around." He made a half circle with his chin. "They're all here for the chum."

"I thought they were here for Paige."

"Sure, that, too."

The pair stood out like tourists at a country club. "Doesn't it bother you? On some level." Lena's face felt very hot.

"Why should it? Money, knowing where and with whom to put it, is the skill I have. No shame. Money makes things, too."

"Honestly, Cal," piped up Artie. "Cut the malarkey and tell the girl how happy you are to have her home."

"He won't say that," Lena said, lifting her chin.

"Oh, Christ, not another one." Artie Green rolled his eyes. "I leave you to yourselves." And bowing like an old-fashioned gent, he backed away.

Cal motioned for the waiter. "What is that?"

"A lemon drop," Lena said proudly.

"Lemon drop? Sounds awful. Never mix sweet with booze. There, that's the night's dictum." To Paco, who was hovering close by, Cal added, "A lemon drop and I'll have another of these." He lifted his highball glass with a bit of whiskey at the bottom. Turning to Lena, he said, "So how are you?"

"The most complicated question in the English language."

"Ah, give it a whack. I'm not listening anyway." In fact, he was listening keenly.

"Then why waste my time?" She made a move to leave, but his hand, so soft and gentle, stopped her.

Cal nodded. "Look, don't pretend to be less than you are, and certainly not for me. If I'm a brute, Helena, I'm not a blind one."

"No," she said spitefully. "You've always had eyes."

"Ah." Cal laughed in his way. "How is your mother?"

"Dandy."

"You see her lots?"

"Not so much."

"By your design or hers?"

Lena shook her head. She wouldn't give him more than he deserved.

Cal studied his shoes. "I regret."

"Regret? What exactly. Screwing your brother's wife, or getting caught? Or was it leaving his family to rot." Her voice rose with feeling, more than she intended.

"Leave it that I do," he said, clearing his throat. "A man can be a fool. How's that?"

"Rich," she stuttered, "one beak short of a lark." If he were seeking forgiveness, she didn't have it. Paco returned with the drinks and Lena took a belt of the lemon drop, which had moved from burning her insides to tasting sickeningly sweet. Oh, where was Charlie? Lena winced and kept slugging. "Speaking of rich, where are my cousins?"

"Christopher is in India, perfecting his headstand," Cal said, looking oddly embarrassed. "As for the bride, Paige is in the tent with the young cats. Why aren't you with them?"

Lena laughed. "I'm not young."

"Bah," he said, the color rising in his cheeks. "I've told them, and you may as well know, it's our intention to give the bulk of the estate to charity. They've got what they need, and the rest we'll gift." Relief opened up his face. He had checked an item off his list.

"I see," she said, not seeing at all.

"So, your Charlie," Cal blundered, moving to the next topic. "Smart guy. Winning concept. Is he good to you?"

Lena nodded. She must not, at all costs, attempt a fourth lemon drop.

"And what are you up to these days? I don't imagine you home with the teat."

Lena winced. He was despicable. He was revolting. She turned to escape and nearly fell.

"Wait a goddamn minute," Cal said, leading her to a nearby chair. "Look. Are you all right?" He was holding her arm.

"How can I be all right? This place . . . I despise this house. I despise you! You could hire twenty teachers for life for what you've spent on this *party*. And I hate that I'm part of it, that I'm trying to . . . impress you. Do I sound like my father? Do I? He was a good man, beloved—not like you at all. And now he's gone from the world. There's only my sisters and me. While you . . ." There were so many words to put at the end of that sentence, she tripped on them all. Despairing, Lena looked around the corner. Charlie and Swanson were talking to that group of serious-looking men and the woman—was she actually wearing a bindi? Lena squinted but couldn't be sure.

"Who are those guys?" she asked.

"My partners."

"Are they good people?"

Cal laughed. "Good? Is that your only yardstick, Lena Rusch? Good? Come on."

"Why not good?"

"Because anyone who attempts anything worth a damn risks mixing with the devil. You know that. Sometimes . . . more than sometimes, the devil wins. At the very least, he's there at the table, ready to make the play. Keep 'em close. Keep 'em entertained, is to keep him this side of you."

She wanted to hate him, but he was eyeing her with appreciation and even respect, and she wasn't immune to that.

"I don't know why I'm here," she said flatly, pushing back her hair.

"We're moving on," Cal said, studying her with those blue lasers of his. "There's no magic to it. You see the next good thing and you move to it. That's why you're here."

"What, like sharks?"

"Don't diss the shark, girl. But I prefer the elephant. Nobody, at least in the animal world, messes with the elephant; he's on the ground. Undeniably *there,* thick-hided, protective, instinctual, sensitive feet. The elephant can feel the tsunami before it's a ripple in the sea. With a memory that goes forever. Can you do that, Lena Rusch?" He put his hand on her shoulder and squeezed.

Eleven

Back in the dining room, Tipper Gore was on the hunt for Dijon mustard to go with her Serrano ham. She would have to find it without Ivy. In all her years of hosting, Ivy never once abdicated the room to chance, but she did so now. Paige, looking every bit the lady of the manor, had come to the living room to be with the older generation; happily encircled by admirers, she didn't need her mother now. Up the stairs Ivy went, a whoosh of skirt, into the private part of the house, with its thirty rooms and a closet lined with felt for the silver, and another closet chilled for furs. Ivy went up.

She had reached the end. Not of this night, not only this night, but of something larger. Something fierce. Her heart went as quick as a rabbit, her long skirt rustled, the voices of the party blended behind her into a singular chorus of yatter. Ivy escaped.

But when she reached the hallway outside the bedroom, she found she wasn't alone: Alessandro was brooding on the Biedermeier settee. Oh, god. They had shared business dinners here and in Napa. Cal certainly liked him, but Ivy remained skeptical. There was something too winning, intense, too lover-boy about Alessandro—and all that Italian ciao-ciao that came with him. Ivy liked her men raw.

"Oh, hello," she said, walking toward him, forcing herself to smile.

"And why is the hostess hiding?" His accent made everything Alessandro said sound suggestive, too.

"Not hiding, dear," she said. "Gathering the lambs."

He turned away, making it clear he wasn't looking to be gathered. She followed his gaze through the balustrade. Downstairs, in the foyer, Lena was talking to Cal.

"Have you met the husband?" Ivy asked. "I hear he's something."

"Something? Something like what?"

Ivy smiled sympathetically. There now. Just when you gave up on a person, they showed you that most vulnerable part of themselves and you had no choice but to welcome them back into the fold.

"Now, darling," Ivy said, sitting beside him. "What did she do to you?"

Alessandro shook his head. Love was impossible to explain.

Ivy knew. She had also been in trouble once, when the children were very young. Before it went too far, an old friend, Edith Tucker, saved her. But Ivy hadn't wanted to be saved, and she wondered, who ever does?

"Come on, duck," she said, knowing with utter certainty that this would be her last party. What was the point of throwing bashes, when you no longer cared about being liked? She stood and expected him to follow, and Alessandro, who followed no one, did just that. Down the hall single file they went, to the back stairs. At one point, going down, Ivy felt dizzy and had to hug the wall.

"Ivy, are you all right?"

For a moment she turned inward, checking underneath the polish to the heart of things, and finding just enough power to push on, she nodded. With Alessandro at her heels, Ivy entered the kitchen.

Paulette was brushing butter onto a tray of Kobe beef filets. Her face shiny with sweat, she radiated triumph. "Tipper Gore asked for the recipe for my *salade Parisienne,*" she shouted with glee over the din. "I did NOT give it!"

Ivy turned to Alessandro. "The library is quieter. I'll bring her there."

With Alessandro tucked away, Ivy searched for Lena in the packed halls and in the living room. Along the way, she smiled and hugged and received praise for the party and for Paige.

Ivy didn't linger. Her kisses were quick and her eyes stayed fixed on the space in front of her, so that everyone understood she was all business.

She found Lena standing next to the tall glass cases of pre-Columbian pots. "Oh, my. When the guests start talking to the art, that's a sure sign the party's deadly dull."

Lena hardly recognized her aunt. "Where are the dogs?" It was all she could think to say.

"We have Angie and Finn now," replied Ivy, not missing a beat. "They would be the great-great-niece and great-nephew of your Gus. Lena, do you have Danes?"

"God, no," Lena replied. "I mean, I would love one, but we couldn't handle . . . oh, god, no." Lena was trying to make out what Ivy had done to her face and, beyond that, why her aunt was looking at her so queerly. "Yikes, Ivy! Why do I have a sinking feeling you're going to ask me if I'm happy or something?"

How familiar she is, thought Ivy; the conviction is what one remembered. Without the excesses of the mother. Lena had the Rusch wiring, and the Rusch ears. Striking, in her way. Though had it been Ivy she would have softened the lips and accented the eyes, instead of the other way.

Ivy put her hand on Lena's arm. "Oh, never ask a mother of young children if she's happy." Ivy deftly eased them toward the library. She was on the verge of deciding that Lena was the worst sort of woman, all feeling with no guile. Such a girl could not be trusted to look out for her best interests, as a practical woman must. "You're happy, miserable—everything in between. Mostly, I'm guessing, you're wrung out. In my day we drank loads of wine at lunch, while you kids ran wild. As I recall, the favorite game was war. Of course, that was Vietnam." Ivy smiled, her face pulling in odd places. "I remember you and your sisters were mad for costumes. Do young girls still want costumes?"

"I'm sorry, what?" Lena had trouble hearing above the roar.

"COSTUMES! Do you like costumes?"

"I hate costumes!" Lena shook her head vehemently, in case Ivy missed her words. Her gaze fell onto a nearby table. The little stone head of Sophia, which she'd coveted as a child, was there, beside a carved bowl. Lena couldn't take her eyes from it.

Ivy picked up the egg-shaped statue and handed it to Lena, who seemed reluctant to take it. "Ah, see that. Your old friend."

"My *only* friend, as I recall," Lena said, her ears going back as she blushed. "Please, take her before Paige sees us. We don't want to upset the bride."

Ivy stared with affection at the statue in Lena's hand. "I've always wondered, what was it you liked about her?"

"Oh, I don't know." Lena sighed. She tipped her head to think. "I guess she seems mysterious . . . content."

"Here's the thing I don't tell," Ivy said. "I found her in a junk shop in Auburn. Years ago, before I met Cal. I paid . . . oh, I guess it was five dollars."

Lena laughed. "Wouldn't that have been my luck: to steal *her* when I could have nabbed a pre-Columbian pot."

"Fa. You weren't going to steal her."

"Oh, yes, Ivy. Oh, yes, I was."

At that moment, Paige, who'd been trying to make her way to them but kept being stopped by well-wishers, cut her way through the crush.

"There you are!" Lena laughed. "My god, you look lovely, Paige." Lena wasn't a trick girl and she wasn't unhappy to see Paige looking good, if only because she had every reason to look good.

"What, no more cow?" Paige replied shyly, the night having elevated her, so that she could make fun of herself and Lena, too.

"Cow? What cow?" Lena frowned, for she'd forgotten that part of the story.

They stopped short for a moment and even Ivy, the pro, didn't have the steam to pick things up. It was Paige, newly energized, who squeezed her cousin's hand and visibly shook off the old ghosts. "You have to meet James."

Lena nodded, feeling the hook of an old envy.

"He's the best," Paige said, a little too robustly, trying it on, for she was still mad at James for telling her that her hair looked better down when she wanted him to say up. Paige noticed the statue in Lena's hand. She shot her mother a look.

Lena set the Sophia on the table. "Really, gang. I don't think I can stoop quite low enough to meet your expectations. I'm here for my husband, that's all."

"Oh, let's not go backwards, dear," Ivy said.

Just then the earth seemed to shake. It was a roller, followed by a quick jolt. The Murano chandeliers in the hall swayed.

"Uh-oh, there goes the NASDAQ," shouted a voice from the living room.

Lena turned toward the library, sensing someone looking at her.

"I should have known," she said. "Earthquake, then you."

The only part Alessandro heard was You.

Had they meant less to each other they would have embraced. Everywhere people were drunk and hugging. It was that kind of a party. But there they were, on the edge. Alessandro couldn't hide his joy, and why should he? The risk of being disappointed by this real Lena, as opposed to the one he carried in his mind, was certain. Yet somehow, he decided quickly, he wasn't going to be disappointed.

"How is it possible?" he asked, continuing his habit of starting conversations in the middle; she was the only other person he knew who did the same.

"It's not," Lena said, her lip shaking just a bit. Getting over him had been a sham; she would never recover. "On the other hand, you—" She swallowed hard. "You look like hell." They both laughed, for although Alessandro Corsini was a little thicker around the chin and the waist, he still walked among the gods.

"*Cara,*" he began, pulling her farther into the library. He had other words in his mouth, but all of them were too private to say. "*Cara,*" he said again.

Why, he's lonely, she thought, not quite believing it could be true. "And where are you in all this?" she asked. Her eyes spanned the room.

Alessandro shrugged. "It is a long story, of course. I'd like to tell you sometime."

"I imagine," Lena said. She wondered if she had on enough lipstick. Then, to make matters worse, she hiccupped. "Oh, god." She covered her mouth with her hand.

Alessandro noticed the ring on her finger, and it bothered him. With a logic that made sense only to him, he felt he had been loyal to her, while she had gone on to have a diamonded life. Reckless despair passed across his face, making him look older. "Can I get you some water?"

She shook her head. It was swimming and all she could think about was the skin on Alessandro's chest—how soft it was, padded almost, as if it had an extra layer of cushion.

Then Paige came round the corner and seized Alessandro's arm, refusing to let go. "Sandro, where have you been hiding?" She smiled agreeably but dismissively at Lena. "Oh, that's right, you two have history, don't you. Oh, my. Very mysterious. Should I go?"

"Stay or go, Paige," Lena said. "It's your night. Though I bet it would be a lot more entertaining out there."

"Have you tried the tent, Lena?" Paige asked.

"No."

"You should. It's fun," Paige went on. "And, Sandro, when are we going to dance?"

Alessandro patted Paige's arm, as if to stop her from talking, and kept his eyes on Lena.

Ivy saved them. Until now, she'd been pinned in the hall by Ellen Silverberg, who had to tell her about all the dreadful changes to the menu at the Big Four. "And then, Ivy, the final straw: they got rid of the chicken pot pie!"

Then Cal appeared in the hallway with Charlie and Swanson, and Ivy was released. "Why, duck," she said, her voice loud enough to be heard in the library. "This must be Charlie."

Hearing his name, Lena walked awkwardly to the door, her face deeply flushed, while in the hall Cal scolded his wife. "You disappeared," Cal said.

Then, as if bored by someone else's brutish behavior, he cast the unpleas-antness aside and introduced Charlie and Swanson to Ivy.

"Charlie," Ivy said, working deftly to pull all boats to shore. She got them only so far. "I was just telling Lena how good it is to have you in this house. Promise me Cal hasn't been working you tonight."

"Not a bit," Charlie said, his face brightening at the sight of Lena. He put his arm around her and, to solidify things, said her name. "Lena."

Her eyes were as shiny as they'd ever been. Greetings were made all around, but none of the players really heard them. They were each caught up in a party that they alone were experiencing. Only Swanson stood tall, hands in his pockets, and listened to every word. He had worn his awful New Year's jacket, and, noting that, Lena winced.

"Now, Charlie, I'm assuming you've met Alessandro," Ivy said.

Charlie glanced at Lena and then at Alessandro, and he understood immediately that they had been talking. He firmed his hold on Lena and said in an unenthusiastic tone, "Sure. How are you doing?"

"Yes, Charlie!" Alessandro beamed, seemingly unworried. "The tal-ented doctor who won the heart of my old friend."

The conversation went on, but Lena couldn't listen. The words flew by as she fixated on shirts, specifically Alessandro's, which was a simple, elegant blue weave, open at the neck, showing his deep tan. It was a shirt that said everything of ease and chic and . . . Oh, why had she come? And why did she make Charlie put on that damn suit and tie?

Behind them, in the living room, Ivy and Cal's guests stood ten deep, enraptured by the magic of Norah Jones.

"Paige, honey, go." Ivy released the almost-bride, who in that moment looked more like a trapped dove. "James is waiting."

Collectively they watched Paige float in her pretty dress toward the music and the lights. Norah Jones finished a song amid a swell of cheers and applause.

"We have to go," Charlie said. "I'm sorry. I have to catch a plane."

"Where are you headed?" Alessandro asked.

"Boston."

"Tonight?"

"Charlie's taking the red-eye," Cal added authoritatively. "He'll sign up Mass General to prototype the Nimbus, then Stanford will follow."

"You'll succeed," said Alessandro with genuine gusto. "You must." And he beamed his confidence onto Charlie and Swanson. Then, turning to Lena, his shine faded a bit and something much more real came up in his eyes. He nodded.

"Yep, gotta go," Swanson said.

In the dining room, Norah Jones was singing "Come Away with Me."

Twelve

Lena and Charlie started for home. The party cast a spell on them and as they walked to the car they had to work to get back to themselves. They had to rebuild the night from an odd stack of parts. Lena was especially quiet. Her heel wobbled in a crack and Charlie had to catch her. He lifted her to the curb and after that, he didn't let go.

"I liked her," Lena said. "Once I got past the face-lift."

"Man, he comes on like god."

"Who?" Lena suspected Charlie meant Alessandro. A beat too late she realized, no, it was Cal. She and Charlie walked on, but the mood between them had changed. They reached the car and climbed in. Charlie paused before starting the motor.

"I wish I could make you happy," he said.

She looked into his kind, serious face. "Happy? When Nimbus goes public, Charlie, will you be happy?"

He didn't torture himself with thoughts of happiness, except when it involved her. But that Charlie wouldn't say. He started the car.

On the plane tonight he would look over four good candidates for VP of engineering and then he was going to wrap his mind around this

Alessandro Corsini, who looked at Lena as if fingering the buttons on her blouse. Charlie detested him. It wasn't just his past with Lena, but his glee, his absolute ease. He was a collector of life, always ready for the next grand time, even if she happened to be someone's wife. A pretty-boy, thought Charlie, who couldn't understand Lena, not in a million years.

Cal Rusch, for all his faults, wasn't like that. He was a worker. He stood in his own great house but was somehow closer to the guy hustling the trays, or the singer belting the song. Of course, Cal was a whole lot of other things, too—and all of this Charlie would think about when he got on the plane.

"So, you talked to Alessandro," he said, turning the corner onto their street. "He isn't over you. Son of a bitch. But then who would be."

"Oh, I think he's moved on—many times," Lena said quickly. "Paige obviously has a crush—"

"Hardly an even trade."

"Well, you're biased."

"Very."

Charlie would be leaving for the airport in less than an hour. He pulled into the driveway and turned off the car. "I said 'very.'"

"I know."

Out of habit they looked at what was directly in front of them—their house. They hoped the sight of it might lift them. But the house was just itself, pink with a scrappy rambling rose. When they first moved in, they swore they'd paint within a month, but they didn't say that anymore.

Charlie ran his hand through Lena's hair. "Sorry. I've got to head up."

I've got to head up: such lines passed every day between husbands and wives—those happy and unhappy. I've got to head up, meaning: I hate leaving you; is Alessandro a real threat?; I've brought it on myself, I know, so I don't dare complain; please, don't be lonely; please believe; hey, are there clean black socks for me to pack? I've got to head up.

"OK," Lena said, meaning: I'm trying to believe; the party was more dangerous than you know; look in your top drawer.

Had the children been healthy; had there been money to spare instead of leveraged credit cards and maxed loans; had the husband stayed home; had the wife been a draft horse instead of a nervy Arabian; had marriage been *at all* flexible—this night wouldn't have mattered. But marriage was a wheel; it was a mousetrap.

Lena went to the kitchen to find Glo. LEGOs, scores of the tiny red, blue, white bricks, were afloat in the kitchen sink. The room stank of chlorine. Glo puffed her bangs from her forehead, and kept on scrubbing, water pouring down her cheeks. She was scouring the LEGOs one by one with a toothbrush, having mopped the floor, restocked the bathrooms with toilet paper and sewn a button on Willa's blue, fuzzy sweater. Earlier in the day, she'd asked for a raise. Now, having put the kids to bed, she was reminding Lena (who did not need reminding) just how valuable she was.

"How's her breathing?"

Glo wiped her forehead with a wet, soapy wrist. "She breathing good. She have one cough, but very small and then she rest good. Theo, he read a book."

"A book? What book?"

Glo tapped the side of her head. "A book in his mind."

Both women smiled, proud.

"*¿Y la fiesta?*"

Lena sighed. "*El mundo de los ricos.*"

The world of the rich. Gloria Angelica Cardenas had been raised in a shack, with a mud floor and a scrap metal roof and a mother who began her days grinding wheat to make the tortillas for her ten children. When Glo was just fifteen, the boy up the road became her husband. A year later she had her first child, quickly followed by another. When Glo was twenty her husband fractured his leg falling off a roof and then turned to drink to stop the pain. Two years later, he was killed in a knife fight in a bar, and Glo had to leave her children with her mother and go find work in the North. How much richer, thought Glo, could anyone be than this?

She drained the sink, put the LEGOs on a towel, dried them, then put them in their basket. She went to the closet to get her bags and coat.

Glo was tiny, not five feet tall. With her coat buttoned to her chin and her plastic purse strung crosswise over her chest she looked like a plump Girl Scout. But her wise eyes took in everything, including the blush on Lena's cheeks.

"Charlie, he goes again?"

Upstairs, Lena checked on the kids first and then went into the bathroom and pumped her milk and tossed it, sparing Willa the effects of the lemon drops.

In the master bedroom, the doctor was packing. He had the garment bag open on the bed and was adding a sport coat, and his lucky shoes.

"You were right about the tie," he said.

Lena sighed into the depths of her closet. Was Charlie lonely, too? Did his bones ache all the time for lack of a touch? Holding the door, she punted her best shoes into the jumble of scarves and belts and sneakers that were Willa's happy hunting grounds each morning as Lena dressed.

She took off her earrings, her necklace, her rings. The urgency moving through her, well, she might as well hump the doorjamb or cry aloud. She glanced behind her as she dropped her jewelry into the glass bowl on the dresser.

At the sound of that particularly feminine, domestic ting, Charlie turned.

They met in the middle of the floor.

"POSH," she whispered, unbuttoning his shirt. "Tell me, Mister, about POSH."

Charlie paused, and like a hound he pointed his nose skyward. "Ocean liners . . . departing England," he said, nuzzling her throat and neck.

There was a spot just below her ear, which long ago they'd nicknamed The Kill. To kiss Lena there cut all her strings. Charlie paused, his lips hovering. "Best cabins were port out, starboard home. That way, you get the sunsets—praise fucking god."

He caught her in his arms.

The bed being occupied, they dropped to the rug.

Clothes and socks were in their way; they got rid of them. Charlie unpeeled Lena's dress, which had been asking for a good peeling since its debut at New Year's. Grunting, he threw it behind him, along with her silk camisole, panties and lace bra. She countered with his shirt and boxers, blindly tossing, seeing them land round the base of the floor lamp, nearly toppling it. This struck them as wickedly funny.

Shush, they said, which only made them get louder.

Everything was familiar, the nipples, the bellies, the cock. They reclaimed the landscape with their mouths and hands. This is mine. And this. Remember?

"Skip the bells and whistles," Lena offered huskily, in deference to the time. She adjusted herself beneath him.

"Come on," Charlie said, grinning, walking his lips south. "At least one whistle for the lady."

Giving herself over, Lena ran a hand through Charlie's thick hair. She was climbing fast and as her knees started to shake, she cried out. He put a hand over her mouth and she happily bit him. He took hold of her jaw and held it, as someone who knows, who owns, those bones and nerves.

He rose from between her thighs and she murmured, "Come here, you," and pulled him onto her, into her, like skin.

It was hey and howdy lovemaking. It was fucking to honor all past fucks: the good, bad, the lazy and the new, the tender; the getting over a fight fuck; the quiet while the baby sleeps fuck; the boring half-zoned half-sick half-hope fuck; the whole damn story. It was lovemaking with children down the hall and the taxi due and no time, no money, the bodies aging, the fantasies wild—the sorrow and the wanting, too. Against all odds, it was everything, and it felt so damn good.

After, as they lay entwined like socks, Lena ran a drowsy, claiming hand along Charlie's rump to his balls. "Mine," she murmured. Charlie responded with a few nonsensical words and wrapping her tightly to him, he nodded off. For a few perfect minutes, they floated to sleep in each other's arms.

If only they could have stayed that way all night—holding, just holding. But instead, forty-five minutes after they'd arrived home, they were dressed and back at the front door.

"Give Glo the raise," Charlie said, putting on his coat. "God knows she's earned it."

"Twenty an hour, Charlie. We can't afford—"

"Hey, lady"—he pulled her to him and kissed her with a mouth that tasted of herself—"hold on to that Glo."

He knew he was out of his mind to leave. Lena was in his pores, and he'd have a long night over the Rockies to be reminded of that. A profound weariness overtook Charlie—all he wanted to do was lie down with his wife. Instead he glanced at his watch, which informed him he had no choice. "Give it to her," he said drily, shifting into business mode. "We can't afford not to."

"Please," she begged. "Stay. Tell them you'll come tomorrow."

"Lena."

Through the open door they could hear the throaty muffler of the cab as it pulled up. Lena lunged for the door and waved furiously at the driver. "I swear to god, if he wakes her—"

"Come on, Lena, the kids are *fine,*" he insisted.

And just like that it turned.

"How would you know?" she cried. "You're never here and the truth is, you don't want to stay." She was trying it on, she'd hardly had time to consider, but now that she'd said it, it became true.

Behind Charlie, Lena caught sight of her face in the hall mirror. She didn't recognize herself. She was haggard and pale. That, and Charlie's raincoat still had the smudge in back. Life was always presenting one with movie-star moments, only to jerk them away.

His tired, red-veined eyes narrowed and he ran his hand through his too-long hair. "Damn! Where is the fucking joy?"

"That's your head talking, Doctor. Talk to me from someplace else."

"I thought we just did!" If a roll on the floor and not one but two whistles didn't buy a man a little leeway, what could? "Did we or did we not!"

She brushed his logic aside with a sweep of the hand. "You assume. You say yes to them, whatever it takes, and no to us. Any second Willa is going to wake up and I'm supposed to handle it—alone, Charlie—always alone, while off you go. It's a kiss and a promise, this life of yours. You brought me back there, to that house, without thinking of the real risk—to me, to us."

He searched her face to see how deep she was going. "Lena, what are you saying?"

"What do you hear?" The veins on her neck stood up like cords.

And then he said something that would come back to haunt him. "Lena, listen, if you're going to write the script, don't make us small."

"*Small*? Did you say *small*?"

"What I meant—Oh, Christ—Hey! Hey!" He shouted, but the cab was pulling away from the curb. It stopped halfway down the block, and Charlie would have to run for it.

"*Small?*" Lena cried, her face wild. "Oh my god. Look at me, Charlie. Small is all I've got."

"There, the last word," he said. Taking his bags, Charlie went out, slamming the door behind him.

Upstairs, Willa woke with a howl.

Anyone who claims that men are the crueler sex has never spent five minutes in the mind of an unhappy woman.

With utter competence, steeled by rage, Lena went upstairs, changed Willa, nursed her, and put her down, all the while sending Charlie to hell—and she sent him there without a dick and without food. She drew herself a bath—hot as she could stand—and got in up to her throat. As she soaked it occurred to her that she had cursed her husband and now her punishment would be that his plane would crash. So, for the next hour, in temperance, she held up the sky. She was on the steep downhill of the lemon drops now, so she wept a bit, too. Afterward she felt a fraction better. She hauled herself from the tub, put on an old shirt of Charlie's and some sweatpants and climbed into bed.

She fell asleep thinking of Alessandro. He'd been there all along. A secret place she visited, sometimes when she was with Charlie. She'd dream of making love with Alessandro. Why hadn't she fought harder for him when she could? When he called to say he'd made a mistake, his marriage was over, why didn't she at least let him try to convince her? He flew to New York and appeared at her door, but she'd only shouted at him; her pride had been more important.

Lena curled in bed. She didn't want to miss her life; she didn't want to miss it at all.

She woke to the sound of the doorbell. Jesse must have forgotten her key again. Throwing back the covers, Lena reached in the dark for Charlie's shirt, which she'd tossed on the floor. Then something passed through her and she stopped. Moving much faster now, she went to the closet for her silk kimono. Her hands were clumsy with agitation. Coming down the stairs, she ran nervous fingers through her tangled hair.

Having wished for Alessandro, she couldn't be surprised to find him there. "The party got very dull after you left," he sighed. "All those tulips without a thing to say."

Lena wrapped her robe tight around her. "I don't know. Seems to me people talk all the time." It was a whole lot of spaghetti, she knew, him coming to the house. "It's pretty much all they do."

He shrugged. "Maybe there was a conversation . . . I didn't hear it."

"San."

He smiled at her special name for him. "But you told me nothing! About your life . . ." He would keep on talking, so as not to be banished. "What are you about; what are your politics these days? How is Helena plotting to take over the world?"

"I don't have any politics."

"That can't be true." He appeared wounded.

"Stop." Lena lowered her eyes. When she had the courage to look again, his smile was thick with lust and old-time afternoon nooky and she didn't want to look away.

The cold bit her skin. She had to be careful. She was being dazzled. She had only to close her eyes and leap. She reminded herself of her children upstairs and Charlie in the sky, in a plane she had cursed and must now hold aloft. The cool air bewitched her nipples, a fact not lost on Alessandro—that was in his smile, too.

"Listen," he said, lulling her with his voice. "Maybe I'd forgotten.

Maybe I thought, ah, it was such a long time ago. But seeing you, I real-
ize . . . some things do not change. Then, now: we can be the closest
of—"

"Friends?" she mocked. "You're no friend. You're smug and—"

He had a wonderful laugh. "See that? You are exactly the same. Tell me,
Elena, have you ever in your life let a man finish a sentence?"

Thirteen

The tent had to disappear by dawn. What took days to construct came down in a few hours. Paige's crowd hauled one of the banquettes and a bucket of Grey Goose into the street to cheer the demolition. When that got dull, the party moved to the Lyon Street steps, but Paige was no longer with them. She was upstairs in her old room with James, whose hair didn't look so much like a hat just then. And in the salon, a strange fellow named Griffin, who'd been showing up at the Rusches' parties since anyone could remember, was playing the piano and singing Roberta Flack's "Killing Me Softly."

Artie and Jules Green were the last to go. They had cozied themselves with Ivy on the salmon sofas, their stocking feet propped up on the Ming coffee table.

"Who is that fellow?" Jules asked, her eyes closed.

"Griffin . . . rum-rum-rum," chimed Ivy and Artie in unison.

Jules cocked an eye open and with a sudden burst of energy, stood. "Artie, darling, get up." She tugged on his arm. He was heavy and drunk, and it was past two in the morning.

"But Ivy promised," Artie said lazily, "to tell again what the bum said."

Ivy touched her fingertips to her temples. "Oh, I just had it. I just—

155

Gratitude, forgiveness . . . I can't remember!" Ivy also couldn't remember when she'd had more wine. "Abundance."

"Well, dear, you have that," Artie assured her. He wobbled, caught himself, rearranged, and sort of stood. But as he bent to kiss Ivy's cheek, he fell into the sofa beside her.

"That's enough," warned Jules, pulling him upright and leading him forcibly toward the door.

And with them went Paige's party.

In the kitchen Paulette was wiping the last of the trays. Her son, Jean-Claude, of whom all had been forgiven, was sitting beside her, sipping Cristal.

"Oh, Paulette," Ivy began.

"Next time less sushi, more pigs en croutc," Paulette announced, and with a sniff she downed her glass of champagne.

Tomorrow the staff would have the day off. Paco, who couldn't bear to leave *his* house at loose ends, would be awake most of the night. Even now, he was bringing the dogs up from their banishment. "Ay, Missus, the bum! I can't believe it!"

"It's all right, Paco. He didn't hurt anyone."

"But where was I?"

Ivy put her hand to his arm, this man who ran their lives, yet who owned neither a cup nor a chair. "You were right where you needed to be. All of you. Thank you."

Ivy had envelopes with cash for each of them, and a pearl necklace for Paulette, and some shares of stock in Google for Paco. "Do you want the dogs up with you, ma'am?"

Ivy followed the Danes upstairs. The loneliness was coming on her, as it always did after a party, when her eyes were too far out of their sockets and all the friends who had walked through her life had left behind their colors and stories. She needed someone to talk to. But Cal was already asleep, too plowed to have kept a light on for her.

Ivy took her wine to her dressing room and, having no one else, called Paige on her cell.

"Mommy," Paige said in whisper, "what's the matter?"

"Nothing, darling. How did you like your party?"

Paige laughed. "Well, it's still going on. Mommy, James and I are here."

"Where?"

"In the *house*."

"This house?"

"Yes! Yes, I'm upstairs."

"In my house."

"Yes!"

"Oh."

"Mommy, are you all right? Didn't you like it?"

"Of course! Of course."

Paige paused to consider. "Is that Griffin Rum-rum playing?"

"I'm afraid so."

"You know, he's not half-bad."

"Well, he's not Norah Jones."

There was a pause then, both of them nodding as they went on thinking their separate thoughts. And then Paige yawned.

"Mommy, James has to get up way early. Is there something—"

"No, no, no," Ivy said, hanging up.

But there were things she wanted. Later, in her sleep, she cried out, shrill as a monkey.

"The fucking ingrates—" bellowed Cal from inside his nightly battle with the titans. He shot the air with his fist.

Ivy struggled, swimming toward the surface of her dream. She tried very hard to see. But the room, shadows and veils, offered nothing; she couldn't make out the window or her hand. Oh, god. There'd been a tunnel with red, slick walls; she had fallen. The dream was her death.

"Cal?" she cried. "Cal?"

"Damn," he said. "A nightmare."

"Me, too." Scared, she put her hand across her heart, across the moon crater that had been her breast, and where, six years earlier, a fine team of doctors had declared her cancer trounced. Ivy thought otherwise. When they asked to rebuild the breast, she said, no, leave it. In her dreams she'd seen cancer like a brown piece of twine unspooling inside her, shooting sparks. I should say something, she thought at the time. But Bruce Noble, their GP—good, able, furry-eared Bruce Noble—was so pleased with her progress, she didn't want to bother him.

"Cal, talk to me a little. Would you?"

"Drifting," he mumbled, his face buried in the pillow.

"I don't care. Say anything."

"You . . . go. I'll listen."

She heard him breathing and knew he was dropping back to sleep. Still, Ivy talked because she had to, she told him about the bum.

Cal snorted. "What do you mean a bum?"

"A bum! A homeless man! He came to the front and rang the bell. He could have walked right in and—"

Awake now, Cal lifted his head. "Did you give him money?"

Ivy paused. She didn't know what the right answer would be so she told the truth. "Yes."

"Well, great. Now he'll come back for sure. I'll make sure Paco keeps an eye out." Cal punched his pillow, his voice syrupy with sleep. "OK. Are we done? I'm wiped." He reached for her hand. "Good job tonight, Iv."

In the dark, she smiled. That was that. A year of preparation came down to "good job." For that matter, almost fifty years cohabiting with this man came down to good job. And if not good job, what? What was marriage anyway, but a daily exchange of preferences and habits—of beef not salmon; coral not pink; Democrats not the other guys; a series of negotiations, and lines shot across rooms, and the mad dash to get out of the house on time: "The Bendels are coming, not the Druckers; the car's in the shop; your breath is heavy. Larry Goldman is a fool. Do you love me? I said I did, and I do, damn it."

Ivy rolled over on her side. It was all running through her, a jumble. She tried focusing on the tulips. The tulips were great. Artie said the guests coming through the tent thought, *Pow*. Bless Artie. He still loved her. Yet Artie could be a schmuck. That time, a hundred years ago, with Ruthie, when he turned to the man seated next to her and said, "Is Ruth boring you yet?" That was the moment he and Ruthie never got beyond. Ivy and Cal were never so grim as that. They always came back.

"Sleep," he said, pulling her to him. They never slept in anything, not in all the years. They were as naked as John Lennon and Yoko Ono. Ivy closed her eyes.

The next morning, after Cal showered and dressed, he stood at the foot of the bed. "Are you home today, or out?"

"Home."

"Good. Rest. For a change don't answer the damn phone. Let your ladies crow over your triumph one day without you." Cal was sliding his wallet into his back pocket, signaling that he was about to go. "I'll be home early. Hey, did Paco pick up my down coat from the cleaners? It was a mess after the inauguration."

Ivy said nothing, knowing she'd packed that down coat, along with a pile of Cal's threadbare sweaters, and made Paco drop the whole lot at Goodwill.

Cal sighed, just to make the point that he had to go. Ivy was in a mood, he could tell by her silence. If it was absolutely necessary, he would say, Hey, come downstairs and let's have a muffin, how about that?

Ivy had spent a lifetime waiting for Let's have a muffin.

"Cal?"

"What." Post-party, she always wanted to analyze the thing. Somewhere in there, she'd have a grievance. With the slightest encouragement she'd take an hour—at the end of which he'd be expected to apologize—for what, he had no clue. Such was the logic of women. For that reason, Cal Rusch had made it a lifelong policy to stand firmly outside the feminine hoop.

But if a man leaves a woman in such a state, he'd better have a reason. "Ivy," Cal declared, "this afternoon I'm telling the two of them, Greg and Bud Cope, to go to hell."

It was coming on to noon when Ivy climbed out of bed and went downstairs to feed the dogs. The house was empty, quiet except for the phone, which had begun ringing at nine and never stopped. In the kitchen she set out breakfast for the Danes, seven cups' worth of kibble and meat each. She put their enormous bowls on top of matching benches that had been specially built for them. Ivy poured herself a tall juice laced with vodka and watched while the dogs ate, their bodies intent down to their tails. She was reading the paper with her feet on a chair, deciding whom among her friends to call, when the doorbell rang.

Harry O'Connor, the carpenter, had come to hang the library doors. He was a month late. Weeks ago Paco had found a new man who'd fixed the doors in half the time for twice the price.

All this Ivy made clear in as few words as possible.

"Oh," Harry said humbly, but not so humbly that he didn't also mention all the projects he'd done for the Rusches over the years. And then he gave an update on his wife, who was an invalid. Ivy had heard it all before.

"You got another fellow," Harry said. "Sure, that's what."

"Harry." Ivy didn't have the heart to send him away. "The cabinets in the salon aren't shutting properly. The locks might be loose. Could you take a look?"

"I'll have to get my other tools," Harry said, looking a little too closely at her.

Once, five years ago, he'd been working on a drawer in Cal's dressing room when Ivy, coming from the bath, walked through the bedroom naked. It was just after lunch and she had a wineglass in her hand. She got as far as the closet before she realized he was there. He'd never seen a woman older than his wife naked, not even his mother, and Harry was awed by the toll: the scar at the breast, the bony knees, and the shocking but somehow girlish absence of hair between her legs. Still and all, Ivy Rusch looked capable, that was the thing. Nothing coy. She noticed him yet she walked slowly, the skin at the bottom of her flat butt jiggling like change in a suede purse.

"Well now," she said, "I'd better get to my roses." She gave the door a playful pat and slowly closed it. Standing with her back to it, she thought, Damn. Sighing, she went to get her jacket and boots.

The fog had lifted and the sun shone clear. The Rusch house was nothing if not private, sitting in the sky on a double lot, bordered by cypress and beds of rhododendron and a strong iron fence. In the back, unseen except from the driveway via a narrow alley, there were lawns and more beds of roses. The roses were Ivy's pride.

From the beds, she could see the Bay through an opening in the hedge. She could see the bridge with its twin orange towers, and beyond the bridge the Marin Headlands. A Japanese container ship with *Hanjin* blazed on its hull coasted like an eel under the bridge, its low-slung snout pointed for the Oakland piers. The world was on the move; the world paused not one second for little Ivy Rusch carting her post-party doldrums over the garden sod.

Ivy started with the Double Delights; they'd been in her wedding bouquet. From there she moved to the Just Joeys and the Brandys. The gardeners were itching to give the roses a hard winter prune, but Ivy had held firm for the sake of the party. She wanted to cut them herself. (Wasn't Paco something, running out here a few weeks back and making tents with foil over each bush to protect them from the hail? She'd watched the scene from the bedroom, with Paulette yammering beside poor Paco, telling him how to do it better and him telling her to shut up and hold the flashlight.)

Ivy had to hurry. She was a thief stealing roses in her own garden. Some of the blooms were far gone, and she wasn't too happy to see traces remaining of the powdery mildew that climbed the canes every August, suffocating them—a fog within every rose. She worked quickly, setting her cuttings in the bucket. Cal's flannel shirt puffed in the wind. Leather gloves protected her hands, leather pads cushioned her knees. From behind, she looked like a boy with a bony ass. That would be Cal talking. She nodded—for what? For knowing. Her heart had many rooms. Ivy studied the next bush, spiking the soil around the base, firking clods with her trowel. Each rose was a puzzle, a question. We know ourselves by our worry, if we know ourselves at all.

"You're all set, Mrs. Rusch." Harry stood on the deck, the Danes on either side of him, their front paws up on the railing, their inquisitive black eyes peering down at Ivy. "Those cabinets shouldn't be any trouble," Harry added.

"Oh, good, Harry. Thank you." She was eager for Harry to go.

He shifted his feet but stayed put.

"Of course, the bill. Harry, would you leave it by the door? Paco will send a check tomorrow."

"Oh, no bother, he can catch me next time," Harry replied, as if that wasn't why he'd come, for help with the rent.

She looked up, shading her eyes. Dignity, she thought.

"Epsom salts, Mrs. Rusch."

"What's that, Harry?"

"Epsom salts, for the roses. That was my mother's trick. That, and coffee grounds."

"Coffee grounds?" Ivy wrinkled her nose. "Wasn't she clever!" She gave a little wave, hoping they were done. Ivy felt tired, her head pounded. It had started awhile ago and was getting worse. The three Advils and the vodka were certainly taking their time kicking in. She pressed her thumb and ring fingers against her temples.

"Want the dogs with you or should I put them up, in the house?" Harry asked.

"Oh, let them stay." She gave a final, limp wave of her gloved hand. The Danes galumphed down the stairs to be near her.

Ivy waited for Harry's truck to roll down the driveway before she dropped to her knees by the next bed. But as soon as she was down, she realized she'd forgotten to bring the bucket. "Oh, damn."

The dogs were barking at the gate, making her head feel worse. She climbed to her feet as the roar grew louder. She turned, suddenly, and that is when she saw him, climbing out of the privet hedge.

"No! No," she cried. "Not you again—"

Something, a bug or something, was tickling her ear. She swatted at it. Her stomach felt queasy; her ear burned. She cried out as her left hand started to tremble. Her arm flapped like a wing at her side. The spasm climbed her elbow, shoulder, neck, then down the ladder of her spine. She was one step behind, mystified, as her body shook then stiffened, turning into wood. Ivy fell to the ground. She saw nothing, heard a distant humming. She felt sweet. Her mouth tasted of blood.

Lying on the sod, Ivy waited for the next thing to happen.

Fourteen

"Hey, quit that! You're eating only the best part," cried Jesse, as she tried snatching the blueberry muffin out of Lena's hand. "Give it here!" Jesse tore off the round top and popped a good chunk of it in her mouth.

Lena didn't care. She had worse problems, starting with the Sophia that had spent the night on her kitchen counter, and was now unceremoniously wedged between a box of Puffins and a jug of juice.

"So, what are you going to do with it?" Jesse gestured toward the statue. When Lena didn't answer, Jesse called, "Hello?"

"I'm taking it back."

"Back? *Why?*"

"Well, for starters, they didn't exactly give it to me."

"You mean you . . . stole it?" Jesse lowered her voice. "Are you out of your mind?" She rolled her eyes in the direction of Lena's two innocent children.

"Yes, yes, I am out of my mind," Lena agreed. She hadn't let Alessandro in the house, but neither had she slept. And now? Violet would be here any minute, and as usual Lena was running late. She focused on spooning the last of the ground chicken into Willa's mouth, a task ridiculously challenging for someone so unmoored. "Ivy handed it to me; I took it."

"She handed it to you."

"In a manner of speaking—yes. It was a symbolic gesture—both sides."

"Symbolic."

"Yes, Perry Mason: symbolic. I wanted to make a point and now that I've made it, I'm taking the head back."

Jesse chewed as she thought. "What was the point? I mean, if pressed—if a gun were put to your head—could you say?"

Lena thought a moment and slowly shook her head.

"Frankly, I expect more from you. " Jesse hopped off her chair to fix the waistband of her tights. "But moving on: What did you say about me? Did they ask?"

Lena considered the question, which had to pass through the far corridors of her sleep-deprived mind. But first she opened the applesauce and spooned a little of it into Willa's bowl, then tap-tapped the table to get Theo restarted on his cereal.

"Hello?" Jesse said. "I'm waiting here." Lena turned and observed her impossibly young, unburdened sister. That week, miraculously, Jesse had landed a job marketing wines. It was commission-only to start, but it was a job. She was even making noise about moving out. Lena felt something close to envy.

"I told them that having survived your impoverished childhood, you've gone on to have a brilliant life."

"You did not." Jesse beamed. "You did not."

Lena bent low to smile adoringly at Willa; Willa grinned back. "Of course, this was before the Grecian bacchanal got under way. Those waiters—in loincloths!"

Jesse opened her mouth wide, so Lena could see down her throat. "Come. On!"

"What's bach-something?" asked Theo, now that he was done with breakfast and had moved to the floor to play with his trains.

Lena was explaining the word *bacchanal* when Violet and Glo arrived at the back door.

"Come on, people!" called Vi. "We should have been on the Bay Bridge five minutes ago."

Lena rose. Was she dreaming? Was she awake? She met Glo at the sink and, focusing intently, talked over the day, giving directions.

Meanwhile, at the table, Theo had taken possession of the Sophia head. "Hey, she's rather sweet. Is she rare?" Vi asked.

"Rare doesn't begin," cracked Jesse. "She's hot. Just ask Lena."

"Careful with her!" Lena demanded, stopping them all. The simple truth was that Ivy could not have picked something that would have spoken more eloquently to Lena's historic heart. Then again, Lena's historic heart had gotten quite a workout in the last twelve hours. She took the head from Theo and kissed him on the hair.

"Stop sniffing me!" Theo complained, liking it just the same.

"Vi," Lena said, deftly shifting topics, "did I tell you Jesse has a new job? Tell her, Jess."

While Violet heaped praise on Jesse, Lena gave the Sophia a last hard look. It was egg-shaped and no bigger than Lena's palm. The girl's eyes were closed, her eyebrows an arched ridge, her mouth a tight bow. She did not look particularly wise but she did look content. Lena picked up one of Theo's socks from the floor, slipped the statue inside it, and dropped it into her large, overstuffed bag.

She was putting on her coat when the doorbell rang. Glo answered it. She returned to the kitchen with an enormous bouquet of peonies, Lena's favorite flower.

"Here," Lena said, hurriedly. "I'll put them in the living room."

"Like hell," Jesse said. "You haven't read the card."

"There's no card."

"Of course there's a card!"

"There's no card!" Lena snapped, making a halfhearted show of rummaging among the leaves.

Violet watched from the sidelines. "Maybe they're not from Charlie," she suggested. As soon as she said this, everyone knew she was right.

Lena left the room quickly. Her hands nervous and clumsy, she put the vase on the table behind the living room sofa. She couldn't believe Alessandro would risk—

She ripped open the envelope.

L,

For me, you have always been the beginning and end of the sentence. You are my days and my nights, my hope. Lean, if I haven't said it enough . . . How I love you, love you so.

— *Charlie*

"Well," said Vi as they drove away from the house. "That was something."

Lena, feigning interest in the view out the side window, said nothing. She was working mightily to push an image of a sleepless, frantic Charlie, phoning Bloomers from slushy Boston and begging them to deliver peonies to the house first thing.

"Marriage," she said at last. "Either the individual or the interest of the species comes out badly, one or the other."

"Says who?"

Lena sighed dramatically. "Me."

"Fa, Missy-pants, try Schopenhauer."

For opposing reasons Lena and Violet both nodded, agreeing with themselves.

"All right."

Vi kept her eyes locked on the traffic, as she weaved in and out of lanes. "Hey, don't make me work here. Who sent the flowers? Alessandro?"

Lena sighed. "Charlie."

"And this is a bad thing?"

Lena tipped her head. Vi knew Lena and Alessandro's story—she'd been their witness from the beginning. She was the one, twenty years ago, who removed a devastated Lena from Sandro's apartment and transferred her, bones and bags, to New York.

Vi shot her friend a very pointed look. "So, the party," she nudged, starting things in a certain direction. "Alessandro?"

"Behaved. Almost."

"And your uncle? And Charlie?"

"We all behaved—almost."

"And?"

Lena threw up her hands. "I don't know!"

Violet appraised her dearest friend. "Yes, you do. Your problem is you can't decide what to do with what you know."

"Oh, shut up."

"You shut up."

They both laughed, one singular bark that turned to silence.

"So. Now what?" Violet asked.

Lena closed her eyes and let the colors and brightness outside the car pass by. "Nothing," she said.

Violet steered decisively. "Nah. I'm looking at you, honey, and that's not the face of nothing."

They were stopped in traffic on the Bay Bridge.

"Listen—" Violet began.

"I know," Lena interrupted. "I know what you're going to say. This middle-aged thing. Did you see it coming? I didn't. Remember when I planned on being governor? Huh, Vi? Instead, I'm living a life that's good for my character. Am I supposed to say it's wonderful?"

Violet bit her lip. Lena was being a brat. Yet, thought Vi, she deserved to be a brat, having been surprisingly noble. So, Violet whizzed across three lanes of traffic to exit at Treasure Island, where she parked in the middle of nowhere, took another serious look at her friend, plunged her hand into the side pocket of Lena's briefcase and plucked out a handful of Theo's drawings. "I would give ten rolls in the sack and fifteen trips to Jamaica for one of these."

Lena nodded sadly. "But if you had these, Vi, do you think you'd stop wanting Jamaica, too?"

"It's not wanting, Lena. You know that. It's not even about some prig-gish sense of right and wrong, or—"

"Vowish obligation."

"That's right."

"The holy wedding cup."

"Exactly. The holy wedding cup. Oh, for chrissakes, Lena, fix it."

"How? Tell me how!"

"I don't know!"

They observed the view before them, which included a stellar sweep of the city and bay. At last Vi said, "Maude lost her gallery in Miami. Don't look at me, I was going to tell you—you were busy, remember? Anyway, she hasn't sold a painting in a year. My first thought, and I'm not proud to admit this, was that maybe she isn't talented. The economy sucks but I'm questioning Maude. I'm thinking, maybe I'm stuck with someone who isn't talented and, if so, what does that make me? So I developed my escape plan. In my head at least, I put some distance, you know, maybe we wouldn't live together anymore, that kind of thing.

"And then one afternoon I came home early. Maude had gone to the farmers' market and bought a sack of beets, the red and orangey ones. She was slicing them into these half-round rainbows. Why, I said. Why'd you get these? And she said, Because you like them."

Lena considered what she'd heard. "You protect. That's just what you do."

"Protect. That's a pretty word. The fact is there are all kinds of pretty words for not caring. Lena, let's be honest, how many shots do you suppose you get at making something lasting? You could've been governor, if I could have been Miss America. But that's not what we chose—all down the line, and I mean way down the line." Violet cracked the window and lit a cigarette. "I love you but I wouldn't trade places with you because I'm tough as hell but you're brave. That said, and this is selfish, mind you: it is ridiculously important *to me* that you and Charlie, against some righteously tough odds, pull this off—" Violet's voice broke. "Otherwise, I don't know, what the hell is the point? Honey, to make something lasting I think you have to let go of secondary distractions that come your way."

Lena seemed to absorb this—so much so, that Vi turned back onto the highway.

"But what if it isn't secondary?" Lena said quietly. "What then?"

Fifteen

After everyone departed and the large tent was packed into trucks and the trucks rolled away, he returned to eat a bit from the cans. It was amazing what these people threw out. The loaves of bread alone would keep him for days. He detected a bit of *poivre* in the ham. He preferred it without, just the honey glaze and maybe a little mustard.

With the dawn he fell asleep in his bag, having found a flat, hidden place between the bushes and the fence.

He'd been asleep all morning when she came out to cut those roses. He watched her from his place, until, that is, the dogs got wind of him. He was just making a quick exit, thank you, when she tried to stand but her arms and legs started to act all hinky. She was thrown flat, poor scamp.

He checked to make sure she was breathing. Then he put his best blanket on top of her and one of the towels he'd borrowed under her head.

His box wrenches. Harry had driven over the bridge as far as Sausalito when he realized he'd left them at the Rusches'. He had to go back. He was always going back, a little embarrassed, a little ashamed. So he finished a small job in Tiburon and turned around. He drove up and rang the bell.

Out back, one of the Danes was going to town—Finn, no doubt. He sounded like a moose calling from the garden. When no one answered the front door, Harry went down the side alley to check. The Danes ran to the fence and sniffed the wrought iron. Harry talked to them. "Quiet, Finn, quiet, Angie." He pressed his eye to the narrow slit in the gate and looked through. Ivy lay akimbo on the sod, a blanket spread over her.

Harry was not a young man, but he got himself up and over the gate. The dogs stood on either side of her, sentinels, with their black, somber eyes, waiting for the human to do something smart. They expected that much at least. They had seen it happen, jumped back as she fell, and afterward, whimpering low, licked her hair and face with their tongues. All afternoon they'd been at it, their long thick nails clacking on the wood and the pavement like women's high heels.

Angie moaned, just to keep Harry in motion.

He ran to get his phone out of the truck.

Soon the siren roared in the distance; the Danes, their ears insulted, turned up their snouts and began to warble.

"Be quiet," Harry said.

Finn paused, looked Harry over, and went on anyway.

Harry put Ivy's head in his lap. Her lips were pulled back from her teeth. There was a fine scar along her hairline, winding behind her ear. He studied that scar as someone who builds things, and takes them apart. Her lips were lined, but her forehead was as smooth as a child's.

"You're going to be fine," he told her. "Don't try too hard. Rest."

Sixteen

That morning, the partners of Rusch & Co.—all except Alessandro and the man whose name was on the sign by the door—arrived early. They'd come to depose a king.

Greg Bettor, who had been with Cal longest, arrived first, and Tony Hatch just after him. They went into Greg's office and Tony took a seat in one of the round chairs closest to the window. Gaspar Neri arrived next, his cheeks flushed and his hair damp. He'd been up early to ride his bike over the grueling pass of La Honda.

"Well, well," Greg said. "The day has come." But he didn't want to say more until the others arrived.

"Here's Bill," Gaspar noted, and the two men watched as Bill Shouts's yellow Lamborghini pulled into the lot.

"Did you stay late at the party?"

"God, no." Greg lived as squeaky clean as a Mormon.

"Norah Jones," Tony said sarcastically. "How much do you think that bit cost?"

Bill Shouts came in and took a seat. His restraint put a damper on the gossip while his clothes, a Brioni suit and a silk scarf that matched his socks, introduced a degree of elegance to the proceedings. His partners looked him over, as if he were a pretty girl.

"On the way home last night," Bill said, crossing his legs, "I said to Alice, sometimes I think Cal's just fucking with us. She didn't disagree." Bill had been a top headhunter on the East Coast. It took Cal years to lure him west. They had lunch once a week, never talking shop. They talked personalities, they talked scenarios; over Cobb salads they played chess with the Valley and its players. Those hours Bill would miss.

Greg was too nervous to sit. He perched on the edge of his desk. He'd been Cal's partner for twenty years and though they were total opposites, they had been a successful team. If only Cal had the grace to know it was time to retire. But no, he had to push things. "Did you look at that term sheet he came up with for Nimbus? Robots. Jesus. Even if we make the terms draconian, it's going to be what—eight, ten years before we see a payout. That is, if they don't screw up, which, let's face it, without an experienced CEO—"

"In this market, to be considering this kind of deal? Please. Cal might as well change the name on the door to Slow & Co.," Bill said.

There was nodding all around.

Among them they had built more than a hundred companies; they thought of themselves as the ultimate champions of entrepreneurs and their ideas. They had always been a team, elbows on the table, working together.

But Cal, with his biting comments, his jokes about slick lads with fancy cars, his inability to incorporate any of their ideas, made him the perennial outlier. They respected him, feared him, and were struck by his talent, but none except Alessandro liked him much. And Alessandro wasn't present at this meeting.

"Look," Greg went on. "I've talked around a bit, to the limited partners. If it comes to it, I feel sure half of them would go with us into a new part-nership. It's a lousy time to think about forming anything new, but, hey, it may be just the moment to start clean. Whoever wants to join is welcome. I'm saying this before the others come. Correct me if I'm missing some-thing, but I don't think Alessandro would—"

"Alessandro will serve his own interests," Gaspar noted.

"Won't we all," Bill said drily.

"As for Cynthia," Greg went on, "well, I don't know."

"You mean you don't know if you want her, or you don't know if she'll come?" Gaspar asked.

Greg shrugged.

Cynthia Dahl had torn her ACL skiing and required a driver, whose car was just pulling up in the lot. The partners watched as Cynthia determinedly hobbled on crutches up the stairs to the front door. "OK," she said, finally reaching Greg's door. Her face was a mixture of anguish and steel. "But let me ask you this: afterward, will we still think of ourselves as nice guys?"

At first, no one responded. Then Greg Bettor cleared his throat and, with more emotion than they thought he possessed, said, "I hope when it's my time, I'll have the grace to go. Cal knows it's coming, but if anyone thinks he won't hit back and hard, they're mistaken."

At nine sharp, Cal parked his vintage Mercedes in the first slot. He climbed the stairs and entered under the sign *Finis in principio pendet.* The phrase still inspired him.

"Morning." Maggie stood on a square of leather, toes turned out, a middle-aged dancer waiting for lights to go on. She'd come alone to the party and left early, and whatever kind of time she'd had he didn't wonder.

A new receptionist, who was still on trial, eyed them nervously.

"Calls," Cal huffed.

"A handful," Maggie replied, keeping up with him as they breezed past the conference rooms. She'd been with Cal since he split with Bud Cope. Maggie was newly divorced back then, with a toddler son she had to support. In the beginning, the hours were brutal, but now Brian was finishing up his doctorate at Yale and she was free to work as hard as she wanted. Her net worth, thanks to Cal, who invested her bonuses himself, was in the millions. On weekends, Maggie played tennis or went to hear jazz, but every Sunday she came into the office and *scoured* the piles, putting Rusch & Co. to rights. And the years went by.

Cal and Maggie were being closely observed as they walked around the outer rim of a large wheel. Inside the wheel, in open cubicles, worked the assistants and associate partners. The relationship between Cal and Maggie, its intensity, was among the favorite office topics—a notch above guessing each partner's net worth or the antics of the partners' spoiled children and wives. The fact that Maggie Gaffney seemed as asexual as Mary Poppins made it more of a guessing game and more fun when the staff got together on Fridays over happy-hour margaritas at El Canto.

It would start like this. "Want to hear Cal's idea of foreplay?" someone would ask. "*For chrissakes, Maggie,* climb up!"

The group roared.

"Fine, Cal, but first"—continued Donna, from research, pointing her finger at the nearest man's lap—"first, we must *cleanse.*"

It passed the time, at El Canto and here, inside the office, where long days were spent catering to the partners, and vetting the steady parade of prospects who trooped across the leather tiles with their change-the-world ideas, to be granted five million here, ten there, or, most recently, nothing at all. The second and third stringers had to keep up their spirits.

On the outer wheel, the partners maintained their large-windowed lairs. Maggie followed Cal into the farthest office, with its view of a madrone grove. Cal's inner sanctum had been wallpapered in a deep Chinese red. A dark mohair sofa lined one wall. At the far end the massive desk was bare except for a phone and an ancient photograph of Ivy, Paige and Christopher that Ivy had put there.

Maggie closed the door.

"Right. Who's up," he asked.

She handed him a folder. "Billybud, Combuy. ArtShop. SourceOne. And then there's Nimbus. I expect the partners' meeting to go long."

"Move Nimbus to the top and bump ArtShop to last." Cal eyed the window through his half-moon reading glasses. "As for ArtShop, Paige knows. I'm going to vote we drop it."

He glanced at Maggie to gauge her reaction. But she was a poker player.

Cal went on, "We have to fast-track Nimbus. It's been weeks since I gave Charlie Pepper the thumbs-up, so let's move this thing along."

Cal knew he was going to have trouble with his partners. No one loves a maverick, even if he happens to be the one who made you rich. No, the man everybody loved was Bud Cope, Cal's original partner and best friend. They split up twenty years ago, and Bud went down the road to start what was arguably the most successful fund outside Rusch & Co.

Cal fixed his gaze on the windows. After breaking his partnership with Bud, Cal had to assuage the limited partners by bringing on a fine-points sort of fellow, a stickler, but Cal and Greg Bettor never really got on. Greg could have left at any time to run his own shop; Cal was glad that he stayed. He'd kept the other guys off Cal's back. Let them have their inside jokes and nights out with the wives; let them have their ski weekends at Sugar Bowl and their summer boat rides at Glenbrook.

"Mag, after lunch, get Bud Cope on the line." He paused. "Bud pulled a move last night. I think he and Greg—"

"Mmm?" If she were surprised, she wouldn't say.

"Is it me, or are the troops preparing a mutiny?" he asked, reading her mind.

"I wouldn't say you're wrong."

"Greedy sons of bitches."

"Young."

"Young!" Cal scoffed. "Greg Bettor is sixty-five years old."

Later that morning, the partners gathered in the conference room for their weekly review of Rusch & Co.'s portfolio companies, and to vote on new investments. In voting, each partner assessed a deal on a scale of one to ten. Cal never lost a vote on a company he'd discovered, and in the past it was pure sport to try to sway him on other deals, to be the partner who brought him something new he could champion.

But in the last couple years, with the deal-flow so heavy and the pace quickening in equal degree as Cal's interest waned, the dynamics changed. It was impossible to be versed on every company in every sector. More than ever, the partners gathered in the conference room and except for the lead partner on the deal, the others might not know more than some background, with maybe a meet and greet along the way. The lead partner had to sell the others and win their votes. This circumstance invited all kinds of backroom horse trading. Cal was the only one who didn't play that game. He didn't need to—as founding partner, his vote counted three times theirs.

Cynthia Dahl hobbled into the conference room and her assistant came behind her with a Diet Coke and a bowl of edamame. "Don't be afraid," Cynthia said to the others. "Have a little soy." She slit the pods with her fingernail, dropped the beans into a bowl, and sprinkled them with salt.

The other partners found their places around the table, their seats long established, with Alessandro arriving last and taking his place at the far end, opposite Cal. Alessandro had been absent all morning, a no-show at the hastily arranged, clandestine meeting that took place in Greg's office earlier that morning. No one, not even Cal, had chatted with him behind closed doors. The partners looked to Alessandro to see which way he'd go. He smiled and made small talk. The truth was he didn't know.

Cal came in and took his usual seat at the curved tip of the egg-shaped conference table, his back to the wall, his eye to the door. He was determined to let the play unfold, his only question being which, if any of them, were still with him.

"All right," he said. "Let's get on with it. We've got a full list. We'll start with new ventures. Nimbus. You've all seen the stuff."

"Hold up, Cal," said Greg. "The agenda says we start with Billybud."

Cal balled the agenda in the mitt of his hand. "Let's forget the agenda and start fresh." He assumed a phony expression of innocence. "OK, so we've got Nimbus. Very exciting. A robot as an übersurgeon. Their medical mapping technology alone is worth—"

"Stop there, Cal," said Greg. "What the hell do we know about robotics? It's outside our purview."

There was nodding all around.

"That, and I have a myriad of legal concerns with this deal," said Tony, inching forward in his seat. "The patent issue, as far as I can tell, has not been fully covered. No, Cal, at every turn I hear the legal question."

"Tony, the thing is, you are always hearing the legal question," Cal declared.

"You say that until we are up to our necks in a lawsuit and then you say, Tony, where the hell were you?"

Cal smirked at the lot of them, the rage building inside. "What is all this negative wishing, eh?" he said. "Come on, we're batting the thing around, OK, let's bat it. But one of you, say something smart. That, or let's move on—"

"How many years, Cal," said Greg, "until you see Nimbus paying out?"

"Ah," Cal hedged. "Six, eight?"

"And if I said ten would you deny it?"

He checked the room. Once there had been such deference he could hear the air puffing through the pipes. Before that, in the beginning, he and Bud Cope had between them a banker and a lawyer and a couple of guys willing to take their calls and a phone that never rang—just that, and guts of steel. They had to beg. They had to imagine. They had to find it.

Cal wanted those days back. He supposed he wanted to be young. And if he couldn't be young, he'd settle for essential; and if he couldn't be essential, risky; and if he couldn't be risky, dead. The game, the pursuit, the next hope was the thing; in love, in money, in talk, in breath.

Greg recrossed his legs and Cal thought: fussy matron wearing panty hose. "To be blunt, Cal, how many on your list won't go public until years from now? Our limiteds, they won't have it. Not in this climate. They see what other firms are doing, holding still, and frankly they've been asking questions. What's the vision here? We agree on one tack, and then you move on your own. SourceOne. ArtShop. Billybud. These are hits, Cal, maybe not this minute, but given a year, eighteen months . . . We need to hold tight and, at best, shore up our companies until the market rebounds. This Nimbus stuff—yeah, maybe, in time. Why don't we agree we'll look at it in six to twelve months?"

"Six months," Cal said bitterly. "In six months they'll have repo'ed the copiers and the phones. Come on. Come on! Don't any of you *get* this? This is the next wave. Now, when everything is crap, we need to *jump*." Cal tossed his pad on the table. "And besides, I've given Charlie Pepper my word."

"Then it's your problem."

"No, Greg, as I'm head of Rusch & Co., it's our problem."

Bill Shouts cleared his throat. "Sorry, Cal, but I'm with Greg on this. For starters, there's untold resources these guys need. They need a real CEO, number one. That's fine, we can find one. But second, they need the cash to get through clinical trials—lots of cash. And they're not the first players. They're number two, with Midas being a formidable One. I don't see it. Where are they going to be in a year? Two years? Not with a product."

"A year proves nothing."

"A year proves what a year proves, Cal. Bottom line."

Around the table there was a whole lot of nodding.

Cynthia Dahl had been waiting for her moment. "The nepotism alone," she said.

"That's right," said Greg, wagging his finger. "Even if we wanted to fund this, Charlie Pepper is your relation. The partnership agreement clearly states that you don't get to fund your own kid, or niece, or husband to the niece, nada. You wrote the damn rules yourself."

"I don't know what business you're in, Greg, but it ain't my business," Cal said drily.

"Twenty years, and you say this to me," said Greg, red-faced and agitated.

"Yeah, well, we have kept our secrets, haven't we, Greg."

"Meaning?"

Cal leaned back in his chair and laced his hands behind his head. "What were you talking about last night with Bud Cope?"

Bill cut in, "Cal, what does this have to do—"

"Ask him," Cal said.

Greg nodded. "Cal, we think it's time you pulled back."

"Ah. And what, Greg, did you think you'd show me my own door?"

"I thought we would walk with you toward an honorable solution."

Cal stood. He planned to be doing deals until he dropped. He thought he would be doing them with this team. But no matter. He'd started out with just one partner, and he could end that way.

"We've never had a clue, that's the thing of it," Cal said. "Beginning at Fairchild, it was a business born of hope and guts. The nineties ruined it by making even the idiots look smart, making the Street believe there's a rule book to follow, with forms in triplicate and such. I've never seen the venture world in worse shape. Run by upstarts and wiggle-handed MBAs. A depression, such as this, is when the real talent stands out. Alessandro, you know what I'm saying."

All eyes turned to that end of the table.

Alessandro, his head bowed, was twisting a paper clip in his hands. He bent it one way and bent it back. "I was remembering the first time I walked under that sign that hangs over the door. I'm sure each of you remembers your first day, yes? Did I come believing in the enterprise? Sure. Did I come wanting to make some money? Absolutely. Did I think I brought some gifts to the table? All right, yes. But were these my biggest concerns? No. I came because I thought the experience, the caliber of the players, would be unlike anything I'd seen before. I'm not alone in this. We all came, at least at first, because of you, Cal." Alessandro shrugged. *"Sono con te."* I'm sticking with you.

Cal cleared his throat but said nothing. Nodding at Alessandro, he left the room and went to his office, where he stayed through lunch. Maggie brought him a sandwich and, later, when he was on the call with Bud Cope, she made sure he wasn't disturbed.

But as he was talking, Maggie received the news of Ivy. She stepped quietly into Cal's office, careful not to distract him.

"Listen, Bud," Cal was saying. "I came to you as a friend. I came *first* to you. And what do you do? Stab me. You and fucking Greg—happy trails, you two."

He listened a moment, his lips pressed into a volcanic pucker. "Pfff. Angry? I'm not angry. Not a bit. It's freeing actually." He laughed bitterly.

"Hey, Bud, as Churchill liked to say, 'It's been nice keeping up pretenses of being gentlemen with you.' "

He banged the phone into its cradle. Bud and his wife, Sandra, were Christopher's godparents. Bud had been Cal's friend for half a century.

"Cal," Maggie said coming toward him, a quaver in her voice.

He turned, thinking he didn't like it. "What now?"

Seventeen

Not knowing what else to do, Lena hugged Harry. She hugged him fiercely. As an afterthought, she introduced herself as Ivy's niece.

"The dogs were calling me," Harry croaked. "I wouldn't have set foot back there otherwise."

Now that the crisis had passed, Harry was on the point of collapse. His only hope for recovery was to tell someone quickly what he'd seen. He had to look into a kind face, and talk, before he could begin to know what had happened.

Lena tried to listen, but Harry's story was chaotic. Beginning far back, with his wife's illness and his failure to attend the Ivy League with his brothers, Harry told her that he'd come to hang Ivy's library doors, and that she'd been nice as ever while she cut the roses. A few details stuck out in Lena's mind: the paramedics had known immediately that it was a stroke; Cal's office had been notified; and the house was empty, though Harry couldn't imagine why.

"And what about that blanket on top of her?" he said. "I can't make heads or tails of it."

Lena hiked Willa higher on her hip and listened while thinking that soon the kids would be hungry. Harry was starting his loop for a third time, when she walked to the back of his truck, rooted around for where he said he'd put his lunch, and, finding a Coke, made him drink it, if only to keep him from talking so much.

She stood in the lee of the mansion, with the late-afternoon wind blowing. The Sophia was in its sock on the front seat of her car. She would get to it later. Meanwhile, Theo was making himself useful by talking to the dogs. He stood by the gate, where Lena could see him, and introduced himself politely. The Danes sniffed at his pockets, where there were plenty of cracker crumbs.

"Do you think they're hungry?" Theo called in a new voice, a voice already smitten. "They sure look hungry. And *massive*."

"Someone needs to put them up for the night," Harry suggested, pausing in his own drama just long enough to add a bit of reason. "I suppose I could." But he had his hand on the door of his truck and he looked eager to get on.

"Mama, could we?" Theo asked.

Lena took the children through the back, the dogs leading the way. She was glad not to have to walk through the foyer. It was enough to see the kitchen through Theo's eyes—his hand going slack in Lena's palm. The kitchen was bigger than all the rooms of their house combined. With the chilled, vaulted air of a cathedral. Dozens of brilliantly shined copper pots hung on one wall. On another wall there was an enormous clock, vouchsafed and unyielding, doling out the minutes. The stove was as large as Lena's car.

Lena pointed Theo to a chair at one of the long slab tables and put Willa in his lap. "Hold her, honey, 'K?"

The Danes, those snobs, kept their distance by the door. Lena opened the cabinets and the pantries, searching for their kibble. "Where is it?" she said aloud, if only to take the spook out of the room.

She was inside the pantry when she heard Alessandro's voice. He was talking to Theo.

"What are you doing here?" she shouted from the closet.

Alessandro was unaccustomed to explaining himself, but he did so anyway. After the partners' meeting, he'd come up to the city for a meeting.

Maggie reached him on his cell, and here he was, summoned to check on things. Paulette and Paco wouldn't be back until evening, he added, though Lena had stopped listening at that point.

She nodded at the two sitting at the table. "These are my children. Theo and Willa. Kids, this is Alessandro. He's an old friend. And now it's time for him to go."

Having said that, Lena disappeared inside the pantry. She paused there, her eyes closed and her heart pounding, not believing anything, and wishing he would just go.

"Do you like horses?" Alessandro asked, peering into Theo and Willa's faces.

They looked back at him with a particular seriousness. They were not especially cute, and they did not offer their souls. At last, Willa smiled goofy-faced, and then she put her hand in her mouth, all the way up to her wrist. Alessandro looked to Theo.

Theo shrugged. He was a dog man.

"And Paige?" Lena asked, coming out of the pantry with her hands on her hips. "Where is Paige?"

"I just talked to her. She's on her way to the hospital. I'll meet her there." Alessandro shook his head. "She acts one way, but she is not strong."

"Yes, she is. You'll see. She's plenty strong." Lena slapped one cabinet closed then opened another.

Alessandro shrugged; he was open to possibility, but he wanted to make clear he was not open to Paige. "Elena, let me help. What are you looking for?"

"Dog food!"

Alessandro turned and began opening cupboards on the far wall. He found the large bucket with the dry dog food and set it down at her feet. Then he backed away, as if she might bite him.

Lena couldn't quite believe she was standing in this kitchen, and that her children were here, too. She was scared for Ivy, irritated at Ivy, and furious at Alessandro. And none of that came close to how she really felt. She poured cup after cup of kibble into the dogs' bowls, put the bowls on top of the special benches and stood back to see if they would eat.

Then Alessandro said something she couldn't refute. "Ivy had cancer a few years back."

"When was that?"

"Ah, it must be five or six years."

He watched as she absorbed this information. She was shaking all over and he had to fight within himself to stay where he was. She went to the sink, found a glass, poured herself some water and drank it down.

"Elena."

"Can't you be quiet? Why is it Italians can never be quiet?"

"And how many Italians do you know well?"

She crossed her arms and smiled into the distance. "One."

The Danes paused to glance at their audience.

"Remember, Mama," warned Theo, "no water after they eat. You don't want them to get bloat." From all the stories he'd heard about Gus, Theo was something of a Great Dane expert. It impressed him that giants such as these two could have such weak stomachs.

"Good thinking, Theo," Lena said.

The dogs finished their meal and were moving on to polishing their bowls with their tongues. Lena picked up the bowls, put them in the sink and washed them. Then she put the bowls upside down on the counter to dry. Tears dripped down her cheeks. She couldn't stop the flow; she didn't try.

"What do you want?" she asked Alessandro. "To hurt Charlie?"

"No! Just the opposite—"

"Don't. Don't *help*."

"Mama?" Theo's small voice came from the side. "Mama, Willa is tipping!"

Theo couldn't hold her. In the late afternoon Willa's muscles got tired and Theo was too small to hold her for very long.

"Here, honey. Thanks. Give her here." Lena picked Willa up and put her where she belonged, on the shelf of Lena's hip. She turned to Theo, leveling at him the look of love and respect he would carry for the rest of his life. "Two minutes," she said, holding up as many fingers. Then she kicked the swinging door that led to the breakfast room and disappeared.

Alessandro followed her.

"San." She turned quickly to face him. "We can't see each other. Just agree, we can't and won't."

"*Tesoro,* you and I, we see each other, we don't—what changes? Nothing." That he'd realized this only a day ago didn't make him any less sure.

Lena glanced at Willa, frowned and, dropping her voice, went on. "Don't you see? I'm full up."

"Are you?" he asked. "Because I am thinking, maybe like me you are just getting through. Maybe like me you have been waiting a long time for a certain . . . knowing." He bent his knees slightly to look under the hood of her eyes. "We can be great friends. We've been everything else. Why not—"

"And the other thing, we'll just put aside?" she mocked him. "Like a dish or a potato. Is that what you're saying, San? We'll pass on the potato?"

He shrugged, as if to say it was all the same to him, which, of course, it wasn't. "I am close to all kinds of people. I want to be close to the one I value most."

"Most? *Most?*" Her face twisted with the certainty she was being mocked. She had indulged this long enough. Kicking the swinging door, she lunged into the kitchen. Theo jumped to his feet and followed her across that long room, past the stove and pots, and the shiny, impervious clock. At the glass door leading to the garden, Lena turned back.

"Do you see this, San?" She nodded at Theo and Willa.

"Elena, yes. But I also see you."

"I'm asking—"

"You don't need to ask."

"I'm asking for a little . . . mercy. I was never good at games but, trust me, I'm really bad at them now." She paused. "That other girl, the one you think you know, she doesn't exist."

He wagged his head, trying to repress a smile. "Oh, she exists. *Amorina,* she exists."

Eighteen

The applause was tempered. Charlie hadn't expected them to hang on every word, but their questions were nitty and uninspired. What if the robot fails midprocedure? How long will it take us to train? Is there the same time delay with the prototype as we've found with the Midas? He'd covered it all in his talk. Even so, he repeated himself, throwing in a bit of voice so it sounded new. Cost savings, time savings, speedier recovery, expanded flexibility, revolution in the surgical suite. Hearing themselves speak, the audience started to listen. It was always that way. Charlie knew he'd converted a few of them, especially in the front rows, but the surgeons of Mass General had yet to embrace the fact that they needed him. Instead they were moving on, to the next patient, to the weekend, to a quick jog before dinner. Charlie felt a growing humiliation. He felt exposed to the extreme. What was this? All right, he thought, leaving the podium. Keep it up.

The chief stopped him at the bottom of the stairs that led from the stage. A beefy fellow, a cardio man, with owlish glasses and the narrow pink face of the Boston Brahmin. He shook Charlie's hand, saying in so many words that he was warming to the idea of prototyping Nimbus, but he wanted Charlie in exchange. One week per month. There was no way Charlie could manage it. Charlie told the chief they could work something out.

He made his way toward the back of the auditorium. Near the doors a table had been set up with coffee, water, a platter of cheese and crackers and some fruit. A short woman in a gray suit, the head of the speaker committee no doubt, stood nearby and catching Charlie's eye, she smiled intensely. She had an old-world look, with black hair, round, dark eyes, and full, red lips and as he drew closer she nodded, prepared to exchange a few words. Charlie felt certain he'd seen her before.

He nodded and kept going, even as it passed through him that he was being rude, that at the very least he should thank her, and for his own shakiness eat a bit of her cheese and fruit. But he just didn't have it in him to stop. He passed through doors, into the wide hallways of the new library wing, which were carpeted in glen plaid. There were a few stragglers present, talking on their phones. Making a clean break, Charlie walked toward the elevators. And then his phone rang.

It was Swanson. "I've got great news, and the worst shit you can imagine. Which do you want?"

"Man, give me something good," Charlie begged.

"This morning," Swanson began, talking in a hushed, excited tone, "Cal Rusch wired us the bridge financing. A million bucks, Charlie, from his personal account."

It took a moment for Charlie to process exactly what had been said. "Wait. The money, it didn't come from Rusch & Co.?"

"Nope. It came from the old man."

Charlie bowed his head, thinking. Why would Cal write a check with his own funds? It didn't make sense. Charlie pressed the sockets of his bone-dry eyes but he couldn't see it.

"What are you thinking?" Swanson said.

"I don't know. I better call him."

"Charlie, the other thing."

"Let's have it."

"Sit down. "

He was in the corridor now. No seats to be had. "OK, I'm sitting."

"No, man, you're not."

"Now, Swan, how would you know?"

"Sit the hell down."

"Hang on." There wasn't a chair in sight so Charlie squatted. "OK. Shoot."

"You sound like you're—"

"Swan!"

Swanson breathed deeply, his voice just a hair above a whisper. "Charlie, Midas is suing us for patent infringement," he croaked. "I've got the goddamn papers in my hand."

Charlie tried to swallow.

"You know it's bogus," Swanson said.

"What grounds?" Charlie asked.

"They say we've impinged on the terms of their software—as if we would want their second-rate shit." Swanson went on in this vein. "Charlie," Swanson pressed, "you know what I'm thinking? I'm thinking it's that snake, Alessandro. He's behind this."

"Don't get paranoid."

"I *am* paranoid. Chrissakes, I am paranoid. Just when things are on the up."

Charlie twisted his jaw. "Don't do anything, Swan. I've got to think. I've got to be quiet and think."

"I know, Cap."

They hung up. But Charlie immediately called back. "Lee, tell Meyer to cut checks for everyone. Back pay, too. Get everyone paid up today."

"You sure?"

"Yeah. Hell yeah."

Charlie hung up and called their lawyer, Sam Friedman, who explained in detail how bad the situation was, and how expensive. "They don't have a leg to stand on, not really. That's the point. Charlie, they have the means to drag this out, and essentially paper you to death. Have you told your VCs?"

Charlie explained that he'd only just heard.

"This kind of thing you have to disclose," Friedman said. "If you lie or hide it, Charlie, listen carefully: if you fail to disclose, it's grounds for retractment, especially as we haven't signed yet. I hate to say it, but a suit of this nature is a deal-killer."

Charlie hung up and, realizing he felt ill, went looking for a men's room. He was washing his hands when his phone rang again.

"Hang on," he shouted, putting the phone on the counter. He was sweating profusely yet his mouth was a blowtorch of dryness. The growl in his stomach reminded him that he hadn't eaten since breakfast. He wet his face, grabbed some paper towels and picked up the phone.

"What," he barked.

"Why are you talking to me that way?"

Of course, it was Lena. She was calling with the news about Ivy. As Charlie listened, he paced. Round the men's room he walked, mopping his forehead with a paper towel. On the fourth or fifth lap, he grunted, swung open the door and returned to the stark hallway.

"What's funny in your voice?" Lena asked.

"Tell you later. Do they know what caused her to stroke?"

Lena sighed. "The CT scan found a brain tumor. Ivy had breast cancer a few years back. Charlie, what do you think?"

They all wanted to know what he thought. They wanted to know what he thought and after he told them, they wanted to know what else he thought.

It was metastasis of cancer. It was an ocean of work, an ocean of apathy, too much information, too little sleep, and not enough picnics on riverbanks—that's what he thought. It was a hundred docs in that auditorium, sitting in the dark, attentive but not there. It was, now that he looked, water spots on his best silk tie. It was a string of gorgeous software, attached to a mechanical arm. It was Nimbus, the dream of Nimbus, to do more, help more, be simple yet bold. It was Midas with enough coin to crush the better thing. Last, first, it was Lena, who failed to mention that she'd received the update on Ivy's condition from her old beau, who'd called the house, having no mercy at all.

"Damn it," Charlie said.

"What?" Lena asked.

"I left my notes."

"What notes?"

"I must have left them on the stage." Growling with impatience, he headed back that way, taking Lena with him.

The auditorium was dark except for two small exit signs on either side of the stage. Charlie knew he should wait for his eyes to adjust to the dark, but he was in a hurry. Blindly lunging, he banged into the last row of seats, hitting himself in the thigh and cursing. Then a thought came to him and he stopped. "Hey, Lean. Did you get the flowers?"

"Oh," she said. "Yes. Yes, I did."

But her voice wasn't right. Charlie winced.

"Charlie, we need to talk. This is too hard." Lena sighed. "So much happens in a day. When can we talk?"

In the darkness, he shrugged.

"Hey! Are you there?" she fumed.

"I'm here," he said. "I'll call you later. We'll talk." Stunned, he hung up, a great sadness overtaking him. He thought he'd better sit down.

"What in god's name could you be thinking?" a voice cried, as the house lights came on with a sudden brightness. Charlie had to shield his eyes. "You can't be in here!" The dark-eyed, red-lipped woman from before was coming up the aisle toward him. "You! You scared me," she accused. "I didn't know who or what. No one is supposed to be in here at this hour. You know that."

Well, he didn't know, but she wasn't interested in the finer points. What was the harm in sitting in the dark? But this little woman in the gray suit wasn't having that.

"I'm sorry I scared you," he said. "You know who I am. I just need a few minutes. I'll turn out the lights when I go."

"And I am the duke of England," she said.

"Excuse me?"

She was close enough now for Charlie to read the name on her badge. Lila Hagopian. His mind went to his first-grade teacher, Mrs. Papasian, who always said Armenian names rhymed with Armenian. You didn't have to be too smart to spot one. Growing up in Boston, Charlie had met any number of these short, plucky, velvet-eyed ladies; they were as common in these parts as pachysandra and chrysanthemums.

She came closer, and Charlie noticed the scar on her neck. There was a story there, thyroid perhaps.

"Pepper," she said. "What kind of name is that?"

He shrugged. "A funny one, no doubt."

"You weren't so funny in your talk."

"Oh, yeah?"

She sighed with a great weariness. "End of the week these doctors are thinking about going home. You want them to listen, to buy your gizmo, you have to loosen 'em up. Would it have killed you to tell a joke?" She lowered her voice a bit. "Don't feel bad. You didn't know."

"A joke. Hardy har-har, that kind of joke, is that what you mean?" he said bitterly. "Is that what you mean?"

"Sure. But even now, I have to tell you, you've got a bit of a grating tone." Lowering her eyes, she shook her head.

"Well, I don't have a joke. Maybe you've got one."

"Nah. My husband, he's the funny one." She made a face. "Ah," she said, "what does it matter? Next time slow down, that's all." She looked him over frankly.

I'm boring the hospitality lady, Charlie thought, his mortification complete. "I have to find my notes," he said grudgingly.

"I didn't see any notes."

"I had them . . . in a folder." He forced himself to push toward the stage, where he hunted in the vicinity of the podium and the few chairs beside it. "Goddamn it," he muttered.

"Work backward . . ." she called, the know-it-all.

Charlie mimicked her, his face turned so she couldn't see. Well, he was feeling small. And if he lost the notes, that was another bad sign.

He gestured at his chair in the front row. "I went from there, to the stage, gave the talk, then the chief came up and shook—"

They were right where he'd left them, on the shelf by the light switches.

"See that," she called. "There you go." She smiled, satisfied. "You know, Doc, you nearly gave me a heart attack, but then, frankly, it's been one nuts of a day."

Charlie could see it from her point of view. He was just some guy walking in the dark like everyone else. He climbed down off the stage.

She was waiting for him at the bottom, and he had the feeling she wasn't done with him, oh no, not this shiny-eyed terrier watching him with unvarnished self-interest.

"You got any more of those cheese and crackers?" he asked.

She nodded at a large Tupperware she'd put down in the front row when she came back to give him hell. Charlie took a seat, opened the lid and grazed.

"Doctor. Let me ask you a quick something. What do you know about Marc Jacobs?" She opened a water bottle and handed it to him.

"Jacobs? What department? He's not a surgeon, is he?"

"No!" She laughed. "Oh, no. Marc Jacobs. He's a hotshot designer, from New York. He makes pocketbooks." She waved her hand encouragingly.

Charlie wiped his mouth with his hand. There was danger in relaxing, he cautioned himself. He needed the food, and then he needed to push on. First, he had to call Cal and talk to him straight. And he needed to call the lawyer and light a fire in his belly.

"Marc Jacobs," she repeated.

Charlie shook his head. "Sorry. I don't know Marc Jacobs. I don't know anything about pocketbooks."

"Me either, turns out." She shrugged. "I know nothing about pocketbooks and nothing about these young girls today, but if I told you Marc Jacobs charges twelve hundred dollars for a pocketbook, what would you say?"

Charlie snorted. "I would say that you and I are in the wrong line of work. That's for sure."

"Bingo," she said. "Now how 'bout I tell you a story and you be the judge." She looked up eagerly. "Last weekend, I threw a baby shower for my youngest daughter. Marc Jacobs, he ruined it. End of story." She took the Kleenex folded neatly in her sleeve and blew in it.

Of course that wasn't the end of her story. On this nuts of a day that much was true. Charlie took a long drink of water. The odd thing, the very odd thing, was that he didn't mind sitting a bit. The shit-storm coming to him could wait another few minutes. Lila Hagopian leaned against the chairs in the next row, wiggling her hips to get comfortable.

"So," she said. "My baby is having her first baby, and, of course, we need to throw the shower. My mother, my sister and me, we cooked for days. Everybody and her sister was coming—I mean everybody. We did up the house; we decorated da and di; we got that baby the Peg Perego, the Boppy, the whole bit. Do you have kids?"

"Uh-huh."

"Then you know. My husband, oh my god, when he saw the bills! 'I'm going to be paying for that Boppy for a year!' he shouts. On the other hand, Nessie, our daughter, was delighted—so how can we do anything less? Her friends, they oohed and aahed. But her best friend, Julianna, came late and missed all that. In she comes with this *thing* . . . this Marc Jacobs purse. Marco who? my mother said. It was chocolate brown and soft—I mean soft. Leather. Buckles everywhere. Heavy as a couple of bricks. Well, the girls couldn't take their eyes off that pocketbook. They all had to hold it, pass it around. They cooed at it as if *it* were the baby. Twelve hundred dollars! You're a doctor, have you ever heard of something so crazy?"

"No. No, I haven't," Charlie admitted, eyeing the doors behind them with nothing short of longing. "That's one beak short of a lark," he said, climbing to his feet.

"Lark?" She squinted, her features condensing like the head of a missile. "What do you mean lark?"

"It's something my wife says. A figure of speech."

"A figure of speech," repeated Lila Hagopian. "How so?"

He'd deal with Cal and then the lawyers, thought Charlie—he'd do that while doubling his efforts at home. Where he would give more love. He would give more love—and make her happy—somehow. As an aside, he would lose the fifteen pounds of lard he'd put on working these last months and buy some clothes and get a haircut and, generally and in every way, get his shit together. He would start to run again, and while he ran, he'd spend the time rejiggering their finances and developing a retirement

193

plan. This much was clear. Charlie took a step toward Lila Hagopian, careful not to hurry and offend for a second time this feisty lady on whose face, moment to moment, passed every emotion from fear to hope to hate to love—reminding Charlie and bringing him back to earth.

He turned slowly for the doors. A few strides, and he'd be in the clear. But a thought possessed him, and he turned back. "Marc Jacobs," he said, "and these docs. They're a bunch of *eshags*, yes?"

"What!" She clapped her hands like a child. "How do you—?"

"A friend of mine. She calls everyone an *eshag*. I've got to think it's her favorite word."

"It's a bad word, Doctor." She mugged disapproval, but the naughtiness won out, and she beamed at him gaily. "A bad word, for sure. But there are times."

"Yeah," Charlie agreed. "There are times."

Nineteen

Willa had to spend her birthday in the hospital, but a few weeks later, at the end of March, she was well again. Her lungs were clear and she was eating regularly. She hadn't had a seizure in weeks. If put on the floor, on her belly, her arms tucked under her, she could, at times, hold up her heavy head and even scoot.

The stairs inside the Pepper house were steep and uncarpeted. In honor of Willa's birthday, Theo decided it was time his sister tried to climb them.

"Look," Theo cried to the group of adults gathered for Willa's party. "I'm teaching her!"

The guests, some thirty souls, included Willa's physicians and therapists, as well as the nurses from the NICU. Everyone trooped to the bottom of the stairs. They'd all come to celebrate the marker that few among them thought Willa would reach. They had helped themselves to wine, toasting Willa, who might not have made it except for their work and a bit of fairy dust.

Theo started Willa off, half a dozen steps from the top. She took to climbing like Quasimodo. One stair, then another, grunting and pausing, her tongue darting in and out, she advanced, with Theo hovering behind her. She was just shy of the top step, when she got stuck. Theo nudged her up and over. Willa swiveled her bottom, fell on her face and then pulled herself forward, so she was perched at the edge of the top stair. The way down was long and hard. She was wearing her party dress, a pale blue velvet with a white, starched collar and soft leather, white shoes. Over her diaper she had a pair of ruffled panties. Recently she'd grown a patch of hair down the center of her head that looked to be the start of dark curls.

With a considered stare Willa looked down at her audience. She tipped forward, pointing her nose like a retriever.

"Catch her, someone!" Beverly cried. "She's gonna fall. She's gonna—Oh, my god, that baby breaks my heart."

Willa rocked back and forth, her hands gripping the top edge.

"She's going to topple. Lena! Lena, stop this at once! Oh, god, I can't look."

"Wait," Lena commanded. "Give her a chance."

"Are you out of your mind? Glo! Someone! Do something." Beverly tugged on Charlie's sleeve.

"Wait," Charlie said. "Willa's got good instincts."

"Good instincts! Ha! There isn't a girl in this house with good instincts." Beverly looked around her. "And I'd say the same applies to the boys!"

"Grandma," said Theo. "Shut the boca."

Everyone laughed, even the hospital crew, all of whom had seen Beverly in action.

"That's not very nice," Beverly said, hurt in her voice.

Jesse, standing nearby, took her mother's hand.

Meanwhile Willa turned around, stuck out a foot, and touched the first step down. Just the way Theo showed her. The next step came almost as easily, though as Willa gained confidence she was also tiring. She was stuck again. With a grunt, she tried to stand. Those watching below gasped, but Theo caught her and hauled her the rest of the way down, where all the adults were whooping and high-fiveing.

It was a huge accomplishment, a birthday flourish from Willa-the-brave. For the second or third time, Charlie felt the need to toast the assembled group, thanking them, his face flushed with gratitude and wine.

Jesse announced there was homemade strawberry-lavender ice cream to go with the cake. Everyone followed her to the dining room, except Lena, who carried a very tired baby upstairs.

Lena was gone a long time. One by one the guests departed, and Beverly, Jesse and Glo went to the kitchen to clean up.

"Charlie's exhausted," Beverly said. "How many trips this week? It's too much."

"Charlie? Charlie!" snapped Jesse. "Why do you only worry about Charlie? Mom, Lena's exhausted."

"Well, sure."

"But you always focus on the man—"

"Don't start with me, Jesse-pa-lunk! Don't you think I know how it is with Lena?" Beverly pulled in her lips and closed her eyes. She took a sponge, dabbed a spot on the counter and hurled it into the sink.

Glo watched them from her seat at the kitchen table. Jesse had insisted that today she was their guest. Glo sat sheepishly, diminutively, her feet hardly touching the ground. She took bites of her cake, pulling the fork slowly, contemplatively from her mouth. "The mommy," she said quietly, "she cry for the other baby girl who didn't have a birthday."

They all stopped. Charlie, playing with Theo in the other room, hurried into the kitchen. "Where is she?"

"I'll go," Beverly said.

"No. Thanks, but no." Charlie pointed at Beverly to make sure she listened.

Lena was on the back deck, on the stairs, the buttery orange cashmere throw she'd given Glo for Valentine's Day pulled around her. She'd put Willa to bed then tiptoed down. There was a bright moon, but her gaze was fixed elsewhere.

"Hey," said Charlie.

"Did you get Theo in bed?" she asked. "I bet that chocolate cake has him wired."

"He's upstairs, tooling around with his planes."

"Mmm."

"Lean."

She didn't answer, so he sat on the step beside her, and took her chilled hand and put it between his warm ones. "I was thinking," he began.

"Thinking," Lena said. "Sometimes I try *not* to think. For days at a time." She squeezed his hand and let go.

"That's not what I'm saying."

"I don't pity us, you know." Her voice was raw. "I just wish I could . . ." Lena wiped her nose with the back of her hand. "So many folks have it worse. That mother in Rwanda who was forced to watch all six of her little children being hacked to death by a boy-soldier with a machete. And then they spared her—for what? Or that father, you remember, in Sonoma, who followed his wife and three kids home in a separate car and witnessed them being hit by the drunk driver, all of them dead right before his eyes. Or, last week, in the paper, that woman, the heroin addict, whose dealer boyfriend got her high then made her watch as he boiled her baby in a soup pot."

"My god," Charlie protested. "Stop!"

"What," she asked dully.

"Lena! Look at me. Is this what goes on in your head?"

Guilty, she turned away. How to explain what had changed in her? It wasn't that she couldn't laugh or that her optimism had abandoned her entirely, or that she couldn't take joy from a happy face or a silly word. Her children still amazed her; she loved them fiercely. She loved Willa's pee-soaked smells, her gibberish, her soft padded hands; she loved Theo's nighttime sighs and his unflappable directness. She loved them as only a mother could. But her estrangement from the rest of the world instead of lessening was getting worse. Lights were too bright, berries tasted too keen, and the large-throated song of the world was too much in Lena's ears.

"I should have taken you someplace," Charlie said. "I should have taken you away."

He was being literal. Thinking of worse stories, the absolute worst, was how she managed the worry and what-ifs. Didn't he know that?

"We both needed to run," she said. "One of us actually did."

Charlie cringed. "Ouch."

"Sorry," she said. "Really. That was mean. Give me tonight, all right? I'll be better tomorrow."

"Lena." Charlie put his arms around her and shook her gently. "Feel this."

She hung her head.

"Let's go somewhere. Cabo. We could go to Cabo. It's not far. Or that place near Carmel, what's it called? We could get there in a couple of hours. You could rest. You could let me take care of you."

But as he spoke she curled herself into a tight ball and sank her chin on her knees. They said nothing for quite some time.

"Say her name, Charlie. I want to hear you say her name."

He swallowed hard, the muscles in his face tightening. "Sylvie."

Lena nodded.

"Sylvie," he repeated. "After that girl in Venice. She was so—"

"Bright," Lena said to her knees.

"Bright," he repeated.

Lena sighed. "I hate that you didn't let me hold her. That I didn't have a chance to say good-bye."

"But you did!"

She shook her head. She'd been drugged and now she couldn't remember. "It's all right," she said, her voice frightening, as it lacked all music. "Tomorrow I'll be fine."

After a long while, Lena came into the house. The lights were off except for the bright ones in the kitchen. Beverly was at the table drinking a beer, her bare feet up on a chair.

"Helena," she said. "I'm through worrying about you."

"OK, Ma."

"Is that all you've got to say?"

Lena nodded.

"Sit down." Beverly nudged the chair next to her with her foot.

"I don't want to."

"Well, I'm not asking."

Lena sat.

"Don't interrupt me until I'm finished," said Beverly, inching forward in her seat. "One, Charlie is only trying to support his family. It's what he knows how to do. You can't blame him for that. Two and three, you need to snap out of this funk. I've got to hand it to you, you got that baby as far as this birthday. I thought it was impossible. But here you are. Thank god you're so stubborn. Now listen to me. I'm going to take the kids and you and Charlie are going to have a long weekend. *Away.*"

"Mom, I can't leave."

"And why not."

Lena looked up at the ceiling.

"Oh, fa. I took care of you, didn't I? How complicated could it be? You'll show me how to work things and make a list of when I have to do this and that. Oh, god, is it that tough? We'll manage. I'll throw some money at Glo and she'll help me. As for Theo, I'll hand him a pipe full of tobacco and tell him to go watch the news."

Lena smiled. "You don't have any money to throw."

"Then I'll throw yours, ninny." Beverly looked fondly at her nice trim ankle. She turned it a bit, checking, then put her foot back into her shoe. "So. Better?"

"Oh, Ma."

"Believe me, girl. Getting over it is not an option. Let's knock that idea from the shelf once and for all. You'll never be the same, but then, who is? Show me someone who's taken a blow who is the same. You have to choose to be happy. Choose it. For him, for yourself, for those kiddles upstairs. No one gives you points for sad, Lena. No one. Not even your old ma. You feel it, now get on. It's been a year."

"Are you always so damn practical?"

"Hardly." Beverly touched her bracelets one by one. "As you know."

"Oh, Ma."

"I'm sure," Beverly replied, defiantly lifting her chin. "Get out your calendars while I'm still offering."

Lena paused "Ma. Tonight. You didn't say a word about Ivy."

Beverly sat up, energized. "What? Is there news? Is she worse?"

Lena smiled.

Beverly cupped her chin in her palm. "Shh. Can you imagine him caretaking? The thought of Cal wiping Ivy's ass."

"Ma!"

"You don't know him like I do."

This Lena couldn't deny.

Twenty

That cancerous string Ivy saw in her dreams, the one shooting sparks, had deposited a tumor in the center of her brain. It was the size of a plum. Surrounding the tumor was a constellation of lesser ones, but, ultimately, the plum, stanching the flow of blood to her brain stem, would kill her. She had six months. There wouldn't be much pain, the doctors said.

Ivy remained in the hospital for some weeks. Cal, having nights on his own in the huge house, found he missed her. One night the urge came on him to poke among her things. He went into Ivy's dressing room, where he'd always made it a point not to go, and saw himself reflected in a dozen mirrors. He opened one closet and then another. Ivy's gowns hung on padded hangers, each with a card attached, written in Ivy's looped, girlish hand, recording the occasion of the purchase and where the dress had been worn. Some she'd worn many times, some just once. The journey of Ivy's clothes comprised her diary, and the gowns themselves were her works of art—no less valuable than what hung on the walls, and just as shrewdly collected, protected, curated, babied. All these years he'd been squiring her to the opera, the symphony, the endless openings, thinking she was blowing a goddamn fortune on looking nice, but in fact Ivy had been at work. And when she died, soon enough, the whole lot would be donated to the Met. The designers who befriended her, and whose bottom line depended on women such as Ivy, understood this. As did Ivy's friends. Cal alone was clueless. He opened every last door. She had rows of hats and purses up top, and drawers of scarves and belts below. She had a safe, of course, and compartments in a cabinet for her lesser jewelry, with each ring or doodad having its own discrete cubby. The drawers, the fabrics, the room smelled of her perfume.

He sat at the desk and found it equally loaded with cards and photographs and odd things she'd saved through the years. He fished a hand through the pile and pulled out a cocktail napkin from the Ritz Paris. On it, in Cal's hand, was a single word: Rome. Why'd she keep that? He couldn't imagine.

She was a mystery to him. It had been that way from the start—the first time he saw her at the bar at Trader Vic's. She'd been at the beach all summer and was dark as a Jamaican. She was wearing a turquoise dress. Gorgeous legs. Her hair was behind her, it went all the way down her back; her skin was as red brown and polished as madrone. He turned to his date, who was a very nice girl from a very nice family and whose father had the means to set Cal up in business. They had been promising him as much, holding their chins just so, while for three rounds of cocktails the father blew platitudes at Cal, not one word remarkable. Cal was penniless, in fact worse than penniless, he was in debt, but that hardly mattered; he was already living in the future.

Ivy was out with her brothers, though Cal didn't know that at the time. They were as tan as she was, but much less refined. They bolted their cocktails and glared into the crowd, as if hoping to fight. The regulars at Trader Vic's took one look and assiduously avoided them. Later, Cal learned that the one with the loud mouth was her older brother, Nate, a ranch manager's son who would become a winning bronc rider until one day he snapped his back. Seeing those three tall boys, Cal felt an old rage.

His date was making a witty remark for his benefit, but Cal didn't hear her. He rose from his chair, leaving behind the possibility of blondes with their nice daddies and matching purses and good manners. He could see the future and in it was a haughty, dark girl looking for a real ride, a girl who didn't always act nice and wouldn't expect the first thing from him to be nice either.

The first night after Ivy came home from the hospital Cal saw what he was in for. The doctors had promised there wouldn't be much pain, but they also warned Cal that mood swings and a certain grumpy affect were not uncommon.

They had dinner in the library. Paco set the card table with a cloth. But Ivy couldn't manage to stay in a hard-back chair, so they moved her to the sofa, and Paco brought up two ancient TV trays from the basement.

Ivy turned slowly and, hooking her finger, she pointed at the trays. Post-stroke, the top part of her face was raised, as if in surprise, while the bottom hung loose. "Ugh. The first . . . ring of hell . . . P-p-p-practical ugly."

"Humph," Cal said. "I see you haven't lost your charm."

"Humph-humph," Ivy stuttered, speaking out of the side of her mouth.

The talk on the evening news was of swine flu and the G-20 summit, but the fate of the world held no consequence for Ivy. She had more immediate problems. She could no longer raise her right arm. She had an itch on her nose she couldn't get to. She'd gone to cut the roses and would never come back. She felt as if she'd heard a compelling story, the details of which she couldn't quite fix. She had a ball of fur in her throat; she had to work to chew. Was Nixon back in office? Cal was sitting next to her and one minute she felt very fond and the next irritated and the next she didn't quite remember who and who.

The dogs with their huge heads couldn't get enough of her. They wanted it made clear how much they'd missed her and so they kept nudging her and stepping on her feet with their huge paws, and whacking her with their tails. She tried to shoo them.

"S-s. S-s-s," she hissed.

Thinking it was a new game, the Danes, with flattened ears and sparkly eyes, tiptoed toward her.

"Get out of here," Cal boomed, clapping his hands. They ignored him and sat at her feet. Cal shouted for Paco and told him to lock them in the kitchen.

"But, sir, they'll only cry and scratch the door."

"Then lock them downstairs," Cal said, with a desperation Paco had never heard before.

Ivy watched as the dogs were dragged off, the door closed behind them.

Later that night, long after Paco had helped put Ivy to bed, Cal came upstairs and found the bed empty. The light was on in Ivy's bathroom. She'd fallen off the commode, gotten stuck between the sink and the toilet, and passed out. He carried her, light as whimsy, to bed. In the morning Ivy awoke to find him there, watching her.

"Who-who," she said.

He didn't go to work those next days; he didn't answer calls. Nimbus and the rest were far from his mind. Cal was suffering from a kind of ecstasy of crisis, sparked by a sudden nearness, once removed, to death. He felt a desire to burn bright, to renew the vows. He felt a desire to care for Ivy. He remembered that as far back as a year ago, Ivy said in passing that she had lost her sense of smell. That was the beginning. Here was the end.

Her personality, dulled by the stroke and drugs, was erratic. She blinked and smiled and stared far off, or came back with a vengeance to bite him. She said strawberry when she meant television; she said frying pan when she needed to pee. Jacked up on steroids, her famously angular face puffed up round as a moon. Her back grew the beginning of a hump. The Decadron also made her tippy, and later that week she fell off the commode a second time and broke her wrist.

Cal interviewed nurses but none was good enough. He called the owners of the agencies and barked his demands.

An agency sent Walker. He came one morning while Cal was out at a meeting. Paco opened the front door expecting to welcome a motherly nurse. Instead there was a black man with slightly buck teeth and the shapely figure of Diana Ross.

Walker asked to use the facilities.

Paco waited outside the powder room as inside Walker took a long time soaping his hands.

Paco supposed, in Mister's absence, he would have to interview Walker.

"If you don't mind, I'd like to meet Mrs. Rusch now," Walker said.

Paco took him up. Let her decide. She was known, after all, to find possibility in the strangest places.

At the doorway, Walker turned to Paco. "Hey, man, it's OK. Better she see me solo, and decide from there."

Ivy, propped up on a mountain of lace pillows, was dozing. At last she opened her eyes.

"Mrs. Rusch, I'm Walker." The nurse stepped to the bed and put his hand on her foot. "How is it today?" he asked.

"If I ask it to go slower, the dizziness . . . my arm ouches. It wants what it wants."

Walker nodded. "Let it have its way, Mrs. Rusch. As a friend of mine, recently passed, used to say: Fight it and you light it."

She looked up at him in a moment of lucidity and wondered if all his friends were fags, or were they rich ladies like her?

"Would you like something for that pain?" Walker asked. "That pain in your arm."

His voice was as sweet as sugar. Who was he? Ivy couldn't remember. She listened very carefully, then her mind wandered, and she dozed, and when she opened her eyes, there was a black man standing beside the bed.

"Who?"

Walker had a Southern way about him. He bent low, his face even with hers. "Walker."

"Will you be staying . . . awhile?"

"If that suits you, Mrs. Rusch, I think we can get along."

It was all decided before Cal came home.

The day Ivy went to see her new oncologist, Cal insisted on taking her himself. He made certain Bruce Noble, their internist of thirty years, would meet them there.

Walker dressed Ivy, then Cal brought her down to the garage. She could not be hurried. To take her arm was to feel that it weighed nothing yet was tight as steel. She refused to get into his old Mercedes; no, she insisted they ride in her car. He told her she was being ridiculous; he had told her that at least four times since breakfast. She stood there like a shirt hanging on a line. So, Cal drove her Jaguar, with its narrow seats and prissy controls. The interior was spotless, and smelled of leather and perfume. The driver's seat put his knees at his ears. He fiddled to adjust the damn thing, and all this took time.

When at last they were on the road, Cal started in. "Paige asked if she should move home to help us, and I said no. Last thing you need is that windstorm."

Ivy shot him a look, her camel lips poised, the information slowly working its way into her mind. She nodded.

"But I called Christopher," Cal went on. "Time for him to get his butt home. He can just as well stand on his head in San Francisco as he can in Pune."

"No," she said hoarsely. "Please, no."

"Ivy, it's done."

Her top lip rose on one side. "Then . . . you . . . un-done it."

The magazines in Dr. Weisman's packed waiting room were heavily used and, Cal imagined, full of germs. One good bug would finish Ivy off. Cal kept his hands in his pockets and made sure that Ivy didn't touch a thing.

A couple who Cal guessed must have been in their sixties came in. The husband was fat as a walrus, Cal noted, but he dressed like a kid, in a baseball cap and sneakers. When a chair opened up, his wife sat while he stood behind her, rocking on his heels so that his thighs kept jarring her seat from the back. She was snapping the pages of a magazine. "John, listen to this," she said. "They've done a new study. Turns out that stress can literally break a person's heart. It says here: 'Women are especially susceptible.'"

"LaNette, you want to worry, worry about *my* heart."

"Your heart, John?"

"Oh, yeah."

"Your heart?"

He nodded, and kept on rocking, reading his paperback detective novel.

"Why are we here, John?"

Now he shot her a look. "You have cancer, LaNette, honey. There's nothing the matter with your heart."

There, thought Cal, I'm much nicer than that guy.

Forty minutes later they were still waiting. Cal checked his iPhone, sent off a dozen emails, checked the weather and his stocks. He paced the room and inquired at the desk. He texted Maggie and had her call Weisman's nurse and ask how much longer they'd be, as he was expected in a meeting.

At last they were led to a small examination room, just large enough for the table, a sink and a single wooden chair. Cal put Ivy in the chair and stood in front of her, as if on a packed train. "They keep these rooms small to humble the patients," he seethed. "Bastards. Bastards with degrees."

He had the great desire to assert his importance. He had the need to throw open the thin little door and shout, I have met with the president. Get this train moving! People! People!

Ivy looked up at Cal. If she gave him any energy now, she wouldn't have it when she needed it, so she released the anger, letting it fall like a heavy shoe. Cal noticed she was drooping a bit. To comfort her, he laid his palm on her back. The weight nearly sent her crashing to the floor. She let her head drop, let it all go. The tape that was her mind had erased unevenly. For instance she couldn't remember what she liked for breakfast. She'd lost some of the colors, their names, and people's faces. Earlier that morning, she couldn't remember the way to the bathroom, but knew that she had been wearing a black turtleneck the first time she'd been kissed. Her gaze fell even with Cal's belt. He had moved to a new, tighter hole. When did he lose weight? She hadn't noticed till now. We should ask Mother, she thought, confused.

And then, drifting, she returned to the hand on her back and thought how heavy it was. Really, she wished he'd knock it off. She tried to wiggle a little, so he'd get the message, but her body didn't respond.

Just outside the door, Bruce Noble was talking with Weisman. They were speaking about Ivy. Cal jerked the door open.

"We're in here. We've been waiting far too long."

The uppity patients, opening doors. Bruce Noble was not amused.

"Cal," he said, tucking his chin like a tom turkey. "Hello, Ivy dear. Sorry to keep you."

The two doctors tried to fit into the space, but there wasn't room.

"Let's go to my office," Weisman said, "where it's more comfortable."

He led them down a hall to a brightly lit room with a suite of furniture and diplomas on the wall and, at Ivy's eye level, a tremendous orchid.

Weisman looked over the chart and then turned to Ivy. He sat in front of her, knee to knee. He had such brightness, she thought, there were stars just behind him, and stars on his shoulders, too. He held her hand. "How are you?"

Ivy managed a one-shoulder shrug.

He couldn't be more than forty, thought Cal, a kid.

Weisman launched into his questions, now looking to Cal for answers. Had she been forgetting things for a while? She had. How long had she smoked? How many glasses of wine did she have in a week? How much vodka? He nodded as Cal answered. The main tumor was in the upper left lobe. It was indeed a metastasis. Inoperable. Stage four.

Ivy leaned on the armrest of her chair and Weisman said, "Ivy, do you have any questions?"

She looked like an angel in a picture, about to sing. She said nothing, gazing above him.

Weisman made notes in his chart.

"Ivy," Bruce Noble said, "we're going to futz with your meds and get it right so you're less sluggish. You'll come out of that fog, and it'll be better."

While Noble talked in nursery tones to Ivy, Weisman stayed back, talking to Cal. They would keep on with the Decadron, he explained, hoping to shrink the tumor. There were side effects: her skin would get very thin; she would continue to bloat. Lesions. Loss of musculature. Before long she would have trouble standing. Someone would have to watch her at all times.

As Weisman spoke, his gaze locked on Cal's face. The young doctor frowned. Cal wondered if Weisman wasn't a little intimidated by him. He expected that, of course. In a meeting he was always the main player.

"And what about her personality?" Cal asked, lowering his voice. "Is she going to be this bossy forever?"

Weisman crossed his arms and leaned in closer. "Mmm. Yes. Well, possibly. Then again, more likely not." The doctor seemed distracted.

Cal stepped back. "What the hell. Is that a yes or a no?"

"Mr. Rusch," Weisman said. "Come here, under the light." Cal expected some disclosure, grave and definitive, regarding Ivy's outbursts; the young doctor would think it appropriate to keep that much private. Cal went eagerly with him to the windows.

"She's been a real handful," he said in a low, confiding voice.

"Mr. Rusch, how long have you had that dark spot? That one, over your eye." He pulled his hands from his lab coat pockets, and touched the spot. "Bruce, excuse me. Bruce, come take a look at this."

Noble tucked Ivy's hand on her lap and took his glasses from his pocket. As he peered at Cal's forehead, Cal caught a glimpse inside Noble's mouth, which was certainly an unpleasant business, a tiramisu of dental work. Bleached teeth, a mess of gold crowns and fillings. It was all disappointingly mortal. Best case, Cal thought, Noble made a few hundred thou a year. His wife, Holly, was tormented by a crazy brother. Everyone had his or her thing. This Weisman no doubt had his thing, too. All this went through Cal's mind.

"Come on, guys. Every year my derm takes out a few more divots. It's nothing. So, I sailed for fifty years before anybody knew to put on a hat."

Bruce and Weisman exchanged skeptical glances.

"Mr. Rusch, look at what I'm seeing here." Weisman motioned Cal to a frameless, round mirror hung on the wall. The doctor pointed with his pen. There was a deep brown, almost purple mark above Cal's eye.

"See the discoloration and uneven margins along the left? There. And again there." His voice was quiet but firm. "We need to take a look at that pronto."

"Oh," Cal said, stepping away from the mirror. "It's nothing. Basal cell bullshit. I've had patches carved out before. Right-o, we'll get on it." He parted his hair to show Weisman his other scars. "Look at that. Look at this one."

"Cal, I'm serious," Noble said. "Dr. Weisman is right. That one looks different from the others. That one is nothing to fool with."

"Oh, hell. What are you driving at?"

"We can't know till we biopsy it."

"Bruce, do I look like your average Joe? I can spot the single good idea among five hundred losers at a packed Hambrecht conference. At your stage, you better be able to do the same. Stop talking to me like I'm some idiot from Weisman's third-world waiting room."

Noble tried not to show any pique. "Cal, these things can look worse than they are," he said. "On the other hand . . ."

Weisman broke in. "Mr. Rusch, you have what I'm fairly certain is a sebaceous carcinoma. Most likely melanoma. It's ulcerated here and here," he said, peering at Cal through the loop he'd taken from his pocket. "It's three, maybe four millimeters to the margin," he said, his voice animated once again.

"Is that big, or what?"

"In a word, yes," Weisman said, nodding at his nurse, who'd appeared out of nowhere, with a clipboard.

"You've seen hundreds."

"I've seen thousands."

"Keep going. Don't hem, man."

"You'd be well advised to take your wife home and come back first thing tomorrow. Lenore, here, will set you up. We'll do the biopsy, and if we can arrange it, we'll run the tests all in the same day."

"Tests?"

"An MRI, pelvic CT, blood work," Weisman said, as Lenore took notes. "After the biopsy, we'll know."

Cal studied the man. "You want to scare me," he said, jutting his lips, even now negotiating the term sheet to his favor. "You're worst-casing things. Scare the shit out of the bugger and then what comes won't strike him as half bad."

"Mr. Rusch, I have no interest in scaring you," said Weisman, having already leaped ahead to probable lymph involvement and the radical neck dissection that would follow. But you do not tell them this at the outset. You lead them through the steps, bringing them along. Third-world waiting room—he wouldn't be forgetting that anytime soon. He said, "At minimum we have to remove it."

"And at the max?"

"How long since you saw a dermatologist?"

Cal shrugged. "Ivy makes me go once a year."

"And when was the last time?"

"I don't know. I'm probably due." He turned to her. "Iv?"

Her eyes were closed, her chin resting on her chest. She was in the space they called twilight, a whole galaxy of stars on the insides of her lids. She looked at peace, as though she were praying.

On the ride home, at the exit for Half Moon Bay, Cal pulled over to the side of the road. In the distance, along the purple hills of Skyline that divided the valley from the ocean, second-growth redwoods were topping their heads. Cars whizzed past them, thousands and thousands of eager souls pushing into the valley. Cal had donated money to clean up the highway and to replant the groves. He'd protected and crushed and insulted and condemned and raised up.

"But I don't feel any different," he cried out. "I don't *feel* a goddamn thing."

She seemed so far away, yet after several minutes she said. "M-m-m-m-may-be you feel too much."

A week later, Bruce Noble sat in his favorite chair—at home, on a spring evening—as his wife, Holly, prepared their cocktails. He was feeling content with his life. He had two sons, both out of college, pursuing respectable careers. The elder, George, was going into medicine; the younger one, Rick, come summer was getting married. Bruce and Holly had been married for thirty-five years, and at the end of a day they still had stories to tell each other.

Holly brought their scotches and a plate of crackers and cheese on a lacquered tray painted with horses.

"So what's the big doings?" Holly had had a full day as well—she was a partner in a downtown law firm. As it was a Tuesday, she'd left work early to take a Pilates class. Yet here she was, fresh from a shower, greeting Noble in her pumps and gold earrings for drinks on the lanai. They had waited all these years to be alone together and so they talked, and eventually they'd go into the dining room and eat from the good plates.

"Cal Rusch," Noble said, giving the headline. "He's got a metastatic melanoma, and a very aggressive form at that. The MRI of the head was a horror show. We stopped counting at eight distinct sites. It's in the sweat glands." Noble took a bite of cheese and cracker. Rusch's cancer would advance down the ear, into the jaw, then into the back of the throat, and there it would suffocate him. It was a terrible, painful way to go.

"He can't beat it, and if he insists on making us treat it aggressively, which he will, it'll be a nightmare. We'll be cutting off parts of his head and scalp, trying to get ahead of it, and in the end . . ." Noble stopped, shaking his head. "It's going to be a race to see who goes first, Cal or Ivy."

Holly set her cracker on her napkin. "Isn't that something. She can't even have her own cancer. He's got to horn in on that, too?"

Noble smiled. It was the same reaction his nurse had had. A woman thing, he figured, as the thought never occurred to him. Over the years, Cal and Ivy never hesitated to interrupt Bruce's family dinners and vacations with their demands for care, their aches and pains, yet the Nobles had never been invited to the Rusches' grand parties. Holly blamed Cal for the slight. The Nobles were Republicans and they were not of the same social circle as the Rusches, and every season the society pages reminded Holly of those facts.

"Hol, believe me, you wouldn't wish this on your worst enemy. And if you look at it another way, who would have thought they'd be so in sync?" Noble put his hand on her knee. "He'll choose the hard way, you can count on that. He'll want every heroic measure, every minute we can buy him. These guys compete from their hospital beds."

Holly studied her husband carefully. "He'll respect you now."

"Oh, darling, no. Don't hope for that. Cal will respect me just enough to use me as a tool. That's how he thinks. There's no getting to him, and who would want to, besides? At the end of the day, he's a dying man."

She gave a little shake of the head. "But in your sphere, you're as talented and as accomplished as Cal is in his."

"Oh, my dear."

She scooted to the edge of the sofa. "Keep talking. I'm just going to heat up the soup," she said.

"Can't it wait a bit?"

She smiled, knowing what he meant. They had been in a hurry forever; no more. "Of course."

Twenty-one

When he grew up, Theo wasn't going to be like his parents. He wasn't going to be *stressed*. He wasn't going to work like a *maniac*. If he ate slowly, if he was always the last in class to raise his hand, if he acted pokey on the soccer field, preferring to track funny-shaped clouds rather than the ball, well, that was him. But if Theo didn't get up from the floor this minute and put on some clothes, his mother would have to come get him. She'd call his name ahead as she marched up the stairs, her lips pressed, her green eyes flecked with gold and brown. At the sight of her near-naked boy, she'd act all angry—then again, she might be amused. There was no telling which mother he'd get, for she was changeable, especially now, and Theo could only search for clues.

Angry, he decided, because that is what his five-year-old heart felt. Listening to the voices downstairs, he wondered, who was she talking to? To know, he'd have to move. He didn't care enough to move. Theo was a dawdler, Mrs. Winters said so, a dawdler. This criticism shamed Theo deeply and gave him one more reason to hate Mrs. Winters, who had a bad hip, and two very smart, grown-up boys, and four hairs—three black, one white—on the underside of her softy chin. If Mrs.

Winters were here, she'd have zero sympathy for a boy who refused to get himself dressed just because he didn't like the feel of his socks. But Mrs. Winters wasn't here now, was she? To mark that fact, Theo hurled his new socks across the room, landing one by the window and another by the bed.

As for his mother's eyes, they were different colors. Theo was the only one who knew. People looked at her and thought green but they were wrong. The left one was lighter, closer to gold. Theo had his father's eyes, dirt brown, no mystery there. In this, Willa was lucky—she got the green eyes. The thought of Willa, napping in her room down the hall, produced an avalanche of feeling inside the heart of Theo Pepper. His parents, he knew, worried that she might die, like Sylvie. Willa was like a lamp, Lena explained, whose wiring isn't quite right. So they kept hauling Willa to the hospital, and staying up all night with her, giving her medicine to keep her from the shakes. "If she goes that will be my breaking," Theo heard Lena confide to Vi. "If she doesn't, that may break me, too."

Thinking of Willa, Theo stuffed his entire drawer of socks, one by one, into the trash. Any minute his mother was going to come up and check on her little savage. Where was she? His heart delicious with fear, Theo roared his fire truck engine 79 into the baseboard, where it made a great satisfying smack. Lying back against the cold floor he noticed for the first time that the house was awfully quiet.

"Mama," he whimpered, quietly at first. " Mommy? . . . *Mommy!*"

"Cut that out," his father called. "Theo, if you want something, come down."

The shock of hearing his father's voice on a workday morning alarmed Theo. His father lived at the office, or on airplanes. At home, he mostly slept.

Theo stormed into the hall and boomed back, "Where's Mommy?"

"Stop shouting!" his father shouted. "Get dressed and come down."

When at last Theo appeared in the kitchen, Lena looked him over as if he'd just been discovered. "Hey, Big!" She beamed at her miracle boy, walking and talking all at the same time. "Come eat."

She was emptying the dishwasher while Charlie sat at the counter talking on his cell. He was talking to Swanson, Theo knew, because when it was Swanson, Charlie's accent sounded more Bostony.

Charlie hung up and put his hand like a mitt on top of Theo's head. "Hey, bud." Then he turned to Lena. "Sorry about that."

She was putting glasses into the cupboard. "What happened?"

"Cal. He's not in the office and no one at Rusch & Co. will take my call. We're this close to a deal and he goes AWOL."

"Could it be Ivy? Is she worse?"

Charlie shrugged. "Anyway, we're not talking about that. We're talking about us. It's all set. I've got the kids covered; Beverly and Glo are fired up to start Thursday. Three days, you and me. I just need to know: Do we go north or south?"

She looked him over as if he were an idiot: she'd never left Willa for more than several hours. "And the whole time you're not going to work?"

"Nope."

"No phone calls, emails, not even a text, sly dog?"

Charlie shook his head. "I'm putting a wall around it. Look, I'm putting up the wall. God knows, come Monday, we'll still be in crisis. But for these days it's just time alone with my lady."

Theo watched as his mother studied the man she'd married, trying to see him with fresh eyes. She didn't believe him. No one would. He had a rash on his left cheek. He hadn't slept, hadn't showered. Yet he was determined. He smiled, ignoring his cell vibrating in small, tight circles on the counter.

Lena heaved a stack of plates into the cupboard and sighed—a faraway sigh she'd been filling the house with lately. "You're nuts, Pepper."

"Yeah, I'm your nuts. And we're going," he said, the company man, the entrepreneur, who was not the man she'd married—ten minutes after the ceremony he was on to the next version of himself. Now all these years later, he was ten, twenty Charlies down the line, with wants and heartaches and compulsions neither of them could have imagined. He was so tired the vein above his right eye throbbed. And what wouldn't she give for him to make her laugh, for one word of surprise.

"South. Big Sur. The place with the cabins and the soaking tub. You'll love it," Charlie said.

Lena smiled despite herself. "Stop trying to sell me a robot."

"Just be ready, Mrs. Pepper. Fine Egyptian cotton sheets and no one to bother you all night, except me." Dispatched, Charlie typed a text as he headed for the living room.

"Mama?"

"Theo," Lena said, turning her beam onto him. "What the heck were you doing up there?"

As they approached the highway, the city disappearing behind them, Charlie made a show of turning off his cell and burying it deep in his pocket.

"Look, Pep," Lena said. "This is all very sweet, but really, if you can't do this, just tell me now. OK? All this fuss. It sort of raises a girl's expectations. And I'm, well, I'm too fragile."

"It's done, sweetheart." He grinned, shooting her the look that was goofy and sexy and just them. He put one hand on the wheel and one on her.

"But what if Swanny—?"

"Swanny isn't invited to *this* show. Come on, come on. Now it's your turn, baby."

"What is this, strip poker?"

"That's right. No work. No talking of children—even the cute, cute stories: banned. No bills, no doctors. One call a day home: that's all you get." He nodded knowingly. "Now give it up, Helena."

"What?"

He tipped his head. "You know."

She was wearing the necklace Theo made when she was first pregnant with the twins. It had a large blue bead etched with *Theo* and another with *Babies*. She took it from her neck, kissed it and stowed it in the glove compartment. Then she kicked off her shoes, hiked her skirt, and planted her bare feet high up on the dash. "All right. I'm unplugged."

"God, I love you unplugged."

"Yeah? How do you know?"

"You serious?"

Lena shrugged.

"I know," he said. "You know, too."

But they didn't know. That's why their hearts were churning faster than the car could fly down the road. They didn't know. Charlie reached into the backseat for the pouch of CDs and handed them to her. "What do we have for music?"

Lena flipped through. "You brought only boys."

"Not so fast. Keep going. I've got you covered. I've got your girls."

And he did. He had her Bonnie Raitt and Dixie Chicks and even the new one, Adele. But to make Charlie happy, Lena put on the Boss and cranked it. They settled in, and just to stay present, they held hands. But after a few songs they drifted to that other place: Charlie looking ahead, grinding his jaw, Lena gazing longingly out the side window.

They arrived late, with ten minutes to spare to pick up the keys before the owner left for the weekend.

"I'm starving," Lena confessed. Starving: that's what she was.

"Why don't I drop you," Charlie said. "You can get settled in the cabin and I'll pick up lunch at that little market."

She looked worried, even a bit panicked.

"What is it, babe?"

"I don't know. I . . . don't think we should be apart."

"Really? You that—?" He ran his hand down her thigh. "A half hour," he said. "I'll be quick."

If he knew what she was thinking, *who* she was thinking about all the time—well. She wanted to get in bed was all: to dive in, to close her eyes. But she was being silly. They had two whole days.

"No," she said. "I'll go. I'll be much faster."

The market was a little roadside place perched on the edge of the cliffs. Shopping put Lena into the spirit. She hadn't heard the name Mama and she hadn't raced down the hall to check on anyone in several hours.

Already she was feeling more relaxed. She chose finger food that would be fun to eat in bed—wine and cheese and salami and a baguette. She bought bars of chocolate and several bottles of wine. By the register, on a rack with maps and crossword puzzles, she spied a book of erotica.

"Looks like a nice weekend," said the woman at the register as she loaded the things into Lena's bag. She was deeply tanned, in her sixties, an old hippie, with thin, loosely pinned-up hair and multiple piercings.

"Oh, let's hope," Lena replied. They grinned, for didn't everyone have a story? Even now, with her phone stowed in the trunk, Lena sensed that Alessandro was calling. He called daily. Her old lover. Most of the time she didn't pick up, but that hardly mattered. He had made himself a bed in her brain. At night, lying next to Charlie, she thought of Alessandro's hands on her, his lips. But then Charlie would roll over and reach for her in his sleep, and there she'd be, both lonely and never alone—there in the real family bed, with its puppy-pile of sleepy husbands and old lovers and sorrow and lust and babies. Oh, for a little levity, a touch. At night, when she got up to tend to Willa, nursing her and clearing her lungs, Lena longed to be the one being flipped over and handled. If anyone could see her, sitting in the vaporized dark of Willa's room: tear-soaked cheeks, face flushed with amazement.

Down the cliff the sea banged the rocks. She carried the shopping bag to her car and thought, Here we go. She was putting the phone calls with Alessandro behind her. All her lusting. Charlie Pepper was going to get some of that.

Charlie honestly thought he had turned off the cell. But for the last hour of their drive, it'd been steadily vibrating in his pocket. Now that he was alone at the cottage with nothing to do, he decided he might as well have a look. Six messages. But when he tried to retrieve them, there was no reception.

The cabin, built on a ridge along Highway One, overlooked the ocean out front and the mountains in back. The mountains were the problem. Charlie carried the phone raised in his hand through the living room, kitchen, bath, and finally he headed out the front door, pausing on the stoop. No matter where he stood, the best he could get was one little bar of reception, then none, then two, then none. He paced the scruffy yard, glaring, holding the phone in front of him like a Geiger counter. The lawn was circled by a ring of oaks. He covered the grounds thoroughly—all the while keeping an ear tuned for the car. If he stood near the fence, in fact, if he leaned his ass *over* the fence while holding the phone at a right angle, he was able to muster two bars. It was enough to get through to voice mail, to hear Swanson shouting: *Sorry for calling, but Charlie, it's a shit storm.* Charlie dialed again; this time there was no signal at all.

The largest of the oaks, a coastal variety, with thin, crooked limbs and sparse, sharp leaves was before him. An inhospitable tree, if ever there was, dwarfed and battered by wind and storm but, nonetheless, the highest point nearby. Charlie pocketed the phone and climbed. The branches could hardly hold him. He made his way slowly, cursing the scratches he was collecting on his ankles and arms. Halfway up, he stopped and dug for the phone in his pocket. Three bars. Even so, he had to stand and, with the wind and all, shout.

I'll really surprise him, Lena decided, parking at the bottom of the hill, where the car couldn't be seen from the house. Laughing, snorting a bit, she climbed out and stripped off her clothes, down to her new black bra and thong. Then, catching her reflection in the window, she gave herself a serious going-over, front then side. Not half bad. Well. Not too bad. She sucked in her stomach then let it go. Oh Christ, let it go, she laughed at herself: forty-two years old and so horny she could hump a post.

She took off her shoes to make her legs look better. She'd tell Charlie now she was really unplugged. She doubted she'd have to say much.

The cottage, painted robin's-egg blue, had white trim and geraniums hanging in baskets on either side of the door. The door was unlocked, of course. Stepping inside, she called out to Charlie. When he didn't answer, she called again.

She hurried through the galley kitchen, then searched the bathroom with its large soaking tub, then on into the living room with its bay window facing the sea. In the bedroom, Lena approached the window that looked over the yard.

Charlie heard the slap of the door, and then Lena shouting.

From his vantage point up in the thorny branches, Lena resembled a bird-watcher at a nudist ranch. Her hand shaded her eyes.

"Oh my god," she cried. "You're up in a goddamn tree."

"I'm really not," he said.

She looked up with a flicker of hope. She looked up willing to see something different. She covered her mouth with her palm. It was her nature to want to believe him, even as her eyes told her otherwise.

But Charlie was in the tree all right. He was in the tree—as she was on the ground. What a picture they made: the middle-aged woman in a thong, the husband up in a tree, hunched back to the wind, talking on his cell. They were fools, she and Charlie, oh yes. She started to cry.

"Wait," he shouted, struggling as the branches whipped his face. "Damn. Damn! Not you. I don't mean you. Oh god, let me get *down,*" he mumbled, then louder, "Fuck! Fuckeroo! Lena, please, please don't cry."

She backed away several paces.

"Lena, talk to me!"

She shook her head.

"Lena!"

"One thing, Charlie Pepper." She held up a finger and waved it wildly. "Say one thing that's true or I'm—"

He had a hundred things to tell her—including the news from Swanson that Nimbus was officially bust; and for all this time away from Lena and the kids he had not a damn thing to show but empty pockets. That, and hope. That, and longing. That, and he had gotten himself bloody from the goddamn branches. But one true thing? No man stuck in a tree can honestly say he had that. If she could only wait a second, one second until he climbed down.

"Lena!"

But she was already running, heading for the driveway. I will not look back, she told herself.

Twenty-two

Alessandro didn't think much of marriage. In his view, marriage was a bourgeois arrangement that favored no one, certainly not the woman, and in which, sooner or later, everyone got tired. Boredom was anathema to Alessandro. Whenever his mind wandered in a meeting, he simply walked out. He dropped conversations at the point at which they cooled—the same for his affairs. Having no desire but desire, he was a most dangerous person.

But he understood some things very well. For example, he understood that when a woman arrives unexpectedly at your door, it's best not to talk too much. It's best not to act too surprised.

"San." Lena wasn't fool enough to think hurt was a justification. She'd left that along with her anger in the Saab. Crossing the threshold willingly, she entered Alessandro's world.

"*Allora*. Lift up your arms."

They did nothing so quaint as smile; they were matter-of-fact, inside the secret that had been waiting for them all these years.

Like a child, she tucked her chin and raised her arms above her head.

As he removed the next layer, the black lace camisole she'd been wearing as her private shroud, she began to weep. He ignored this. He unclasped the bra. "Ah," he said. She kept her eyes down and let him look. Having only recently stopped nursing, her breasts weren't what they had been. I should be embarrassed, she thought, but for now she was on the other side of humiliation.

Moreover, Alessandro wasn't about to let her be distracted. He had spent all those years acquiring knowledge for such an occasion. One particular book he'd discovered in, of all places, a gift shop inside a deluxe car wash in L.A. The book had been of greater use than perhaps any other volume in his library. It was a handbook, really, its subject being women's pleasure, with a particularly creative approach to female anatomy and to something the authors defined as "the cake," which for illustrative purposes was divided into four quadrants: the upper left quadrant being the inner cake.

He carried her to the bathtub. He laved hot water over her and, starting at her feet, moved up her legs, touching her artfully, almost there, then not, almost there, then not.

Lena rested her head back against the cool tub, and closing her eyes halfway, tried to remember, had it always been like this?

She looked at the side of Alessandro's head, older now, with a few lines. "San." She smiled. She'd always like that soft place where the ear met his cheek. He *was* her old friend. And now her old friend was touching her in a way that was altogether familiar yet new. She was being brought along. OK, she thought. She stopped looking at him and, closing her eyes, focused. First she let go of her face. Next she let go of the stretch marks on her breasts and at her hips, those silver fish, those snail tracks of childbearing. She let go of the gray hairs; let go of her hands, working hands; she let them go. He had always been the best, no question, but what was this new trick? She nodded to the women whose bodies had taught Alessandro. He was touching her in the most precise and perfect way, *good for them, thank you, girls*. She waited for the peak, anticipating it with a touch of regret, that it would be over, but it was followed by another and another, gentle and perfect, over and over—my god, there were scores of them—on and on and on. Lena laughed aloud.

She awoke to the smell of . . . rice? It was stunning, how relaxed she felt. Her life had moved on without her. Men in white overalls, competent and silent fellows, had come into the room of her life and carted it all away. She was in trouble, no question, but there would be time soon enough to worry about that.

She found Alessandro in his kitchen, slicing vegetables. Behind him, pots bubbled on the stove. *"Allora."* He grinned. "She rises."

From the doorway Lena smiled.

"You look much better," he said.

"San."

"Ah," he said, shrugging. "We both know I owe you."

"Come on, you can't owe someone *that*."

His gaze then was so keen—as happy as she was unhappy, as relieved of his loneliness as she was not.

"Ti voglio bene da sempre," he said. "An interesting phrase—*Ti voglio bene.* We say I love you, but literally it means I want well for you." He shrugged. *"Da sempre.* I always have."

He had such a nice face. Already she was missing it. She crossed the room and took that nice face in her hands, and kissed Alessandro's cheeks, his forehead, his ears, his mouth. What did people do with their lives but this. What more was there? He cupped her ass, lifting her, and as she wrapped her legs around him he carried her to the counter. He could have her here, and in the living room, and in the bedroom, or anywhere else he wanted. He could have that much.

The next morning, at dawn, the phone rang. It was April 14, the anniversary of the sinking of the *Titanic*. The Dow was plummeting. The price of oil had tumbled below fifty dollars a barrel.

Twenty-three

On the second day of his parents' absence, Theo, restless and lonely, realized that if adults could take flight, so could boys. The thought came to him shortly after lunch. He was in the main room at school, where the juice cups were being collected and the trash put in bins. The children stood on line to go to the roof and play. Mrs. Winters turned to Theo, who was particularly quiet as there was a song in his head just now, his lips moving, his eyes fixed dreamily on nothing. Mrs. Winters asked Theo if he wanted to be her messenger. It was an honor. No way could he say no. He had to go downstairs, find Mr. Henry, the janitor, and tell him the exact number of chairs needed for the audience at the Spring Sing.

Riding the elevator to the lobby, Theo found Mr. Henry in the supply closet, that secret place where children were forbidden to go. Yet they all knew about Mr. Henry's sanctuary, with its long workbench and a vise large enough for a child's head.

Theo stared long and hard at the vise. "Please, Mr. Henry, seventy-nine chairs."

"Seventy-nine!" gasped Mr. Henry, as if he'd never heard such a thing in his work-to-the-bone life. He leaned back in his creaky metal chair, the calendar just above his head with an X across all the days he had endured. Rolling his eyes and slapping his knee, Mr. Henry moaned, "Not eighty. Not a hundred. She's got to have seventy-break-my-back-nine."

Theo studied Mr. Henry's whiskery, dark face, and nodded.

"And she's gonna count 'em. What do you bet?"

Theo shrugged. This seemed a likely possibility.

Mr. Henry thought so, too. He went on speaking, a few curses thrown in, as Theo inched backward, toward the door.

As he retraced his steps to the elevator, Theo had the odd feeling that he was tethered by strings: one to Mr. Henry, another to Mrs. Winters, and still another to his parents, who were gone. Theo pulled a bit. The strings didn't stop him. He pulled a bit more, stepping to the far side of the lobby, where children absolutely were not allowed. Nothing bad happened. In fact, from this new angle Theo noticed a few things. The double doors leading to the courtyard were propped open, revealing a world of birches, flowers, wooden benches and a multi-spouting fountain. The Episcopal church next door shared the courtyard. Theo had never been allowed out there, though he'd seen the courtyard from the roof. A nice afternoon breeze was coming on. What could be the harm of looking? Theo stepped, he stepped again, and soon he was outside among the birches. He looked up to where the other kids were playing on the roof, their voices a kind of music carried on the wind. He looked over his shoulder then stuck a finger into the splash of the cold fountain. On the other side of the courtyard the church doors were open. What could be the harm? He stepped in there. The two-tiered nave was empty, though Theo didn't know it was a nave. He'd never been in a church before. Not once in his five confuddled years. Where was everybody? He walked up the central aisle to the altar, drawn by the array of shiny objects arranged on a high, narrow table.

The silent majesty of the church deeply impressed him. "Hello," he said, and *Hello* called back, filling his chest. The tall, brass candlesticks and thick candles loomed above him. The golden chalice, too. He put a finger to its shiny surface. Then he climbed the pulpit and, standing on tiptoe, managed to open the great book. He ran his finger along the lines of print.

The air in the nave seemed thick and slow. He coughed, just to hear how that sounded. He was reaching for something courageous and independent in himself, a solemn spark, something beyond being just an odd boy.

But Theo was expected by Mrs. Winters, and with a nod as if to an imagined great future, he hustled off stage. Instead of going back the way he came, he headed to the back of the church, to the heavy, wooden doors, and pushed. The wing of that heavy door flowing outward was nothing short of electrifying. Theo stepped outside. The door closed behind him, but he wasn't worried, even as he discovered that the door didn't have a handle and was flush to the wall. Theo tried the other doors, four in all, but they were locked. He went around to the entrance of the school, which, for security reasons, was also locked. He peered through the windows but no one was in sight.

The bell by the door rang in two places: the first being Mr. Henry's workroom, where the old man was banging chairs and couldn't hear him, and the second being Mrs. Winters's office. If Theo pressed the bell now, he would summon Mrs. Winters herself.

For the first time, Theo was on his own. He lingered for a moment, feeling it. His heart beat rabbity, there in the fullness of the sun. The air smelled of tar. They were putting on a new roof next door. Chinese fellows on top were shouting down to the Chinese men on the ground. Up went the bucket of hot tar fixed to a rope and pulley. Down came an empty pail. Why did it scare Theo? He didn't know. It was an inexact process—a single loop of the rope and the shaky pail went up, carrying that load of hot tar. Theo thought it unsafe. Especially as the men were talking, not paying full attention. What were they thinking? Fooling around that way. He was certain the pail would fall. He covered his face with his hands, imagining the men's cries as the hot tar hit them. The bucket went up, and Theo could see plainly it wasn't right. Up top, a man shouted.

Theo ran. But not before pressing the bell at the front of the school. He dashed along Fillmore, in the general direction of home. At Union Street, at the bottom of the hill, he turned right when he ought to have gone left, but by a lucky coincidence the turn delivered him to the door of Union Street Toys.

He didn't have the heart for shopping, but he went inside just the same and, finding a dark corner by the stuffed animals, hid. No one noticed him. There weren't a lot of people in the store at that hour, just a couple of mothers with babies, perusing the aisle of infant toys. Theo regained himself. He wiped his face. Walking with a slight tip forward, a version of his father's gait, he addressed the airplane section with the seriousness of someone who knew the world. Soon he moved to the bins of magnets. He studied the LEGO kits, comparing the size of each box and the price. He looked so busy, so industrious, the adults assumed he belonged to someone.

And he did. Theo belonged to himself.

He went outside. The great world, with its cars and pigeons and recycling bins, took him up. Theo headed north to the library, smiling a private smile, feeling very good about himself. Independent life was as he thought: heart-racing, a swing of the legs, a lark.

Inside the library, he directed his search among the reference books in the children's section and for once there was no one hurrying him along. "Is your mother here?" the children's librarian asked. Theo pointed to the other room and without a moment's hesitation said, "She's over by Fiction."

Meanwhile, an ambulance had been called for the seriously injured workers next door to the school. The commotion disrupted recess and art period, and afternoon pickup was thrown off. Theo's disappearance went unnoticed until Glo and Beverly rolled down the sidewalk with Willa in the stroller. Theo Pepper could not be found.

He was not on line or in the boy's room. He was not in any of the usual places, or hiding in a closet or cupboard. Mrs. Winters scouted the area herself—in front of the school and in the play yard and on the roof; throughout the building she shouted for Theo.

"He's flown the coop, that's what," Beverly said, knitting her mouth.

"Impossible," replied Mrs. Winters, though she was already dialing the police.

Beverly turned the stroller and headed down the sidewalk with Glo. "Where would he go?" she asked.

Meanwhile Theo was finishing his tour of the library. On his way out the doors, he gathered several brochures and studied them carefully as he ambled along the sidewalk. One brochure detailed the capital campaign on behalf of the library's renovation. It had 3-D graphics. The library was going modern. Theo had the brochure open large as a kite as he crossed Laguna Street. He never saw the bicyclist shooting down the steep hill. Theo was lucky to break only an arm.

Later that afternoon, Lena pulled into her own driveway and sat with the motor turned off. She'd been gone only a day and a half, but she knew it would feel to the kids like it felt to her: before and after. The moment her key touched the lock, Theo would come running, his face full of exquisite joy and want. And questions. She wondered if Charlie was back, and if he would ask her directly, hoping she'd been at Violet's, or Jesse's. And knowing otherwise.

Later he'd say, What have you done? A shudder went through her. Lena, what have you done?

But the house was empty. On the kitchen counter a note in Charlie's hand had been tucked under a glass. *Hospital*. There it was: Willa was dead. That would be Lena's punishment. She tried Charlie's cell, to hear him say it, to get it over with—the ending she'd been waiting for.

He wasn't answering his phone. She cursed him and then she remembered: cell service was spotty inside the thick walls of California Pacific Medical Center.

She found them in the dingy nook of the ER waiting room, under the blasting TV. Charlie had Willa in his lap. There was blood on his sweater, but Willa, propped against him holding a doll, looked fine.

"It's Theo," Charlie called across the room as she came toward them. "He broke his arm. They're setting the bone and then they'll call us."

"Oh, god, I thought—"

"I know." Charlie glanced at Willa, his whole face softening. "Aside from the scare, I think Theo's pleased with himself. He's proven he's a kid after all." Charlie talked on, in a tone approximating conversation, but he couldn't bring himself to look at Lena.

Overhead, the TV blared news of another day of world economic crisis. "There it goes," Charlie said. "There it goes."

They brought Theo home and put him on the sofa to rest. Soon after, Charlie left the house and was gone for hours. Lena didn't know what to do but cook. She roasted a chicken with potatoes and artichokes and beets, all the while trying to think of what next, but there was no next. She put a pot of cannellini beans to soak. There were some apples in a bowl and she peeled them for a pie. As long as she cooked, her hands were steady and her mind occupied. She fed Theo early on the sofa; she cut up the chicken and vegetables and had a picnic with Willa on the floor beside Theo. Then Lena noticed the time and took the kids upstairs. She nebulized Willa, gave Theo a Vicodin and sang them songs until each fell into a heavy sleep.

The phone rang, but she didn't answer it. She washed pots and pans and wiped down the table and the counters. As she was leaving the kitchen she realized she hadn't eaten all day. She opened the refrigerator and stared at the bowls and sealed containers she'd put there. She closed the fridge and went upstairs.

While Lena was taking a bath, Charlie came home. She heard him downstairs in the kitchen, the tines of his fork tapping his plate, worry making each movement slow.

He cleared his dishes. He took a fresh glass from the cabinet and the last of Swanson's New Year's tequila, along with a few limes and a knife, into the living room.

The world had changed, and while he tried it on, he was going to drink. He was supposed to be on holiday. He had no surgeries and he wasn't on call. Come Monday he would lay off ten more employees. Soon they would all be gone, and only Charlie and Swanson and a couple of fancy desks would remain, and those they'd sell, too.

Charlie took the lime between his teeth and drank. It turned out he didn't need the lime. Ditto the ice. Finally, he didn't need the booze. He didn't need anything to cut the bitterness inside him.

When he heard Lena coming down the stairs, he called to her. She appeared in the doorway dressed in sweats, her hair wet, no makeup—looking the way he liked her best. *Another man*—it was a thought he couldn't finish. He was disgusted. He supposed he didn't love her anymore. Ah, what a load of bull, he thought, mocking himself. He'd love her until he died.

"So, Lena, have you found grace?"

She stared at him intently and he had the sudden feeling he was no match for her. Then Lena said the last thing Charlie expected. "What happened at Nimbus?"

He wanted to reply spitefully, but she was looking at him with such seriousness that he gave up and told her about Cal. How it wasn't the lawsuit but cancer that decided things. How Ivy and Cal's bad luck had become his and Lena's.

"Oh, Charlie, what a rotten turn. I'm so sorry."

"Yeah." He laughed bitterly. "Me, too. I'm as sorry as I can be." He studied his glass. "So, obviously, that's why I had to take the call. If you knew, maybe you wouldn't have run off so fast."

"You're wrong about that," she said, not proud, but there it was.

"Ah." He nodded.

For a time they were quiet, lost in their mutual but distinct agony. Then, Lena, thinking of Cal and Ivy, said, "My god. That they would both be dying? The synchronicity." She weighed it, curious and sad, trying to make sense of the mysteries.

He had always enjoyed that part of her, but it did nothing for him now.

He saw her struggling to understand their lives and what a wasted effort that was. Cal and Ivy, all of it. He realized that since hearing the news, he hadn't thought of Cal and Ivy in terms of Lena, only in terms of Nimbus.

He took a drink just to busy his hands. "Why did you marry me?"

She squinted toward the kitchen. "I don't know."

"Yes, you do. You know everything."

"Because you weren't anyone else."

"Not him."

"Not any of them."

The pain on Charlie's face made him more interesting, more present to her than he had been in a year. "Because you were good, smart. Steady. Loving. Kind."

"Stop, for crying out loud!" Charlie held up his hands. "You make it sound like you were choosing . . . an old Volvo."

Just then a thin human cry came from somewhere nearby.

"Shh. Was that Theo?"

"No. It came from outside."

"Are you sure? God, listen to that—" The cry was piercing.

"Is it a . . . cat?"

Outside, a woman called, "Leoni! Come, Leoni!" Then a door slammed and the night was quiet.

They didn't move for a moment, their faces lit with the communion of all the nights spent listening for their children's cries.

"Sorry," Lena said softly. "I didn't mean an old Volvo."

"Yes, you did." He wagged his finger at her. "That's the thing about you. You always *mean* it." Charlie poured himself another glass and looked at it. "Well, I guess I made it easy for you to rationalize—"

"Rationalize? Charlie, I don't need to rationalize."

"Oh, no?"

"*Lonely*. Humans, Charlie, we get *lonely*. We break down. We get sick with worry and not sleeping and fucking up—of being unsure we can handle what's next, when what's next is the thing we fear most. We get tired of holding on. And then we want to laugh. We want to laugh. How stupid is that? Do you have a robot to excise that one? Do you? I'd like to see it."

"All right." Charlie sat up. "Tell me, if sadness were a gun, Lena, how many times this past year do you think you've shot me? Huh? How many times." He made a pistol of his hand and pointed it at her.

"If I could find you," she said.

"Oh, you found me, you found me," Charlie said. He looked around the room for proof, everywhere but at her. "You and I . . . we've been places so fine—no one knows." Charlie glanced at Lena and seeing he had her full attention, he said, "I was wrong to make you hold to a bargain. Knowing you, I was wrong. And I was wrong to leave you alone. But is it unforgivable? Maybe. And if it is, if it's my sorry-ass luck to lose us, Lena, it wasn't from lack of love."

"I know."

"I'm the guy." He shook his glass, so the tequila sloshed onto the arm of the chair. "*I'm the guy.* And this is your house—damn you—your house, with your boring, tired failure of a capitalist, and upstairs those two non-perfect children, and you, least perfect of all. Oh, for chrissakes, Lena, grow up." And with that Charlie drained his tequila and hurled his glass against the wall.

Lena turned on him with a look of womanly assessment that contained every minute she'd been alive and every minute she'd been with him. She went into the kitchen and got the broom.

"Leave it," he said.

She nodded and kept on sweeping. Their kind of love wouldn't just end. It was harder to break than that. They'd acted unpardonably, self-ishly, and, in her case, shabbily, and the world didn't stop and they didn't kill each other and, as yet, they didn't quit. Their punishment was worse. They would go on. There was a teacher conference to attend, Willa's ther-apist appointments, an orientation at Theo's new school come May, client meetings, patients. But looking into each other's faces and seeing no love or desire, how were they going to manage that?

Charlie climbed to his feet and went upstairs to check on Theo, who was moaning in his sleep, his arm in its cast hugged to his ribs. The Vicodin had dropped him into a deep, noisy, twitchy slumber. Charlie sat on the side of the bed and smoothed Theo's forehead and watched him breathe. On the bedside table, there was a small pad where, each night, Lena wrote words for Theo to find in the morning. *May. Play. Hay. Stay.* At the bottom, she'd left a lipstick kiss.

Charlie went to their room and packed a bag. He lumbered down-stairs to the basement, and unearthed a sleeping bag and backpack and took them to the front door.

"One question," he said. "Is it him you want?"

She looked at Charlie, her face blotchy, tears fresh on her cheeks. She turned away.

"What, then?"

Even now, after she'd decided that she no longer loved Charlie, had never really loved him, she saw that he had his sweater on backward. She'd noticed it in the hospital that afternoon, a lifetime ago. Even now she wanted to help him with it, so much her fingers itched.

Lena wrapped her arms around herself.

"You want to be young," Charlie said, mocking her. "You want to be fancy-free. You want to forget."

"Yes, Charlie. To forget. That's it," she said, her voice heavy with despair.

He raised his fists skyward. "What, then? *What?*"

Within the hour, Charlie was gone. Lena checked on Willa and then she went to Theo's room and sat at the foot of his bed and held his feet. When Theo woke moaning again, she gave him another Vicodin and some applesauce. Soon it was morning. Charlie had left money, as he always did at the start of a trip, on the dresser by the cup with Lena's rings.

Talk

Twenty-four

At that moment in a case when things turned south—the patient's pressure started falling, or the disease proved more widespread than the initial scans indicated, Charlie pressed on. Indecision or failure of confidence weren't options for a surgeon, and Charlie had suffered those palsies only once—just after the twins' birth. He'd put himself on leave then, for a month. Meanwhile, the bills grew staggering and Nimbus threatened to falter. So, unhealed, Charlie went back. If redemption could be found in work, Charlie worked. He pressed on.

Now, with Lena's words haunting him—what she said and did not say—Charlie drove north, grinding his teeth, across the Golden Gate.

He went as far as Mount Tam, parked in a pull-out, stowed his cell phone in the glove box and waited for the sun to rise. At first light, he set out on a narrow trail. The air refreshed him. The walking, the steady movement uphill and down, calmed his mind. He walked ten miles, energized by rage. When that lessened, his drumming steps echoed the bitterness of his grief. He blamed himself. He should never, *ever*, have entertained Cal's offer. Everything had come from that. He'd lost her;

he'd lost them. Losing the company would be a distant third. He was sick to the bottom of his soul.

He followed one trail then switched to another—anything so as not to be linear. He worked the lines by not working them and in this manner willy-nilly he went. Where the space opened out, he walked through the high grass. He decided that if the fog rolled in, he'd take it as a sign and turn back. But the skies were brilliant.

He camped out that night, and the next one as well. By this time he'd walked up and down the mountain at least half a dozen times. He kept going until he had decided a few things.

As he drove toward the city, Charlie made some calls. He checked into an inn, showered, then stepped to the mirror to shave. There reflected in the glass he found a forty-seven-year-old man with the face of deter-mination. He had a three-day-old beard and, on his waist, demi-handles of middle-aged pooch. With a couple more years like the last one, he'd resemble the teapot men of his father's generation, done even before they retired, with their round bellies covering their belts. His hair, like a shamed army, had retreated; his nose, Theo recently reminded him, was growing larger. He had good bones, OK teeth and dark rings under his eyes. Charlie put down the razor and called room service. While camping, he hardly ate. Now he devoured a salad, steak and fries, and a large piece of chocolate cake. He washed them down with a decent red. Then he slept for ten hours.

In the morning, he drove up the hill past his own street and at the top he turned west onto Broadway. He had an appointment to see an old man.

Paco had warned Dahlia about her humming. She'd been warned about her sloppiness, too. Likewise her tight uniform, which only accentuated her rather ample "pumpkin." She'd been warned but still she couldn't help herself. She ate and hummed. Her new boyfriend, Jorge, was the rea-son for today's song. He was very sweet, Jorge. And if his toothache didn't cost too much (he had an appointment with the dentist that morning), he was going to take her dancing after she got off work. Thinking of Jorge,

Dahlia forgot where she was going with the fresh towels stacked high in her arms. She missed the door to the bathroom and instead walked into the master bedroom, where she found Mister standing in the arch of the window, naked to Dahlia and the rest of the world.

Dahlia immediately backed up. Her heart roaring, Dahlia turned sharply around and tiptoed into the bathroom, the rubber soles of her shoes making the tiniest of squeaks. With shaking hands, she opened the warming drawer, and stuffed the towels in. But the thought of Mr. Rusch's skinny legs and his *pene*—three sticks—well, she couldn't help herself; she started to laugh.

"Dahlia."

She covered her face with a towel. *Dios mío,* she begged.

"Dahlia!"

"I am putting the towels, Mr. Rusch!"

She waited for him to say more. When he failed to answer she had no choice but to return to the room. Please, please, she prayed, don't fire me and please don't make me look at that face. The *pene* was one thing—what man didn't have one?—but the face was something else. It wasn't that she didn't feel compassion for a dying man, but ever since the boss's surgery, his scarred and seeping head gave her nightmares.

He was sitting in his chair now, looking out the window as before, but at least he'd put on his robe. And then, perhaps out of modesty or in an effort not to scare her, he'd turned the other way.

"Where is Paco? Where is Raoul?" he asked.

On the surface, these questions seemed simple enough. But with Señor Rusch nothing was ever simple. Everything was *una tita pregunta.* He knew, as well as Dahlia, that the doctor said no more massages until Señor Rusch's face healed from the surgery and radiation.

"I am no certain," Dahlia hemmed, nervously tugging the rings from her fingers.

"Was that you singing?"

"I don't know. I—"

"And what are you so happy about, eh, Dahlia? Did you find coins in the bottom of the hamper again? Or do you know something?"

Downstairs, locked behind the gate, the dogs began to bark.

"Ah," Dahlia said, backing up slowly. "You have a visitor."

All his life Cal had been longing for silence. He built one enterprise after another—his family, his partnership and countless companies—while wishing to be left alone.

Then, in the witch of things, cancer gave him exactly what he wanted. He spent his days alone in his room. He was scarcely able to speak for the pain in his jaw; he could hardly hear for the cancer that had swollen his glands and ear canal; and he could hardly see, what with one eye swollen and the other rheumy with fluid.

They'd gone in to cut out the tumor and found all hell underneath. They removed the tumor and part of his skull, from the midline of his forehead to above the ear. To cover the wound, a skin graft was taken from his leg. The pain in his jaw and leg was tremendous. The roar in his ear was the cancer—himself crunching on himself.

But that wasn't the worst part. They'd begun to burn his face raw. When he wasn't at the hospital for radiation treatments, he had to wear a contraption called a sponge-vac. The idea was to bring the nerves back to life so the skin graft would take hold. Day and night, the sponge-vac, fitted to his face like a skin, went about its sucking torture.

Paco showed Charlie into the bedroom and brought the tea.

"Ah, what a sight is me, eh, Charlie." Cal's shoulders shook to approximate a laugh. "Come on. I'm dying and you're pissed. We make quite the pair. But then this isn't a sympathy call, is it?"

"No, it isn't." Charlie sat by the window on the long curved sofa, with a view past Cal of the northern tip of the city and the windy bay.

Cal huffed, "Yeah, let's say we've got two concerns here. Yours and mine. Mine, we know is . . . ah, grave? Ha, it's a mess. Let's indulge me by starting there." He gestured at a stack of binders on the table beside him. They contained Cal's records and pathology reports and the coordinated efforts of doctors on both coasts. There was a binder from a Spanish group who was doing enzyme research on advanced brain cancer patients in Calcutta. "Want to have a look, Doc, and see if there's something worth shouting about?"

"That's all right," Charlie said, preferring to take his clues directly. He studied Cal's masked face and his first thought was: a hooded falcon. Then, looking deeper, Charlie saw the man, who, at the end of the day, was just a man, fighting even in his last days. Charlie's natural sympathy returned to him. "Weisman's team is top-notch. I wouldn't argue with what they're doing. But, Cal, they're treating you very aggressively when the prognosis is . . . grim. I'm sorry, but that's a fact. A month longer is a month of extreme pain. So I would ask, how far do you plan to go with these extreme measures?"

"As far as I can," Cal replied. "Wouldn't you, Doc?"

Charlie paused, the irony playing across his face. "Would I go so far as to have no quality of life? No, I wouldn't." Charlie rubbed his new beard. He'd dropped some weight while hiking; there were hollows in his cheeks, yet his eyes were clear. "I say that, but I'll admit it's a recent shift in my thinking."

"Ah," Cal said. "You've had an epiphany. God help us all." He wet what was left of his lips. "Look, Charlie, you awoke the giant."

"No, Cal. We did."

Cal ignored this. "Yes, yes, it was bound to happen. Midas saw you upstarts getting too close. Though to claim that you are violating the integrity of the market—it's a ballsy line Midas is taking. Frankly, I'm surprised they came up with it."

"I don't think they did," Charlie said. "Not on their own."

"Who then?"

"You know as well as I do that Alessandro works with them."

Cal closed his eyes. "You're wrong there, Charlie. Sandro's many things, but he's straight up when it comes to business. He's been on the phone all week working the angles for you."

"I'll bet," Charlie said bitterly.

Cal pressed on. "I'll tell you how it's gonna look, Doc. Soon Midas will call with an offer. Their lawyer will whisper something in your lawyer's ear. Make sure you listen. Selling is the only way out."

"Sell to Midas? Never."

"Ah, pride. Where does it end? I've been thinking of my own pride, and I can say the one good thing about dying is that when at last I go to hell I will no longer have to see the faces of all those nice folks who wished to send me there." With the tips of his fingers, Cal touched his mask, trying to relieve the pressure. "Look, Charlie, I'm not so deep in my own stuff that I don't know I let you down. I've thought around it a hundred ways. I don't see but one way out. Sell. Do what you have to do."

"No," Charlie corrected. "Nimbus is the same company it was a month ago, when you agreed, when you gave your word, to fund it. I'm here to remind you of that understanding. We need eight months. That's eight million instead of the twenty you've promised. That's nothing to a man whose immortality hinges on the hope that his vision will outlive him. I can get Mass General to beta-test the robot, and at that point, if Midas buys us, they'll have to pay real money."

"You're inexperienced at playing the hard-ass, son," Cal said quietly. "And don't think you can talk to them as you talk to me. You'll end up looking weak." Once again, Cal touched his face, cringing at the pain. "Ah, Charlie. Come on. What if you don't meet the mark? Six months? Eight months? It's a minute. The litigation alone will chew up the next year. Nah. Sell to them. It's the clean break. They'll offer you ten mil—which, knowing you, you'll take as an insult and want to piss all over. Do not. I say, Do not. Look at ten as a place to start. Listen up. Don't negotiate with your feely parts."

Charlie stood. He'd had enough. "Earlier you asked how far I'd go. If I were you, Cal, I'd give some thought to what comes next. And I'd be damn sure I was clean this time around. If not for your own peace, in hell or otherwise, then for your daughter. For Lena."

"Sweet Jesus!" Cal could not have been more surprised. He sputtered and then finally asked, just the hint of relief in the asking, "Does she know?"

"No," Charlie said drily. "I hadn't figured it out myself until a day ago. Actually, I wasn't sure until just now."

"Yeah? What was it?"

"You, Cal," Charlie replied. "Like you, and only you, Lena negotiates with her feely parts."

Charlie left the Rusch house immediately and drove south to Buck's where he met Swanson, who hadn't heard a peep from Charlie in days. Charlie told his friend everything about his tête-à-tête with Cal (everything except the part concerning Lena, which he kept private).

"And then?" Swanson asked. "What did Mr. Visionary say?"

"Nada," Charlie replied.

"Nada?"

"I left him sitting on high in the window of his bedroom, the world laid at his feet."

"That may have been the ultimate boner move, my friend." Swanson held up his empty mug so the waitress would know to bring the pot. Recently he'd spent so much time in the lab that every moment on the outside felt illicit and nothing short of a miracle. But Swanson's pacing was off. The waitress was pouring the coffee at the same time he added milk, making a mess of things. He beamed sheepishly. "Crying out loud."

Charlie took a call on his cell. As he talked, Swanson ate all of his fruit salad and then moved on to Charlie's chocolate croissant.

Charlie put his hand protectively on the remainder of the croissant while into the phone he barked, "Say it again," then handed the phone to Swanson.

It was Friedman, their lawyer. Midas had called with a "peace feeler," a lowball offer to buy Nimbus, just as Cal said they would. They were offering ten million for the company, providing that Swanson agreed to stay on as chief technical officer. They offered Charlie a one-year contract with a modest stipend, as medical consultant.

Swanson closed the phone and studied his empty plate.

"Medical consultant," Charlie said. "They really loaded the dagger there." He said it so Swanson knew there would be no weirdness between them.

"It's a fucking insult, is what it is," Swanson replied, slamming his hand on the table. "A man builds a company and this is his thanks. On the other hand, by the way, you look like shit. If they could see you, Cap, with this Paul Bunyan thing you got going, they might think a year with you is too damn long. Lousy bastards."

Charlie shrugged. "Ah, Swan, we almost made it."

"What's this? You giving up? Come on. You heard the old man: this offer is just the preamble."

"You know, Lee, when someone decides not to play by the rules we always thought should be givens—I mean a certain degree of fairness— well, the whole system buckles; it sinks to its knees. And, inevitably, that person wins."

"I don't believe that, Charlie," said Swanson. "And by the way, neither do you."

"I'm not so sure."

"Well, I'll be sure for the two of us, till you come around." Swanson winced as he drank his coffee. "Damn, Charlie, I think I'm getting an ulcer. Should I add more milk?"

"How many cups of coffee? Start there." Charlie checked his watch. The lawyers on both sides were due to meet at Midas's headquarters in a couple of hours. Midas wouldn't expect an answer so soon, but they'd certainly managed to skew the conversation.

"Hey," Swanson said. "I told the guys in the lab I'd be back by eleven. I better run."

Charlie tossed some bills on the table. "I've got a better idea. Come take a ride with me."

Midas's offices were based north of San Diego, in Carlsbad. Charlie and Swanson hopped on a Southwest flight and arrived at the company's door a few minutes before the meeting with the lawyers started.

Sam Friedman, Nimbus's lawyer, met them at the elevator. "If only I had a muzzle," he said by way of greeting. "Charlie, don't go in there."

"And why not," said Charlie. "Where's Tisen?"

Friedman shook his head. He liked Charlie, but he believed a lawyer ought to lawyer and a doctor ought to doctor and that didn't make either of them the right guy to be running a start-up. "He's doing what guys with successful companies do, Charlie. He's letting the lawyers duke it out, while he gets on with business. You should try it."

Charlie kept moving. He was a surgeon and what he knew was to take action by examining the wound. As he entered the conference room with Swanson and Friedman close behind him, the other lawyers stood in surprise and then there was a scramble to find chairs.

"No worries," Charlie said. "We'll stand." It occurred to him that he hadn't felt quite so free in a long time. Then his phone rang. Charlie held up a finger and answered it while the room observed him. "You have a hell of a nerve," he said sharply. And then Charlie left the meeting.

It was Corsini on the line. They didn't speak long. As Charlie listened to what Alessandro had to say, Tisen, Midas's CEO, came out of his office into the hall. Tisen, a Nordic fellow, favored a uniform of pressed shirts and khakis. He was the sort of a man who liked things kept in tidy rows. Charlie knew the type. For a deal to happen, Tisen would have to believe he was the lead dog. Charlie hung up and suggested they take a walk. Within the hour, Charlie and Swanson were back in the car, heading to the airport.

"Thirty mil?" cried Swanson. "Sweet Jesus, where did you get that figure? And what now?"

"They will give it a think." Charlie laughed. "They will give it a good, hard think."

Swanson glanced out the window. He had never liked San Diego, but it was growing on him. "So who was that on the phone?"

For a moment Charlie was silent, the contradictions very much alive in him. "Alessandro Corsini," he said, almost wistfully.

"Get outta town."

"What an accent that guy's got."

"An accent."

"Yeah. He told me to forget about the prototype and start the negotiations at twenty mil. He said it was all about the software—they need it badly, it turns out. And it would be a whole lot cheaper to buy us than develop it. We got there first and they know it."

"Damn straight," Swanson chimed.

"He said he got that from one of his guys, a Jimmy Sachs, who got it from Tisen's number two. I figured the Italian was lying, twisting me, you know, and then, Swanny, he said something interesting. An Italian phrase. I had him repeat it, so I could write it down. Here." Charlie fished in his jacket pocket for a crumpled scrap of paper. He handed it to Swanson.

"Jesus, I can't read this scratch," Swanson said.

"Yes you can—*Tanto soldi*—"

"Yeah, yeah. *Tanto soldi quanto insulto,*" Swanson said. "What the hell is that?"

"Basically, it translates to 'Add as much money as insult.'" Charlie grinned. "And then we got off the phone."

Delighted, Swanson looked out the window. "So, you, ah, added the insult."

"Part of the insult," Charlie corrected.

Twenty-five

It shouldn't be difficult—that was the phrase Alessandro told himself at the start of a difficult task. It shouldn't be difficult, he said—the way a conjurer invokes "hocus-pocus," or a storyteller starts with "once upon a time"—if only to clear the path ahead and summon the gods. Until now, Alessandro's methods worked brilliantly. But spring had turned to summer and things were only getting worse for Alessandro. Any day he expected happiness to turn up again at his door, but happiness was keeping her distance.

On Sand Hill Road the venture business was in worse shape. And taking sides with Cal didn't win Alessandro any love from the other partners. They loaded his calendar with meetings, endless meetings, with nervous, strung-out entrepreneurs who wanted reassurance and guidance and, more than anything, money. But money was the one thing Rusch & Co. wasn't giving. And with Greg Bettor in control, Alessandro's patience was tested hour to hour.

And then, of course, there was the problem of Lena. He hadn't seen her since their night together, months ago, and she was avoiding his calls. What was she up to? Her attitude chafed Alessandro, particularly as it hinted he might end up with much less than he deserved. As for other women, Alessandro broke up with his girlfriend and saw no reason to replace her. He just didn't have the interest.

Meanwhile, Alessandro decided to launch a new program of seriousness, to counter his loneliness with good deeds. He helped Charlie, knowing from Lena's cryptic emails that husband and wife were living apart, at least for the summer. And on this news alone, Alessandro based his hope.

While waiting, often in the morning before work, Alessandro drove to the city to sit with Cal. Alessandro would read the newspaper aloud, now that the old man couldn't, or he would tell him the latest doings in Silicon Valley, or air his complaints about the partners and the deals Greg was nixing at Rusch & Co.

One day, as Alessandro was reading a bit from the business section of the *Times,* Cal interrupted him. "Enough, Sandro. What else have you got going?"

"Ah, Cal. It's been quiet."

"Really?" Cal's voice was barely a scratch. He coughed. "You will find . . . a man in my position has time only for what's real. Humor me?"

"Of course." Alessandro leaned forward in his chair to show he was an open book.

"Good. Because I'm wondering about this other deal of yours. You know, the one where you're talking sweethearts to Lena but helping out her old man? How does that go?"

Alessandro could not have been more shocked, and on his face he had the crooked smiled of someone guilty but also a bit relieved to be found out. "Ah, Cal—"

"No blame, Sandro! Quite the contrary. I'm interested in knowing how the new thinking comes. It's with new thinking that new deals get made, yes? Humor me. Let me see if I can string this one *solo mio.* You've been saying to yourself, on the one hand, I've got work. And on the other, love. The one hand doesn't fight the other, though they happen to be part of the same guy. And therefore I can't possibly be a shit because I work with the husband—hey, I help the guy—and, well, I also happen to be in love with his wife." Cal leaned back his head. "Am I getting warm?"

"It's not like that . . . it's not cynical at all!" Alessandro cut the air in front of him to emphasize his point.

"Stop," Cal said. "I'm hardly the one to judge. Thing is, I invented that deal, Sandro. It should be in the dictionary under my name. Different players. Different story. Still, the *definition* of a shit."

Alessandro's voice rose with passion. "He ignored her! A woman like that. I would never, ever ignore."

"Of course he did," Cal replied. "He screwed up ten ways." Cal pressed his temples with his fingertips and winced. "Ay, you cannot imagine this vise. Sandro, on the table, the bottle of pills."

Alessandro handed Cal his pills and the glass of water by the bed. Cal drank, gulping loudly, the water dripping from his chin. He fell back into the pillows, exhausted. He was quiet for some time. "In the end, eh, Sandro? The classy move is to leave her alone."

Alessandro didn't agree. His feelings wouldn't allow it. But as the weeks passed he began to think he was looking foolish, at least to himself. Finally, Lena called and asked him to lunch. She chose a restaurant in, of all places, San Bruno and made the reservation late, so the room would be empty. She arrived first and took a table in back.

As he approached her, he could see she was wearing a high-necked blouse. He smiled, thinking of how they'd play off that primness, but when he kissed her, she hardly kissed him back. They talked of small things, ordered quickly, and when her food came she didn't touch it.

"San," she said.

"What is it, *cara*?"

Her hair was dark and her skin incredibly white, and just as he was thinking that he loved her as much as he'd always loved her, it came to him that he shouldn't.

"How could we not do this?" she asked, her face open and vulnerable—his again. "You are so—" she stopped herself from saying more. "And it kills me that it will be for some other girl."

"You are the girl," he said, only a little more worried and wanting very

251

much to stop her silly hand from fingering the tablecloth. Finally, after some inward struggle, he put his hand on hers. "You are the girl."

But even as he said this, it was obvious to him that she was not *his* girl. She and Charlie had been separated for weeks yet she hadn't called. Why was that?

As if hearing his thoughts, Lena took back her hand to finger the creases in the tablecloth. "I've been thinking, San. My god, all I've been doing is working, getting the kids around, and thinking. It's been awhile now."

"Since we were together."

"Since I was with either of you," she said. And pulling the hair back from her face, she studied him with an even gaze. "San, what the heck are we doing?"

"What we're compelled to do. Look, it is as much a surprise to me, that I would feel this way now. But how can you fight life? You shouldn't."

She frowned. "It's got to be more than that—more than impulse."

"Impulse is good enough for me."

"Is it?" Her eyes read his and then she shook her head. "Grace, San. When I think about the moments of grace, there's the two of us—back there, at the beginning, when we were so damn young. And since then—I know you don't want to hear this—but all the places with Charlie. San, look at me. The night Theo was born, holding him, like this, here, on my chest, while he slept. And Willa, once they let me. I'd waited forever, it seemed— weeks. I held her all night, as I had her brother, and the next night, and the next. They come out of you, and it is only when you are touching, skin to skin, that you feel whole. You feel as if you've found your purpose. I didn't expect that." She paused, laughing at herself in a new, detached manner. "I thought we were supposed to invent the world . . . but no."

"I thought," Alessandro said, "at least it felt to me . . . like we invented something, no?" But as soon as he said this, he realized he was talking in the past.

She bit her lip, hearing it, too.

"*Cara.*"

"You and I, we're magic, San. Lovely magic we keep alive, like a secret in our minds. We'll always be our young, bright, fuckable selves—"

"Elena!" He scooted his chair closer to her. "You've got to believe me. I'm not interested in a fantasy." He gripped her arm to prove it.

Lena smiled, more sure and more distant. She was ahead of him only in that she was less afraid. "One night before the twins were born, Theo said to me, 'Mama, you say that you love me with your whole heart, but when the babies are born you'll love them, too, and then there'll only be half your heart for me.' And I said, 'Theo, that's not how it works. My heart has many rooms. One room is yours and yours alone. No one else's. It can only grow larger. It has all the things we've ever done and said and my wishes for you and all the little things about you I love. When the babies are born, my heart will make two more rooms.' "

Coming to the restaurant, she'd wavered, but talking this way, about the kids, firmed her resolve. As she talked, she realized she was missing Charlie, who had gone first to Mbarara—as far away as he could go—and was now staying with Swanson, visiting the kids on the weekends. It was still too raw for Charlie and Lena to talk—and for that reason she couldn't mention him. She was keeping Charlie private. "San, I could drive us both insane trying to explain—"

"The rooms," he said grimly. "Trying to explain the rooms."

And seeing those rooms through her eyes, with their rugs and fireplaces and bric-a-brac, Alessandro grimaced and bowed his head.

"Listen to me, San." She took his hands and turned them over and covered the inside of his wrists with kisses and tears. "You are *my* desire," she said. "But you are not my life. You, Alessandro Corsini, are not my life. And I am not yours."

When at last he looked up, she saw the contempt in his eyes—and behind that, the emptiness. It took her breath away. She had come so close to being lost.

"Ah, *cara*," he said. "What a thing. I don't know how—"

"Of course you don't," she said, her tenderness devastating him. "Sandro, who knows?"

They walked together to their cars.

Twenty-six

Paco carried Cal's medicine and syringe on a silver tray. As he passed the far bedroom, he knocked.

Walker was there with Ivy. At her insistence they'd moved her down the hall to the guest room, an airy space a quarter the size of the master suite. She'd always liked the pale blue walls and the windows facing the garden.

The roses had bloomed all summer without her. Ivy was too busy, holding her life in her arms. In just a few more months she'd be dead. She didn't want to eat; she didn't care what she wore. In that house where they'd lived and slept and tossed love over their shoulders as if it were only a penny, she took up her life.

Walker was giving her a sponge bath. They started the day with it. He washed her fingers one by one.

"I'm remembering," she said sleepily. "All kinds of things."

Walker chuckled. "That's right, Ivy. Cleaning out the files."

Some time later, outside Ivy's bedroom, Walker and Paco talked in low tones, in shorthand, intimate now with the intimacy of others. Hearing them, Paige came down from her room upstairs and joined them in the hall by the large Francis Bacon self-portrait. It was seven in the morning. Through the days and nights the three caretakers looked after Ivy and Cal round the clock in eight-hour shifts.

"He's complaining about that eye. Wanting the morphine worse than bad," reported Paco. "And Missus?"

"In and out," Walker said. "Some lucid. Earlier, she was telling stories."

"What did she say? Tell me exactly," Paige insisted.

The men smiled kindly at her. In the beginning, they were certain Paige would be too fey for this kind of work, but she'd proven them wrong. When she could have hired more nurses, she took on extra shifts, and changed the bedpans and the dressings just like they did. It wasn't the dying Ivy Paige served, but the mother she never got to know. For until now Ivy had never held still. Her legions of friends came and went, as in the past, bringing her flowers and gossip. But more often now she sent them all away, preferring to spend hours with Paige lying next to her on the bed, reading to her or just drifting.

Ivy's lucid mornings were increasingly rare, but this was the start of the last good patch, when, as Walker liked to say, she was getting the job done. Ivy was sweet; she was goofy; she was irreverent. And her speech had come back just in time for some last-minute truth-telling. None of it she remembered.

"You'll do fine," she told Paige as they lay on top of the bed facing each other. Ivy, weighing less than ninety pounds, shivered under the covers. Paige got up to find another blanket.

"What was I saying?"

"You were saying that I will do fine."

"When?"

Paige tucked the blanket around Ivy's bony knees and soon Ivy was launched again. "Your father, he'll marry quickly, you can count on that . . . Thank god I'll be dead or *that* would kill me. Now, I don't want you giving Maggie any trouble. But don't let her near my house." At this Ivy wagged an emaciated finger.

"Mommy," Paige said softly, "Dad's not going to get better."

"Oh, shush. He's putting it on. The big baby. He'll be fine."

Paige didn't correct her. What would be the point? Instead, she punched the pillow under her head and looked at her mother's face, memorizing it.

"Cig me?" Ivy demanded. She looked impishly at her daughter. Of course she'd started smoking again. On the grounds that what difference could it make now?

"It'll kill you," Paige said.

"And how."

Of course, the tricky part was that Ivy's hands shook, and when she didn't have the shakes, she had the forgets. The ash would get longer and longer before she thought to bring the cig to her lips. And so the Aubusson carpet was burned in patches, and the cashmere blankets and antique bedside table.

Paige fixed the pillows behind Ivy's bony spine. She lit a cigarette and handed it to her. Then she crawled to the other side of the bed and stacked her own pillows the way she liked. They sat together like the princess and queen.

"Couple of things," Ivy said, sucking deeply and exhaling in a thick slur.

"Mommy, you don't have to—"

"Couple of things," Ivy said. "I have a list—look in my top drawer. You decide who gets what. Maybe a piece of jewelry. Maybe a good purse. Hermès. You decide. Spread a few things among your friends. It will make you happy later on. Like finding us when you aren't looking. I want your daughters—and you will have daughters—I can see them, duck, give the short pearls and the first diamond he gave me. You decide who and who."

Paige squeezed her own thin hand. "Oh, Mommy. And what if there aren't any daughters?"

"Ho-ho," Ivy shot back. For she could see them—two boys and two girls, four in six years, with James. "You'll do fine with them, lovey," she said, wagging the cigarette, the ash flying. "You'll be much stricter than I was. I was tentative. I left you too much on your own. You won't do that. God bless them, you'll be on them like a freight train. They would have come over here for a reprieve. I'd like to have been the good guy, damn it.

"I am sorry," Ivy went on. "I am sorry I didn't know to love you enough to counter you. I'm sorry I didn't hold you more. Like this. Isn't this nice? Like this. You know, you smell good. You smell so good to me."

Paige had heard few real compliments in her life. She thought about petting Ivy's hair and then she did. It was heavy, Indian hair.

"Simple," Ivy said. "Simple."

And because it was simple, Paige felt an irrepressible need to confess. "Mommy. I did a terrible thing."

"Mmm," said Ivy, taking a drag and waving the butt in the air until Paige got the ashtray and put it out. "What could that be?"

"You know that company Cal wanted to invest in. Nimbus?"

"Mmm."

"Well." Paige took a deep breath and went on. One day, months ago, before her engagement party, and after her father told her he was going to ditch ArtShop, Paige met Alessandro at the office to work on finding a way to save her idea from the scrap heap. She and Alessandro were going out to lunch. He was tied up on a group call in the conference room, so Alessandro asked her to wait in his office, which she was happy to do. For fun, she sat in his nice partner chair. And, well, she wasn't trying to be nosy but she did glance at the papers on his desk, and at his computer screen, where he was drafting a memo analyzing Nimbus's strengths and weaknesses in the area of patent protection. And maybe, well maybe, Paige put that information into the wrong hands, on purpose.

"Oh." Ivy frowned. "Why?"

Paige shrugged. She had been so angry with her father for shelving ArtShop. And then all this rah-rah having to do with Lena and Nimbus. Paige supposed she'd been angry for a very long time. But that feeling was far from her now.

"That's all right," Ivy said, growing fuzzy. She patted Paige's hand and her speech, slurring as she tired, came out in a whisper. "When . . . you were quite young, five or six, your father, he said . . . he said you had the makings of a real bitch." Ivy smiled brightly. "He never liked you much . . . I don't think he liked me much either. But that is not to say we didn't have something very . . . ." Her voice trailed off. She closed her eyes.

"Mommy! What are you saying?"

Ivy frowned. "Who? What's that?"

"Mommy, what did you just say?"

Ivy tried to go back. But the scrim tumbled down and she forgot Paige. She closed her eyes. "Ah!" she said brightly. "Inhabit your life. That's the key. I learned it . . . yesterday." Ivy smiled, deeply pleased. "Walker told me. Such a nice man. Gay as a peacock, of course."

Down the hall, Cal's jaw was in fact killing him. The radiation hadn't worked. And still they carved him, inch by inch. In the second surgery, they took his cheek and part of his ear. The next time, they removed a portion of his skull, along with his left eye. Next, they took what remained of his left ear, leaving behind a tube for drainage. They took the skin from his face and scalp, peeled it back and replaced it with yet more skin grafted from his thigh. He was burning up. He was being eaten alive. Keep cutting, he told Weisman.

After Walker gave him a shot, as the narcotic took hold, Cal's life floated over him. He was buried in a shallow grave of sand; on top, there were piles of dry leaves. Shadows, a canopy of redwoods, sunlight fading. He was at the center, alone. He didn't mind. He had waited his whole life not to be bothered. The light was orange. He could smell it more than see it. He'd done the best he could, yes. He had been born with the gift of a prescient gut. But he hadn't known love, not as the great men know it. He had been unable to open himself. He'd been born on short legs to a depressed mother and a philandering pater. He'd been small; his father was at pains to remind him of that fact. Ted had the heart; Teddy. Now, blind, Cal could see on a different level. The world, with all its gizmos and blow jobs, its arias and limited partnerships went by, and all that remained was the primitive, the world beneath unceasing, the woodpecker pecking, the bull driving among the cows, the eagle following the trail of a mouse.

Now, at last, when he had every reason not to talk, being contrary, Cal wanted to. He called in his lawyers and reviewed the details of his will. He sent for Maggie, whose eyes welled with tears at the sight of him.

"Turn the chair, Mag, so you don't have to look."

She faced him squarely with her files and laptop. "It's not so bad," she said, feet planted, skirt covering her knees—no house ever built more solid than Maggie.

Ah, the good Catholic girl, thought Cal, recalling that Maggie had been raised on the face of the bloody eviscerated Jesus.

It was Maggie's idea to lift his spirits by bringing in some visitors. Alessandro came most frequently, but the other partners put in their time, too. Maggie made sure that Cal and Greg Bettor mended things.

To Greg, Cal said, "Don't be too happy."

Bud Cope couldn't bear the sight of Cal's face. The rawness. And something else: the end of their time. Cal had taken a piece out of everyone he knew and now the pieces were being taken out of him. Bud didn't enjoy seeing it. He began the conversation by saying, "Sandra and I—"

Cal cut him off. "Here's the deal, Bud. First the shit goes gray, then yellow, now it's white. I am shitting death. You no doubt will think I am getting my just rewards."

"No, Cal."

"Liar!" insisted Cal with a certain valor. The two men were silent for a while. "Hey. It was good of you to come. Now that my checkbook is in the drawer, I don't get a lot of visitors."

"Ah, they'll be writing books about the dark prince of Silicon Valley. You'll be immortal," Bud said, only stating what he knew to be true.

"I'll be as dead as your aunt Bertha," Cal said.

"Yes, but Aunt Bertha didn't build like you."

"That's the thing of it, Bud. We did some stuff. I thought I'd do more stuff before the bell rang."

Bud was two years younger, and only luck separated him from where Cal was sitting now. "What's stopping you?" Bud said. "You want me to send you some young Turks? You can run them through their paces. You'd be doing me a favor."

"Run them through their paces, eh? And what if I find one I want to keep?"

Bud wagged his head, laughing. "I would be thrilled to go in with you on any deal, but I won't expect it."

"And how," Cal snorted.

That same week Bud kept to his promise: he sent the young Turks. Word got around that Cal would see them now. If they could get past the face, he would see them. Maggie made the arrangements and Paco served tea, and one by one they took their places on the sofa by the window.

"Start at the top," Cal said, closing his one good eye.

So they laid their problems at his feet: it was the engineering hanging them up, or marketing, or a lack of funds, or a hundred other details that went into revolutionizing an inch of the world.

When Cal heard the blip, he barked, "Back up! You're fudging. Start again, first-year revenue." Or he might say, "Good. You've got the roll-out in your pocket. Now the other nightmare—" And he'd tip his jack-o'-lantern head against the pillows and wave them on.

One morning Maggie brought an Indian kid to the house who couldn't have been more than twenty-four years old. He was Maggie's find. He'd ranked third in his class at IIT in Delhi, which won him a full ride at Stanford. The head of Stanford's engineering department claimed he was special. His name was Sakim Nair.

"All right, Sakim. Maggie says you've come up with the next thing the world desperately needs. Amaze me."

Cal's one good eye glanced at Sakim's Italian loafers. Men today, Cal scoffed: from the ankle up they look like gas station attendants, and from the ankle down, like gigolos. This one was small and wiry.

Sakim Nair relaxed into Cal's velvet sofa and laughed. "Ah, Mr. Rusch. Did Bill Gates or Steve Jobs know what they had on their hands? I don't think so. They had urgency, yes?"

"Hey, Sakim. What's on your mind?"

"Forgive me. Am I going slow? Ah. I was just asking a friend of mine who is working at Google, tell me, Joss, in this stinking economy, what gets the most searches? You want to know what he said?"

"Let me guess," the old man jumped in. "Self-help. Fitness."

"Yes! That's it. And cooking! Exactly, Mr. Rusch. All the things of comfort you can do at home with no money. And when the economy turns, what will the top searches be then? I had to ask myself this question."

"Restaurants. Shopping. Movie and music tickets. What, Sakim, are you going to sell movie tickets?"

"Cars, Mr. Rusch. When the economy turns, it is going to be cars."

"Cars!"

"And not just any car. The car that will come several years from now will speak to the green movement, of course, and it will be a car that also talks to the man who has come out the other side. A car that is so cool, so fast, so quiet, sooooo sexy, well . . ." Sakim held up his hands.

"Your plan then is to go up against the big car makers with what—a hybrid. A tribrid?"

Sakim shrugged. "The car business is in crisis, Mr. Rusch. Survival city. In the center of the chaos, I see a window of time, maybe a few years, when someone small can come in and capture a good deal of the market. It is new thinking that is required to nudge Japan and Detroit into the twenty-first century. Of course I am speaking of solar. We take what is plentiful and turn it to our uses. We're not there yet with the motor, not just yet. I can tell you, Mr. Rusch, I have some very interesting problems."

Clear-eyed, unafraid, Sakim beamed confidence into the divots and bruises and missing parts that were the great Cal Rusch.

"Tell me your problems," Cal said. "Start at the top."

So Sakim Nair began to talk, from the inside out. The smart ones always took things that way. They started with a common question, then pushed through to the heart, with simplicity and elegance. Cal rarely mistook the sound. Their problems were the genesis of a new world. This young man was going to revolutionize the auto industry.

"But how are you going to get your customer? In this economy no one is buying fads," Cal said.

"Excuse me," Sakim countered. "They aren't buying duds. They aren't buying go-carts for fogies. The internal combustion engine is dead. We are in the pockets of the Saudis. And that, as any man will tell you, is not a good place to be."

Cal nodded.

"This customer is going to come to me because he thinks he has to compromise his desire. He thinks for the good of the planet he has to drive the equivalent of an ugly Earth Shoe. A hybrid. He hates this idea—of course. Ah, but I am going to give him so much more. I am going to give him a race car. A studmobile. With speed and looks, but which doesn't pollute. Even better, it makes hardly a sound. Silence, Mr. Rusch. Nothing to interfere with the engine of the human heart. He's a bird, a panther; he's speeding across the earth yet he's the earth's friend." Sakim paused. "Of course, we have to address the conversion issue—the drivetrain and cloudy days are my greatest nightmares."

"Bah," said Cal. "You're talking a niche market."

"At first, yes. But, Mr. Rusch, you and I are in it for the next cars and the next. Isn't that so?"

Cal met with Sakim several times. And each time he pressed him and each time Sakim came back with more sound thinking. Cal arranged for Alessandro and Greg to meet him. He brought in Bud Cope to be the second. When Rusch & Co. funded Sakim Nair, Cal put Maggie in for a piece.

And when, years later, Maggie finally retired, her holdings in Rusch & Co. made her one of the wealthiest women in Silicon Valley.

They were nearing the end of visitors.

But one morning in late September Paco brought Beverly up the back stairs to Cal's room. She came dressed for the races, in dark glasses, a black bolero jacket and heels. The outfit made Paco nervous. And then there was her voice. He all but shushed her as she came up the stairs.

She sat in a chair at the end of the bed and drank her tea and talked to Cal of the old days. He wanted to hear stories about Ted.

But at a point Cal said, "Hey! That didn't happen. You're making things up."

"Of course I'm making things up!" she cried even louder, giving his foot a robust squeeze.

Down the hall, Ivy heard the jingle-bangles. She'd been silent all day, waving in the twilight.

"Walker?"

"Yes, Ivy."

"How . . . much longer?"

"Oh, I couldn't say." Walker came round beside the bed and looked into her troubled face. "And it's not me holding out on you either. Lord, I've been surprised so many times. Many times. But where you are I'd say is what we call the sweet spot. It will get bad in a while, but I'll keep it from getting real bad, I promise you that. We'll put that out of our minds. But right here, Ivy, this is the magic time. I've seen people doing all kinds of wonders with it."

"Thank you, Walker. Can I have . . . my pill?"

The next morning she woke with a gust of energy. "Walker? I want . . . to see him."

She skipped her sponge bath. Instead, Paige helped Ivy into her purple silk robe. She brushed Ivy's hair and put lipstick on her and a little rouge. Then Walker rolled Ivy down the hall to the master bedroom.

Cal was napping, looking small on the huge raft that had been their bed.

"Up . . . up . . . next . . ." Ivy whispered none too softly, in the toddler-esque staccato that was now her talk.

Walker lifted her onto the bed and put a blanket on top of her and tucked it around her little feet. The movement exhausted her. She and Cal lay side by side for the better part of an hour with their eyes closed.

"Ivy," Cal said, with a start. "I want to talk about the future."

"All right."

They said nothing for the next half hour.

"Christ, it hurts," he said, waking with a start.

"Poor duck." She scratched at the covers for his hand.

They lay on their backs, hand in hand, propped up on pillows, their eyes closed, like sun worshippers on the beach at Capri.

"No one comes to see me," he said. "Where are all those bastards? You're the popular one."

Each phrase was long drawn. Their mouths didn't work right, for one. Ivy didn't think to answer for another long spell. "I told Walker . . . this dying . . . best thing that ever happened to me. I think I meant it."

He turned very slowly and studied her with his one good eye. She looked awful, all gullies and knobs. The effects of all her meds had turned her once thin face to twice its normal size. Her teeth and ears looked huge.

"Ivy," he said, "I've been a pain in the ass."

"Mmm."

"You as well."

"Don't . . . blow it. You were doing fine."

"Iv."

"Mmm."

"For the record, I did *not* bed Maggie. We were above board. I want to drill that point home."

"OK," Ivy said.

"That's it? *OK?*"

The shadows of the trees outside were fans and veils gliding across the walls. But Ivy didn't see them. She was watching the film of their lives with her eyes closed.

"Well," she said at last. "You had *one* visitor. Mrs. Jingle-jangles."

"Iv—"

"You know, you could have been a whole lot—*tidier*." She paused, her shaky tongue trying to itch the roof of her mouth. "Le—Lena. Does she . . . know?"

He wasn't sure how to answer, so he told the truth. "No."

"What the hell are you waiting for?"

Another hour passed. Walker peeked in on them. They were asleep with their mouths open. He left them to it.

Twenty-seven

By October—one year after the crash—the market was up again, but on the ground things remained shaky. Obama had been president for nine whole months but in all that time he hadn't managed to fix the economy, pass universal health care, stop global warming, close Guantánamo, or finish the wars in Iraq and Afghanistan. In all that time Obama had only proved he wasn't a god after all. Worse, he was aloof, proud; he compromised when he should have stood firm. The newspapers, as could have been predicted, blasted him. The Republicans called him a fake.

Lena, in protest, stopped reading the papers. Her middle-of-the-night sojourns with the political blogs ceased. Knowing things, she couldn't not know them. She had a fullness of the brain and heart. Besides, she already had the polar bears up north to monitor and the penguins in trouble down south. Ditto the lions and the lemurs. She had Israel and Palestine, no advance there; Iceland and California bankrupt; Madonna having taken up with a boyfriend named Jesus, who was twenty-two years old. Lena had to worry about swine flu and the larger question of vaccines, pro or con. Just when soy felt right it was wrong. And so on, until it seemed that only Queen Elizabeth and bin Laden were secure.

Lena had to remember paper then plastic then paper now hemp—and it wasn't enough to own the bags, she had to remember to bring them to the store. Dementia, what to do about dementia? Madoff was bullying the cons in prison. Lena had to stop.

Theo, accepted on scholarship to a good school, was starting his new life. His cast came off, and he announced he was now a soccer player. Willa had to have tubes put in her ears. Of all her surgeries, this was the one regular parents understood. But it meant Lena was out of work for another week. At the end of that week, Violet called, her voice shaky and urgent. The clients were complaining again and this time Violet couldn't fix it. She met Lena one evening when Glo could cover; they walked from the house to a nearby wine bar.

"Babes," Violet began.

"It's OK, Vi." Lena felt her cheeks shake, and though she forced herself to be strong, she wasn't so strong. She was shocked and gobsmacked and now she was out of work. And worse, she had strained Vi. "It's OK," she repeated. "Let's drink this bottle and maybe another, and agree that for reasons neither of us could control I've been a sucky employee and you have been a class act to keep me on. Let's leave it at that. Thank you and please don't worry about this for a minute."

Violet protested more than she needed to. "It's just that the phone isn't ringing. I don't know when things are going to pick up again and I can't—"

"You can't carry me, Vi. Come on. I don't expect it."

"Do you need money? I can give you money."

"Yes, I need money; and, no, you won't." Lena smiled reassuringly though she didn't have any idea what to do.

Vi wiped her nose with a tissue. "Oh, Christ, I'm sorry."

"It's going to be fine, Vi," Lena said, giving it her best.

"Who said it's going to be fine?" Vi snorted. "Show me one thing that's going to be fine."

"This," Lena said, taking her hand.

———————————————————

Glo was in the kitchen sewing a button on Willa's blue, fuzzy sweater.

"¿Y tu trabajo?" Glo asked, knowing that Lena had come from a special meeting with Violet.

Lena shrugged. "Ah, Glo. ¿Dondé está la suerte?"

Where is the luck? Back in January, as Willa was hospitalized with pneumonia, Gloria Angelica was enjoying the first vacation of her life. She'd gone to Yosemite with her church group and for the first time had seen snow. She ran through it in her sneakers, cupping balls of it in her icy hands; she'd licked it as if it were sugar. Then, in the evening, the group of them led by the pastor and a fellow named Manny, who was by day a pizza chef, gathered in a field under a cloudless, moony sky. Elated, Glo fell back into the snow and flapped her arms and legs, making an angel of herself. Manny took her picture. Glo's children had never seen snow, not even in books, of which they had few, and all of them hand-me-downs from Theo. They had Theo's books and they had their mother's voice on the phone every other Sunday. But they did not have her, not even in her own wake-dreams. For it was true, as Glo flapped an angel in the Yosemite snow, as she looked up at Half Dome, which had to be a step up to god, her thoughts went to Lena, Theo and Willa. She pictured their delighted faces as she told them that she'd made an angel of herself in the snow.

By Easter, Glo had moved in with Manny. For the first time she was in love. But Manny had false papers to start with and then he'd ignored a summons to file for amnesty. Two months later, the INS made a sweep of the restaurants in the Mission and Manny was deported. She hadn't heard from him in months.

Glo bit the thread with her teeth, knotted it and then tucked the needle and sweater away. Glo's friends told her that she should have gotten a raise a year ago, when Willa needed care round the clock. Lena couldn't have refused her. But Glo, knowing how extreme everything was, didn't have the heart. She loved this family. She loved Lena, who was a demonstrative boss, kissing and hugging Glo hello and good-bye, who sent her to English class and gossiped with her in Spanish and who knew the smallest details regarding Glo's children. To this, Glo's friends at the park replied, "But, Gloria Angelica, tell us, can your children eat kindness?"

Now there was no money to pay her and Lena couldn't put off saying that anymore. They sat across from each other at the kitchen table.

"Lena, I give you twenty hours a week for the room downstairs and meals."

"But, Glo, what are you going to do for money? You need money."

Glo shrugged. "Find another yob."

"Job," Lena corrected as she reached across the table. "Oh my god, Glo." And so it was settled. Glo got up and went to the closet to fetch her bags and coat.

Lena followed her to the door. "But if Charlie and I div—"

"No," Glo said.

That night, Lena couldn't sleep. She went downstairs to the desk in the living room and wrote the last of the scripts she owed Violet. Then she moved to the kitchen and made coffee. With a space heater going full blast, she spread the mess of unpaid bills out on the kitchen table. Beside a thick pad and the laptop, she arranged things in piles: pay now, put off till next month, put off longer, medical (no hope). The simple bills, PG&E, trash and telephone, she paid. The mortgage she would come back to. The property taxes were overdue. On it went. The credit cards, amounting to sixty thousand total, she addressed by paying the minimums and moving on. That left her with five hundred dollars for the month. She'd never make it. She needed to find another job quickly. And she needed to talk to Charlie. The thought of him, of how much she missed him and feared they would never find a way back, sent her into another flurry of activity. She cleaned out the junk drawer. When that was done, Lena sat in the living room, in Charlie's chair. She held very still, like a sparrow on a branch, head slightly tipped, keen to the rustling.

She heard a sound and went upstairs to check on the kids.

Willa was awake, sitting up in her crib. Her calm, expectant eyes lifted. She smiled.

"Hey, Brave, what is it?"

It was as if the ocean had summoned the shore.

Weeks passed with Lena unable to find work, and then one morning she received an odd call.

"Ah, Lena. Cal Rusch here." The gravel in the voice was so thick she could hardly understand him.

"Oh." She hesitated. "How are you?" The words were out of her mouth before she remembered she was asking that of a dying man.

"No small complaints. You?"

She paused. "I'm OK."

"Good. Listen. I wonder if you would come up to the house tomorrow. No big deal, just a chat. I'm terrible to look at and such, but I wonder how would ten o'clock strike you? Paco likes to serve tea but you can have that, or a lemon-thingy or whatever you want. How does that sound?"

"I have an appointment."

"When?"

"Tomorrow."

"Is it at ten?"

"No."

"Good. Come at ten and we won't take long." And with that, he hung up.

Paco answered the door.

"I made a cake," Lena confessed. "Isn't that silly. I made a cake."

Paco nodded. "What kind?"

"Chocolate."

"Ah, she used to be crazy for chocolate."

"But she's not now? What about Cal? Does he—"

Paco's face had an extraordinary ability to pull inward. He looked blankly at Lena and in that blankness she was struck by his sorrow. Other things about him had changed, too. He no longer wore a suit. Instead his uniform was a black jogging outfit with matching black sneakers. Of all people, Paco looked a bit worn. Neat, clean, but worn. Lena thought, So this is who loves them.

"Is it any good?" Cal asked, as she entered the room with Paco carrying the cake. Cal was seated in a chair by the window, his feet on an ottoman and pillows all around him. Bandages covered most of his face, and a scarf covered the bandages. With his jaw and chin so far extended, he looked like Ichabod Crane.

"What do you mean?" she said. "Of course it's good."

"No worries," Cal fired back. "Paulette can put lipstick on any pig. Eh, Paco?"

Though Cal's face was mostly covered, the parts Lena could see were raw. Looking at him, Lena realized two things: one, he was very shy and two, he was trying to be playful with her.

"Well, I'm not a baker," she admitted, "but the guy who sold me the cake promised it would taste better than homemade."

Paco coughed. Smiling with his lips shut, he set out the tea things and left them.

"How are your kids?" Cal asked.

"What? They're fine." She wasn't good at small talk under normal circumstances and even less so here. He was having an awful time—that much was obvious. Cal was down to perhaps a hundred and twenty pounds. Yet she resisted the urge to feel sorry for him. Instead, she narrowed her sights and addressed his question by talking to one of her worries. "Theo. He's started a new school and it's going a bit rough and with everything in flux—"

"Ah, hang on . . . fading here. Hang on," he said. His head dropped into the pillows and he seemed to pass out. She wondered if he was playacting. Then she saw the syringe on the table next to him.

Five, perhaps ten minutes passed.

"Has he got some smarts?" Cal said, waking with a start. "Theo. Has he got some smarts?"

She nodded.

"Is he responsible?"

"Yes. Perhaps too much."

"Good. Channel it. Find something he can do and put him in charge. Got it?" He gave a little wave of the hand, as if to move on, and then stopped. "Hey," he said, "why doesn't Theo take the Danes?"

"The Danes? Oh, god, no."

"Yes. That's it. The boy needs a dog. Why not two?" Cal trailed off, then caught the thread again. "Paige doesn't want them. It would help us if you'd take them."

"I don't know what to say."

"Say yes, for chrissakes. I don't have a hell of a lot of time here, you know." He pressed his lips together as if irked, but really he was only trying to hold on, working through his list. He had only a set amount of energy before the next wave of pain. But even while trying to be quick, he talked slowly, with many halts. "Which brings me to— Listen. Ivy and I, we've got a foundation. The director, he's leaving—well, I fired him. I'd like you to think about coming aboard. There's an administrator—she's excellent—so you wouldn't have to do the boring part. It's vision we need. Pay isn't bad, with benefits including health for . . . Damn, what's the other child's name?"

"Willa."

"Willa. Best of all you could set the agenda and have the pleasure of giving my money away."

Lena stared at him, her mouth open. She wondered if maybe the drugs had addled his mind. But he didn't look crazy. He looked awful, god-awful, but not crazy. "I don't know the first thing about running a foundation."

"You never got grants for your documentaries?"

"Yes, but—"

"So it'd be a different but not altogether new challenge. You're scared? That's good."

"Not exactly."

"Nothing scares you, eh, Helena Rusch?"

She shrugged, gathering her nerve. "I'm scared of the dark and of ending up alone, and of crawly things in my hair—and, maybe most of all, of pilfering love. I just don't know enough about foundation work and I am unwilling to be beholden to you—in any way."

271

She was on her feet again. Truthfully, she was afraid. She was afraid of him.

"So, you dislike me," he said. "*Big deal.* It's decent pay. You could do worse. And, need I say, I won't be here to bug you."

"Why? Why do you keep coming at *me*? Stop it."

He paused for a long moment. "As I said, having money and knowing who to put with it is the talent I have. I have a feeling about you. And I've made my assessment based on that. I'm asking you to help me. And in the process help yourself. And even, god help us all, do something right for the world."

"You play with people," she said fiercely, her fury nearly as intense as her confusion. For though she hated Cal, she was energized by talking with him. "You use money in place of real connection, and when it goes sour you move on."

"Christ, girl. Do I need your lectures?" Wincing, his hands flew up and hovered above his awful face. "This is different."

"How?"

He looked at her from the one eye, testing himself and finding that he didn't have the goods to tell her. "You have to trust me, it is."

Lena scoffed. There was a hardness in her she didn't understand, but it came over her when she was near him, and it was all the years and all the hurt and she was caught in it. "Trust you? How could I trust *you*? No. I feel sorry for you. Nobody should suffer like this. But I won't help you. I can't."

He let her get as far as the door. "Bravo. Bravo! Send the old bastard to hell, and then walk out thinking you're the berries. My god. If there was any doubt you were my daughter, you sure as hell just proved it."

Lena turned.

"Yes," he said thickly.

She thought he was putting it on, the cruelty and tricks unending. But no. She stood in the doorway, refusing to believe him, yet knowing what he said was true. "Why?" she asked. "Why now?"

"Your mother," he replied. "She told me, and she also asked me to look at Nimbus. No obligation, either way."

"No obligation?" Lena echoed, too stunned to say more.

"That's right, she was very subtle. Cautious. Uncharacteristically so," Cal added, thinking it for the hundredth time. "Your mother, she is easy to underestimate. Her affections are fierce—you must know that," he went on. "But I wouldn't have gone ahead if I didn't believe Nimbus was viable—more than viable. My interest was real. You might tell Charlie that. As for you"—he stopped short, the pain coming on him from all quarters—"promise me you'll give it a think: the dogs, the job. I have no business asking, it's true, but it would be a comfort if you'd at least consider before telling me to take a hike, Lena."

She didn't hear half the words he spoke, but she felt them deeply. "I'll consider the job," she said, after a time, fighting to keep her voice even. "But the Danes, yes. For Theo, I'll take them."

As Lena made her way down the steep driveway, she spotted Beverly sitting behind the wheel of her car, which was parked across the street. Beverly motioned with a tip of her head, and Lena begrudgingly walked over to the passenger side and climbed in.

"So," Beverly sniffed. "He beat me to it, did he? He beat me to it and now you think you know enough to be giving me that look." Beverly managed to lift her chin.

"Is that what you have to say to me? Is that all?" Lena cried.

Beverly looked at Lena with more longing than love, more guilt than hope, the halfway glance she'd been sending Lena's way for as far back as she could remember, but only now did it make sense.

Lena moaned. It would be a long time before she could make peace with any of it, and until then it would sit like a knot in her throat. She couldn't stop picturing Cal's wretched face. "He's awful," she said, after a time. "He looks . . . Frankensteinian."

Beverly mused on that as she turned the rings on her fingers round and round. "For all the bluster, they're not sturdy, those Rusch boys." She took a tissue from her little purse and blew her nose.

"Why? Ma, why didn't you tell me?"

"Tell you what? Ted raised you. You were his and he was yours. No one can convince me otherwise."

"And Didi . . . and Jesse?"

"Didi was Ted's." Beverly smiled with a fading spark. "You . . . from day one you were different." She paused, adding as an aside. "Of course, Jesse came much later, with Paul."

Lena looked away, recalling how unlike her sisters she'd always felt. "I don't know how to think about this. Did you even love Dad? Why didn't you just marry Cal?"

"Fa!" cried Beverly. "I loved *them both*. You're a woman—tell me you don't know how it is." Beverly shifted irritably. "I should be immune to you by now. You want me to be wise. I'm not. I should have all kinds of things to tell you, things I've been saving; I don't. I didn't tell until I thought it was necessary. Until I thought it could—"

"Help," Lena said, understanding at last. "You thought it could help Charlie and me."

"Fat good it did. I'm sorry for that."

"No, Ma," Lena said, for it was the first time she could remember Beverly going out of her way. "It was good you tried."

They were quiet, thinking on that.

Then Beverly said, "Choose one of them? Is that what you said? Where we grew up, Helena, there was a whole lot of grass and a whole lot of dust and not much else. As bad as you think it was, trust me, it was lots worse. Grimsville. All I knew is that I had to get the hell out. Two brothers lived down the block. They were both skinny birds, but of course I was a skinny bird, too. The one was full of beans, I mean smart. Such heat he had. You could see he was going to do something, if he didn't explode or kill someone sooner. Cal had a real chip on his shoulder. Not a talker. But when he fixed on you, well, it was a compliment but also a little dire, if you know what I mean.

"I had my nerve. I snuck out with him at night. The first time he kissed me, the bolt went through my heels." She paused, feeling it yet. "My father, he said Cal was too old and wild, and I was too young. He forbade me to see him. When that didn't work, he all but tied me to the house.

"My brother was friends with Ted, and I would see him when he came over. Ted was funny. He always had a joke and a sweet word. Ah, I suppose he scared me less. I looked down his road and saw we'd have a good time." Beverly bit her lip, still deciding. "You have to know we're talking about little houses and little lives, Lena, and I thought, well, isn't it better to be happy?"

Beverly checked her nails. "I didn't understand, of course, that because of me they had come to hate each other. And every night they had to sleep with their heads not three feet apart," she said. "One day Cal disappeared. He vanished. He took it upon himself to decide for all of us."

Beverly dabbed her nose. "So, miss, now you be the judge."

"I don't want to judge, Ma."

"Well, I'm sure that's not true. But you see, the point is, Lena, you don't have to be a fool to have lived a foolish life." Beverly shuddered and for a time they were quiet. Then Beverly turned her beam onto Lena and gently said, "I suppose the question now is, What's this girl next to me going to do?"

Lena shrugged. "The best we can. That's what Charlie says."

"Oh, my," Beverly said. "He really doesn't have the talk, does he?"

"Yes, he does. Sometimes."

"That's not to say he isn't right for you."

At this Lena cried out. "Oh, Ma! I've been such a stupid cow. He was the love of my life . . . what a corny phrase. But I think, somehow he was."

"Love of your life? Wait. Are we talking about Charlie or the other one?"

"Charlie!"

"Oh, fa. If you still want that, it's not done." Beverly waved the worry away.

"You don't know. He's proud."

"Honey, there's only one way to lose a man like Charlie, and that is to convince him he never had the goods to make you happy in the first place. Now, have you done that?" Beverly looked appraisingly at her daughter. "As for pride, men are only as proud as the next time you tell them they're great, then, pow, like magic, they're yours again."

"You make them sound like simpletons."

"Well, darling, they are! Thank god. I mean they're nothing like *women*. Men just put it in, if you know what I mean. That went for Ted, and for the one up there, in the big house—and the same goes for your Charlie. I may not know much, but I know that." Beverly patted Lena's hand.

Lena veered from skeptical to grateful, and finally, overcome, she threw her arms around Beverly's neck. Beverly gave a small cry and tapped her small hand on Lena's back.

"All right," Beverly said at last, for a little hugging with her daughter was a lot.

Regaining herself, Lena sat up and wiped her face. "Ma. Come for dinner on Sunday."

"Really? You're inviting me? With the kids?"

"I can't promise it's going to be gourmet."

"Oh, I don't care." For a brief moment, Beverly smiled, and then she pointed her nose at Lena's door. It was time for her to go.

Twenty-eight

On the morning Paco brought the Danes, Lena let Theo skip school. Paco parked the Mercedes wagon in the narrow driveway and unloaded all of the dogs' gear while Theo, busting with pride, held the door. In came the chocolate linen velvet beds and the leashes and brushes. In came two newly varnished benches and their hand-painted porcelain bowls. Each Dane ate the equivalent of fourteen cans of dog food daily, seven hundred pounds a month. The food, Paco assured Lena, would be delivered on the first of every month, prepaid. He handed Lena a typed sheet of paper with the numbers for the vet and the groomer. "Also paid," he said.

He drove back up the hill, returning a half hour later with Angie and Finn. The dogs came up the front stoop, which was only large enough for their front ends.

"Paco," Lena said welcoming them inside, whereby they immediately made the house feel much smaller.

"My number is on the paper, should they need anything," he replied, avoiding her gaze, while the Danes, those lethargic ponies, sat on his left and right, their heads as high as his ribs.

Paco put his hand on each of the large foreheads and talked straight to Theo. "They like to be scratched here, behind and under the ears, and here, on the chest." He showed how it was done. "Don't worry about being gentle so much as . . . *vigorous.*"

Theo nodded. He would not have to be told twice.

"They have been with me, and me with them, for a long time." Paco sighed. "They are good dogs."

Taking their leashes from Paco's hands, Theo rubbed the dogs behind the ears so that Paco would know it was going to be done correctly, and then he took them outside to the backyard.

That night, Lena put the velvet beds under the window in Theo's room, but the dogs refused to go there. They remained downstairs, walking from the front door to the back, circling all night, their nails click-clacking on the wood floor.

"Theo," Lena said the next afternoon, "if you feed them, they'll think you're their master, and then, in a while, they'll sleep in your room."

And so he did. Theo took them outside and ran them round and round in the small yard. He hopped on Finn's back and went for a ride. They were patient with him. If he said Sit, they sat; if he said Down, they thought a minute, you could almost see the words moving slowly through the thick knot of brains, then down they went; when Theo fed them liver treats, they sniffed his hand before opening their enormous mouths to show giant teeth and an even larger tongue and then, very gingerly, as if nibbling on a tea sandwich, the Danes took the treat from him.

But all the while they were waiting. At dinner and in the morning, they watched Lena to see when, at last, this game would end and they could go home. They went from door to door, checking.

Angie had it the worst.

Late at night, Angie followed Lena into the small, narrow bathroom. Finn came in behind her, the two of them squeezing into the doorway to observe Lena as she sat on the john and then as she brushed her teeth.

The loneliness was on them and she told them about it. She patted their heads and told them what good dogs they were and that it was a crazy time all around, but somehow things would turn out. Basically, she talked so they would know her voice. "Come," she commanded as she led them into Theo's bedroom. She sat on the floor between their beds with Theo's sleeping bag wrapped around her.

"Settle," Lena said and snapped her fingers.

Angie's ears pinned flat as she stepped gingerly onto her bed. Finn followed. Round and round they went, until at last Angie's legs buckled and with a moan she collapsed, and then Finn after her. Lena stroked their thick necks and rubbed their chests, palming their large loyal canine hearts. Finally, they dropped their heavy heads into each of her hands.

Lena looked at the dark and the dark looked back. The one person she wanted to speak to, the one person who could help her make sense of things, was the one person she couldn't call: Charlie. If he wasn't still working, he'd be at Swanson's, sleeping. She went for her phone, but as she fingered the buttons, she stopped herself.

The next morning, she drove to Nimbus. She had to see him. She had to see Charlie's face and tell him how much she missed him.

He wasn't there. Swanson was alone, packing his office.

"Hey, Lee."

"Oh, Lena. Hey. You looking for Charlie? He's at Stanford. You want me to call him? Find out when he's coming back?"

Lena refused Swanson's offer and only then noticed the condition of the room. There were boxes everywhere. The talk of the bust was hyperbolic. It was graphs on the news, with angry arrows shooting downward. But in reality it was a whole lot of meetings with lawyers and calls to the phone company and talks with employees that involved the taking back of keys. The taking back of a dream. It was Swanson in his office, packing his futon. He took a box from a folding chair and motioned her to sit.

"Swanny, I'm so sorry."

"Ah, we almost got there. Now those bastards will get the glory. But we know what we know. Still, I'm going to miss it."

"And Charlie?"

Swanson shook his head. "He's not talking much."

It occurred to Lena that Swanson was looking at her differently, in that he wasn't looking at her at all. "Lee, do you hate me, too?"

"Hate you? Of course not."

"Then what do you really think?" She stared at him with an almost rabid intensity.

"I don't know, Lena. I'm not very wise in these matters," he admitted.

She laughed bitterly. "Come on, Swanny. You are the wisest man we know."

"Oh, god, no." Swanson looked at her with a terrific sadness. He opened his large, empty hands and folded them again.

"So much has happened, Lee. And Charlie, he's the one person—" Embarrassed, she buried her face in her hands.

"Gee, can't be as bad as that. Can't be."

"But it is. It is as bad as that."

Swanson looked around the room for help. "Hey, Lena, you want something. A soda? Let me get you something."

She perked up a bit. "Do you have chocolate? I seem to be living on nerves and chocolate."

"Oh," he said. "Sorry. I'm sort of taking a breather from the junk."

Lena picked up her head and studied Swanson with fresh eyes. He was buttoned up, his hair combed, his shirt tucked. He had lost a good ten pounds.

"Lee Swanson, have you got a lady?"

He blushed and beamed. "Jesus Christ. Isn't it time I got a life? Yeah, I've been seeing someone—a few times—though she's not exactly your Harvard type."

"That's probably good," Lena said, truly pleased for him.

Swanson sighed, clearly smitten. "She's a nurse. At Stanford. Charlie introduced us."

"A nurse," Lena said, thinking of Charlie matchmaking, when his own life was a ruin.

"Her name is Briana. She's divorced with a young kid. A boy. Four years old. Ryan," he said proudly.

"Oh, Swanny, a little boy."

"Yeah. But it gets real bad from there." Swanson shuddered.

Lena steeled herself for a tragic turn, a violent ex-husband, an illness.

"Sweet Jesus," Swanson said, "they're Yankees fans."

Lena slapped her hands to her heart. "Oh, Swan!" She laughed. "You've got to be kidding me."

He laughed with her, and then he remembered and his smiled faded. "Hey, Lena, I wish I could do something for you guys. I'll tell you what my nana used to say. She had a whole bit about cups."

"Cups?" Lena said.

"Yeah. She cooked all her life and so I guess her frame of reference was naturally cup-based. Anyway, she was always telling us, in her way, to make the best of things. To be tough. 'Life is a chipped cup,' she'd say. 'There's no fixing. You just learn to drink around.' "

Lena couldn't help feeling amused and awfully glad for Swanson. "Lee, you and Briana are going to be very happy."

"Yeah. I'm sure she's been waiting all her life to fall for a bum with no job."

Lena pulled up. "Wait. Aren't you going to work for Midas?"

"Nah. I've got maybe another thing going. Anyway, in the final-final we didn't get the deal we'd hoped for, but Charlie nailed it without my having to commit to a contract. Did you know that?"

She didn't.

Swanson watched her carefully, deciding on the fly to give Lena more of a picture, even if Charlie wouldn't like it, on the chance that it might help them. "Charlie made sure all of our initial investors were covered, and our debts. After that there was enough left over for me and the guys in the lab to walk away with a little something. He took less, of course, being Charlie. I wouldn't have let him pull that trick, but he sort of went around my back, if you know what I mean. All he cared about was paying off Willa's medical bills and socking away some for Theo and Willa's college. So that's a couple of worries off the table."

Lena could only nod. Swanny's unshakable belief in Charlie shamed her. She got up and walked to the window as Swanny kept on talking.

"Listen, Lena. I'm not saying he's a saint or anything, 'cause let's face it . . . but Charlie, well, he's not like anyone I know. Most guys in his situation would . . ." Swanson stumbled and then charged ahead. "Anyway, I'll tell you what he told me. He said, 'I wouldn't for the world want to stand in the way of her light.' " Swanson dropped his large hands on his thighs. "That's Charlie for you."

Later that night, after the kids were asleep, Lena picked up the phone. It was two o'clock in the morning.

"Charlie?"

"Are you all right? Are the kids—"

In her mind's eye, she saw him listening with the furrow between his eyes.

"Charlie."

"Yeah. OK."

"Charlie, Swanny told me."

"Yeah? What—what did Swan say?"

"He said—" She sighed and he sighed back at her.

"Swanny tends to exaggerate," Charlie went on. "You know that. He means well, but—"

"Charlie?"

"Yeah?"

She didn't know where to start. There was so much and they were so far behind in talking. "Did you know about Cal? Cal and me."

"Only very recently. I kept turning over what happened this past year, asking myself, really, why did Cal come after us in the first place? It was the only thing that made sense. I figured he or Beverly should be the ones to tell you."

She took that in and for a while she couldn't speak. "Charlie, he offered me a job. A job!"

"Doing what?"

She told him and at first Charlie was quiet, thinking of Lena—who she used to be and who she was now. At last he said, "I hate to say it, but it's perfect for you. You could fund the clinic in Mbarara. You could fund various documentaries. Research. Climate change. All the crazy shit you follow in the newspaper."

"I know."

"What did you tell him?"

Lena's head was splitting. "I said, in a nutshell, I'd have to think about it. But before that I basically told him to go screw himself. I told a dying man to go screw."

"Well, he's a tough bird. He would have expected that."

"Charlie, he said to tell you his interest in Nimbus was real."

"I know. I know it was, if only because he wouldn't do it any other way."

"Charlie, I—"

"Can you sleep, Lena? Can you just lay it down for the night and rest? See where you are in the morning."

She nodded. "OK."

"I'll pick the kids up early on Saturday," he said. "Give you the day. We can talk when I bring them home. How's that?"

"OK. But—"

"Good night, Lean."

Wincing, she bit the back of her hand and nodded.

"Sleep well," he said.

A few days later she took Theo with her up the hill to Cal and Ivy's house. Lena had Theo wait outside in the hall with Paco, where the two of them talked about the Danes, while she went into Cal's room and stood before him.

Cal was in the bed, the pillows all around him. If possible, his chin looked even more distended.

"Changed your mind?" he said.

"Sort of."

"Sort of? Well, I'm sort of glad then."

Shaky, Lena charged ahead. "Why don't you hear me out first?"

"OK."

"I'll accept the job on the following conditions," she said. "One, I choose what we fund. Two, I am guaranteed a two-year contract. Three, I can work from home when I need to tend to Willa."

"Fine-fine," Cal said. "Paige will be on the board, you have to know that. And Maggie, my right hand, and an old friend of mine Bud Cope. They won't be any trouble; they'll look to you to hold the rudder."

Lena thought about that, about Paige. At last, she nodded. "Four, I want the foundation or at least specific large gifts to also bear my father's name. Ted's name."

He grunted, thinking it over. "All right. All right. No doubt it's just."

Relieved and stunned, she forgot what else. "Thank you," she said.

He watched her with a great stillness and she had the thought that he didn't want her to leave. That hideous man, her father. "And the Danes?" he asked in that hoarse awful voice. "How are they getting on?"

"Better," she said. "On that score, there's someone I'd like you to meet." She went to the door and brought in Theo.

"He wants to thank you for Angie and Finn," Lena prompted.

"The boy can talk, can't he?" Cal turned his head slightly and, with his one remaining eye, studied the boy who was studying him.

"Ah, pretty gross, eh, Theo?" Cal prompted. "You ever seen anything grosser?"

Theo shrugged. "Does it hurt?"

"Like hell."

Theo nodded. And for a time they were silent while Theo took in the face and the enormous room, and then the face again. "Are you cold? Is that why you have so many covers on you?" he asked the old man.

"Yep."

Theo's eyes traveled over to the window. He itched to go look at all the world out there, but Lena squeezed his hand and he knew he had to stay put. "Mama said you like elephants."

"Right you are."

"But she said that you told her no one preys on them. That's not true. Lions prey on elephants, especially the sick and the young ones. I saw it on TV. And then there's the poachers. There's not much an elephant can do against a poacher." Theo paused, covering his mouth with both hands.

"In that case, Theo, what would you advise?" Cal asked.

Theo shrugged. "Look sharp, I guess."

Cal grunted, amused or agreeing, it was hard to tell. Soon Paco came in and it was time for them to leave.

Twenty-nine

That next Saturday Charlie took the kids and the Danes hiking in the Marin Headlands. They returned home late, coming into the kitchen with their dusty day packs, shoes and paws. Lena was waiting. The beard Charlie started in the spring had grown bushy, but that didn't mean it looked any better. She smiled with relief as she gazed from one woodland creature to another. Willa, who'd ridden on Charlie's back, had twigs stuck to her jacket. Theo had tripped and banged his knee, and they all seemed to think it was a riot.

"Ba-ba," Willa said, her hearing only partial, but better than it had been; she was starting to make sounds.

"Oh, that's right!" cried Theo. "Willa spotted a *bobcat*."

"We were on a ridge," Charlie explained. "He was a hundred yards ahead of us, up the slope, looking very—"

"Curious!" Theo cried.

"Curious," Charlie agreed. "He looked right at us."

"And then?" Lena tipped her head as Charlie took off Willa's jacket and handed it to her.

Theo watched the familiar domestic dance, and all the missing he'd

285

been doing was in his eyes. "Mama, Dad has a new job. He's just going to be a doctor again. Tell her, Dad."

Charlie nodded. "Stanford. They've asked me to come on full-time, as part of the robotic surgical team."

"Charlie, that's . . . wonderful. I mean, is it wonderful?"

He shrugged as he took Willa and Theo to the sink and washed their hands. "Half clinical with teaching. Half research. Not bad at all." He paused. "Swan said he told you about the deal that went down with Nimbus."

Of course, Charlie would make a point of finding out exactly what Swanson said. Lena nodded, aware that Theo was watching them.

"Hey, buddy," she said. "After that long car ride those dogs might need to go out."

Theo took the Danes to the backyard.

"Cal was right," Charlie said. "He's great with them."

"He is," Lena agreed.

"Yeah," Charlie said, "but now Mass General has come up with a counteroffer. They want me to start up a new robotics department. I'd have my pick of any team and enough money to really advance—"

"But Boston, Charlie."

"I haven't decided anything. I thought we should talk."

"You'd like to be back there, wouldn't you? Leave this place. Go home."

Charlie pointed toward the door. Theo was coming up the deck stairs. "But it's not just about me, is it?"

Later, after they'd split the tasks of giving each kid a bath and putting them to bed, Charlie sat with Lena at the kitchen table.

"So," he said. "What did you decide about Cal?"

"You mean the job, or the fact that he's my father?"

Charlie nodded—for both things.

"I'll take the job—I'll try it—but in terms of how I feel about Cal, I haven't begun to figure that out." Lena paused, choosing her words carefully. "It's odd, but I think I understand him. I pity him. The wasted heart."

Charlie nodded, understanding as no one else could what Lena wasn't saying, too. "You should know that Alessandro helped us negotiate with

Midas. And Cal picked up the legal bills." Charlie watched Lena, gauging her reaction. "Anyway, it's done. Nimbus is over. No looking back."

He got up from his chair and she thought he was coming toward her. She hoped. Instead, Charlie picked up Willa's tiny, fleece jacket and folded it. It was a simple gesture but it spoke volumes to her heart. He put the folded jacket and then the hat on top and moved the small pile to the counter, by the bowl of keys, where it would be ready for the morning, as they had done a hundred times.

She said, "I don't love Alessandro, Charlie. I don't think I ever did."

"No, but you liked the idea of him. He isn't an old Volvo."

"Neither are you," she said. "Are you really going to Boston?"

He turned to her with that odd, unsettling look of his, both curious and severe. "What do you want, Lean?"

"You're asking?"

"Oh, for chrissakes."

She loved when his voice cracked and she could see all the way to the bottom.

"Charlie, I want—" She stopped. "I want it to be good."

"Yeah," he said. "I know." He looked out the window. "I've been thinking, the house, it needs painting. I've got a couple of weeks. I could do it. I mean, I wouldn't be in your hair."

"Do you *know* how to paint a house?"

"Haven't a clue."

A slow smile spread across her face. "Charlie, you're my people. You and Theo and Willa."

If he heard it, he put it in his pocket for later. "Go ahead and pick out a color, 'K? Just make sure it's got lots of pigment. It's going to be hell to cover that pink."

"Charlie—"

He pushed in his chair. "Anyway, let me know what you decide, color-wise. I'll just go up and kiss them good night."

Several afternoons later, Lena came home with the kids to find Charlie at the top of a very tall ladder. She had never seen that particular ladder and certainly she had never seen Charlie on top of one. There was a step stool in the kitchen, and she had never seen him on that either. Now he was twenty-five feet in the air and if he heard them, he didn't turn around. He had a boom box blasting. He was applying primer with a roller attached to a pole. A rag was tucked into his waistband and his shirt was off. If there was anything sexier than a half-dressed man up on a ladder painting for free a house he doesn't like and doesn't live in, well, she didn't know what it could be. She stared at the back she knew so well.

Theo was calling him.

Charlie turned and looked down at them—at her—and grinned. "Hey."

Thirty

In 2009 even the weather was extreme. And that autumn San Francisco never got its promised blast of heat. The winter rains started early, though on the morning that Obama won the Nobel Peace Prize the sun shone brilliant and cold. Half the world said he deserved the prize; half said not even close. By November the last of the dahlias and roses in Ivy's garden were just hanging on and Ivy was nearing the end.

Paige and Christopher kept vigil in her room, with Paige holding one of Ivy's hands, and Christopher, just arrived from India, holding the other. He had come at last, after Paige begged him to; he came for his sister. They lit candles, read poems and, at points, Christopher chanted, a kind of buzzing, nasal invocation that put everyone on edge. Late at night, Paulette climbed the stairs from the kitchen to say her rosary quietly. Ivy drifted in and out, never opening her eyes. Her feet and hands turned blue, and they all thought, Here's the end, but then her heart quickened and her limbs pinked and the cycle began again.

They stayed beside her all night, watching the life come and go, saying what they needed to say though she couldn't hear. Christopher was particularly stunned. A thin, sharp-boned man of forty, he peered at his mother with a face very much like Ivy's from years ago, and wondered, Where are you?

Just before dawn, Ivy sighed her last sigh, and an hour later Paige and Christopher left while Walker washed her and put her in the de la Renta cream and black polka-dot sheath, cut on the bias, with a nice ruffle at the neckline, as Ivy had requested. They came back and Paige laid roses from the garden around Ivy's pillow, and Christopher, who had come farther than mere miles, having fled this house for a room in India with a crude table and a pallet on the floor, took his mother's cooling hand and bowed his head.

They could have stayed a long time. But then, around eight that morning, Walker hurried down the hall and said, "By god, it is getting to be Cal's time, too." This surprised them. They'd assumed he had weeks left. But Walker knew his business, he had proven that, so they left Ivy and hustled down the hall to join Maggie and Paco in the master bedroom.

"Did she?" Cal asked as his children came near.

"Yes, Dad," Christopher said.

The one eye flicked on the son. A slight nod. And that was all.

The hours passed, Cal's breathing grew labored; he was as noisy in death as he was in life.

Paige read her father the eulogy she'd written, thinking he couldn't hear.

"You . . . got me," he said, in a halting whisper. "Now cut it in half."

Those were his final words. A few minutes shy of midnight, he died, and the day of Ivy and Cal ended.

Cremate me. Cal wrote in his will, "Drive *Thirst* at full sail so she's lined up with the flagpole at the Yacht Club, on a line with Alcatraz and the bridge, and toss my ashes there, into the Bay. No song, no fuss. And, damn it, no memorial!"

He was dead, though, wasn't he. Paige made the arrangements, and where her parents' desires conflicted, she let Ivy's prevail.

A month later, on a wintry December day, more than a thousand mourners came to Grace Cathedral for Cal and Ivy's last party. All of San Francisco society turned out, and much of Silicon Valley as well. Cal's partners and lawyers came, as did Ivy's shoe repairman, and the billionaires and the technogeeks, and Harry the carpenter, who had a special place in the proceedings, if only in his mind. The church garage filled early. Town Cars and limos lined the block. Governor Schwarzenegger escorted Maria Shriver. Gavin Newsom, the mayor, was giving a eulogy. Al Gore, who had business in town, arrived without Tipper.

"Party attire. No black," Ivy had specified in a codicil to her will. But to her best friends, the symphony and opera matrons, she added, "No sad sacks and ashes. Come in what makes you feel beautiful." So they wore their reds and canary yellows. They wore their jewels. Their men donned garish vests and bright jackets. The photographers from the *Nob Hill Gazette* and the *Chronicle* snapped their pictures as they climbed the long, wide stairs.

"Is it too much?" Paige asked James, pausing outside the car to adjust her hair. She was wearing one of Ivy's Yves Saint Laurents from the sixties and a hat Ivy had worn to Royal Ascot. It had a long turquoise plume.

"Never." James beamed. He took her hand and led her, his soon-to-be-bride, through a special door at the side of the cathedral.

Christopher followed in a Nehru jacket and sandals. He had a dusty quality to him, and a remoteness that would not be displaced by his parents' deaths or a thousand sun salutations.

Walker and Paco arrived together, as they'd been those several months. Paco wore his best blue suit. Paulette carried the Hermès shawl and Birkin bag Ivy left to her. Dahlia wore Ivy's red satin Manolos.

"Remember, darling," Ivy often warned Cal, "people won't remember what you did, but how you made them feel."

As the mourners passed into the cathedral, it was remarked that money died in 2009, and Ivy went with it.

The Ghiberti Gates of Paradise were open in honor of the bishop, who was presiding. But most of the mourners assumed they were open to honor Ivy and Cal.

Lena came up the stairs alone. Earlier, Charlie phoned and offered to take her, but she said no, she'd see him there. The moment she topped the long set of stairs she realized her mistake. The crowd was thick, moving through the gates, taking her with it. She looked back, slightly panicked, through the doors to the city, a place of hills and sand, of rise and fall, of gold to ashes to gold again. She hugged a wall, holding firm, thinking of Cal, her father.

This home, this lark, had talked to the hopes of a boy from Santa Rosa. He had come to this city built by gold-struck miners, on shifting sand dunes and dry, precipitous hills. The first homes were tents and shanties, and the first professions prostitution and gambling. From that start grew a town of foggy morals and loosey-goosey politics. The city had been crushed three times by fires and earthquakes, and each time it rose again. Lovely, whitewashed, beguiling, it was built by dreamers on seven square miles of whim. Part of its splendor was knowing, as Cal had known, that any moment, with a terrific shake, it might all collapse.

Lena would not. She moved into the church, looking for Charlie, as the cathedral boys' choir, dressed in black shoes and starched surplices, entered the choir stall. In the farthest pews in back, the clerks and shopkeepers Ivy had befriended took seats where they could gossip and watch the parade of mourners.

"Can you believe they went on the same day? Such devotion. To the end."

"What a load of garbage. Everyone knew they fought like wolverines."

"Well, I couldn't have stood a single day with him."

"With all that money? Sweetie, you could have lasted a long time."

Lena was late, of course. The best pews were already filled, with everyone dressed to the nines, talking excitedly. The blue of the windows and the gray concrete walls and buttresses and the holy smells of the church overwhelmed Lena. Where were Paige and Christopher? They were sequestered, as they'd always been, in a private room, protected before the service began. Lena felt the old sting of being left out, but she wasn't surprised. She looked up to the angels sitting on small shelves near the top of the nave's pillars. And she thought, God's house is very tall but narrow.

The organ played Bach. The seats were nearly gone. Lena headed down the aisle to her left when a familiar hand took hold of her arm.

Alessandro had been awake for two nights writing Cal's eulogy. His face was pale, and though she hadn't seen him in months, it felt like no time at all. She knew instinctively that he was frightened.

"Elena! I've been looking all over for you. Where have you been? Did you find your seat? Come. Come up front. I'll walk you. You shouldn't sit alone."

"I'm fine," she insisted, freeing her arm. "Really."

"But, but?" Alessandro fixed on her, even as a man walked up and tried to shake his hand.

"Please," Alessandro said, speaking close to her ear. "How are you?"

"San, I'm OK. You?"

He smiled sheepishly. "I'm a wreck—"

"It's all right." Out of habit, she rose on tiptoe to hug him.

Alessandro pulled her in tight against him and pressed his lips to her neck.

Surprised, she opened her eyes. Charlie was standing there, watching them. Disgusted, he turned and disappeared into the crowd.

"No!" Lena cried, pushing Alessandro away, and searching for Charlie. But the bright faces of the crowd had absorbed him and, despairing, Lena retreated to a pew near the back.

The service began with the bishop leading, and one by one the speakers talked of Ivy and Cal. Lena hardly heard them. She was in agony, reliving the pained expression on Charlie's face, and blaming herself.

A boy from the choir, a towheaded twelve-year-old, rose and sang in a soaring pitch:

> *Ye watchers and ye holy ones,*
> *bright seraphs, cherubim and thrones,*
> *Raise the glad strain, Alleluia!*

The hymn ran on, louder, the organ blasting its notes like men with barrel chests and women dressed in good wool. Hymns always struck Lena that way—as people. She grasped her hands together to get a hold of herself. It didn't work. She was alone. The ceiling receded, the angels looked down, snug on their perches. Lena wiped her eyes.

From behind, someone dropped a Kleenex into her lap. She looked back to say thanks and spotted Charlie moving at a fast clip down the aisle, heading for the doors.

She followed, walking where he walked, toward the back. Where the pews ended, there was a labyrinth. She plowed across it. She was air and damp spirit and, for that matter, damp sleeves, and one day she, too, would be dust. The choirboy held his note.

Lena burst through the doors.

"Charlie!"

He turned, his face more familiar to her than her own. She'd once thought she knew everything about him. She didn't think that anymore. She ran down the stairs to him.

"It's no good," he declared. "I came here to say, OK, let's start again. But what good is it?" He searched her face.

"What do you mean?" she cried.

"Lena, I'm done," he said grimly.

"But we can't be done."

Eventually, the service ended; Charlie and Lena hardly noticed. The mourners emerged from the cathedral and started down the wide expanse of stairs. The shopkeeper and the scion, the maid and the mayor, in their high heels and fancy suits, navigated what felt like a mile of steps. Halfway down, the governor had his picture taken with a group of Japanese tourists. Al Gore was escorted by the Secret Service into an armored SUV.

A briny, stiff breeze was rising from the Bay; it carried Lena and Charlie's pitched voices.

Jules Green shielded her eyes against the sun. "Artie, look. It's Lena. Why didn't she sit up front with us? Are those trousers she's wearing? Artie?"

Now that Ivy was gone, Artie Green had become a husk filled with sighs. "To all your questions," he said, "dearie, I don't know."

Jules made a sour face. She hadn't liked the service. It went on and on while she suffered, the waistband of her skirt too tight. And she couldn't quite feel sad about Ivy. The dead had her day, and in Artie's case, the dead had had a lifetime.

"Can you believe it?" Jules said. "My, they're really going at it. So public! Artie, listen to that. She said fuck. Shouldn't we do something? Shouldn't we at least go down there? I mean really."

Artie removed his glasses, wiped them and looked again. There on the inlaid stone of the courtyard labyrinth, Charlie and Lena gesticulated like bad actors. Charlie was jealous; Lena was stung. They cursed. They growled. They gave up. They went beyond giving up. Artie Green smiled knowingly. "No, Jules, we stay right here."

Lena crossed her arms. "I said I was sorry."

"Right. Now, if only you meant it," Charlie said.

"I *do* mean it."

"You *mean it* as a lever to get me to move. There's a difference."

"Oh, Christ, Pepper!"

They had broken the windows and collapsed the arches. Now they stomped their careless hooves on the rubble. Things that must never be said, they said. Their dream was flimsy from the start, a wisp of a thing, a grand and perilous hope. They were sorry, ashamed and not a lick wiser. Having torn it to the ground, they stood among the wreckage.

"Please," Lena begged. "Let's try one more time. I won't interrupt. Please. What did you want to say?"

She bowed her head, and in that subtle gesture, Charlie gained ground. He looked across Taylor Street into Huntington Park, where city dogs relieved themselves on the green sod, and children played on the swings, and a half dozen Chinese seniors practiced qigong. Closer, on the corner, he saw the Huntington Hotel's Big Four restaurant, named after railroad barons—Collis Huntington, Leland Stanford, Charles Crocker, Mark Hopkins. One had been a grocer; one, a dry goods merchant; and the other two, hardware store owners. Out of their dreams, they built the railroads.

Out of their dreams they built.

Coming to the church, Charlie thought he had the right words. He needed to find them now. But they were not at the Huntington and they weren't in the park.

They weren't new words or especially grand—that much he was clear on. They had to fit in the mouth of a plumber's son. Then, too, they had to be the opposite of grief, which, it turned out, wasn't Charlie working-till-he-dropped, or Lena dallying with an old beau. Charlie needed to find the one thing that until this year of mortification would have sounded un-American in its modesty.

Enough. That was it. Looking over Huntington Park, Charlie found enough.

"Be with me." The doctor's empty hands reached out to her. "I will talk to you, Lena, I promise we'll talk and never stop. Be with me. Be with Theo, Willa and me." Having said all he had, Charlie nodded. "That's it."

A slow smile spread across Lena's face. So simple, yet she had hardly dared to hope.

"You're a poet, Charlie Pepper."

"Not so much, Helena Rose." But he kept on talking as if to prove he was. Then, being just wise enough, he shut the boca and let her come to him.

She stepped across the stones. She was laughing or crying, what did it matter? It had been a time, such a time. Charlie took this hope, this woman, this life and wrapped his arms around her.

They were in it now. They were in it.

Acknowledgments

Thanks be to Dr. Richard Babayan, Dr. David Bangsberg, Dr. Gary Rogers and Dr. Robert Seymour, who offered invaluable advice, medical and otherwise. And thanks to Jeffrey Crowe and the late Tommy Davis, who shared views of the venture world. Thanks to Temple St. Clair Carr, Lacy Crawford, Jennifer Egan, Rebecca Kaden, Jane Lancellotti, Lori Ogden Moore, Judith Rascoe, Nancy Shelby, Tricia Stone, Jeffry Weisman and Daniel Wheeler, who read early drafts and otherwise kept me on course, body and soul. To the best staff and supporters anywhere at *Narrative,* my undying respect and appreciation. To Jennifer Rudolph Walsh and Nan Graham: it's an honor and a pleasure. And thanks simply aren't enough for the ones who sustain me: Liv Far, Lucy Honor, Anne Riley and Tom.